Praise for Juliet E.

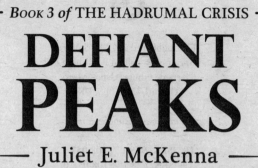

— BOOK 3 *of* THE HADRUMAL CRISIS —

DEFIANT PEAKS

— Juliet E. McKenna —

SOLARIS

First published 2012 by Solaris
an imprint of Rebellion Publishing Ltd,
Riverside House, Osney Mead,
Oxford, OX2 0ES, UK

www.solarisbooks.com

UK ISBN: 978 1 78108 057 3
US ISBN: 978 1 78108 058 0

10 9 8 7 6 5 4 3 2 1

A CIP catalogue record for this book is available from the
British Library.

Designed & typeset by Rebellion Publishing

Printed in the US

For my nephew, Rowan
and for my niece, Millie

— ACKNOWLEDGEMENTS —

As EVER, FAMILY and friends, long-standing and newly made, have sustained me as I wrote this book, and indeed, this trilogy, through what have proved testing times for this whole household, at school, college and work. My profound gratitude to you all.

Thanks to the wonders of modern communications, I have drawn invaluable inspiration and energy from the enthusiasm of those readers who have followed these adventures from that thief's first gamble so long ago in an unremarkable Ensaimin tavern, as well as from those who have joined in along the way, in the Archipelago, in Lescar and now in Hadrumal and Caladhria. To all of you who have asked me unexpected questions via email or at conventions, who have reminded me of throwaway lines (or letters) and characters with unexplored potential, who have shared your appreciation of these stories through blogs, reviews or chance conversation, my sincerest thanks.

In this time of flux in publishing (though I wonder if publishing ever sees anything but constant change) I am indebted to my fellow writers for camaraderie, perspective and encouragement, along with so many sociable and amiable editors, agents, booksellers and others within the SF&Fantasy genre and in the wider world of books beyond.

My thanks to Jon, David, Ben and Mike at Solaris and Rebellion for editorial, administrative and marketing support. Over and above the usual acknowledgements, I am most grateful that they commissioned Clint Langley to paint the covers for these books. Having the complete triptych to hand as I wrote has both focused and stimulated my imagination in truly rewarding fashion as I'm sure you will agree, when you find out exactly what Archmage Planir is doing...

— CHAPTER ONE —

Halferan Manor, Caladhria

Winter Solstice Festival, 3rd Day

In the 10th Year of Tadriol the Provident of Tormalin

SHE STOOD AMID the silent statues and contemplated the crystal urn holding her husband's ashes; footed with silver leaves and crowned with a five-petalled flower sparkling in the light of the shrine's candles.

The Archmage himself had fashioned the beautiful vessel from a humble tisane glass. Was this a tangible expression of Planir of Hadrumal's remorse? An apology for his obdurate insistence on observing the wizard isle's merciless edicts? Did he privately regret refusing to allow his mages to help the Halferan barony, when her lost beloved had begged for wizardly aid, time and again as this coast was plagued year after year by thieving corsairs sailing up from the southern seas?

Zurenne hadn't ever dared ask Planir such questions. Now she didn't think she ever would. Her husband, the father of her darling daughters, was dead. No answer could change that. No magic could bring him back. Besides, the corsairs were dead and gone; their whole island sunk beneath unknown Aldabreshin seas by the most terrifying wizardry after a renegade mage had dared to challenge Planir. If they wouldn't defend anyone else, it seemed the wizards would rip land and sea asunder to defend their own authority over magecraft. Well, that was no concern of hers.

11

'It's Neeny's birth festival, my love,' she said softly. 'You wouldn't credit how tall she has grown.'

Zurenne could scarcely believe that this was the sixth midwinter since their second daughter's joyous arrival. That carefree For-Winter season when she had been so happily pregnant seemed like a different lifetime. A life secure in her husband's love and in the manor's prosperity, with little Lysha so excited to welcome an infant brother or sister. After Halferan's heartbreaking troubles through this past handful of years, such peace seemed as remote and unreal as the Otherworld which the priests insisted lay beyond Saedrin's door.

Hooded Poldrion gazed down at the crystal urn set on the shrine table, the god's statue garlanded with myrtle, mistletoe and ivy. This was his festival; guard and guide of the dead, shepherding the pious and honest alongside the deceitful and worse, all to face Saedrin's judgement.

Zurenne didn't need festival or shrine to bring her beloved husband to mind. She communed every day with her memories. She contemplated the berries on the garlands; shining like pearls and dull as beads of jet, ripe with the promise of life to come.

Priests said that the shades of those truly remorseful for their errors or offences in life passed through Saedrin's doorway to blissfully ignorant rebirth in the Otherworld. The greatest of gods condemned the unrepentant to torment at Poldrion's demons' claws though, until pain and contrition expiated their sins.

Zurenne's eyes prickled with tears as she imagined her lost husband's anguish, forced to admit the misjudgements which had been the death of him. Surely Saedrin would consider his honest intentions, his righteous devotion to the Halferan barony and to its people, even if his endeavours had ended in fatal miscalculation, trusting in a treacherous wizard who'd been as ready to betray him as he had betrayed all his oaths to Hadrumal.

She could not blame Planir for her husband's death, not entirely. Let Saedrin judge the Archmage whenever the wizard finally stood before the Doorkeeper. Winter Solstice marked the New Year and that was time to make a new beginning, leaving all grudges behind.

'You would be so proud of Lysha. She is determined to be the finest Lady of Halferan since the barony's foundation.'

Zurenne smiled even as she wondered how her husband was supposed to hear her, if he was already reborn to a new life with no memory of this world. No priest ever explained that.

The statues of the gods and goddesses offered no answers, silent on their plinths. The candles cast their shadows on the shrine's empty shelves behind them. With all remembrance of the manor's ancient dead swept away in the destruction wrought by the corsairs, the only funeral urn in the shrine was her husband's.

Long may it remain so, Zurenne prayed with silent fervour. She extricated a length of ivy from one of Poldrion's garlands and twisted it into an offering to lay before Maewelin's statue, for the sake of the very young and the very old alike under the Winter Hag's protection.

This For-Winter season had been mercifully mild. No funeral pyres had burned beside the brook beyond the manor's wall. No new urns would be set on these shelves tonight. That was one more thing for the household and the manor's demesne folk to celebrate on this Souls' Ease Night, highest and holiest day of the festival.

Noon's five chimes sounded from the timepiece now installed in the gable end of the restored kitchen buildings across the courtyard. Zurenne turned towards the shrine's inner door leading into the manor's great hall. Her business was with the living now and there was still a great deal to do before the revels began at dusk. She went through the doorway to the wooden dais raised above the long sweep of the hall's flagstone floor.

'Mama!' Ilysh stood beside a high-backed chair golden with new varnish. Elegant though it was, it was no match for the ancient and ornate baronial seat which had once dominated the hall. That had burned, buried beneath the old roof's timbers when the corsairs had set fire to the manor and its buildings.

Ilysh's violet silk gown shone in the sunlight falling through the newly reglazed windows. While the style suited her maidenly years, the costly cloth and her gleaming gold necklace and rings proclaimed the resurgent barony's resources. Amethyst tipped pins adorned her light brown hair as befitted a wife, even though no one seeing her youth could doubt her virginity.

Zurenne's own modest gown of charcoal grey velvet befitted her dowager status as did the twist of lace securing her dark braid on the nape of her neck. She was merely the mother of the barony's lady now, for all that she was still young enough to have had hopes of bearing a son to inherit his father's honours before her husband had died in the barony's defence. But that was merely one more regret to leave on Poldrion's altar at this turn of the year.

'My lady.' The manor's steward covered the newly-finished oak of the high table with a maroon drape. The cloth was so fresh from the loom that Zurenne could smell the faint tang of dyestuff.

'Master Rauffe, have you recorded the accusations and pleas from the lesser assize to your satisfaction?'

Festivals at solstice and equinox saw the living judged as well as the dead so the steward had spent the morning in the village rising from the wreckage of houses, workshops and tithe barns beyond the brook. Those accused of minor infractions were called to answer in the market place, with their neighbours standing witness for good or ill.

'Mama!'

Zurenne braced herself for renewed argument. 'You may be Halferan's lady but you are still far too young to hear the quarrels and excuses of adulterers, drunkards and cheating tradesmen.'

When he returned from Caladhria's midwinter parliament in Duryea, Corrain could issue verdicts from Master Rauffe's written evidence of claim and counter claim. He might be Halferan's baron in name only but his previous career as a guard captain left him well prepared for this particular lordly duty. Better prepared than many born to noble rank.

'That's not what I want to talk about,' Ilysh said impatiently. 'Can we not at least forgive the people half of their tithe? We know full well how hard everyone is still toiling to recover their fortunes.'

Zurenne saw Master Rauffe's lips tighten and guessed that Lysha had already been arguing with him, presumably in hopes that his agreement would sway her mother.

'My lady Ilysh—' she saw her daughter's eyes widen at such formality '—we are only asking the people to give us a tenth share of what they might have over and above their own needs. If they have little or nothing to give at this season, so be it. The coin isn't important. Resuming the custom is what matters, to further restore Halferan's morale.'

15

She held out her hand to her daughter. 'Our people should be given this chance to prove to you, their liege lady, to their neighbours and to themselves that their hard work through Aft-Autumn and For-Winter has restored our peace and prosperity after all our grievous losses. Do you understand, Lysha?'

Ilysh nodded slowly, her hazel eyes thoughtful and so reminiscent of her father that Zurenne's heart twisted within her.

'I—' Whatever the girl might have said was lost as the tall door at the far end of the great hall opened. Torches already lit in their brackets in the shadows of the side aisles flickered in the draught.

'Mama? Mama?' Esnina's slippered footsteps were drowned out by her appeals as she ran the length of the hall. 'Why can't I stay up for the feast? It is my birth festival.' She halted below the dais, looking up with winsome hope. 'Please, Mama? I promise I'll be good.'

Zurenne reminded herself to lay some grateful acknowledgement before Drianon's statue, to thank the goddess of hearth, home and motherhood for this past season of peace and quiet. Restored to her home which she had known since birth, albeit so extensively rebuilt and remade, Neeny's tantrums were now few and far between. After the trials and tribulations of living with the entire household crammed into the Taw Ricks hunting lodge after the manor burned, everyone was thankful for that.

She looked at the young man following Esnina. Smartly liveried in pewter and maroon as befitted the newly-confirmed captain of Halferan's guard, Kusint had brought an iron-bound coffer up from the strong room below the muniment room of the baronial tower at the other end of the great hall.

Not so long ago, Zurenne reflected, Kusint's red hair, mark of his Forest blood, would have prompted suspicion if not outright hostility in Halferan. Chimney-corner wisdom condemned such wandering folk as thieves and deceivers. Now household and demesne folk alike accepted Kusint as one of their own, acknowledging their debt.

Without the Forest youth's skills with a boat, he and Corrain would never have escaped from the corsairs who had enslaved them. If Corrain hadn't escaped and returned, the dogged guardsman would never have been able to force the Archmage's hand and secure Madam Jilseth's wizardry to save them all. At least, that's what the barony's folk believed, with a handful of different theories as to why the Archmage had changed his mind.

Only Corrain, Kusint and Zurenne knew the truth. That Corrain had defied Hadrumal to bring a renegade mage south from the unknown lands north of remote Solura. It was that mage who had defeated the corsairs only to enslave the remnants of their forces himself, threatening to renew their murderous attacks on the mainland, this time bolstered by his magic. That had compelled Planir to act.

'Where is Raselle?' Zurenne's personal maid should have been keeping Neeny busy in their private apartments on the tower's top floor.

'Doratine sent word that she needed her in the kitchen.' Kusint climbed the three steps of the dais and set the heavy box down on the table.

'Thank you.' Master Rauffe was setting out his ledger, his pens and an impressive brass and enamel inkstand.

'I said I would bring Lady Esnina to ask your permission for a later bedtime.' Kusint fished in his breeches' pocket for the strongbox's key before turning to look at the little girl still waiting down below. 'She gave me her oath that she would abide by your decision.'

'I did.' Neeny looked up at her mother with mute appeal.

'Let her stay up, Mama.' Lysha narrowed her eyes at her little sister all the same. 'As long as she behaves.'

'I will, I will,' Neeny promised fervently before scrambling up the dais steps.

Zurenne could see the first of Halferan's loyal tenants appearing in the far doorway, summoned by the noon chimes.

'Very well, Neeny, as long as you are good.' She hoped her stern words left no room for doubt. Like Lysha, her younger daughter could twist any statement towards her own advantage.

'Come and sit here, chick.' Kusint led the little girl around the table to lift her onto a chair beside the heavier, more ornate seat prepared for Ilysh. He pulled the latter back. 'My lady of Halferan.'

'Thank you, Captain.' Ilysh settled her skirts, folding her hands modestly in her lap as he pushed her forwards.

Kusint straightened the matching chair beside her before walking to the far end of the table to stand guard beside Master Rauffe and the strongbox. Zurenne made no move to sit. That second carved seat was for the present Baron Halferan, even if Corrain only held his title by virtue of Lysha's marriage of convenience.

'Let all with tithes to pay approach and make themselves known.'

As the steward's words rang through the hall, the first of the dutiful tenantry began walking towards the dais and their young liege lady.

Had she done the right thing by her daughters and by the barony? Zurenne longed to ask her dead husband that question above all others. Binding Lysha in this charade of marriage to secure their freedom from whomever the Caladhrian parliament would have set in authority over them. In the absence of a true grant from her lost father, their guardian would have been one of the barony's neighbouring lords or Zurenne's older sisters' husbands. Because Caladhrian law couldn't countenance a widow and her orphan daughters living without a man to rule over them.

Zurenne resolutely reminded herself how her beloved husband had trusted Corrain, even knowing the guardsman's flaws and failings. He had believed in the man's worth, despite the scandal when Corrain had been caught seducing the former manor steward's wife. He had retained him, albeit stripped of rank, in the barony's troop.

Corrain had been the only man to offer Halferan any hope of salvation from the corsairs. Even if his scheming had seen the manor itself devastated while the wider barony had been saved.

A belated thought struck Zurenne. Should she have sent Madam Jilseth some festival gift or greeting? What of Master Tornauld and Madam Merenel? Did mages exchange such courtesies at the solstice and equinox seasons? It was strange to think of the mages who had slaughtered the corsairs' would-be wizardly tyrant and helped to rebuild Halferan celebrating like ordinary folk.

As Zurenne's hand strayed to the triangular silver pendant which she wore threaded on a black ribbon around her neck, she noticed the gazes of the first tenants to approach the dais fix on the necklace.

The device itself held no significance, beyond making up Zurenne's personal seal formed from the three runes drawn by ancient custom at her birth, arrayed around the sun rune to show she had been born in the daytime. What mattered to Halferan's folk was knowing that the Archmage had given their widowed lady that pendant imbued with his very own magic. So she could call for his aid, if the corsairs who had murdered so many of their kith and kin ever reappeared.

Zurenne let her hand fall to her side. Saedrin send that she would never have to do such a thing, that Lysha would never need to use the ensorcelled pendant wrought from her own birth runes. Saedrin grant them all that blessing, and Dastennin god of storms and Raeponin god of justice and any other deity who might be listening. If there was any fair dealing from the gods, as this new year began, Halferan was done with magic.

The crowd was swelling in the manor's great hall. Kusint opened the brass-bound coffer to receive the baronial dues. Master Rauffe trimmed his quill's nib with a penknife and uncapped his inkwell, ready to inscribe names and sums in his ledger.

Both men looked expectantly at Zurenne. She drew a steadying breath, grateful for the elevation of the dais's three steps. Now she could look even the tallest men in the eye despite her own modest stature. She spared a moment to thank Halcarion, goddess of maidens, that Ilysh took after her father in the promise of elegant height when she was full grown as well as in her strong features.

The murmur of conversation died away as the tenantry realised that she awaited their attention.

'Fair festival to you all.'

Zurenne had barely spoken two words before

exultant cheers rang up to the restored roof, echoing among the bare rafters unsoftened by the generations of hanging banners that had once proclaimed Lysha and Neeny's heritage. Like the ancient baronial chair, those standards had burned to ashes, never to be salvaged.

As the echoes died away, Zurenne continued. 'We have no need to hold any high assize—'

Once again, noisy approval drowned out her words, even though everyone knew that Kusint's guardsmen had no violent malefactors locked up in the barrack-hall's cellar.

The demesne folk and the tenantry had ensured that their maiden lady need not insist on her duty to sit in judgement even over murderers and rapists, compelled to condemn such evildoers to the gallows and the gibbet by the high road. They knew full well that Ilysh had only seen her thirteenth summer solstice this past year, however determined she might be to assume all of her dead father's responsibilities.

So, as Zurenne had learned, overhearing the maidservants gossiping, Halferan's villagers and yeomen had administered their own swift and rough justice whenever some villain had been discovered selfishly seeking to profit at others' expense while everyone else strove to rebuild their homes and to re-establish their flocks and herds.

She stole a glance at Kusint. He gazed blandly over the heads of the joyful throng, as if he'd never had to intervene to make sure that such punishment stopped just short of murder, when an egg-seller whose wares all proved addled had been pelted with filth and stones or a day-labourer caught sleeping under a hedge rather than work for his bread and ale had been stripped naked and beaten bloody. And Zurenne had no doubt those incidents were only the whiskers on that rat's nose.

Of course several neighbouring barons had seized on such incidents, claiming that Halferan was slipping into anarchy. Baron Karpis in particular didn't cease to prophesy disaster. How could any barony hope to prosper without the guiding hand of a nobleman reared to manage such responsibilities?

Upstairs in her sitting room, Zurenne had a box of letters from concerned lords' gracious wives offering their support when she came to her senses and sought to set Ilysh's scandalous marriage aside in favour of a more suitable alliance.

Such letters would go unanswered and if any noble lord thought to take advantage of Corrain's absence by arriving unannounced, intent on browbeating her, Zurenne would remind them how Baron Karpis and his men had been so thoroughly humiliated when the magewoman Madam Jilseth had rusted their swords and armour to dust in the blink of an eye with her wizardry. Those lords weren't to know that Halferan had forsworn magic's aid henceforth.

As a smile of recollection curved her rose-petal lips, Zurenne realised that letting her thoughts wander had allowed the tenantry's cheers to subside into idle chatter and jovial exchanges of festival greetings. She must command this crowd's attention and respect, for her daughter's sake.

'Today—' Zurenne cleared her throat and repeated herself more loudly. 'Today we ask you to pay your fealty in coin, to enable your lord and baron to safeguard your interests through the year to come as his—as his oath to you all demands.'

With the cheers this time more respectfully muted, she noted Ilysh shifting on her seat.

Had her daughter caught that stumble in her words? Zurenne had so nearly repeated the form of words which her dead husband had always used, which his stewards had used on his behalf when he had been away attending the festival parliament.

Her lost beloved had laid claim to this seasonal levy both as his birthright and by virtue of his oath to Saedrin. He had been Baron Halferan by blood just as his father had been and countless grandsires before that.

Now it was Lady Ilysh who commanded these people's loyalty and their love. Zurenne's heart warmed to see the affection in their faces as they stepped up onto the dais, eagerly laying down their coin as tangible proof of their devotion.

Corrain would never be more than an erstwhile guard captain to these people, his sham marriage merely one more service he was rendering to the barony to keep their true lady safe.

— CHAPTER TWO —

'YOUR CLOAK, MY lord Halferan.' A lackey hurried forward to offer him the heavy grey wool, scarlet-dyed fur at the collar thick to foil the cold. Winter was appreciably more bitter here, so much further north with almost the whole length of Caladhria between him and home.

'Thank you.' Corrain tossed the man a silver penny before taking the cloak to sling it around his own shoulders. Though he didn't imagine a Duryea inn's doorkeeper would try to strangle him, lifelong habit wouldn't see him allowing another man's hands so close to his throat.

'Will you be sharing some festival cheer with your friends, my lord?' The porter smiled, genial and guileless.

'No.' Corrain didn't offer the man any more than that as he emerged into the bright sunlight. He shivered unexpectedly.

'Did some Eldritch Kin walk over your shadow?' A dark-haired youth in Halferan livery strolled over from the brazier where he'd been enjoying the warmth of the glowing charcoal. His breath smoked with the warmth of the sausage he was eating, wedged into a sliced heel of bread with a generous spoonful of fried onions.

Reven might be young but Corrain found it hard to credit he still believed in the black-eyed, blue-skinned

24

half-men of chimney-corner tales. In the echo of their footsteps crossing whatever ground corresponded to this marketplace in the unknown Otherworld.

Corrain was concerned with more tangible mischief-makers than Eldritch Kin defying Saedrin's authority and slipping into this world for their own nefarious purposes as the Keyholder's door stood open on this shortest quarter day of the year.

'Find out who's paying that doorman for whatever he might overhear,' he ordered without preamble, fastening his cloak. 'Whose maids and lackeys will be clearing up after the parliament's debates today? Who will be guarding the merchants' hall's doors?'

Corrain had different battles to fight now that the cursed corsairs were all dead and drowned, now that he was finally free from the uneasy and unequal alliances he had made with Hadrumal's wizards. Now he needed the information which he had always supplied to his own true Lord Halferan, to be used amid the rivalries and squabbles of Caladhria's nobles, especially as he pursued his current conspiracy with the barons of Saldiray, Taine and Myrist.

Reven chewed and swallowed quickly. 'Lord Pertynd supplies the servants to tidy the merchants' exchange hall every day. Erbale will watch the door until today's debate concludes and Vildare will have the night's duty after that.'

Corrain nodded. 'Find out the name of Lord Erbale's guard captain. Find out where his troopers are drinking this evening. Go along in a plain jerkin with a fat purse and a harmless face. See what gossip they might have picked up from the barons going to and fro through the day.'

'Aye—my lord.' Reven ducked his head to cover his instant of hesitation.

Corrain hid a smile. The lad's first instinct was still to call him captain. That was no great concern, as long as there was no one around to overhear them. What was important was Reven learning all the skills that a good guard sergeant needed to serve his lord when the quarterly parliament was in session.

He considered suggesting that the lad seek out Lord Pertynd's maidservants. To see if Reven could inveigle his way between some adventurous girl's sheets, the better to search her bedchamber for whatever notes she had gathered up, passed between the barons' tables during their debates and carelessly discarded. Corrain's own reputation as a trooper with a keen appetite for festival dalliance hadn't only stemmed from his willingness to oblige any woman whose wandering eye caught his own.

He thought better of it, and not only because he didn't think that Reven had ever so much as untied a giggling girl's garters. The barony would be better served if every Halferan guardsman kept his breeches laced. He jerked his head backwards towards the Silver Boar's grandly carved and painted entrance.

'Has anyone come sniffing around the laundry baskets at the inn, looking for stained sheets? Asking the chambermaids if I've been sleeping alone?'

Corrain hoped there had. Anyone looking to undermine the marriage making him Baron Halferan by catching him in adultery was doomed to disappointment and the sooner that word spread, the better.

He had married his dead lord's daughter to keep her and her mother and sister out of any would-be guardian's grasp. He would no more give Halferan's enemies cause to challenge his right to protect them than he would humiliate the child by tupping some tawdry whore. Until he found a husband worthy of Ilysh, he would stay as celibate as she was virgin.

Besides, these days he found that no trial, though his drinking companions of old would find that hard to believe. Plenty of troopers sworn to other lords could tell lurid tales of sharing their festival liberty in the same gambling dens and brothels as the new Baron Halferan.

'Well?' he prompted Reven.

'No, my lord.'

Corrain noted the swift blush rising from the boy's collar. 'Then what have they been asking?'

He hadn't served in Halferan's guard for more than twenty years without learning to recognise a junior trooper with something to hide.

Reven's cheeks were burning as furiously as the sausage vendor's brazier. 'They say, my lord—' he couldn't bring himself to look at Corrain '—that you're no longer fit to share any woman's bed.'

'Why not?' Corrain was honestly puzzled.

'They say, my lord, that the Archipelagans—' Reven forced the words out in a rush '—that the Archipelagans geld their slaves.'

Corrain's first instinct was to laugh. He curbed it. 'They're saying that I've left my stones on some Aldabreshin beach?'

Reven nodded. 'Everyone knows that the warlords geld the house slaves who watch their wives.'

Corrain shook his head. 'The corsairs would gain nothing by cutting a galley's rowers. They'd lose half of them to blood loss or wound rot or just the shock of it.'

He could feel his groin tightening just at the revolting thought.

'So try thinking with your brain not your shrivelling cock, Sergeant,' he said curtly. 'What does anyone have to gain by spreading this new rumour about me?'

Reven hesitated. 'To make you a figure of fun?'

'That's doubtless part of it,' Corrain agreed, 'but what does it mean for Halferan? What's to become of the barony if there's no chance of me begetting an heir? That's what they want people asking themselves,' he concluded grimly.

'My lord.' Reven's blush had been fading. Now he coloured more luridly than before, doubtless at the thought of Corrain sharing Lady Ilysh's bed.

Corrain clapped a reassuring hand on the lad's shoulder. 'Well, if whoever's behind this rumour has the stones to challenge my right to Halferan on these grounds, I can just drop my breeches and show all the lords of the parliament that I've still got both my berries attached to my twig.'

That won him a choked laugh from Reven.

'Meantime, you can drop a few tantalizing hints when you're drinking with Lord Erbale's men this evening,' Corrain said thoughtfully. 'Just make sure you take their coin before you disappoint them with your certain knowledge of my intact manhood, my lonely bed notwithstanding, and my unshakeable devotion to Lady Ilysh.'

'Yes, my lord.' Reven ducked his head. 'Would you like to see what I have bought her for a festival fairing?'

'By all means.' Corrain eyed the lad thoughtfully. Was he just trying to change the subject?

'Look at this.' Reven took a rag-wrapped lump from his pocket. Carefully unfolding the cloth, he revealed an ordinary pebble with one smoothly polished face.

'See?' Reven turned the shining stone so that Corrain could see it was patterned like a feather fern.

No, it was a feather fern, or at least, that's what the hucksters who sold such stones insisted. Somehow in aeons past, the plant had been trapped in mud which had gradually turned to rock. Any wizard would swear to it, the peddlers assured their customers.

'Do you think she'll like it?' Reven asked, suddenly uncertain.

Corrain was tempted to lie. He'd brought Reven on this trip for a good many reasons. Newly installed as sergeant, the lad needed to establish his authority over the troop without Kusint always at hand to prompt the men to toe Reven's line. Added to that, Corrain wanted Kusint watching over the manor, in case someone like Baron Karpis was fool enough to try taking advantage of Zurenne while she and her children were left alone.

That wasn't all. Over this past half-season, Corrain and Zurenne had agreed that Reven's obvious devotion to Ilysh looked far too likely to slip into infatuation. One thoughtless midwinter kiss amid the license of the festival could prompt no end of complications.

'I think she'll like it well enough.' He kept his approval muted. 'Now, once you're done drinking, you're welcome to find some girl to share your pillow for the night. The cleanest whorehouses are by the Peorle Gate. Best to be sure you don't take any unwelcome gifts back to some Halferan sweetheart.'

'I don't—' Reven thrust his barely whiskered chin forward. 'It's my duty to serve you, my lord.'

'As you wish.' Well, he could hardly order the boy to go out and flip a lightskirt's frills.

Noon's five chimes sounded out across the town, every

timepiece attuned to the great bell in the merchants' exchange tower. Corrain reminded himself of the shorter days at this season so much further north than home. The barons would be summoned to their next debate by the sixth chime of the ten dividing the daylight. He had scant time to waste if he was to carry through his avowed intent to mark the turning of the year.

'Come with me.' He headed across the marketplace.

Reven's stride nearly matched his own; For-Winter might have just passed but the lad had grown like a weed flourishing in Aft-Spring.

A black-gowned dancer trailing white ribbons from her hands wheeled into their path. As she pirouetted around them, drawing fleeting, silken designs in the sunlight, her smile invited them to spare some small coin in return for her festival entertainment.

Perhaps she had innocently noted Reven's pewter and maroon livery matching Corrain's cloak, marking them as noble and escort, one of them bound to carry a full purse.

Perhaps her calculating accomplice was coming up behind them. A slim knife could cut through a belt or even into a pocket to steal a purse unnoticed, especially if the girl were to stumble on these slick cobbles in her flimsy dancing slippers. Either the nobleman or his loyal trooper would surely dash gallantly forward to save the dark-haired beauty from a painful fall.

Perhaps mingling with barons and their plotting was making him too suspicious. All the same, Corrain twitched his cloak back to leave his sword hilt unencumbered.

'Fair festival.' He smiled at the dancer. 'Reven, a few coppers for the fair maiden.'

As the boy obliged, the girl plucked the coins from the air amid a deft spiral of silk. The glint of tossed wealth prompted other entertainers to drift in their direction.

'This way.' Corrain disappointed them by cutting a straight route across the cobbles towards a narrow alley.

'Where are we going?' Reven made sure that his own cloak wouldn't foil his blade if he needed to use it.

'To fulfil an oath.' Corrain felt for the new dagger sheathed on the opposite hip to his sword belt. He'd spent the last chime of the night before dawn honing the expensive steel with his whetstone. It would be sharp enough.

'You should learn your way round these ginnels.' He left the alley for a narrower path dividing the back yards of two long terraces. 'Here and in Ferl, Trebin, Tresia and Adrulle. You must be able to find your way around any such town blindfold before the parliament returns.'

As they emerged on to a cobbled street, Corrain watched to see how long it took Reven to recognise their surroundings. Good. The first thing the boy looked for was a tavern. As soon as he found the Elm Tree, recognition gleamed in his eyes.

'Where are we headed?' Reven asked.

'Talagrin's shrine.' Corrain crossed the broad thoroughfare and took another alleyway to reach a square of worn turf with a circular building in its centre.

The door stood half open to reveal the glow of candles within the windowless gloom. Hilts of broken daggers were nailed around the entrance and to the door itself, inside and out. Chipped enamel pommels, fraying wire bindings on hilts and fractured steel blades turned the portal into a sharp-toothed maw.

'My lord?' Reven was understandably bemused. The

god of the hunt's season was For-Autumn, with his rites celebrated at the turn from Aft-Summer.

'Wait here.' Corrain entered the shrine and closed the door behind him. Today the lad could learn that even a trusted sergeant didn't know all a baron's business.

He looked up at the god's statue. Talagrin stared blindly ahead, his marble eyes blank. With Duryea so close to Caladhria's border with Ensaimin, Corrain guessed at some Forest blood in this particular sculptor's veins. The bow-wielding, pelt-draped effigy could have stepped out of the tales which Kusint told, of the god of wild places whom his mother's folk worshipped as one of their own.

Corrain had been raised to call Talagrin the swordsman's god. The little statue in Halferan's manor shrine carried a sword and wore a chainmail hauberk in the same style as every baron and the men who rode behind him. That statue had been smashed along with the others when the corsairs had despoiled the shrine.

Once Corrain had done what he intended today, he was done with all the gods, however they were carved. He no longer believed in any of them. Why should he, when they had so completely failed him and his fellow guardsmen when the corsairs had enslaved them and murdered their lord?

'I swore an oath,' Corrain drew the dagger from his belt, 'that I would see Hosh brought safely home. That I would see Halferan saved from those accursed raiders. That I would do it all myself without any god's aid, for my dead lord's sake.'

Turning his head, he drew the long braid of his uncut hair free from his cloak's collar. Pulling it hard and taut, he severed it with a swift stroke of the razor-sharp dagger.

'So much for my ambitions. I was a fool to meddle with magic. But Hosh is home and the barony is safe—'

About to throw the fraying braid at the statue's feet, Corrain halted. 'Maybe I should give this to Drianon. How does it feel for a warrior god to be outdone by a goddess armed with a broom? She's done more to save Halferan than you.'

He remembered the night when he had cut Ilysh's ribbon-bedecked wedding plait, to lay it before the divine guardian of hearth and home, yielding to Zurenne's desperate plea for the fiction of legal protection for her children.

So much for his oath to save his dead lord's family by cutting down their enemies with his mighty sword. Who was he to mock even this lifeless statue of an imaginary god? Who was he to boast of his heroism?

Corrain had sworn to avenge his dead lord but Hosh had slain Lord Halferan's murderer. Alone, unarmed, suffering from unhealed wounds, the boy had survived in the corsair lair after Corrain and Kusint had escaped. More incredible still, he had escaped the slaughter when that cursed Mandarkin mage had held the whole island in magical thrall.

Corrain dropped the severed hair to the earthen floor and drove the dagger deep into the wooden pillar closest to hand. Now he turned his attention to his manacled wrist. Plenty of the parliament's barons had sneaked covert glances at the slave iron he still wore, trailing its short length of broken chain. He'd wager that none of them had noticed that the manacle's iron ring was now secured with a discreet twist of wire.

No one, Corrain included, could possibly have imagined how long it would take him to pick that cursed

Archipelagan lock. At least he'd had plenty of time, sitting alone at night in his truckle bed set up in the baronial tower's muniment room. When the time came to give Ilysh's hand to a worthy suitor, plenty of Halferan servants would be able to swear that the two of them had never shared a bedchamber. Meantime, no one would be able to sneak up the tower's stairs without Corrain knowing.

'Have this as well and much good it may do you.'

Corrain dropped the unlocked manacle beside his discarded hair. Let that baffle the shrine's priest or whoever else might find it. Perhaps someone would recognise it for the low-born Lord Halferan's slave-iron and go running to some other baron.

Good luck to them and he hoped that they would ask for its weight in silver before handing the cursed thing over. Who ever bought it would get no joy of their purchase. He wouldn't answer any of their questions. This was between Corrain and his dead lord.

Now his honour was satisfied. He had made good on his oath to lay these tokens before Talagrin when Hosh and Halferan were safe and he'd done so far from home, to avoid sullying the manor's shrine at this turn of a new year with these reminders of past sorrows and tribulation. Now it was time to make a fresh start without gods or wizards or any such fetters.

Corrain turned his back on the god and opened the shrine's door.

'Cap—' Reven's eyes widened to see Corrain's hair cut short above his cloak collar. His gaze dropped instantly to fasten on the older man's wrist, the scars where the manacle had galled him now plain for all to see. 'My lord?'

Corrain wasn't about to answer his sergeant's questions either. The only person with any right to ask him what he had done was Hosh, though Corrain still shrank from the prospect of explaining his follies and failures to the inexplicably trusting youth. One day, perhaps. Many years from now.

'Do you think that the Elm Tree will serve us a decent mug of ale and a bowl of stew before the parliament begins its debate?'

'Perhaps, my lord,' Reven said uncertainly.

Corrain left the shrine door ajar as they had found it and headed towards the jovial noises of the street. It wasn't only his head and his hand which felt lighter, relieved of those burdens of his oath and his servitude.

He was done with the gods and goddesses and their deceits and uncertainties. Now it only remained for him to cut Halferan's last ties to wizardry and be free from the perils of consorting with mages.

More than that, for his dead lord's sake and with the help of Baron Saldiray and Baron Taine, he'd see all of Caladhria guarded against Hadrumal's influence before this midwinter parliament dissolved.

— CHAPTER THREE —

The residence of Mellitha Esterlin, Relshaz
Winter Solstice Festival, 3rd Day
In the 10th Year of Tadriol the Provident of Tormalin

THE ARM-RING lay in the centre of the rosewood table. A gaudy ornament, it showed its age in its florid styling as well through evidence of hard wear. Several of the rock crystals studding the circle were chipped and the inner surface had lost its gilding, the silver dull with scratches.

'What did the boy Hosh say to you about his experience of its ensorcellement? His exact words if you please, Velindre.' The oldest of the four wizards seated around the table looked intently at the tall, blonde magewoman sat opposite.

'Forgive me, Madam Mellitha, but what is the point of this?' the youngest of the four asked curtly. 'We have been striving all afternoon with nothing to show for our efforts.'

'Merenel?' Jilseth looked at her friend with concern. She could feel the warmth of Merenel's fire magic fading from the arm-ring.

The nexus which the four magewomen had wrought, in hopes of penetrating the silver gilt ornament's secrets, was already unravelling. Jilseth would never have imagined such a thing when she and Merenel had perfected their skills with Tornauld and Nolyen, the two other wizards handpicked by the Archmage to learn quintessential magic's secrets alongside them.

It was all the more puzzling since Merenel's ability to work individual fire spells seemed largely unaffected although her skills with quadrate magic, combining all four of the wizardly elements, had become markedly erratic.

'We know that this trinket bestows a stoneskin spell on whoever wears it. Granted, that's no trivial wizardry but any of us could work it if we wished.' Merenel ran a hand through her curling black hair. The Tormalin magewoman's olive complexion was sallow with exhaustion and her shoulders sagged beneath her long-sleeved crimson jerkin.

'Stoneskin isn't the only enchantment instilled into the thing,' Velindre observed. 'No mundane born who wears it can remove it. Doing so requires a mage's touch and I would very much like to understand that spellcrafting.'

'I wish to understand how an inanimate object can still confer such benefits when the mage who first wove that wizardry is ten generations dead,' Mellitha added.

'Then I suggest that you find another mage to make up your nexus.' The Tormalin wizard stood up and left the elegant sitting room. As she slammed the door to relieve her frustration, the angry draught stirred the long velvet curtains shielding the tall windows.

Hearing the clack of Merenel's boot heels retreating down the marble floored hallway, Jilseth wondered if she should go after her. She knew something of such distress; of being suddenly unable to rely on the magic which one had so carefully nurtured and studied ever since that first manifestation of one's affinity, thrilling and terrifying in equal measure.

Though their situations weren't wholly the same. In that last desperate defence of Halferan Manor as the corsairs attacked, Jilseth had feared for her own life as much as anyone else. She had willingly poured her strength of mind and body into her innate link with the elemental earth, to harness the complex spells which Hadrumal's great mages had devised.

Merenel had been given no such choice. She had been swept up in the Archmage's magic, unable to resist as Planir had woven fifteen other wizards' power together to secure the destruction of the corsairs' lair. Ever since, it seemed that the Tormalin magewoman's intuitive grasp of quintessential magic's complexities had deserted her.

Quintessential magic could only be wielded by four mages working together to double and redouble their united strength in a nexus of sorcery uniting their affinities with air, earth, fire and water. Its secrets were among Hadrumal's most closely guarded lore.

Ever since that catastrophic night, Jilseth found herself wondering what other secrets were hidden in books and scrolls held in the wizard isle's tallest towers? Had the Masters and Mistress of the elements known that Planir could unite four separate quartets of wizards into one still greater nexus? Did they understand how he had been able to control that immense magic, an order of magnitude stronger than the quintessential magecraft which Jilseth had always been told was the summit of Hadrumal's wizardry?

It had been the only way to defeat the murderous magic wielded against them by the renegade Mandarkin mage who had sought to claim the corsairs' island and to enslave hitherto-unsuspected Aldabreshi mageborn for his own vicious purposes. So the Archmage had explained, offering his regrets but no apology to those who had suffered as badly as Merenel.

'I don't believe that the problem is with our nexus.' Mellitha studied the silver-gilt arm-ring.

'What nexus?' Velindre retorted. 'We cannot—'

Mellitha looked across the table. 'We know that a precise combination of all four elements must have ensorcelled the thing. I am beginning to suspect that this particular blending has also been crafted to disrupt any subsequent union of wizardry which might seek to nullify the spells within it.'

Jilseth decided she could leave Merenel's temper to cool while she learned what she could from these far more experienced wizards. There were few to rival either magewoman, even in Hadrumal. Velindre had been widely expected to rise to the rank of Cloud Mistress not so long ago. All the wine shop sages agreed that Mellitha could become Flood Mistress whenever she chose to challenge Troanna, even after her decades away from the wizard isle.

Perhaps Merenel felt even more out of place than Jilseth sometimes did, caught between these two who could boast elemental understanding and expertise so vastly outstripping her own.

Then she realised that Velindre was looking at her intently, a frown of concentration sharpening the woman's angular features.

'The underlying sorcery is tied to the metal and the crystals, making this inherently an earth-magic artefact. You should focus your affinity on it alone while we three ward you and the piece alike from other elemental influences.' Velindre glanced towards the closed door, her lips thinning with irritation. 'If we can persuade Merenel to rejoin us.'

'I'll try,' Jilseth temporised.

'Let Merenel rest for the moment.' Mellitha rose, gracious despite her comfortable curves and the years threading silver through her chestnut hair. Her costly green silk gown rustled as she picked up the silver-gilt arm-ring and carried it away to a side table. She returned with a shallow silver bowl and a finger-long purple glass vial.

Resuming her seat, she rested her fingertips on the bowl's rim. Beads of water swelled in the base, wrung from the empty air to swiftly fill the bowl. Mellitha let a single drop of blended oils fall from the little vial. Emerald magelight suffused the water and then the spell called up a vision of some featureless sea.

'We're already losing the daylight.' Velindre shook out the loose sleeves of her azure tunic, cut in the flowing Aldabreshin style so common in this port city, and cupped the bowl with her long-fingered hands. The sun's afterglow gilded white-tipped wavelets two hundred leagues and more away. The Archipelago's more swiftly falling night would soon shroud those southerly seas.

Aquamarine mist thickened over the remote waters and foaming crests surged across the bowl to vanish into the scrying spell's emerald rim.

Velindre withdrew her hands, sitting back. 'Nothing has changed as far as I can see.'

'Jilseth?' The green magelight striking upwards deepened the fine wrinkles around Mellitha's grey eyes.

Jilseth focused her concentration on the scrying and then reached through the ensorcelled water to assess the swirling confusion of the elements in those distant seas where the corsair island had been.

As she touched the bowl, her innate tie to all things born of the earth recognised the essence of elemental silver. Its touch soothed and strengthened her wizard senses. It seemed absurd to recall that not so long ago she had feared that her affinity was crippled beyond recovery. Now she must concentrate on curbing powers awakened by the shock of being caught up in Planir's assault on the Mandarkin mage. Where Merenel's wizardry had been thrown into confusion, Jilseth had discovered myriad unsuspected facets of her affinity to explore.

Infinitely careful, she threaded her wizardry through Mellitha's scrying and sought any sorcery swirling through those remote waters scanned by the scrying spell. Tangled amber magelight surfaced briefly amid the roiling waves. The amber skein unravelled and sank away.

'Is that something new?' Velindre leaned forward.

Jilseth shook her head. 'Nothing prompted by wizardry. Just currents of molten rock shifting beneath the seabed.'

The sweetness of the oils blended with the scrying perfumed the room as though the bowlful of water was being warmed by that distant heat under the southern sea. Mellitha's spell didn't falter, unruffled by the elemental fire's antipathy to her water affinity. Jilseth marvelled, not for the first time, at the serene magewoman's skills.

Velindre contemplated the shadowy vision, her eyes hooded. 'Elemental upheaval still lingers even after a full quarter of the year.'

Jilseth was still waiting for the right time to ask these eminent magewomen what they thought of Planir's actions. Had they agreed when the Archmage and Stone Master of Hadrumal had declared the Mandarkin mage guilty of the most heinous crimes against wizardry? Had they concurred when the Element Masters of Cloud and Hearth and the Mistress of the Flood had agreed that Anskal's abuses of those mageborn whom he had enslaved mandated his death?

Had anyone foreseen the consequences when Planir had woven his first nexus with Rafrid, Kalion and Troanna? Did even the most revered among Hadrumal's Council know how mercilessly the Mandarkin Anskal would be confined by their quintessential magic? That his belligerent magecraft would merely rebound from that implacably constricting barrier? That his struggles to escape this incarceration would only hasten the moment when his control over his innate affinity failed? That his unbridled wizardry would be lethally destructive trapped within the adamant prison woven by the Archmage's nexus?

Jilseth longed to ask Planir when he had realised that even this initial union of Hadrumal's greatest wizards wasn't going to suffice. That the Mandarkin was calling on some vile unknown sorcery; a spell to suck all elemental strength from those enslaved mageborn, to add their power to his own, not caring that he would kill them.

When had Planir decided to abandon Hadrumal's original hope of rescuing at least some of those mageborn captives by confining their wizardry in less lethal fashion until they surrendered to judgement?

When had the Archmage realised that only the unprecedented four-fold nexus could possibly defeat the elemental maelstrom whipped up by the Mandarkin? Had Planir hesitated for even an instant before risking the lives, the sanity and the affinity of those wizards whom he had summoned to work with him, by weaving their elemental powers inextricably into his elemental lattice?

Jilseth could only be grateful that Planir had been able to drive that devastating power down into the bedrock deep below the corsair harbour. That he had cast it out into the seas surrounding the remote island and hurled it into the winds that scoured the Aldabreshin sky. The destruction of the raiders' island wasn't so great a calamity, not compared with the catastrophe that could have befallen so many of Hadrumal's greatest mages and so many of her friends.

'There's no trace of any other ensorcelled artefacts sunk to the sea floor.' Velindre ran a thoughtful hand through her close-cropped golden hair. 'Is there any way that the renegade could have sent some of his loot to an ally?'

'We don't know that he had any allies in Mandarkin or anywhere else.' Mellitha drummed impeccably manicured fingers on the rosewood table top. She looked at Jilseth. 'Have our esteemed colleagues in Hadrumal made any progress in learning just what his homeland's magical traditions might be?'

'Not beyond confirming that Solura's Orders of Wizardry condemn all Mandarkin's mages as venal and as violent as Anskal proved,' Jilseth replied.

'His ambitions went beyond mere wealth,' Velindre argued. 'Why else would he gather a circle of Aldabreshi mageborn to train in his own tradition? If all he sought was gold, he could have gathered ten times such riches by simply lying to the corsairs about which of their treasures had some wizardry bound within them. The Archipelagans have no way to know. They would have handed over whatever he pointed to, repelled by even the suspicion of magic's contaminating influence.'

'Perhaps but we still have no reason to think that any artefacts escaped us,' Mellitha said firmly. She gestured and a tall oil lamp obediently glowed to relieve the gloom deepening in the long room.

Now Velindre turned to Jilseth. 'How are Hadrumal's own investigations into the Mandarkin's loot progressing?'

'No better than our attempts here today,' Jilseth saw nothing to be gained by dissembling.

'I never came across any such things, not in all my time in the Archipelago.' Velindre scowled at the arm-ring.

Jilseth wondered why the magewoman took it so sorely amiss that she hadn't encountered any trinkets or jewelled ornaments imbued with spells, when she had been travelling the Archipelago in the guise of a eunuch scholar a handful of years before.

'Why should you?' Mellitha challenged Velindre. 'You weren't looking. Besides, if you had admitted to sensing magic within some warlord's treasure, you'd have seen your own flayed skin nailed to a gatepost before you died.'

Jilseth shuddered at the thought of the Aldabreshin hatred of magic; so absolute that such atrocities were deemed essential to preserve the purity of the omens of earth and sky which governed every Archipelagan's life.

Had the past year's events given any Aldabreshin warlord pause for thought? Had the Archipelagans realised their savagery was a two-edged sword? With no wizards to call on, they could have no defences against a mage as vicious as Anskal.

Velindre scowled, still brooding. 'I might have noticed ensorcelled trinkets being passed from hand to hand if the art of crafting such things wasn't so scorned in Hadrumal.'

Mellitha looked at Jilseth. 'I take it the Soluran Orders of Wizardry are still refusing to share what lore they hold on such things?'

Jilseth nodded. 'As long as Hadrumal refuses to share the secrets of quintessential magic.'

Velindre folded her arms. 'If you and Merenel haven't come here with any news, you must have come with questions from the Archmage. What does Planir want?'

'He asks what you know of the current situation in the Archipelago, of the consequences of last For-Autumn's events.'

When they had arrived though, the senior magewomen had immediately sought their assistance in making a nexus in hopes of prying open the gilt and crystal armring's secrets. Jilseth and Merenel had both been just as eager to try.

'The winds are still unsettled in that reach of the Nahik domain and are likely to remain so.' Velindre gazed towards the long windows, as though she could see across the hundreds of leagues to the Archipelago. 'Without the corsair island on the western fringes several important sea lanes are now left unshielded from approaching storms.'

'The sea currents are similarly reshaping themselves and everything else under the waves,' Mellitha added. 'What should concern Planir is we've seen no ships sailing northward from the Miris domain since the corsair island's destruction, or passing through the Miris islands from anywhere further south. While we wouldn't expect to see Archipelagan galleys risking the winter sailing from the islands to the mainland, the usual trading between the warlords' domains should have continued.'

'Do you think that the galleys and triremes will sail north again once they have got the measure of the shifts in the currents and winds?' Jilseth watched the scrying spell fading to leave clear water glossed with the rainbow sheen of the perfume's oils. 'Such changes are a natural consequence of the corsair island's loss even if such destruction itself was magewrought.'

'The Aldabreshi won't make any such distinction,'

Velindre asserted, 'not as long as they see the omens and portents around those islands thrown into chaos.'

Jilseth pictured the map which Velindre had once shown her, of the northernmost islands and the two neighbouring domains whose sea lanes were the conduit for all trade between the mainland and the Archipelago.

'What does this mean for the Khusro and Jagai warlords?'

'I have no idea.' Now Mellitha sounded just as affronted as Velindre had done earlier. 'The Aldabreshi have managed to convince the Relshazri to shun any dealings with wizardry.'

'Still?' Jilseth knew that the locals here had sought to placate the Archipelagans after the shocking news from the south had caused initial panic among the galleys and triremes tied up along the dockside. After a full season had passed, she had imagined that this city of traders and merchants would resume their pragmatic and profitable ways, turning magecraft to their own advantage as they always had.

If Mellitha didn't use her wizardry directly in her lucrative business of collecting taxes for the Relshazri magistrates, her magebirth was no secret after three decades living in the city. Indeed, as she had cheerfully told Jilseth, her underlings tactfully let newcomers know that they were dealing with a wizard, in case those optimists fondly believed that a second set of ledgers or some concealed stash of coin could escape her mage-enhanced eyes. As a result, Mellitha rarely had to work any actual spells to uncover such deceits.

Velindre traded openly on her wizardly skills, surveying the skies and winds and selling her knowledge of incoming storms and sea states to mariners charting a course towards the Archipelago or heading eastward across the Gulf of Lescar to Tormalin's ports.

'No ship's captain sailing anywhere from Col to Toremal who has dealings with the Aldabreshi dares to be seen in my company.' The blond magewoman scowled.

Mellitha sighed. 'We haven't been idle. Tell Planir that we've sent ciphered letters to Kheda by a range of different routes. Though I cannot say how long it will be before we get a reply. Such a letter must pass through ten or twenty hands to conceal its origin and its destination.'

'Planir will know who this Kheda is?' Jilseth knew that was a foolish question; of course the Archmage would know, but she didn't and she was curious, having heard this Archipelagan mentioned a few times in this house. He had been involved Velindre's own mysterious and perilous travels in the Archipelago some years before.

Mellitha smiled with wry understanding and answered Jilseth's unspoken query. 'Kheda is that rarest of Aldabreshi, one who understands that magic is no more good nor evil than any other tool or authority. What matters is the use which it's put to. He travels between the Archipelago and the mainland, trading in knowledge and practical solutions to common problems. He believes that hostility between the islanders and the northerners stems from ignorance more than anything else.'

Velindre snorted. 'It would be as well to remind Planir—'

All three women looked around as the door opened and a chill draught prompted a combative glow in the charcoal brazier set between the table and a trio of silken settles further down the room.

'Forgive me.' Merenel stood in the doorway, a blush of embarrassment on her cheekbones. 'You're quite right,

— CHAPTER FOUR —

'MIN GARTAS.' THE balding demesne reeve opened his purse with fingers stained and scarred from working alongside the manor's craftsmen as they restored their village.

'...fourteen, fifteen and sixteen.'

Master Rauffe carefully counted each silver mark aloud before these witnesses and then wrote the tally in his ledger.

'Our most sincere thanks, Master Gartas,' Ilysh said warmly.

'And our admiration,' Zurenne added quickly. 'You must have worked long days and most diligently.'

Truth be told, she refused to believe that this was a tenth of whatever Gartas had earned on his own account since autumn's equinox. Of necessity Zurenne had taught herself the intricacies of the barony's finances since her husband's death and during Corrain's absences pursuing corsairs. This much silver must be nearer to a fifth of Gartas's share of the trading dues he'd collected through this past quarter year. The tenth-day market in Halferan village was still barely worth the name and no merchants or casual peddlers had passed this way since the turn of For-Winter.

She saw the same realisation in Ilysh's eyes. They had educated themselves together, defying all tradition which insisted that a manor's accounting was none of a noblewoman's concern.

'Athim Sirstin.' The tall man stooped to set his coins down on the table, the breadth of his shoulders as impressive as his height. Softly spoken as he was, there was no mistaking the pride in his voice at being able to make this payment.

'Twelve silver marks.' Master Rauffe recorded the total with brisk pen strokes.

'Our thanks.' Ilysh smiled with sincere gratitude.

Zurenne echoed her daughter, even as she calculated that the blacksmith's skills would have earned him the coin to pay at least half as much again in a year of peace and plenty.

'It's my honour, my lady.' Sirstin favoured Lysha with a fatherly grin. 'My lady Esnina.'

Neeny giggled as the smith bowed to her, still pink-cheeked with elation at being so honoured. Zurenne spared her younger daughter a smile, privately surprised that boredom or weariness hadn't yet overcome the little girl's earlier promises to behave.

'Our thanks for your son's service.' Sirstin's lad Linset was the most youthful of the barony's guards currently accompanying Corrain to the Duryea parliament.

Zurenne spoke loudly enough for her words to reach those in the hall below the dais. Let them remember that their tithe would be spent feeding and equipping the troopers who defended Halferan's roads and herds from any villains still seeking easy pickings after the barony's recent troubles.

'Tye Fitrel.' The old man climbed stiffly up onto the dais, a surprisingly fat purse in his weathered hand, and scars of swordplay visible across his knuckles.

'Fair festival.' Zurenne greeted the veteran guardsman warmly.

'Master Fitrel, you are most welcome to our feast.' Lysha's eyes shone with equal gratitude for the old man's stalwart service.

Neeny bounced forward in her chair. 'Sergeant!'

'Not any more, moppet, I'm retired. Now, here's something for your festival.' Fitrel opened the purse to take out a little toy rabbit, fashioned from the fur of the real coneys which he raised in pens around his house.

Corrain had helped the old warrior rebuild his holding on the edge of the village across the brook. Comparing the manor's newly drawn tithe map with one surviving from the old archive Zurenne had noticed shifting boundaries had favoured the old man significantly.

She didn't begrudge him a finger-width of the ground. Fitrel hadn't only rallied old men and beardless boys to the manor's defence this past year. A generation ago, barely older than Lysha was now, Corrain had been bereft of both parents. Fitrel had taken him under his roof. Zurenne had come to realise just how much Halferan owed to the loyalty which the old man had instilled in the guardsman.

As Neeny squealed with delight over her new toy, stroking the little rabbit's stitched face, Fitrel chuckled with affection.

'Four silver make a gold star and one silver mark over.' Master Rauffe recorded the tally of coin in the correct columns.

Zurenne saw that this second strong box was nearly full, soon to join the first which Kusint had already stowed behind the iron gate barring the stair to the cellars beneath the muniment room.

'Thank you, Sergeant Fitrel.' The red-headed captain echoed Ilysh.

'I plan on staying retired.' The old man looked at Kusint with a glint in his eye. 'Don't give me cause to come back to the barrack hall to show you how to keep your troopers properly harnessed.'

'You can sleep easy,' Kusint assured him with a grin.

'Once I've got a meal and some ale in my belly.' Fitrel nodded to them all and went on his way

Zurenne saw that someone had sent word to Doratine that the old sergeant was the last waiting to pay his tithe. Trestles had already been set up, supporting long tabletops. Now kitchen lackeys and maidservants appeared at the far end of the hall carrying platters and bowls. The demesne folk cheered, breaking off their conversations around the broad fireplaces newly built on either side of the hall to replace the old-fashioned central hearth.

Zurenne noted few roast birds or haunches of mutton and pork amid the festival bounty. With Halferan's herds and flocks so sorely reduced, the young bullocks and rams usually supplying tender, flavoursome meat would see an unexpected spring, to be fattened up to a greater weight or to be sold on to neighbouring baronies.

This feast offered a preponderance of stews; the best way to cook the tough cuts from older, barren heifers and ewes earmarked for autumn slaughter, not worth the fodder to see them through winter. Fortunately Doratine knew how to render such meat palatable with spices and long simmering. Zurenne also saw plenty of pies doubtless filled with bottled fruit salvaged from the back shelves of storerooms across the barony, mixed with the last shreds of meat stripped from the carcasses.

The dishes were interspersed with decorative evergreen garlands, the better to fill the tables. Zurenne also saw bowls of nuts and rounds of cheeses and wrinkled apples from the hay barn lofts; humble fare normally never seen at a festival.

She smiled as Halferan's assembled tenantry and yeomen greeted their feast with loud cheers. They didn't care that these tables weren't laden with extravagant delicacies. Halferan barony was renewed and a new year was opening and that was reason enough for celebration.

Precious little would be left for Halferan's hounds, Zurenne reflected, beyond bones to crack for their marrow. Still, better that the manor's dogs went hungry instead of the household. Besides, well-fed hounds would be more inclined to doze in their kennels instead of staying alert for sneak thieves hoping to take advantage of the manor's festival generosity.

She turned to Kusint as Master Rauffe totted up his ledger's columns. 'Have any beggars knocked at the gatehouse today?

The truly indigent could still expect a share of this feast, insofar as Halferan could afford to honour Ostrin, god of hospitality.

'Just one sturdy rogue looking for a handout instead of doing a day's work to fill his belly.' Kusint closed the coin coffer and locked it. 'He got a stale crust and a cup of water and then young Linset escorted him back to the high road.'

He broke off as a louder cheer than any yet greeted the appearance of three kitchen maids carrying foaming jugs of ale in each hand.

Zurenne heard Corrain's name saluted with several upraised tankards. She smiled. The demesne folk should certainly be grateful. Their new baron had ridden out time and again with his newly-drilled troopers before the turn of For-Winter left the roads hock-deep in mud. They had recovered most of Halferan's scattered herds and taken back the grain illicitly harvested by Baron Karpis's henchmen. Now none of Halferan's villages would go without bread for lack of wheat this winter and there was enough barley to keep the manor's brew house and most taverns' tuns from idleness.

'My lady?' Zurenne's personal maid arrived at her side, offering a pewter goblet on a linen-covered silver tray.

'Thank you.' Zurenne took a sip of the darkly glinting liquid rimmed with creamy foam. She summoned up a smile to hide her desire for wine instead. This time next year, perhaps, as long as Halferan's fortunes were sufficiently restored for such self-indulgence. 'Raselle, take Esnina to choose something to eat, before she gets too tired.'

So far the little girl hadn't provoked Ilysh's irritation or inconvenienced Master Rauffe but it could only be a matter of time. The last thing Zurenne wanted was Neeny's hopping rabbit spilling ink over the steward's ledger.

'Yes, my lady.'

Zurenne watched Neeny agree to Raselle's suggestion with telling alacrity. The little girl headed straight for the table where Doratine's maids were now setting out dishes of honey cakes.

'Lady Ilysh? Shall we join the feast?' Zurenne turned to her daughter but before Lysha could push her chair back, a woman stumped heavily up the dais steps and approached the table.

'Saedrin and all the gods bless you, my lady.' Mistress Rotharle reached across the table to lay her age-spotted hand on Ilysh's slender one.

'Fair festival to you and yours,' the girl replied with a smile.

'And many more to come, Poldrion willing.' Mistress Rotharle looked over Ilysh's head to the narrow doorway at the back of the dais. Giving the young girl's hand a final pat, she continued on her way to the shrine.

Despite the heat from the fires down in the hall and the logs smouldering in the smaller hearth up here on the dais, Zurenne shivered in the cold draft as the old woman opened the door. This festival-night would see a steady procession to the shrine as those who had survived the corsairs remembered loved ones sent to Saedrin's judgement in brutal and untimely fashion.

'Mama?' Lysha twisted around in her seat as Mistress Rotharle called out, startled, within the shadowed shrine.

Zurenne instantly recognised the other voice. Just as swiftly, she was ashamed to realise she hadn't noted his absence. She walked hurried into the shrine to see Hosh disappearing through the outer door.

Mistress Rotharle looked at Zurenne, distressed. 'I just want a moment to remember my Tull but the poor boy can stay—'

'I'll tell him.' As Zurenne opened the outer door, she looked this way and that. The cobbled expanse between the hall and the range of kitchen buildings was deserted. Had Hosh returned to the guards' barrack hall opposite? She looked towards the gatehouse. Had he already passed beneath that arch and through the porter's door in the barred and iron-bound oak, fleeing to his widowed mother's house across the brook in the village?

'My lady?' Hosh was standing behind the shrine's door.

'Oh!' Startled, Zurenne took a hasty step back. 'No, forgive me.'

She reached out to lay a gentle hand on Hosh's sleeve when the boy would have retreated. Stepping out into the night, she closed the shrine door behind her. 'Please sit with me for a moment.'

'As you wish, my lady.' Reluctant but obedient, Hosh sat down on the bench by the shrine wall.

The rough-hewn seat had been set up while the manor was being rebuilt. So many folk had come to the shrine to beseech divine favour to speed their labours or to seek solace for their grief over slain kin and valued friends. The men nailed silver and copper pennies to the outer face of the door while the women pinned twists of cloth or scraps of lace and ribbon on the inside; tokens of faithfulness to each deity they prayed to.

'Mistress Rotharle won't be long,' Zurenne assured the boy. 'You can return to your prayers.'

'I can wait.' He gazed up at the sky.

Zurenne looked up to see what fascinated him so.

'They call it the Opal, in the Archipelago,' he said, unprompted, pointing at the Greater Moon. 'The Lesser Moon's the Pearl, according their heavenly compass.'

'Oh.' Zurenne knew nothing of Aldabreshin stargazing.

'I only learned to interpret the skies to keep watch for ill omens.' Hosh turned to look anxiously at her. 'Then I could warn the other slaves and maybe they wouldn't give me a kicking so they could steal my food.'

'That sounds very wise.' As Zurenne smiled reassurance, she tried desperately to hide her pity.

Close to, Hosh's injuries were cruelly visible, even in the moonlight. The deep dent in his cheekbone drew his eyelids askew while his sunken lips betrayed the loss of so many teeth on that side of his mouth. The cold night air prompted a trickle of moisture from his sagging eye and a glistening smear beneath his grotesquely broken nose.

Corrain had told her how a corsair's sword pommel

had smashed the boy's face, when Minelas had drawn them into a deadly ambush. The wizard's promises had all been lies; that his magic would bolster Halferan's attack as her husband and Halferan's best guardsmen fell upon the unsuspecting corsairs laired in the coastal marshes. Instead the waiting raiders had killed or enslaved them while Minelas had returned to make prisoners of Zurenne and her children in order to plunder Lysha and Neeny's inheritance.

She and Corrain had been in the muniment room in the rebuilt tower's ground floor. Zurenne had brought the letters and ledgers amassed during her sojourn at the Taw Ricks' hunting lodge to be added to the scant manor records salvaged by Master Rauffe before they had fled the corsairs' final assault.

Corrain had been writing the new muster roll of Halferan's guardsmen. He broke off to take Zurenne entirely unawares with a sudden outburst. It was his fault and his alone that the corsairs had captured so many Halferan men. Hosh would have fought to the death, Corrain had insisted. He was the one who had ordered the boy and the rest to throw down their swords in hopes of living to fight another day. He had brought that disgrace on Halferan.

Falling silent as abruptly as he had spoken, Corrain had left his list unfinished, hurrying from the tower to call for a horse. Zurenne hadn't seen him for the next two days. After that, Corrain had said nothing more of his time enslaved in the islands and Zurenne had no intention of asking him.

'Forgive me, my lady.' Hosh flinched and turned away. Stricken, Zurenne realised he thought that she'd been staring at his injuries, rather than overtaken by recollection. But she couldn't think how she might explain. She had to do something though or the boy would flee to hide himself away with his misery.

'Tell me what you make of this sky, in the Aldabreshin fashion.'

'My lady?' Hosh was startled into looking back at her.

'Is there anything in these heavens to encourage the southern savages to come north again?' Zurenne looked up at the moon, realising why that question had come to mind.

Even though Corrain and Jilseth had assured her that all the corsairs were dead, she was still mortally afraid of seeing warning beacons lit on the seaward horizon.

'The Aldabreshi don't sail north in the winter, my lady.' Hosh fell silent for a long moment then said slowly, 'But looking to the future, the Amethyst is below the horizon, along with the stars of the Sea Serpent. That jewel warns against arrogance and anger while the Sea Serpent warns of unseen forces and foes. Both are in the arc of the heavenly compass where the islanders look for omens of home and family. You've shown yourself a worthy mother, my lady, and a steadfast defender of your daughters. Any Aldabreshin would consider those stars a warning against attacking you again.'

'Truly?'

Zurenne wasn't asking about the stars. Was that how the household saw her? She so often felt wretchedly inadequate, far from a worthy parent. Or was Hosh just echoing his own loyal mother, Abiath?

'There's the Ruby.' Hosh was still intent on the skies. 'See, my lady, over in the west?'

As he pointed, Zurenne saw a star glimmering faintly red amid a spray of white pinpricks. One outshone the rest.

'That's the Diamond along with it, both within the stars of the Canthira Tree.' Hosh's tone grew unexpectedly animated. 'The Archipelagans hold that plant dear, my lady, not just for its flowers' beauty and fragrance. It will regrow from burned stumps and black ash, even when fire sweeps right across an island and kills every living thing.'

'What does such a portent mean?' Zurenne was growing curious.

'That's the arc of foes, my lady. They count twelve such regions around the whole compass of the sky.' Hosh gazed at the star-filled darkness. 'Halferan is renewed, like a Canthira tree, and the Ruby is a talisman against fire. The Diamond is a talisman for leaders, and you and the captain have both proven yourself against the corsairs. Those are omens in your favour, not for anyone who would attack you.'

'But surely the southern barbarians would read the skies to favour themselves?' Now Zurenne was intrigued.

Hosh shook his head, pointing to the sky halfway between north and east. 'Not since the Emerald moved into the arc of death.'

Zurenne shivered as she searched in vain for the merest speck of green. 'That sounds ill-omened.'

'Not for us,' Hosh reassured her. 'As long as the Emerald lies in that arc of the sky, the Archipelagans will look for warnings above all else in their heavenly omens. The stars of the Spear are there at present so that's counselling caution for warlike men. A clear portent against aggression especially with the Opal in the arc of travel with the stars of the Walking Hawk.'

Hosh pointed but Zurenne could only see the pale round of the Greater Moon. She could make out nothing among the stars that might signify the exotic and unknown creatures which Hosh was talking about.

'The Walking Hawk's a sign for watchfulness and the Opal's a talisman against magic, so that would warn of wizardly hazards facing anyone venturing to the mainland. The Pearl's on the other side of the Emerald, in the arc of marriage and all things beloved. The Pearl's another talisman against magic but the Winged Snake with it is an emblem of courageous defence. So that means if they stay close to home, such omens should keep them safe. With three heavenly jewels in the same quarter of the sky, the Aldabreshi will take those omens to heart.'

Hosh fell silent and then shrugged. 'For whatever good such hopes may do them.'

Had he ever seen anything to uphold the savages' faith in such stars? Zurenne's chattering teeth cut off that question. She stood up, rubbing her hands briskly together to warm them. 'I should return to the feast, but come back into the shrine. You have as much claim to the gods' and goddesses' favour as anyone else. Then you must come and have your share of the food and ale.'

'Very well, my lady.' Hosh was clearly reluctant but more unwilling to gainsay Zurenne.

She opened the shrine door to find that Mistress Rotharle had departed. Ushering Hosh inside, she left him to his private devotions and went through the inner door onto the empty dais.

Zurenne lingered, ready to deny entry to anyone else stepping up to enter the shrine, just for a little while. She searched the gathering down on the hall's floor, looking for Lysha mingling with her people. Kusint's red head soon indicated her daughter's presence. The young captain was standing close at her shoulder as the throng circled around them. Everyone in the household was eager to offer their lady a festival greeting.

A few moments later Zurenne heard the outer door to the shrine open and close. So Hosh would rather go hungry than show his wounded face to this hall full of people, even if the demesne folk should surely be counted as friends and his own mother was here among them.

She saw Abiath smiling in the midst of a circle of the village's elder matrons. Hosh might be only a handful of years older than Lysha but Abiath had been all but past hope of children when he had been born. Since her husband had been killed so soon after in an accident, life's burdens had weighed the diminutive woman down further. Did the return of her only son, given up for dead, balance those scales? Hardly.

Zurenne found her joy in the festival tarnished. It was so unfair, that Hosh should have endured so much, that he should have survived such travail, only to return and find himself still distanced from his kith and kin by disfigurement.

The poor boy couldn't leave his tribulations behind him as this new year started. If only someone could take away Hosh's sufferings as quickly and as easily as Madam Jilseth and the tall blonde magewoman had relieved him of that strange arm-ring which the Mandarkin wizard had used to enslave him.

— CHAPTER FIVE —

The residence of Mellitha Esterlin, Relshaz
Winter Solstice Festival, 3rd Evening

THIS TIME VELINDRE called a halt to their endeavours. 'Jilseth, unless you see some crack in the ensorcellement, I suggest we abandon this approach.'

'There might be something—' Seeing Merenel's involuntary grimace, Jilseth broke off and nodded her agreement. 'I may well be imagining it.'

'It is long past time we had something to eat and to drink.' Mellitha looked towards the side table and a silver hand bell stirred itself to ring a summons.

'Madam?' As always, a handsome lackey answered her call within moments.

'Wine for us all, if you please, and whatever festival delicacies have been waiting in the kitchen. Please offer my profound apologies to Seomina,' Mellitha added ruefully.

Tired as she was, Jilseth smiled. On her earlier visits here she had seen how Mellitha's cook would forgive her mistress anything.

'At once, Madam, and this arrived just before the last chime.' The lackey presented an ink-smudged and hastily sealed letter.

Mellitha read it and frowned as the servant headed for the door. 'Master Resnada says that Kerrit Osier has taken a turn for the worse. He asks for your help, Jilseth.'

'Help with what?' Velindre demanded. 'Resnada's the apothecary.'

'He merely asks for Jilseth's assistance. See for yourself.' Mellitha passed the grimy reed paper to Velindre and snapped her fingers to attract her lackey's attention before he left the room. 'Nishail! Who brought the note?'

'One of Master Resnada's boys. He wouldn't wait for a reply.'

'Intent on his festival fun,' Mellitha wondered aloud, 'or unwilling to be seen loitering at a wizard's gates?'

'The latter, I would guess, Madam,' the lackey said unhappily.

Velindre looked over her shoulder. 'The mood on the streets is still ugly?'

'Yes, Madam Mage.'

As Nishail nodded, Jilseth was already rising to her feet. 'I'll go. I'm unlikely to be recognised.'

She had visited Kerrit often enough in his convalescence through the fading days of For-Autumn. When news had first broken of wizardry loose in the Archipelago, Aldabreshi hotheads had attacked a number of Relshaz's better-known wizards. Kerrit had suffered by far the worst assault. The scholarly mage had been so badly beaten that his life had hung in the balance.

'I'll come with you,' Merenel offered.

Jilseth shook her head. 'I'd rather you stayed here, ready to bespeak Planir once I know if there's truly cause for concern.'

Alas, she had no doubt that there would be. Master Resnada wouldn't send such a note for no reason, still less write it in such haste. The apothecary was as level-headed as he was skilled.

'Send word as soon as you can.' Mellitha exchanged

a look with Velindre suggesting they both thought the same.

Nishail opened the door to usher Jilseth into the marble-floored hallway. 'Shall I fetch you a lantern, my lady?'

He knew better than to ask if a wizard needed him to summon a carriage in this emergency.

'No need.' She pulled her grey cloak from its peg beside the front door, mindful of the cool of the cloudless night outside.

Nishail opened the front door and Jilseth stood on the white stone house's steps. She looked with some misgiving at the heavy wooden gates in the high wall encircling the residence. This prosperous and decorous district was normally so peaceful that the lyrical songbirds in the orchard beyond Mellitha's lawns could be clearly heard inside the house. She glanced at the bare-branched fruit trees framing the immaculate flower beds sleeping through the short Relshazri winter. Elegant redcanes waved fronds like scarlet feathers.

This evening it sounded as though the modest tavern on the corner of the broad road at the end of this quiet side street was packed to the rafters. The cheering, jeering and shouts had an unpleasantly harsh edge.

'Is this the usual revelry?' Jilseth reminded herself that she had never spent a solstice holiday in Relshaz. Festivities in Hadrumal were bound to be decorous by comparison. Those mainland-born still cherishing fond memories of their families' rites made their seasonal observances before whatever statues they kept in their rooms. Few wizards paid much heed to whatever liturgies and deities they had been raised with.

'There seems to be more excitement than usual.' Nishail looked apprehensive.

Jilseth was tempted to ask him to open the gate, so she could look outside and judge for herself. No, Master Resnada had asked for her help. Kerrit was a mage and Hadrumal's interests must always come first.

'Tell Mistress Esterlin that I'll be as quick as I can.'

Her affinity reached down through the flagstones to the delta mud far beneath. That rich darkness was resonant with every fragment of rock and earth which the mighty River Rel had carried down from its springs amid the broken uplands where Dalasor butted up against Ensaimin and Caladhria. More than that, Jilseth could trace every successive tributary's load of silt added to this great city's shifting foundations.

With her wizardry solidly rooted, Jilseth reached upwards into the air. Not so long ago, this had been one of her least favourite workings, the elemental air so irritatingly elusive. Now she wove her translocation with ease and assurance, deftly blending the hints of fire and water that were integral to the spell. Now she could thread her knowledge of the streets around Master Kerrit's house through the interstices of the airborn wizardry that would carry her there.

The yard and Mellitha's gardens disappeared as white light enveloped her. Jilseth felt her feet leave the flagstones. In the next breath, she felt cobbles and something unpleasantly slimy beneath her leather half-boots' soles.

As the magelight faded, she looked down to see what she had landed in. What was it her first teacher in Hadrumal had said so often? Chance can always be relied on to curb any mage's inclination to arrogance.

At least whoever had celebrated the solstice so early and so unwisely wasn't still here vomiting. Jilseth scraped the noisome mess off the side of her boot as she looked around to see if anyone might have noticed her arrival.

Kerrit Osier's house was a narrow three-storey dwelling, one of a handful surrounding the yard tucked back from the bustling street. This was one of Relshaz's more humble districts. The buildings were white with lime wash not marble, brick-built tenements five and six storeys high. The residents lived their lives on their balconies and with open doors and windows rather than hidden behind high walls and gates.

Looking through the yard's entry to the street, Jilseth saw the festival's jollities well underway. Leather and clay flagons of wine were passed from hand to hand and tossed from one garland-bedecked window to the next.

Directly opposite this alley, locals sat upon a sturdy flight of steps leading up to the first apartments built above the damp-prone cellars. Sharing wine and stronger liquors, they gnawed on skewers of spiced and salted meat cooked over a charcoal brazier set beside the steps.

'Fair festival, fair maiden!' An exuberant youth noticed Jilseth. He raised a glass bottle to salute her, the contents sloshing in the flickering light of torches lashed to the balcony overhead. Despite the seasonal chill, he wore only loose cotton trews in the Archipelagan style, his bare chest bronzed with mixed mainland and Aldabreshin blood.

Jilseth cursed herself for a fool for catching his eye. She climbed the steps to Kerrit's front door and lifted the brass ring to knock briskly.

'Fair maiden!'

She turned to see the bare-chested youth running towards her with the graceless ease of the spectacularly drunk. Jilseth knocked again but the door stayed obdurately shut, the windows still dark.

'That's not a festival dress,' he scolded.

Jilseth could hardly deny it. Her grey wool gown was buttoned high to the neck and tight to the wrist, wholly unlike the loosely draped and low cut dresses which Relshazri women favoured, in silks dyed every colour to be found in a sunset and often slashed to reveal curves of bosom and thigh.

She knocked on Kerrit's door again. Where was Master Resnada?

The lad sprang up the steps and slid an arm around her waist. Before Jilseth realised what he intended, he pulled her close and kissed her hard. When she cried out in instinctive protest, his tongue slid into her mouth. The pungent fumes of white brandy nearly choked her as he dropped his bottle to grope for her breasts.

Jilseth didn't know whether to be more outraged or astonished. She punched the bare-chested youth hard in the midriff with an unseen fist of elemental air. He collapsed and tumbled coughing down the steps to sprawl amid the shards of his brandy bottle.

A key turned in the lock and the door opened to reveal Master Resnada's bearded face and the tip of a wickedly pointed knife.

'Madam Mage?' Alarmed, he opened the door wider. 'Are you all right?'

The apothecary was a sturdily built man of common height with greying hair and tidily trimmed whiskers. He could have passed without comment through any marketplace across Ensaimin or Caladhria, though the leathery tan of his skin and his accent indicated a lifetime spent in Relshaz.

'It's nothing of consequence.' Jilseth left her would-be assailant fighting for the breath to curse his misfortune. 'Where is Kerrit?'

'This way.' Resnada relocked the door as she entered.

'Are you alone?' Jilseth was surprised not to see the usual covey of apprentices eager to learn whatever the master apothecary could teach them.

'Since I'm tending a wizard, yes.' Resnada led her through the tidily furnished sitting room where Kerrit was accustomed to debate with his friends and visitors.

Not only to debate. Jilseth noted a small table with a white raven board and all the other pieces set ready for a game. The carved and painted wooden figures waited motionless to see if the forest fowl could drive the fabled bird out of the woodland or if the raven could find sanctuary from their mobbing amid the trees and thickets. She wondered which side Master Kerrit preferred to play.

Resnada continued into the neat, tiled kitchen at the rear. 'Upstairs.'

'Do your other customers resent you tending Kerrit?' Jilseth wondered if Mellitha and Velindre knew that the apothecary's trade was suffering from his association with wizardry.

'Some have seen fit to rebuke me.' Resnada smiled without much humour. 'Their indignation generally fades when they find themselves in need of more medicaments.'

'The Archmage will make good on your losses as well as paying for your care of Master Kerrit,' Jilseth began stiffly.

He waved her to silence. 'Kerrit is my friend. I've known him since he first came to the city. I would no more abandon him than I would my own brother and I assuredly don't look for payment. Upstairs, if you please.'

Dropping her cloak on a chair, Jilseth followed the apothecary up the boxed staircase curving through a tight half circle to reach the upper floor. Two doors set at right angles stood open. One revealed the larger chamber at the front of the house. It was lined with crowded bookcases surrounding a leather-topped table thickly layered with papers. The rear room was Kerrit's bedchamber, although at first glance, the only difference was the bed amid the book-laden shelving rather than a table.

A single lamp burned on a hook beside the door. Resnada skirted the bed to lay his surgical knife on the windowsill beside a sturdy leather coffer holding other mysterious instruments, a multitude of small bottles and a silver cup for mixing doses. The window overlooked an alley where revellers ran back and forth, hollering and whooping.

'Master Kerrit?' Apprehensive, Jilseth approached the rumpled bed. 'How are you this evening? Is your ankle troubling you?'

The stick Kerrit had been using ever since he'd been so brutally attacked was propped against the bed. The apothecary had guessed that the wizard's foot had been repeatedly stamped on, to break so many of the small bones as well as his ankle itself.

Kerrit lay amid the pillows and quilts in breeches and a creased shirt. He hugged a tattered shawl around his hunched shoulders and glared at Jilseth. 'Who are you? How did you get into my house?'

Jilseth raised placating hands. 'Master Resnada—'

'Meddling fool!' Kerrit spat at the apothecary.

Jilseth was startled. Kerrit had always been an amiable and courteous patient, even in those most painful early days following his injuries.

Resnada ignored the mage's hostility. 'How is your headache?'

'Murderous.' Kerrit clutched at his thinning hair.

Jilseth could see a lurid scar beneath his pale fingers. She recalled the gash in Kerrit's scalp which had bled so long and so profusely. She also realised that he had lost weight markedly since she had last seen him. With sagging jowls and dark shadows under his eyes he looked far older than his middle years.

'Master Mage! Do you not remember me?'

Kerrit looked up, blinking. 'Of course. You... you are...'

Jilseth saw a haunted look in his eyes. In the next instant, he snapped at her.

'Of course I remember you, though I do not recall inviting you into my home. Please leave. I have a most tiresome headache—'

'Drink this.' Resnada passed him the silver cup.

Jilseth was both surprised and relieved to see Kerrit dutifully swallow the nostrum.

'I'll see Madam Jilseth to the door.' The apothecary nodded towards the staircase.

Kerrit merely grunted, settling himself amid his pillows and quilts.

Jilseth took the hint and went downstairs. Resnada followed her as far as the kitchen. He took a bottle of wine from a high shelf along with two goblets of coloured Aldabreshin glass.

'These headaches are getting worse and his memory and temper alike are becoming more erratic.' He took a small knife from the drawer in the well-scrubbed table and pared the wax from the bottle's neck.

Jilseth sat on a stool. 'If he's in a great deal of pain—'

'That's not the reason.' Resnada's tone allowed for no argument as he levered the cork out with the knife tip. 'I have seen this before following a head wound, even long after the patient seems to have recovered. There's more besides. He hasn't touched a book for the last four days. He says that he's too tired but I believe he now struggles to read. He will not admit it though so I cannot establish if the problem is with his eyes or his ability to comprehend the words on the page.'

Now Jilseth was seriously worried. 'What do you want from Hadrumal?'

The apothecary poured two modest glassfuls of wine and hooked a second stool out from under the table with a deft foot.

'You are a mage born to the earth?' He betrayed the usual mix of curiosity and nervousness of the mundane born broaching the subject of wizardly affinity.

'I am.' Jilseth took a sip of wine to allow Resnada a moment to ask his next question.

'Do you have any skill with bones?' He rolled a pellet of wax between his stubby fingers.

'Bones?' Jilseth hadn't expected this. 'No, I'm sorry.'

She knew of earth mages who made a study of skeletons of men and beasts, striving to understand the slow processes that bound minerals into living tissue. Some of those pursued the challenge of crafting spells to mend broken bones or to reshape those which had mended awry. It was a slow and painstaking process, according to the few accounts in Hadrumal's libraries.

Such studies held no appeal for Jilseth. She had been fascinated from the first by the far more complex magic of necromancy. Only an earth mage could use the infinitesimal traces which lingered in dead flesh to discover how a life had ended. Precious few of the small number who tried proved able to master the necessary spells.

Resnada swallowed a mouthful of wine. 'I fear the fracture to Kerrit's skull has left something amiss within. There may be slow bleeding or some splinter of bone making mischief.'

The fine vintage soured on Jilseth's tongue. 'Let me bespeak Hadrumal.' Planir would know of any mage with the skills to help.

The apothecary shook his head. 'If you cannot help with your own magic, we'll be better served by the temple. Can you bring one of Ostrin's priesthood here?' He glanced up at the ceiling. 'I dare not leave him alone.'

'Tonight?' Jilseth hadn't thought that Kerrit looked mortally ill.

Resnada looked at her, beseeching. 'If his brain is swelling, the longer that goes unchecked, the more his wits will suffer. I can try a trepanning but that brings its own risks. Ostrin's priests will be able to learn what Kerrit cannot tell me, so we can decide the best course of action.'

Jilseth wondered if the apothecary realised that the local priests' healing lore was in truth aetheric magic, the last tattered remnants of the Artifice which had once underpinned the Old Tormalin Empire. Those arcane enchantments were now reduced to meaningless syllables learned by rote and mouthed over the sick and dying to inconsistent and often indifferent effect.

This was what Kerrit had studied for these past ten years, filling his house with gleanings from temple and shrine archives, ancient letters sent between Relshaz's merchant houses, even copies of the Magistracy's proclamations from generations ago.

Jilseth had no argument with seeking knowledge for its own sake. That ideal underpinned Hadrumal's existence. But she was at a loss to see the value of studying an obsolete magic which Kerrit couldn't even use, precluded by his own magebirth from working even the most insignificant aetheric enchantment.

But if the apothecary was confident that Relshaz's priests could help show him how best to succour Kerrit, Jilseth would ask for their help without delay.

'Is there anyone particular I should ask for?'

'Brother Tinoan,' Resnada said promptly. 'One of Ostrin's senior deacons.'

The title meant nothing to Jilseth. Hadrumal had no shrines and she was Hadrumal-born, her family settled on the wizard isle for five generations. She looked around the immaculate kitchen. 'Please open the window.'

Ordinarily she wouldn't risk a translocation from within a building but at present she judged it would be more hazardous to be seen working magic outside this house.

Resnada shoved at the metal window frame. It squealed open to allow muted music and sounds of celebration into the silent kitchen.

Jilseth wove her spell. This time she sought the hidden niche which Velindre had first shown her, tucked between two buttresses on the seaward side of Relshaz's great marble temple. She took care to ward her magic against the elemental power of the waters, bolstered by the tidal surge summoned by the Greater Moon's full. Jilseth could only be thankful that the Lesser had barely reached its first quarter.

As soon as her affinity was safely balanced, Master Resnada's inarticulate astonishment faded from her hearing. All sensation was overwhelmed by the spell and then she felt solid ground beneath her boot soles once again.

She stood on the temple's wide foundation. Jilseth could sense that this ground had once been the highest hillock in the delta, even before the river had been tamed by the Relshazri network of canals linking the inland wharves facing Caladhria and Lescar with the deep-water docks for sea-going vessels.

She smelled the salt wind from the sea. For a timeless instant, the elemental power of those boundless waters surged into her spell. She didn't merely feel the sullen brine confined within Relshaz's harbour walls, nor even the greater expanse of the Gulf of Lescar, bounded to the east by Tormalin's long thrust southwards and to the west by the bulwark of Caladhria overlooking the northernmost Archipelagan islands.

Jilseth's mage senses brushed against the immensity of the oceans, beyond the Cape of Winds to the east and past Cape Attar to the west. She could even feel, infinitely faint and some impossible distance away, the ties between those two oceans, divided by the Archipelago. Every sea and ocean was ultimately linked through the endless circulation of water through river and tide, cloud and rain.

Gasping, she thrust out a hand and welcomed the cold shock of the temple's marble wall, luminous in the moonlight. Her affinity drew her backwards through the rock's aeons-old existence. She felt the ring of the mason's chisels and then the shuddering crack as the block was prized from the quarries in the hills above Feverad in distant Tormalin. The tremors faded, soothed by the calm of countless undisturbed generations until she felt the warmth of the rising fires deep beneath the earth which had transformed the once humble limestone into this radiant marble.

Jilseth opened her eyes and smoothed her skirts. Shivering, she realised that she'd left her cloak on the chair in Kerrit's kitchen. There was nothing to be done about that beyond summoning up a breath of elemental fire to ward off the cold sea breeze. She took a cautious step forward and looked to either side.

The harbour-side path separating the temple from the low wall lapped by the gulf's dark waters was deserted. Jilseth made her way cautiously along this windowless face of the mighty temple. The uproar from the crowds in the vast square on the inland side grew louder.

As she turned the corner and walked to the front of the temple, she contemplated the unruly celebrations swirling around the two great fountains in the centre of the flagstoned expanse. Silk-clad Relshazri bedecked with jewels mingled unconcerned with the city's ragged and filthy, bottles and flagons passed from hand to hand.

Snatches of music rose above the tumult. Jilseth picked out several huddles of pipers and viol players around the fringes of the crowd. In the open space between the fountains and the temple, jugglers tossed rainbow knots of tasselled cords and glittering glass balls. Painted tumblers displayed their skills; girls flipping themselves from hands to feet and back again before their partners tossed them high onto a waiting strongman's broad shoulders.

Would-be worshippers waited quietly in long lines four and five abreast. Every few moments they advanced a little further up the steps towards the temple's great double doors. Torches burned in brackets high on the white marble pillars supporting the pediment laden with statues of the gods and goddesses. The flames struck a golden sheen from the hammered bronze sheathing the recessed entrances all across the front of the temple.

The hollow darkness within was guarded by priests and priestesses barring every one of those thresholds. No one entered without dropping some offering into the deep wooden bowls presented by these guardians.

Jilseth recalled that her coin purse was in her cloak pocket in Kerrit's kitchen and besides, it only held a few silver marks and pennies for Hadrumal's wine- and cook-shops. Mainlanders in taverns claimed that Archmage Planir could pluck solid coin out of thin air but if that was truly one of his secrets, he'd never shared it with Jilseth. Drawing pure metal from ore-bearing rock was a slow process by wizardly standards and besides, she no more carried such ore around than she did gold coin.

Would these supposedly pious men and women let her into the temple without paying their fee? She might be doing the Relshazri religious a disservice but Jilseth doubted it.

Since she had embarked on her travels around the mainland at the Archmage's request, Jilseth had met priests and priestesses as varied in character as any other selection of humanity. Among those nobles who so often inherited a shrine and its obligations with the rest of their holdings, she had encountered both the truly devout and the mindlessly sanctimonious. Among those who had chosen to swear their life away in the service of some unseen, unquantifiable deity, she had met both the calculatedly venal and those whose dedication was clearly rewarded in some intangible fashion far beyond the food and shelter bought by the alms given to their shrine.

Master Resnada had said that time was of the essence. Jilseth retreated into the shadows and wrapped a veil of air around herself. Walking out unseen into the torchlight, she headed for the nearest door.

A dutifully generous trio were being ushered past two broad shouldered and thick necked acolytes by a prosperously plump priestess whose charcoal silk robe could have been sewn by Mellitha's own seamstress. Even twenty paces away, Jilseth's wizard senses told her that the rubies in the golden amulet hanging around the woman's neck were of the finest clarity and colour.

'May Poldrion see you safe to Saedrin's threshold if that's your fate in the year to come.' The priestess peered into the bowl to see the suppliants' offering. She looked up with a complacent smile. 'May you see many more midwinters before Poldrion's summons comes.'

Jilseth approached, using another swathe of elemental air to muffle her footsteps on the white stone. Master Resnada's words echoed in her memory. How long was she prepared to wait for a chance to slide past these mercenary guardians unseen when Kerrit was in sore of need of whatever healing lore might be held within by more genuine priests?

— CHAPTER SIX —

Halferan Manor, Caladhria
Winter Solstice Festival, 3rd Evening

AT THE FAR end of the manor compound, beyond the storehouses and the drying ground for laundry, Hosh rubbed at his face and grimaced. The cold gnawed at the deep dent beside his broken nose and woke the lurking ache on the toothless side of his jaw.

He ran his tongue carefully along his gums. He could no longer feel the empty sockets where he'd recently lost two more teeth and he couldn't taste or smell the foulness of pus. The chewing herbs which Doratine pressed on him were keeping such corruption at bay so Hosh was daring to hope he might yet keep his remaining teeth. If only the wise woman had something as efficacious for the pains he suffered.

The only way to find any relief would be to go somewhere warmer. Where could he wait until his loving mum had eaten and drunk her fill with her friends in the great hall? The village women would still be sharing the burden of each other's sorrows and losses as well as taking comfort in his mother's joy at his unimagined return. It would be close to midnight before she would be ready to go home to the village beyond the brook.

Hosh looked around the storehouses and contemplated their cellars, bins and lofts now filled with the season's tithes from the farms which paid their dues in kind rather than coin. He liked to make these circuits of the compound, alone and unobserved, to reassure himself that this wasn't some tantalizing dream. Every day when he woke, he still had to remind himself that he was truly safe home in Halferan where the manor had risen, better than new, better than ever before, from the ruination left by the corsairs.

He walked past the well-house and the smithy and contemplated the barracks beyond the steward's residence. A lantern glowed in the window of the wide hall and the door stood ajar. Doubtless a handful of troopers had retreated there to drink ale warmed through with white brandy while they shared choicely obscene stories.

He wasn't about to join them. Those who hadn't shared in that final assault on the corsair island would pester him with questions about that terrible night. Those who had followed Corrain alongside the guardsmen from Licanin, Tallat and Antathele would be happy to relive their own elation at surviving what had seemed like certain death.

Hosh could repeat himself till his tongue withered, insisting that he had no wish to remember that night. The other troopers still demanded to hear how he had cut down the black-bearded corsair who had murdered the true Lord Halferan. How he wrestled with the blind trireme master who had commanded that unconquerable raiding fleet, apparently by means of insights into heavenly omens, in truth thanks to the wizardly spells held within weapons and trinkets; magic which was anathema to true Archipelagans.

He had tried telling them that he had only picked up a sword because he was so certain that his life was already lost. Until then he'd done all he could to stay

Defiant Peaks

alive, meekly serving the Mandarkin mage. He was
no hero but none of them would accept that, insisting
that he tell them how he had plotted his revenge and
connived against the vile wizard from the outset.

Since they didn't want to hear the truth, Hosh now
refused to be drawn into such conversations. He would
answer for his deeds, for good and ill, when he finally
stood at Saedrin's door. Until then, he wanted to look to
the future, not dwell on past horrors.

He glanced at the shuttered dormitory windows above
the barrack hall. Could he slip up the stairs unnoticed
and lie quietly on his own bed? No such luck. A candle's
glimmer through the cracks above suggested some lucky
trooper had persuaded his sweetheart to share a festival
frolic.

Hosh heaved an incautious sigh and winced as the cold
air bit deep at the back of his nose. He couldn't see a
sweetheart in his own future, let alone the grandchildren
his beloved mum silently longed for. Who would marry
a man with a face ugly enough to sour milk, never mind
one who refused to accept the accolades and surely the
fat purse that should be his reward for slaying the true
baron's murderer?

The manor's maidservants had grown sufficiently used
to his disfigurement not to let their revulsion show but
Hosh still saw the pity in their eyes before they swiftly
looked away. He heard the incautious comments and
guessed at the whispers behind raised hands whenever
he visited the village.

He contemplated the gatehouse. The windows to the
guest apartments up above were dark; Halferan had no
noble visitors at this festival season. Only a couple of
troopers would be sitting in the guard room beside the

archway, to answer any knock at the heavy oak gates. They would be the most junior of the autumn's recruits, too awed to ask him impertinent questions. They would also have a warm fire. Hosh could sit beside that until his mother was ready to go home.

He walked quickly across the cobbles and knocked on the guard room door. As he opened it, he halted. Kusint sat at the table within. More astonishing, so did Lady Ilysh.

'Hosh, fair festival.' Lady Ilysh greeted him warmly. In her eyes, no mutilation could possibly signify after the service which Hosh had done her father by avenging him.

'Come in and shut the door.' Kusint invited.

Hosh did as he was bid. There was no danger of the Forest man wheedling for some titillating tale of slavery among the barbarian Aldabreshi. Kusint had rowed in chains himself after being captured in the battles between Lescar's rival dukes, lured to a mercenary's life by tavern tales of high heroics and riches. So he knew all about the pain and fear which pervaded a slave's every waking moment and which still plagued Hosh's nightmares.

Hosh took a chair and looked at the rune bones spread on the table. 'What are the stakes?'

He couldn't see any coin waiting to wager on the roll of the three-sided pieces, not even the copper pennies cut into halves and quarters which the troopers were supposed to limit themselves to in their gambling.

'We're not gaming,' Lady Ilysh quickly assured him. 'We're casting fortunes for the turn of the year, according to Forest lore.'

She gathered up the nine stubby triangular bones, battered and scratched on their three oblong faces where the runes themselves were carved. Slipping them into a tattered leather bag, she tucked it into a pocket hidden in the side seam of her gown.

'How do you read fortunes in runes?' Hosh had heard about the new captain's habit of seeking such guidance but he'd never had occasion to learn how it might be done.

Kusint looked at him for a long moment before producing a wholly different set of runes. These were long wooden sticks as long as the Forest man's hand and no thicker than his smallest finger. A leather thong tied them together, triangular shapes nested together to form a single larger triangle.

The captain unknotted the leather and set aside the stick with the symbols for the sun and lesser and greater moons. 'Each of the nine sticks has three sides to give us twenty-seven runes. Once we take away the heavens, that leaves twenty-four. Have you never considered how those divide into six quartets embracing every aspect of life?'

'Air, Earth, Fire and Water, for the substances that make up all things. The Forest, the Mountain, the Plain, and the Sea, for the places where we live.'

Now Ilysh was nimbly sorting through Kusint's runes to show Hosh each set of four symbols. The black lines seemed to have been burned into the wood with hot metal rather than carved.

'Deer, Wolf, Eagle, and Salmon, for the creatures that live alongside us. Oak and Pine and Broom and Reed, for the growing things which shelter and feed us. Chime, Drum, Horn and Harp for music and all that delights us. The Storm, the Calm, the Cold Mountain Wind and the Warm Sea Breeze for the weather and such unseen mysteries.'

'You've heard of Artifice?' Kusint looked at Hosh. 'Aetheric magic, not the wizardry of the mages? Among the Forest Folk, these weather runes also speak of such enchantments; of the strength to overrule what surrounds you, or to stand unharmed by an assault. Of Artifice to drive away foes or to lure them close, all unknowing.'

Hosh looked at him, awe-struck. 'Can Forest enchanters truly do so such things?'

He'd heard the usual stories of Artifice's lost wonders in tavern tales; how one adept could speak to another unheard over a thousand leagues or see through some unwitting dupe's eyes. Like everyone else, he hadn't believed half of what he'd heard. Besides, as everyone in the barrack hall agreed, such eerie magic was long lost amid the collapse of the Old Tormalin Empire twenty-five generations ago.

Kusint smiled. 'Forest lore has humbler ambitions. The enchantments which the Folk still cherish help secure food and shelter and keep the peace when families cross paths and mingle on their journeys through the greenwood. The true masters of Artifice are the *sheltya* who live in the far mountains, but they keep themselves to themselves and guard their secrets closely.'

'The Forest Folk have lore enough to see what lies ahead for their kith and kin,' Lady Ilysh said firmly. 'Why not see what the new year will bring you, Hosh?'

Her determined urging reminded him so powerfully of her fallen father giving an order that he reached for the rune sticks. The new manor timepiece rang the third chime of the night.

'Oh, I hadn't realised it was so late.' Lady Ilysh sprang to her feet. 'Mama will wonder where I am.'

Before, she had been a self-confident maiden on the verge of womanhood. Now she was a child caught in mischief like little Esnina.

Kusint was already on his way to open the door. She curtseyed a swift farewell. 'Captain. Hosh. Fair festival to you.'

'Saedrin send a fine year ahead for us all, my lady.' Hosh watched Kusint linger in the doorway, watching Lady Ilysh all the way back to the great hall.

As a slave among the corsairs, Hosh's life had depended on his attentiveness to every shift in mood and expression around him. He hadn't expected to find much use for such skills on his return home. As it turned out, being able to watch what went on around him without anyone noticing was an unforeseen benefit of everyone so diligently avoiding him.

'The captain has been concerned that Reven is growing too fond of our lady.' Hosh blotted insidious moisture from his skewed eye with his cuff. 'Should he be concerned that she is growing fond of you?'

He didn't need to explain to Kusint. Corrain would always be Halferan's captain as far as the two of them were concerned.

'I know she is.' Kusint carefully closed the door.

'What of your feelings for her?' Since Corrain wasn't here, Hosh steeled himself to ask. After all, he and Kusint were both only a handful or so years older than their lady.

'She is still a child.' Kusint smiled affectionately nevertheless. 'When she's grown?' He shrugged as he took his seat at the table again, his expression unexpectedly serious.

'I'll settle for seeing her grow into the woman she has the promise to become if she is allowed to think for herself, to read her father's books of history and natural philosophy and to rule this barony in truth as well as in name. If she is allowed to look beyond this manor's walls and beyond a life circumscribed by marriage and motherhood.'

He shook his head, exasperated. 'I cannot believe how little you Caladhrians value your womenfolk's strengths. Perhaps it's because your land is so fertile and so peaceful. We would never survive in Solura or in the Forest with half our people kept so idle and blinkered.'

Kusint warmed to his theme. 'It's not as if there aren't strong women closer to home so you can see their worth. When I was fighting in Lescar, the Duke of Marlier's mercenaries were commanded by his concubine, the woman they call Ridianne the Vixen, and she proved a warrior to equal any man. Did you know that she was Caladhrian born? When your parliament's unjust laws saw her thrown out of her home with no more than the clothes on her back, only because she couldn't give her husband a son, she made herself a new life, using wits as sharp as the sword she took up!'

'I didn't know that.' Hosh wanted to argue with the Forest man's assessment of his countrywomen but he was recalling what his mother had told him of Halferan's helplessness when Lady Zurenne had been left widowed.

Reared to manage a household and nurture children, their gentle lady had been left undefended and unprepared for the predators who had so swiftly circled the barony while her distant sisters' husbands had placidly agreed that her dead husband's barony's affairs were none of their concern.

'When Lady Ilysh is grown?' Kusint smiled again, reflective. 'I will stand at Corrain's shoulder and see if any Caladhrian noble youth deserves a wife with her strength of will and character. If not, then we will see if she looks on me as a brother or something more.'

Hosh looked at the wooden rune sticks tied tight with the leather thong. 'Is that what you see in her future through your lore and these runes?'

Though he knew what Corrain would say. That such fortune-telling could be nothing but wishful thinking and maybe even benign deceit, to persuade Lady Ilysh to follow her own natural inclination for independence.

Corrain had dismissed the Archipelagans' stargazing as folly and superstition only fit for gulling savage barbarians. But just as Hosh had learned that not every Aldabreshi was his enemy, he had come at least to respect their belief in portents. His beloved mum had always said that man or woman, one earned respect by returning it.

'That stays between me and her.' Kusint smiled to take the sting out of his words. 'Do you want to see what the year to come might bring for you?'

Hosh couldn't deny that he was tempted. 'How might I do that? Just for curiosity's sake?'

'Just out of curiosity.' Kusint proffered the bundle of nine rune sticks, loosely held and end on, so Hosh couldn't see any of the runes seared onto their long sides. 'Take any six and lay them in two crosswise rows of three.'

Hosh did so. Kusint laid his hand on the table beside the three sticks closer to him. 'These upright runes offer insights into good things to come. These runes which are reversed should be studied for warnings.' He reached forward to spread his fingers over the trio on Hosh's side of the table.

That made sense to Hosh. A tossed rune always landed with one face hidden, one carved symbol upright and the third one upside down. It was those upright runes which won a gambling throw and surely planning for the future was a series of wagers. 'What do these tell you?'

Kusint tapped each stick in turn. 'The Wellspring for water promises a desire fulfilled and the Eagle counsels hope and confidence as well as speaking of a journey. The Chime hints at a new beginning but you should consider your decisions carefully. Once made, such a choice cannot be undone, any more than a bell can be unrung.'

'I see.' Hosh was inclined to think that Corrain would be rightly sceptical. After his unwilling sojourn in the Archipelago, Hosh had no intention of travelling anywhere ever again. He nodded at the second trio. 'And these?'

Kusint's coppery brows drew together in a puzzled frown. 'Surely these runes speak more of the year just gone. The Earth speaks of upheaval when it's reversed and the Wolf's counter meaning is greed.'

Hosh understood. Kusint had been with Corrain when the corsair island was torn asunder and the Forest captain had been one of the first to know of the Mandarkin mage Anskal's avid search for ensorcelled artefacts.

'What does this one mean?' Hosh picked up the last stick, showing the rune symbolising the cold North wind rolling down from the mountains, upside down.

'That is a riddle,' Kusint admitted. 'In the first three, it would have meant trouble ahead.'

'Then surely that means good fortune if it's reversed?' If Hosh didn't plan on trusting in this Forest lore, he would still rather not carry an ill omen into the new year.

'No,' Kusint rubbed his chin, stubble rasping at the end of this long day. 'It's still a warning, but I think it means that whatever fate lies ahead isn't fixed.'

He surprised Hosh by gathering up the rune sticks and tying them tight together. 'I know little enough of Forest lore. My mother lost her family to Mandarkin raiders when she was little more than a child and Solurans took her in. A true adept raised in the wildwood would most likely find quite different meanings. Shall we share some festival ale in hopes of a prosperous new year here in Halferan?'

The red-headed man rose and went to the sideboard, filling two tankards from the jug before Hosh had a chance to reply.

'I'll drink to that.' Hosh was also unexpectedly content with that reading of the last rune. After all, stubborn hope that he wasn't destined to die on the corsair island had sustained him through that ordeal, even if abandoning that conviction had goaded him into his final act of despairing bravery.

He raised his tankard to Kusint. 'May we see so many midwinters that our hair is white as snow before we hear Poldrion's summons.'

That was a more fitting wish for this festival than dabbling in half-understood mysteries of Forest Artifice.

— CHAPTER SEVEN —

The Temple Square, Relshaz
Winter Solstice Festival, 3rd Evening

IF THIS TEMPLE'S scarcely-remembered Artifice was to offer Kerrit any help, she had to get inside. Jilseth wasn't prepared to wait any longer for a chance to slip though some opening in this steady procession. Still veiled with ensorcelled air, she caught a fugitive breeze and made ready.

The next suppliant approached. The hard-faced priestess stepped forward and thrust her wooden bowl towards him. The man had his coin ready.

Jilseth snagged the bowl's rim with an invisible hook. Caught unawares, the complacent priestess dropped it to spill silver and gold minted in every mainland realm across the smooth marble.

'Quickly!' The priestess dropped to her knees, frantic hands sweeping coin back towards her. Pious worshippers scooped up handfuls of marks and pennies. Some dropped the money into the wooden bowl. The priestess's burly attendants hurried forward to seize those more interested in pocketing this unexpected bounty.

As soon as Jilseth crossed the threshold into the temple, she unveiled herself to appear like any other suppliant coming in through the vast temple's many doors. She slowed and looked around with a fair imitation of their uncertainty in this shadowy candlelight as she searched for an altar to Ostrin.

He was the god of hospitality as well as healing and
Jilseth knew that his shrines across Ensaimin, Caladhria
and Lescar were variously adorned with bunches of grapes
or sheaves of barley. Did the Relshazri favour wine or ale?

Screens of carved and pierced stone separated the
shrines to every god and goddess whom the all-conquering
Tormalin had first honoured here. Smoke from incense
and candles burning before each statue drifted upwards
into the gloomy void. The soft murmur of prayer was
punctuated by the occasional stifled sob of grief.

Most suppliants were waiting for their moment before
Poldrion's statue. Once they had commemorated their
dead, most headed for the narrow door where watchful
priests oversaw their departure. A few made obeisance
before some other deity.

That must surely be Ostrin. Jilseth cut across the
empty heart of the temple towards the statue of a curly-
haired man wearing a simple tunic belted with a rope
which made a mockery of the priests and priestesses'
opulent garb. He cradled a wineskin while offering a
stout-stemmed goblet with his other hand.

A single priest served this god tonight; a round faced
man of Tormalin complexion with close-cropped
dark hair. He was exchanging a few quiet words with
a priestess whose stole was embroidered with ears of
wheat, reminiscent of the sheaf carried by Drianon's
neighbouring statue. Both their plain woollen robes
were girdled with honest hemp.

'Excuse me.' Jilseth approached, her voice muted. 'I
wish to speak to Brother Tinoan.'

'Indeed?' The priest raised questioning eyebrows. 'A
visitor from Hadrumal? Are you a friend of Master
Kerrit's?'

That made matters simpler. 'Apothecary Resnada sent me. Master Kerrit is increasingly unwell.'

'This way.' With the briefest of nods to the priestess, the man led Jilseth around to the back of the altar where small rooms had been built into the thickness of the temple wall.

Entering the central recess, she saw chambers stuffed with scrolls and ledgers on either side. An elderly man in a faded robe sat at a sloped desk amid yet more shelves of records.

Jilseth's first thought was astonishment at seeing him reading with an unguarded candle amid so much paper. Hadrumal's librarians forbade any naked flame within their doors and any apprentice wizard arguing for magic's command over elemental fire could expect to be forbidden admittance until they returned with some new-learned humility.

'Brother?' Her guide spoke more loudly than Jilseth expected. 'Brother!'

'Barmin?' The old man looked up with the hazy amiability of someone unable to see beyond the length of his arms. Wisps of fine white hair fringed his age-spotted scalp.

As the priest wasted no time on introductions or explanations, Jilseth did weave a little air to carry his words clearly to the old man's deaf ears.

'Master Resnada seeks your help for Master Kerrit.'

'By all means.'

As Brother Tinoan slipped spryly from his high stool, Jilseth revised her first impression of his decrepitude. Moreover, Hadrumal's most aged mages might have stiff limbs and aching joints but their minds were still formidably sharp.

He peered at her. 'What concerns Resnada most?'

'Kerrit has increasingly severe headaches and he's prone to uncharacteristic anger. He didn't seem to know me, although he tried to hide it.'

'I see.' The old man hurried off to lay an unerring hand on a tattered scroll. Searching quickly for something else, he halted with a hiss of irritation and crossed to another shelf.

Jilseth looked around the cramped room. Before she could offer to help, a scarlet pinprick appeared in the air, swiftly opening into a circle of magefire.

'Where are you?'

Jilseth answered Velindre through the bespeaking spell. 'At the temple. Resnada seeks a priest with some expertise in healing Artifice.'

'Take some temple servants with you. Big ones with cudgels. We have troublemakers kicking at the gates here and trying to get over the wall. There may be other attacks on wizards in the city.'

'I'll come as soon—'

'No. See what the healer can do for Kerrit. Mellitha has sent word to the Watch.'

As Velindre's spell winked into nothingness, Jilseth recalled how highly the city's guardians valued the magewoman. Her tax collections paid their stipends and equipped them with the best armour and weapons produced by Relshaz's justly famed smiths.

She must warn Kerrit though. But would he respond to a bespeaking in his muddled state of mind? Even if he did, would Jilseth be able to persuade him to summon Resnada so she could convey Velindre's warning to the apothecary?

'You don't need your spells.' The old priest was rolling a scroll tight.

Before Jilseth could explain, Brother Tinoan closed his eyes, a smile deepening his wrinkles. A moment later, he nodded, his expression solemn. He opened his eyes.

'Your friend was right to be concerned. Master Resnada says that the house is being pelted with filth and insults.'

So the priest knew the apothecary well enough to speak to him by means of Artifice? Jilseth was relieved to think that they need not send some messenger through the crowded streets with a note. 'I'll bespeak Madam Esterlin. She can send word to the Watch—'

'Barmin can do that,' the old priest said mildly. 'We are used to managing our affairs without wizardly help. But you may use your skills to take us to Kerrit's house. It will take half the night to cross the city by carriage.'

The younger priest reappeared with four burly men carrying iron-bound staves longer than they were tall. Jilseth contemplated their broad shoulders and reflected on the wealth which this temple gleaned from the city. Those hard-eyed priests and priestesses watching the doors would naturally ensure that their coffers were protected. But how had Brother Barmin known to return with these guards?

The younger priest glanced sideways at her. 'Brother Tinoan thought it best to share Master Resnada's thoughts with me.'

'Are you using your Artifice to know what I was wondering?' Jilseth was too startled for courtesy.

Barmin smiled. 'No, I've simply spent half a generation seeing men and women beseech Ostrin's favour in times of sore trial.'

'You are clearly an astute observer.' Though Jilseth wasn't overly pleased that he had read her face so easily.

Still, she had to allow that she had never particularly cultivated a stony expression. She didn't play tedious games like white raven where some incautious blink or the wry twist of a lip could betray an entire strategy.

'You're not very trusting.' Barmin was more curious than critical. 'I give you my word that I'm using no lore.'

'Forgive me,' Jilseth said curtly. 'I am anxious about my fellow mage.'

Brother Tinoan turned around. 'Please wield your wizardry, Madam Mage.'

'By all means.' Jilseth recalled Hearth Master Kalion saying how difficult aetheric adepts found it to move themselves from place to place. She was less inclined to feel so superior now she that knew aetheric communications could be shared among several adepts. Wizardly bespeaking could only reach one mage at a time.

'We each have our different skills.' The old man smiled serenely.

Was he reading her unspoken thoughts? Jilseth elected not to ask. Master Kerrit was her priority so she would bring Brother Tinoan to work his healing Artifice while these burly temple acolytes dealt with whatever malice might threaten them.

Drawing strength from the immenseness of the marble edifice, Jilseth carefully encompassed the temple guards and the old man within her spell, leaving Brother Barmin untouched. As the temple's gloom yielded to the brightness of translocation, the last thing she heard was his unguarded astonishment. She smiled with satisfaction as the yard outside Kerrit's house appeared.

A venomous shout greeted her. 'There she is, the whore! Where did you go, bitch?'

Jilseth was astonished to recognise the bare-chested youth who'd tried to force his intoxicated lust upon her earlier.

'Do you know this man?' Though her burly escort's tone was respectful, his eyes were sharp with displeasure.

'No, I do not,' Jilseth retorted.

A metal-framed window grated overhead and Jilseth sensed a fine hail of rust falling through the air.

'They were shouting for her to come out of the wizard's house.' A woman's disapproving voice floated down. 'When they got no answer, they started hurling stones and I don't know what else.'

By stones, Jilseth presumed the neighbour meant the broken lumps of plaster and brick strewn across the paving. The stink of human ordure indicated these ne'er-do-wells had also smashed the night soil jars tidily tucked beneath each house's front steps, to pelt Kerrit's windows with filth.

Something had extinguished the lantern by the door. Jilseth held up her hand, her forefinger tipped with crimson magefire. 'I'm here now. What do you want?'

The amorous youth was staring at her now, agape with horror. 'I only—'

His companions were already running away.

'You only sought an ill-advised kiss. Fair festival and Poldrion's blessings on us all.' Brother Tinoan waved the boy away before turning to climb the steps to the door. 'Calirn, you and Acal keep watch. Virsem and Dires, tidy up.'

As the temple guards did the old man's bidding, Master Resnada opened the door, gripping his surgical knife once again. 'Thank Ostrin you're here.'

'How is he?' Tinoan reached for Resnada's hand.

'Failing much faster than I had feared,' the apothecary said unhappily.

The priest hurried through the shadowed sitting room. Resnada followed. The two men were halfway up the cramped stairs before Jilseth caught up with them.

She waited by the door as Brother Tinoan approached Kerrit's bed. Resnada watched anxiously from beside the window.

Kerrit lay back against his pillows, the quilt draped over his legs. Even unaccustomed to sickrooms, Jilseth could see this wasn't the stillness of healing sleep. The mage's eyes were pressed tight closed and deep grooves shadowed his downturned mouth. Laboured breath rasped in his throat and even in the warm lamplight, the mage's face was ashen.

Brother Tinoan perched on the edge of the bed. 'Kerrit?'

He took the wizard's limp hand between his own but there was no sign of any response, no change in that laboured breathing.

'He is dying.' Tinoan gently stroked Kerrit's forearm.

Jilseth stared at the priest. 'I thought you came here to heal him.'

'I came to see what was amiss,' he corrected her. 'If I could heal him, I would, but he is as far beyond my lore as he is Master Resnada's skills.'

'How did I fail him?' the apothecary asked wretchedly.

'You didn't.' Tinoan's gaze never left Kerrit's face. 'I don't believe that he ever fully recovered from that first attack. Not that anyone knew it, least of all poor Kerrit. Subtle injuries within his skull have been slowly bleeding from time to time, each instance leaving clots to do further harm. Now he has reached this crisis, his memories have begun to unravel. Soon his body will forget how to breathe and his heart will forget how to beat.'

'There must be something you can do.' Jilseth insisted. If not, what good was this Artifice?

'Can your wizardry restore a broken egg?' Brother Tinoan enquired. 'Not merely mend the shattered shell but see a healthy chick hatched from it? No, no manner of magic can do that. But I can fashion a sanctuary for Kerrit, from the oldest and fondest memories which he still cherishes. Those will be the last to fade.'

Master Resnada heaved a sigh and sank down to sit on the windowsill, an unheeded tear glistening on his cheek.

Tinoan smiled at the dying man. 'He will feel neither pain nor distress, surrounded by those dearest to him until the time comes for him to leave this life and discover whatever truth lies beyond the mysteries of death.'

'Should we—?' Jilseth realised that she had no idea who might wish to be at Kerrit's deathbed. She didn't even know if he had been mainland or Hadrumal born. Were there kinsfolk somewhere who deserved to be told of his death? Were there Relshazri with a claim on him?

Someone would have to settle his affairs. Who would know what bequests he had promised in coin or property? What of the quantities of books and scrolls stored throughout this house, the fruits of ten years and more of diligent, scholarly work? Of incalculable value for Hadrumal's libraries or limitless irrelevance? Someone would need to find out, now that Kerrit would never be able tell them.

She swallowed to clear her throat of unexpected burning grief at this amiable wizard's undeserved fate.

'I will carry this sad news to Mellitha, and then bespeak the Archmage. There may be mages in Hadrumal who will wish to make their farewells.'

Resnada nodded, all his attention on Kerrit. Brother Tinoan didn't even seem to hear her, eyes closed as he silently mouthed his enchantments.

Jilseth went quietly downstairs to the kitchen. Resnada had closed the window but that didn't concern her. Mellitha's house was as familiar as her own rooms in Hadrumal's Terrene Hall. She blended the magics of air and fire with the shifting nature of water, underpinned by her own ties to the earth. Kerrit's kitchen faded away and—

Jilseth cast the translocation spell to the four winds and let the elements reclaim the wizardry. Someone else's magic was at work in this house. Jilseth looked around with the wizard sight that was Hadrumal's first lesson for every newly-apprenticed mageborn. No, there was nothing here to cause her concern.

Walking through to the front room, she looked up at the ceiling. Overhead, in that upper chamber, some skulking mage was hiding. Some paltry, thieving hedge wizard; one of those who fled Hadrumal for the mainland, too ill-disciplined to sustain the study to make the most of their innate talents. Word must be spreading that Kerrit was finally succumbing to his injuries and this charlatan had sneaked in to scavenge.

Jilseth threw a dense web of elemental water around the entire building. In the next instant, she felt a surge of elemental fire attack her spell. The assault was stronger than she expected. Catching this villain unawares would require some thought.

He was doubtless waiting for her to come up the stairs.

She studied the ceiling, using her wizard senses to assess the laths beneath the plaster, and the rafters supporting the floorboards above. Foiling such expectation would demand precise timing and an immediate switch between such antagonistic magics. Not so long ago she would never have dared to try it. Now she didn't hesitate.

A surge of air took her halfway to the ceiling. As a second step thrust her upwards, Jilseth released the elemental air and summoned her earth affinity to pass through the upper floor as the last remnant of rising air faded away. Her feet landed solidly on the dusty boards.

'Despin!' Wizard sight showed her the shabbily dressed mage in a corner, vainly trying to hide himself within a swirling spiral of air.

'I—' He let his invisibility spell uncoil and fade away. 'I came to pay my respects to Master Kerrit.'

'He lies.' Brother Tinoan said mildly from the doorway.

'I don't need Artifice to tell me that.' Jilseth looked at Despin with incredulous contempt.

Kerrit's table was strewn with scrolls and books, haphazard where everything had been so neatly piled before.

Despin folded his arms, bearded chin jutting. 'Mind your manners, Madam Pupil. I am a member of Hadrumal's Council. I do not answer to the likes of you.'

'You can answer to Planir.' She felt the surge of Despin's wizardry attempt to carry him away. Once again, her magic web around the house held firm, even against the searing heat of his unrestrained affinity.

'What are you doing here?' she demanded.

Before Despin could answer though, Jilseth remembered sitting in the neat sitting room below not half a year ago. Kerrit had explained at frankly tedious length precisely how he proposed to search for any mention of ensorcelled artefacts in Relshaz's temple archives. She remembered Velindre relating that conversation to Hadrumal's Council in the first of the endless debates over what should be done with the magical loot won from the renegade Anskal.

'You're looking for lore on the wizardry of instilling spells into some object.'

'Quite so,' Brother Tinoan confirmed.

Jilseth couldn't help a shiver of unease. Was the old priest prompting her memories as well as Despin's unspoken answers?

The shabby mage clenched furious fists. 'We have no more insight into those cursed artefacts than we did on that first day when we took them from the Mandarkin. The Solurans demand a price which we will never pay for their help yet Planir just folds his hands and accepts their arrogance and insults. Where will we find the secrets of crafting such things for ourselves? Nowhere—'

He broke off, his eyes widening, to thrust an accusing finger at Tinoan. 'What are you doing to me? How dare you?'

Despin hurled elemental fire at the old priest. Jilseth threw up a cold wall of emerald mist to consume the vicious wizardry.

Her distraction gave Despin his chance. With a swiftness that swept books and papers from table and shelves alike, the bearded mage disappeared.

Jilseth would have followed him. Where else would he be heading but Hadrumal? But as she reached for her affinity, she felt the first tremor of weariness run through her wizardry.

'You have done a great deal today,' Brother Tinoan observed.

Jilseth spun around. 'What did you do to him?'

The old priest shrugged. 'I merely encouraged him to speak so that you would know what you were facing.'

'What was he doing?'

This time Jilseth was asking herself but Brother Tinoan answered.

'You heard what he said. More than that, he seeks advancement and acclaim for being the first mage to unravel the mysteries of these magical treasures. He is by no means alone,' the old priest reflected. 'If you thought that the renegade mage's destruction would see an end to Archmage Planir's troubles, think again. The echoes of such violent upheavals haven't even begun to die away.'

'Brother?' Resnada opened Kerrit's bedroom door. 'I think he's fading.'

Jilseth smoothed her skirts. Carrying herself back to Mellitha's house would be less demanding, than returning to Hadrumal. She could bespeak Planir, to inform him of Despin's appalling behaviour and ask what he wished her to do.

Tinoan looked at Jilseth, his gaze penetrating with disapproval. 'Can you not spare the time to sit with us as we see Kerrit to Saedrin's threshold? To honour the price he has paid for Hadrumal's sake?'

'Of course, forgive me.' Jilseth was ashamed to think that she could have even thought of being so callous. Kerrit deserved far better than that.

Nevertheless, as she followed the old man back to the blameless mage's deathbed, she found herself beset by growing fears as well as distress at Kerrit's undeserved fate.

Whether or not through means of his Artifice, Brother Tinoan had been right. Jilseth had assumed that the Mandarkin's death would see Hadrumal's customary serenity restored. There would be no more disputes over Planir's authority in the Council Chamber, especially now that even the most contentious mages had the puzzle of these ensorcelled artefacts to fascinate them.

Beyond the wizard isle, there would be no more challenges to Hadrumal's hegemony prompted by Corrain of Halferan's infuriating obstinacy and his unshakable resolve to find magic to save his people from the corsairs, never imagining what unforeseen disasters would follow.

So she had blithely assumed. Jilseth was no longer so certain. None of them, not her, Velindre or Mellitha had foreseen the murderous attack which was now proving the death of poor Kerrit. What further unanticipated consequences might yet unfold?

— CHAPTER EIGHT —

The Merchants' Exchange, Duryea, Caladhria
Winter Solstice Festival, 3rd Evening

Was there any chance of achieving what he had come here to do before this parliament ended? How soon before someone called for a recess tonight? Whoever it might be, Corrain couldn't blame him. He would have emptied his own purse for a breath of fresh air. The atmosphere in this room was somewhere between stale and stifling at the end of this tedious day.

Four hundred and more Caladhrian barons had journeyed to Duryea, fulfilling their sworn duty to attend at least one quarterly parliament a year. They sat on benches at long tables on either side of the aisle running from the lectern beneath the great chamber's north-facing window to the double door in the southern wall. Twenty tables, each one set with flagons and fine goblets for twenty lords and at the moment, at least twice that number were trying to talk, every one intent on having his say without listening to anyone else's opinion.

This vast chamber easily accommodated them. Duryea's merchants' exchange was larger than any other in the realm. This most northerly of Caladhria's market towns prospered whatever the season or the weather's vagaries, thanks to the east-west high road carrying trade between the independent fiefdoms and towns of Ensaimin and the wealthy princes ruling the great houses of Tormalin. Lesser roads brought goods from Dalasor, and still more northerly Gidesta. Duryea had separate market places for linen and dyestuffs, for raw wool and leather, for livestock still on the hoof and for the wheat, oats and barley harvested from these Caladhrian barons' fertile fields.

And none of these wealthy lords had been willing to spare a copper cut-piece to defend the coastal baronies from the corsairs.

Corrain took care to hide his abiding resentment as he sat on a chair an arm's length from one of the middle tables claimed by a coterie of barons who held lands around Trebin. The local lords had needed to send lackeys to fetch extra seating on the festival's first morning. The number of barons attending this midwinter parliament was unprecedented.

Corrain and his allies had worked hard to make sure of that, drawing on Lord Saldiray and Lord Taine's detailed knowledge of the barons' countless factions, some united by location and common interests and others divided by personal dislikes and enduring rivalries.

'My lords! It is clear that no one will prevail this evening!' Standing at the lectern by right of his local pre-eminence, Baron Gyrice shouted, hoarse and exasperated.

The assembled Caladhrian nobles were so startled that silence swept through the room. Those barons still intent on arguing were hastily hushed by their neighbours. Those who had been dozing belatedly stirred, trying to pretend that they had merely closed their eyes in contemplation.

Corrain would send such dullards to keep a night watch with their own barony's guard troop. They could learn the skills of staying alert and unwearied from first chime to last. Then they might appreciate the discipline required of the men who defended their homes and families, always ready to make obedient haste and fulfil any liege lord's request.

'Thank you, my lords.' Baron Gyrice took a sip of water from a goblet on the shelf of his lectern. 'Let us adjourn to observe Souls' Ease Night's rites. A show of hands?'

Corrain was on his feet. He ignored the outraged faces, more than one lord ready to rebuke him for resuming this endless wrangling.

Other lords looked bemused. He knew they considered a jumped-up guardsman had no right to be heard, even if some disgraceful contrivance had annulled Baron Licanin's rightful guardianship of the Widow Halferan, sister to his own wife.

Corrain spoke quickly to forestall any interruption. 'My lords, we are debating this proposal to enshrine in Caladhrian law a complete and eternal prohibition on the use of wizardry in warfare by any baron using force of arms on behalf of the Caladhrian populace against enemies from beyond our borders...'

He spoke slowly and clearly, for the benefit of Lord Matase who was proving his worth as a scribe, though the noble baron could not have imagined this undertaking when he had volunteered on the parliament's first morning. Customarily the official archive only needed summary notes of those attending and of the show of hands should a vote be called.

But today the noble lords of Saldiray, Myrist, Taine and Blancass had proposed this ban on wizardry throughout Caladhria. For the past two days, Duryea's taverns had heard terrifying tales of wild magic from those guardsmen of Licanin, Tallat and Antathele who had returned home from the Archipelago.

They had expected Hadrumal's spells would merely carry them to the corsairs' anchorage so they could put the villains to the sword. They had agreed to help the Archmage because Planir had told them that the corsairs had amassed a collection of ensorcelled items which they would use to renew their attacks on the mainland. Since Hadrumal's ancient edicts forbade the use of wizardry in warfare, the Archmage had a duty to stop such abuses of magic.

What the Caladhrian warriors had experienced was destruction beyond imagining.

Now Corrain would play his part, as agreed in ciphered letters exchanged long before he arrived in Duryea.

'...I propose one further amendment to our new law. We must recognise that dire circumstances can drive any man to truly desperate measures. We must all admit, in our heart of hearts, that even the most honest among us would steal before seeing his children starve.'

He looked around, uncompromising.

'My own true lord, the former Baron Halferan, was driven to seek wizardly aid for lack of any other hope for his people. I followed his example because I had no other recourse. Even after the Archmage's wizardry swept away the ground beneath my feet, as the southern seas swept over my head—'

Cold recollection slid down Corrain's spine to shrivel his manhood. He steeled himself not to shiver

'—I would follow that same path again, if so vile and murderous a foe threatened Halferan. If I still lacked any other ally.'

He noted the eyes drawn to his wrist now bare of that

slave manacle. He knew the taverns would be rife with speculation as to why he had cut his hair. Reven and young Linset and Halferan's other troopers were ready with answers for Duryea's taprooms.

Archipelagan corsairs denied their galley slaves any blade, not merely to stop them taking their own lives or some captor's. Matted hairiness marked out such slaves on any shore, even when they were released from their chains to undertake some task.

Corrain had maintained his unbarbered state, since making his unprecedented escape, in memory of those Halferan men captured with him. Those whose bones now lay unburied and unburned on some Aldabreshin isle, to leave their innocent shades trapped between death and Saedrin's threshold, tormented by Poldrion's demons alongside the vilest, unrepentant evildoers.

Reven and Linset's explanation would be carried back to these noble lords by their own loyal retainers. If Corrain no longer believed in the gods, he assuredly believed in guilt. Let every baron remember their cowardice in successive parliaments as the former Lord Halferan had begged for their men and swords to drive the corsairs from his own and his neighbours' shores.

But now, so Reven and Linset would confide over their ale, Corrain had given up any hope of rescuing any surviving Halferans after the utter destruction of the corsairs' isle. Now these noble lordships could consider the terrifying rumours of Hadrumal's cataclysmic power whenever his raggedly shorn head caught their attention.

They didn't need to know that the Archmage's sole concern had been destroying the renegade Mandarkin mage whom Corrain had so foolishly offered the pick of the raiders' plunder, only for that thrice-cursed villain to turn traitor and threaten Caladhria with still more lethal malice as he discovered unsuspected mageborn and still more unexpected magic among the corsairs' treasures.

The barons didn't need to know that Corrain had wept bitter tears in Halferan's silent muniment room as he had worked through those lonely nights to free himself from that manacle. He would never forgive himself for failing those lost men. All he could do to honour their memory was ensure that no Caladhrian barony was ever left so shamefully undefended again, their honest troopers abandoned to fight such hopeless battles alone.

He swept the room with a searching gaze. 'Let us agree on a duty in law, to be laid on our heirs in perpetuity. If a barony is attacked, we must join forces in that lord's defence, whether that attack comes from beyond Caladhria's borders or from malevolence within. Then no barony need ever seek wizardly aid to drive off their foes.'

He took care not to catch Lord Saldiray's eye. The noble lord had assured Corrain that he would remind selected barons of Baron Karpis's humiliation at the lady wizard Jilseth's hands.

The story of a mild-faced maiden reducing the Karpis troops' armour and weapons to rust and warped scraps of leather had passed through the previous year's parliaments quicker than counterfeit coin. That had been a fine joke but an Archipelagan island being so comprehensively ravaged that not a rock remained above water wasn't nearly so amusing.

However tempting these noble lords might find the prospect of calling on wizardly assistance, to inflict Baron Karpis's mortification on some rival of their own, let them imagine their fiefdom facing a hostile mage capable of wreaking such utter destruction.

As soon as he had recovered from his ordeal in the Archipelago, Corrain had begun writing to the barons of Saldiray, Myrist, Taine and Blancass, erstwhile allies of the true Baron Halferan. Reading his chilling testimony they had agreed with him that such magic must never be loosed on Caladhrian soil.

'An interesting proposal, though it comes very late in the day.' Baron Gyrice made the mistake of taking another sip of water.

A baron from the Tresia region sprang to his feet. 'If Caladhria is to forswear wizardry, we must urge those dominions which border our lands to follow our example.'

'For our safety as much as their own. Only a fool discards a weapon to leave it where some enemy can pick it up.' One of his neighbours stood to support him.

Baron Myrist had played his part well in preparing them. Corrain resumed his seat, hiding his satisfaction.

'Assuming this proposal is passed, we must write first and foremost to Tadriol the Provident, Emperor of Tormalin—'

'We owe Tormalin no fealty!' Some backwoods baron was so outraged at the notion he shouted out unbidden.

'We owe the Imperial throne due respect,' Baron Gyrice retorted from the lectern.

'Caladhria has been independent of Tormalin since the first decade of the Chaos, for twenty and more generations!' A lean nobleman didn't wait for Lord Gyrice to call on him to stand. 'Our independence is our most cherished freedom, won by our forefathers driving their Tormalin conquerors back over the river Rel—'

'Thank you, Lord Torlef, I don't need a lesson in history from you.' Baron Gyrice slammed his goblet down on the lectern's shelf, spilling water over his hand.

Baron Myrist took advantage of his distraction. 'If his Imperial Majesty proposes a similar law to the Convocation of Princes, explicitly forbidding the use of wizardry in warfare, we can surely hope that the lawmakers of Lescar and Ensaimin will follow Tormalin's example.'

Corrain made sure not to catch Baron Taine or Baron Saldiray's eye. Those noble lords had already written to their friends among the sieurs and esquires of Tormalin's princely Houses to endorse just such a law.

A hand shot up from a knot of barons huddled around a central table. Baron Tulbec rose to his feet at Gyrice's nod. 'I propose that we write to the Relshazri Magistracy to apprise them of our new law.'

'This law hasn't yet been put the vote,' Baron Saunor snapped.

'Anyone voting against it is an arrant fool,' Baron Tulbec said tightly.

Corrain noted nods of support from every noble with lands within two or three days' wagon travel of the River Rel. Their wealth in timber and grain customarily filled the barges floating down to Relshaz, where it was turned into good gold coin.

'Has your trade with the Relshazri been truly so undermined by their new shunning of wizardry?' A baron with no such concerns thanks to his fiefdom's border with Ensaimin was openly sceptical.

Baron Tulbec's tone sharpened. 'Do not underestimate the Archipelagan's loathing of magecraft, my lord of Estoel. Since the eruption of wizardry in their islands, for which they blame Caladhria—'

Corrain parried Baron Tulbec's condemning glare with an expressionless face.

'—the Aldabreshi have scorned all our goods or

wares. They refuse to do business with any Relshazri merchants trading with Caladhria. They look instead to Ensaimin, Dalasor or Gidesta—'

'Those realms cannot supply our wheat and barley and flax—'

Baron Tulbec rounded on the complacent Baron of Ferl. 'The Lescari are eager to steal that trade now they have peace to plough their fields.'

Lord Dalthran lurched to his feet. From his high colour on plump cheeks, he'd been paying more attention to a wine flagon than to the debate. 'This so-called Conclave in Lescar is merely a rabble of rebels! They encompassed the deaths of the Dukes of Parnilesse, Carluse and Sharlac.' His voice thickened with outrage. 'Their Graces of Marlier, Draximal and Triolle escaped with their lives through merest chance. If we acknowledge such malcontents and murderers as Lescar's rightful rulers, what does that tell our own dissenters?'

Corrain narrowed his eyes at the belligerent lord. This was what he and the lords conspiring with him had feared. All too often Caladhria's parliaments' debates descended into irrelevant and inconclusive wrangling.

'Forgive me, my lord of Dalthran.' Baron Saldiray didn't sound in the least apologetic as he stood up and waved a pale parchment, its broken wax seal stark as a clot of blood.

'The whereabouts of Duke Iruvain formerly of Triolle and Duke Ferdain formerly of Marlier are currently unknown, much to the distress of their creditors in Abray, Adrulle and Relshaz,' he observed drily. 'Duke Secaris formerly of Draximal remains in Savorgan in northern Tormalin, still forswearing any desire to return to his former dominion.'

'My lords, Lescar's affairs are none of our concern and the evening draws on!' Baron Gyrice gestured curtly towards the candlesticks on the tables. His servants had brought tapers to light each handful of flames as soon as dusk had drawn its veil across the room's tall windows. Now the candles were visibly shorter.

'This of all nights in the year requires reverence rather than argument,' he continued crossly. 'It is long past time we adjourned. May I have your assent?'

Hands rose at every table and some were already rising to their feet, taking the vote as given and eager to eat their festival dinner.

Corrain remained in his chair as Baron Gyrice's lackeys opened the double doors at the far end of the room, to admit a welcome draft to set the candles flickering and the sounds of festival revelry in the market place outside.

He watched the lords of Saldiray, Myrist, Taine and Blancass depart amid the throng, each unobtrusively following a particular lord. They had not secured their new law today but by tomorrow those noblemen would have shared a few choice thoughts on the perils of isolation so vividly demonstrated by Halferan's fate with the barons most easily persuaded to vote in favour of such mutual support.

Maidservants began straightening the benches and chairs and clearing away flagons and goblets. One gave a silver wine jug a hopeful shake. Opening its lid, her expression brightened and she hurried to add the jug to a handful of others set aside on the table by the door. Other servants carried silver and glassware briskly away.

A pointed cough echoed through the room. Baron Gyrice was conferring with Lord Pertynd and Baron

Matase by the lectern beneath the tall north window. Matase in particular glared suspiciously at Corrain.

He rose to his feet and strolled towards the door. Were those barons innocently intent on feasting with families and friends before piously remembering their dead? Or would they go seeking some illicit partner to share a bottle, a wager or a bed? Every parliament offered opportunity for a little wildness away from hearth and home to set the heart racing, blood pumping through noble and humble veins alike, celebrating life's vigour by defying midwinter's stillness.

Corrain smiled, recalling one summer parliament in Trebin. The local lords had supplied so much excellent wine on the festival eve that Corrain and his fellow guard captains had spent the following morning carrying apologies from their masters who apparently found themselves belatedly stricken by an excess of sun on the road.

They had also been asked to discreetly discover exactly what had been debated and decided the previous day. Corrain and his friends had amused themselves concocting ever more outrageous possibilities to horrify their wine-sick liege lords. Then they had simply asked the servants who'd fetched and carried the flagons and goblets.

So which of the youthful Halferan guards would have most success wheedling information out of these maidens? Corrain considered Linset's beguiling manner as he continued unhurried down the broad staircase to the entrance hall. Liveried guardsmen stood by the bottommost steps.

Baron Erbale's men, crumpled and heavy-eyed after this overlong day on watch, were yielding their duty to a crisply-dressed contingent. Fresh-faced from a day's rest, Lord Vildare's men were ready to stand sentry through the night, midwinter feast or not. Corrain acknowledged the troopers with a lordly nod while assessing them with a guard captain's sharp eye.

A couple looked back, their expressions more knowing than deferential. Had they heard barrack hall stories from guard captains who'd known Corrain of old? Was deliberate malice prompting such stories of his erstwhile taste for festival dalliance? Those nobles still outraged by Corrain's elevation to their rank would be delighted to wound him with truth rather than lies.

Those runes could roll either way; it made no difference to him. Corrain would return to The Silver Boar, to eat his festival dinner with a modest measure of ale and take to his solitary bed. He'd be rising as early as any guardsman tomorrow, to see the vote on Caladhria's edict forbidding wizardry formally proposed and carried through this parliament.

Outside, the market place was lit with lamps hung outside every doorway. Iron fire-baskets warded off night's chill, as ale, wine and white brandy were sold from the open windows of every inn. Peddlers offered trinkets for sale while hucksters extolled the virtues of any number of taverns and brothels. Sharp-eyed tricksters sought the drunk or gullible, offering a few trios of runes cast on an empty barrel top, just for a friendly wager.

'Lord Halferan!' Baron Dalthran stepped out of an alley.

Corrain noted the guardsman a few paces behind him. A swift glance reassured him that neither man's hand rested on a blade so Corrain held off reaching for his own sword. 'Fair festival, my lord.'

Baron Dalthran took an unsteady step forward. 'We'll look to you for recompense when the Relshazri beggar us all.'

'I beg your pardon?' Corrain was wrong-footed by this attack.

'How much of the corsairs' loot did those wizards help you bring home, you and Lord Tallat's men?' Dalthran demanded. 'And Licanin and Antathele?'

'There was no booty,' Corrain assured him. 'We didn't think we'd get back alive, still less have time to stuff our pockets. Ask Lord Tallat if you don't believe me or Licanin or Antathele.'

'You think they will admit to such ill-gotten gains?' Dalthran spat. 'Did you think that you wouldn't be called on to surrender such plunder? Those corsairs raided up and down the Caladhrian coast, thieving from countless fiefdoms. Every barony deserves reparations.'

Corrain reminded himself of the folly of debating with drunks. Besides, Dalthran was doubtless only repeating other barons' gossip. He was too idle and blinkered to have thought of this unprompted.

'I have no notion what happened to the corsairs' loot. I can tell you that we have none of it, nor ever sought it, and I'll swear to that on any altar you propose.'

'Do you think anyone will believe you?' Dalthran's finger wavered in the air before he jabbed at Corrain's shoulder. 'We will send our own messengers to the Archmage to find out how much treasure you're hiding, and curses on your law forbidding dealings with wizardry. Don't imagine we don't see your reasons for shunning Hadrumal's mages. You simply want to hide your own thievery.'

Corrain looked past the nobleman to Dalthran's guardsman. 'Take him to his bed. When he sobers up, tell him how I dealt with insults in my days as Halferan's captain. He can count himself lucky I respect my new rank and those worthy of it.'

He turned away, not checking his stride when he heard a yelp from Dalthran suggesting that the guardsman had forcibly restrained his inebriated lord.

Corrain was already composing the message he must now send to Lady Zurenne, brief and miniscule on a slip of onionskin paper to be rolled tight and stowed in the silver cylinder fastened to a courier dove's leg. She needed to know of this new rumour of undeserved riches in Halferan's strong room, to go with their hoard of wizardly gold. Though that tale was somewhat more inconveniently true, or at least it had been before rebuilding the manor and restoring the demesne had seen most of Planir's coin spent.

He would have to wait until morning before loosing one of the handful of Halferan-hatched birds which Sergeant Reven was so diligently tending in his bedroom. Still, he could send messengers tonight to warn the lords of Tallat, Antathele and Licanin of these accusations, if he could find anyone sober enough to reliably carry a discreet note.

Would Dalthran repeat his claims before the whole parliament? Would some other lord who might be listened to more readily? Corrain decided to send notes to the barons of Myrist, Saldiray and Taine as well, to warn them of such potential distraction when debate on this new law resumed.

At least no one had yet levelled the accusation which Corrain feared most. He didn't relish having to stand up in front of the entire parliament and swear to a blatant lie, even if he no longer feared divine retribution.

That secret should be safe though, held close between the two of them. No one else could possibly know that Planir had demanded Corrain's endeavours to pass this law as the final price for his wizards' assistance in saving Halferan.

No one would believe that the Archmage wanted to see Caladhrian law forbidding the suborning of magecraft in warfare, still less that Planir hoped to see similar decrees signed and sealed by every mainland realm and dominion.

Corrain had readily agreed to do whatever he could to convince Caladhria's parliament. He wanted all accounts settled with Hadrumal, so he need have nothing more to do with any other wizard, not even a mild-faced maiden like Madam Jilseth.

— CHAPTER NINE —

The residence of Mellitha Esterlin, Relshaz
Winter Solstice Festival, 3rd Night

JILSETH DREW A deep breath and wove her translocation. Kerrit was dead but she must set aside her grief and anger for the moment. Unrestrained emotion provoked untamed magic. Every mageborn newly come to Hadrumal, homesick, fearful or defiant, was warned of the dire consequences when wizards gave way to unbridled passion. Those inclined to scoff were sent to read the chilling letters and journals detailing the stomach-churning destruction which followed.

As pure white light enveloped her, she considered what she would say to Mellitha and Velindre about Despin's attempted theft. What would Planir—

Sapphire magelight dazzled her. Jilseth lost any sense of elemental earth, the very foundation of her magecraft. She was buffeted by elemental air as brutal as a hurricane. Fire escaped her mastery next and the punishing winds scorched her like furnace blasts.

Jilseth fought for composure. Panic would be the death of her. She realised that her wizardly strength was untouched. That was no great relief. Not when she had lost all ability to harness and channel such perilous power. No prentice-mistress or pupil-master had ever taught her how to handle this particular circumstance. How could she regain control of her magecraft when she was denied her own affinity? Despite her best efforts, dread threatened to choke her.

'Jilseth!'

She heard Mellitha through the deafening roar and felt the soothing touch of elemental water. Coolness flowed between her wizard senses and the chaotic brutality of fire and air. In that moment of respite Jilseth sensed the elemental earth. Channelling her learning and strength, she anchored herself amid all four elements. The turmoil enveloping her paled into the white mist of translocation.

'Jilseth!' Mellitha grabbed her arm even before she felt solid ground beneath her feet.

'What's going on?' They stood on the paving between the lawn and the white stone house's gates. Jilseth was chilled to realise that she had lost any sense of where her disrupted spell might have carried her.

'The local malcontents are no longer satisfied with hurling abuse.' Velindre's contempt was scathing as she drew a curtain of azure magelight along the top of the wall to shatter a volley of stones into a shower of gravel.

Jilseth realised that her translocation must have become entangled with Velindre's warding spells. Ordinarily, she would have demanded her immediate attention. They must establish precisely what elemental conflicts had arisen as the spells clashed. Disseminating their conclusions through Hadrumal's halls would be vital to warn other mages of such a hazard.

Such wizardly concerns would have to wait. The air crackled as though a thunderstorm were about to break over their heads. Inside the stables Jilseth heard a horse whinnying uneasily and the thud of hooves against wood. Bricks hurled over the wall were reduced to dust by

Velindre's shimmering magic. Jilseth noted that these attackers had found far larger missiles than anything lobbed at Kerrit's house. Her throat tightened painfully at the thought of the guiltless wizard's death. 'I must tell you—'

'Do these fools imagine they can defeat our spells with such nonsense?' Mellitha flung up her hands and emerald mist captured and quenched a blazing bottle.

'They know that mages must tire eventually,' Velindre said grimly.

A handful of bottles stuffed with burning rags followed the first. Mellitha's magic reduced them to a rain of molten glass pattering harmlessly onto the paving.

'Where is the Watch?' she raged.

Jilseth found the customarily serene magewoman's fury more disconcerting than this unprecedented attack.

'Jilseth, scry beyond the wall. Find out what we are facing.' Velindre repulsed another wave of broken masonry and cobblestones. Rage-filled shouts turned to choking and coughing as she sent the resulting cloud of dust to swirl around their attackers.

'Find out why the cursed Watch aren't here,' Mellitha snapped.

'Of course.' Jilseth ran into the house.

Mellitha's servants were gathered in the marble-floored hallway.

'The mistress said—'

'I'm sure.' Jilseth didn't wait to hear Mellitha's instructions repeated. It was enough to know that the vulnerable were safely out of harm's way.

Flinging the salon door open, she wrung water out of the air to fill the scrying bowl on the distant table. With Mellitha's magecraft pervading the house, Jilseth barely had to brush against the element. She didn't waste time with ink or oils, simply cupping her hands around the overflowing bowl. Emerald brightness banished every shadow to the far corners of the room

Usually the cool touch of pure silver soothed her. Now apprehension chilled Jilseth as she contemplated the scene in the scrying, as clear as if she walked, invisible and insubstantial, along the coping stones of the tall white wall.

This was no mob of drunken fools to be easily scared away. The crowd was ten deep in places. The street outside the gates was impassable and the path circling the house was choked with people.

Jilseth could see fearful men and women trying to fight their way free of this stifling throng. Some were plainly regretting whatever hatred or hysteria had swept them here, drink-fuelled ire cooling. A few had visible reason to leave; bleeding heads wounded by missiles falling short of their target.

None could get away. For every one trying to depart, a handful more arrived, their faces ugly with mindless viciousness. Shoving turned into scuffling, restrained only by the crushing lack of space to throw punches. More people struggled to escape the spreading fracas. Their frantic efforts only provoked more hostility from those thinking themselves attacked. Dagger blades flashed in the moonlight.

A tremor sent ripples across the scrying water. Jilseth snatched her hands from the bowl and dropped to one knee. As she pressed her hand against the floor, she felt the ominous disturbance more clearly.

Abandoning the silver bowl, her untended spell fading, Jilseth ran out of the salon and through the hall. She waved away the servants desperate to ask her questions, flinging a trivial cantrip ahead to open the door.

'Mellitha! Velindre!' She stood on the topmost step, a dart of air carrying her words to each magewoman's ear.

'What?' Velindre crossed the thirty paces to her side in a single step.

More stones soared upwards only to disintegrate amid the blonde magewoman's magic.

'Where are they still getting these cobbles?' Mellitha demanded, irate. 'Have they stripped every street between here and the Rel?'

All the older woman's attention was focused on the gates. Jilseth's wizard sight showed her the water magic suffusing the sturdy barrier. Despite the assaults of sharp-edged stones, boots and belt-knives, Mellitha's wizardry was repairing every splinter and crack, the wood as solid as though it flourished uncut in some distant coppice.

'The wall is about to fall!' Though only an earth mage would sense the strain in the close-fitted and mortared joints, the shifting in the foundations below the ground, Jilseth knew beyond any possibility of doubt that the press of this crowd would soon overwhelm the masonry.

Mellitha stared at her in momentary disbelief. 'Use your magic to hold it firm.'

'Then those being crushed against the stones by the rest will surely die.' Jilseth had already glimpsed unconscious faces in the crowd, only saved from falling to be trampled to death by the press of people around them.

'If the wall falls, those closest will fall with it,' Velindre said grimly. 'They'll be crushed underfoot by the rest rushing forward to attack us or to loot the house.'

Unable to deny that horrible truth, Mellitha narrowed her eyes. 'Where is Merenel? If we have a fire mage, we can form a nexus—'

'Do you honestly believe we could work quintessential magic with rocks raining down on our heads?' Velindre demanded before glancing at Jilseth. 'Besides, Merenel has gone back to Hadrumal to tell Planir what's amiss.'

Jilseth felt another tremor running through the wall's foundations. The masonry was close to fracturing in a handful of places. She reached deep into the earth to buttress the stones with the memory of the mountains they had been hewn from. It was no easy task, standing on delta mud threaded through with the city's constrained streams.

'How much longer can you defend those gates?' Velindre challenged Mellitha. 'How long until Jilseth exhausts herself keeping that wall intact? I am already weary of pounding bricks into dust.'

'What do you suggest?' Mellitha asked Velindre acidly. 'A wall of fire to burn the closest to ashes and send the rest fleeing in terror? An ice storm to freeze them to the ground and bad luck to those who lose fingers or feet to the frost? How many friends will that win Hadrumal? How will that reassure those merchants harassed by Aldabreshin demands to shun all wizardry?'

Before the blonde magewoman could answer, an uprush of flames framed the top of the gate. Oil or pitch had been hurled against the wood swiftly followed by a burning brand. Mellitha's eyes glistened green; unshed tears reflecting the emerald radiance quenching the fire beyond any possibility of relighting.

A scream rose above the tumult beyond the wall only to be cut short with eerie abruptness. Then countless screams and shrieks of pain ripped through the silence.

Mellitha spun a globe of swirling water out of the empty air between her hands. The ensorcelled water flowed into a floating disc and a vision of the street outside floated across the water's surface.

Before Jilseth could marvel at this unsupported scrying, she was shocked at the mayhem it revealed.

The Relshazri Watch had arrived to find themselves unable to force a path through the crowd with their polearms' staves. So they were using their weapons' blades. Blood glistened on churned mud where cobbles had been dug from underfoot. Bodies slumped motionless or curled in agonies around some murderous thrust. Those wounded who could still walk lurched and stumbled away. Those beyond reach of the biting steel took flight as best they could.

Not everyone was fleeing. Jilseth watched, dry-mouthed, as a double handful of men and boys drew up into a ragged line, armed with knives and swords. Even in the uncertain moonlight they looked Aldabreshin in features and complexion despite their mainland clothing. Were they Archipelagan born living in Relshaz or some of the many born of mixed blood? Did that matter?

'This will be a slaughter.' She turned to the other magewomen. 'We could keep them apart—'

'No,' Mellitha said bleakly. 'Using magic against the Watch will turn the whole Magistracy against wizardry.'

'Those Aldabreshi won't thank you for your help.' Velindre was equally sombre. 'They'll only seek to kill you more quickly to cleanse themselves of magic's stain with your blood.'

Jilseth felt sick to her stomach as she saw the Watch sergeant gesture with his halberd, warning off some stragglers caught between the urge to run for safety and a callous desire to see what happened next.

One of the belligerents hurled a knife. It struck a Watchman in the neck. The blade fell away, leaving the man unharmed thanks to his steel gorget. The Watch contingent levelled their polearms and charged.

A bearded man in a long tunic died skewered on a halberd's point. A boy tried to attack the Watchman wielding it. The Watchman pulled his weapon free to rip open the boy's belly with a scything stroke.

One man had retreated to wrap a cloak around his off-hand, a curved Aldabreshi sword in the other. As a Watchman approached, he darted forward to get inside the polearm's reach. He hacked at the Watchman's foremost wrist while looking to tangle the halberd's deadly blade in the cloak.

The Watchman stepped adroitly aside. Swiftly flipping his weapon end to end put the blade beyond reach of the smothering cloth. The same movement smashed his assailant's sword arm with the iron-shod foot. The man dropped to his knees. The Watchman spun his halberd again. This time the killing blade hacked his assailant's head from his shoulders. Blood soared into the air, glittering in the moonlight.

Another swordsman thrust at a Watchman. The armoured man used the flat of his halberd's blade to force the sword down to the broken earth and cobbles. As the attacker stumbled forward, the Watchman swept his blade up the sword and into the man's undefended face.

Jilseth longed to block her ears with magic to silence the screams. She wanted to look away from Mellitha's scrying. But she would have to bear witness to this slaughter for Planir. She wondered what the Archmage would do if he was here. Were he and Merenel watching this carnage through a scrying wrought in Hadrumal?

Mellitha heaved a sigh. 'That's over at least.'

The last defiant attacker threw down his knife as his remaining allies took to their heels. Half the Watchmen pursued them while the rest subdued those few who'd surrendered with brutal blows.

'What will happen to them?' Jilseth wondered aloud.

'They'll be thrown in the Magistracy's lock-up until they're sold as slaves,' Velindre said sourly. 'This night's work may weigh in their favour. Some Aldabreshi will want to own men who've fought so bravely against wizardry.'

A fist hammered on the gate outside, a courteous yet uncompromising voice shouting. 'Madam Esterlin. Open for the Magistracy, if you please.'

Mellitha let the extraordinary scrying dissolve into a cloud of mist and gestured. The gate swung open. 'Yes?'

The Watch sergeant bowed low, though Jilseth noted his eyes scanning the gardens, the stables and the house. The men behind him gaped more openly at Mellitha's opulent residence.

The sergeant produced a twice-folded and thrice-sealed letter from a pouch at his belt. 'This is for you.'

Mellitha took it and examined the seals. 'From the Magistracy, no less.'

Velindre stepped forward to question the sergeant. 'Has there been much trouble in the city tonight?'

'For the mageborn? Yes.'

Jilseth was about to ask what he meant when Mellitha set the parchment in her hand ablaze with scarlet magefire.

Even Velindre was taken aback. 'What is it?'

'I am ordered to leave the city.' Mellitha clenched

her fist around the blood-red flames. 'For the sake of continued good order.'

'I am ordered to defend your property until circumstances permit your return.'

The sergeant took an involuntary step backwards as Mellitha glared at him.

'Really? And what are your orders if I choose not to leave?'

The man squared his shoulders. 'To leave you and your property unguarded.'

Jilseth recalled Velindre's warning that even mundane mainlanders knew that any wizard's strength must eventually fail.

The blonde magewoman snapped imperious fingers to demand the sergeant's attention. 'How long do we have to arrange our affairs?'

'I am to be gone before dawn.' Mellitha's voice broke somewhere between grief and anger.

'Then guard those gates while we make ready to depart.' Velindre narrowed her eyes ominously at the sergeant.

He bowed again, even lower. 'Madam Mage.'

As the sergeant and his men retreated, Mellitha gestured. The gates slammed closed and she rounded on Velindre, incredulity outweighing her anger.

'You think I will abandon my home to be looted by the Magistracy's lackeys? That I will turn my household onto the streets to face that mob unprotected? Shall we abandon Kerrit to their mercies as well?'

'Master Kerrit is dead.' Jilseth hadn't meant to break the grievous news so bluntly but Mellitha's attack startled her into the truth.

'He—' The older magewoman stared at her, appalled. 'But the priest—?'

'There was nothing his lore could do.' Jilseth's eyes stung with painful recollection. 'Temple guards are watching Kerrit's house though. That should keep his property safe.'

'There is nothing more we can do here,' Velindre said forcefully. 'Do you intend to set the whole of the Magistracy against Hadrumal?'

The echo of Mellitha's earlier words hung in the silence between them.

'Very well.' She began walking towards the house.

Jilseth found this abrupt calmness more unnerving than Mellitha's earlier fury. She followed Velindre up the steps and onto the threshold. A handful of young men, as handsome as the magewoman's hirelings invariably were, stood in the hallway with an equal number of women ranging from a fresh-faced girl twisting nervous hands to a stolid female of Mellitha's own age perfumed with the lingering savour of kitchen spices.

'I'm sorry beyond words that this festival has become a nightmare for our household,' Mellitha said crisply. 'I wish that we could wake from an evil dream prompted by too much white brandy. Alas, that will not happen and now we have been forsaken by the Magistracy.'

The magewoman drew a breath, visibly struggling to rein in her temper.

'I have a duty to keep you all safe and that means I must take you to Hadrumal. I will see that you go wherever you wish after that but I cannot allow you to risk trying to cross the city tonight. Please gather up your most precious belongings. Please make haste.'

Jilseth watched the silent servants scurry away before raising a hand to request Velindre's attention. 'Will we take them with us in a collective spell or individually one by one? Where will we take them?'

'We'll go to the sundial courtyard in Wellery's Hall.' Mellitha said decisively. 'Rafrid and I have long been friends.'

'What do you want to take with you?' Velindre glanced around the hallway and through the open door into the long room overlooking the garden.

'What should I take?' Mellitha raised her finely shaped brows. 'My sitting room furniture? Gowns from my dressing chamber? Why should I want any reminders of everything which I cannot salvage? What of my happy memories of raising my children here? My impeccable reputation among Relshaz's merchants, both as a most discerning customer and their truest confidante concerning their taxes?'

She bit her lip and turned away, only to stop short. 'My horses. They must be taken to the Watch stables. Tanilo is spending the festival with his family. He can collect them—'

'I'll tell the sergeant.' Velindre vanished to reappear by the gates, hauling them open with sapphire magic before giving the Watchman his orders with forceful gestures.

'We can get a message to Tanilo once we're in Hadrumal.' Jilseth hated to think of the magewoman's faithful coachman not knowing that his mistress and the other servants were safe. That he might already have heard of this uproar and been caught up in the mayhem outside didn't bear contemplating.

'Madam.' Nishail struggled into the hallway dragging a heavy chest. 'Your jewels.'

For one appalling moment, Jilseth thought Mellitha would lash out at the boy. Instead the magewoman smiled at him with apparent gratitude.

'Do put that down before you suffer a rupture.'

She clapped her hands as the other servants returned. 'Everyone stand in a circle.'

The servants meekly piled their belongings around the chest and ringed it, linking hands. They looked at Mellitha with unfailing trust.

'I will lead the spell.' Velindre reappeared on the far side.

Jilseth felt the chill of elemental air pass behind her back. She caught a swirling wisp and braided her own grasp on such wizardry into it. Now she was bound to Velindre's magecraft. She felt Mellitha do the same. A rush of fire swiftly followed the azure breeze and then Jilseth felt the smoothness of Mellitha's wizardry coursing towards her. Binding her own understanding of water into the spell she channelled the blended elements onwards to Velindre.

She followed the flow of water with her own magecraft, reaching out with her affinity to the distant stones of Hadrumal's towers. Quarried from the wizard isle's own hills, they shared their essence with the minerals in her own bones, island born as she was. Jilseth felt Velindre take firm hold of the interwoven magic and was momentarily surprised to realise how evenly their wizardry was now matched in their respective disciplines.

Threads of magic only visible to mage senses shifted into a rainbow haze. Magelight visible to all bleached the mist to purest white.

'Now.' Velindre's wizardry coursed through the spell like lightning through storm clouds.

In the next instant, Jilseth felt the familiar stones of Hadrumal beneath her grateful feet.

'What—?' A startled wizard's exclamation echoed around the dark quadrangle.

'Where—?' Mellitha's cook quavered between relief and apprehension.

Jilseth sought to reassure her. 'You're safe in the wizard city.'

The cool whiteness faded to reveal the courtyard in Wellery's Hall with the ancient sundial at its centre.

'Jilseth!' Canfor strode forward. 'What do you think you are doing?'

He was the last mage she wanted to see. Canfor seemed to treat the strength which he'd gained from Planir's fourfold nexus as no more than his due. Several mages had told Jilseth that he confidently expected to be offered the next Council seat to become available.

'Where is Cloud Master Rafrid?' Jilseth looked towards Wellery's tower and was relieved to see lamplight in the windows.

Now Canfor had seen Mellitha. 'Would you care to explain this precipitate arrival, Madam Mage?'

'A little respect for Madam Esterlin, if you please,' Velindre snapped.

Mellitha ignored them both, surveying the courtyard. Curtains were being pulled back from windows as shutters were thrust open, querulous voices demanding answers.

'Hadrumal,' she muttered with loathing.

Jilseth wondered if she would learn why the magewoman disliked the wizard city so. She certainly didn't think that Mellitha would stay here any longer than she must. Where would she go?

She wondered if the magewoman would consider visiting Halferan. Lady Zurenne and most particularly young Lady Ilysh would surely find Mellitha a fine example of a woman commanding authority and respect on equal terms with any man.

— CHAPTER TEN —

'MY LADY?' HOSH rapped on the jamb, although the door was securely wedged open. Zurenne didn't want anyone thinking that she was appropriating the baronial audience room in its rightful master's absence.

So many people sought her advice though. Using this larger chamber on the tower's ground floor with its anteroom opening from the hallway was far more sensible than having them tramp up the stairs to her sitting room and crowd the landing.It wasn't as if she was encroaching on the muniment room securely locked behind her.

Hosh proffered a closely folded and securely sealed parchment. 'A letter—'

'From Corrain?' Ilysh hastily corrected herself. 'From the Baron?'

'Mama?' Esnina looked up hopefully from her copybook on the opposite side of the table beyond a branch of flickering candles. This was a dark chamber on dull winter days, with every wall fitted with oak shelves. Most were empty as yet, waiting expectantly for generations of bound and rolled parchments which would renew the manor's archive while the barony's ledgers and sealed, oath-bound agreements were further safeguarded in the muniment room's locked chests.

'The baron would send a courier dove.' Unless, Zurenne realised, the last birds which Reven was tending had succumbed to wet or cold. But any rider from Duryea would still have had to set out before the parliament opened to arrive back here so soon. Whatever news such a letter brought would already have been overtaken by the messages which the doves had carried.

Hosh handed the letter over. 'A rider from Licanin brought this. He says it's urgent news.'

The boy's hand momentarily shielded the disfigured side of his face. Zurenne had noticed him do that before, though Hosh seemed unaware of the gesture.

'For my husband?' Ilysh glanced towards the coffer on a side table where Zurenne had stowed the few letters addressed to the Baron Halferan which had arrived in Corrain's absence. While she had accepted her mother's decree that such missives must remain unread, she had done so with marked ill-grace.

'It's addressed to me.' Zurenne was momentarily surprised until she recognised her sister Beresa's personal seal. 'It's from your aunt, Lady Licanin.'

Who would have calculated her own husband's journey back from Duryea, over four-fifths of Caladhria's length. Beresa would know equally well that Corrain must still be at least a double handful of days ride away from Halferan. What news was so pressing that it couldn't wait for either baron to reach home?

'Has her man accepted a bed for the night?' Zurenne snapped the wax seals and unfolded the stiff parchment. 'Has he been asked to await my reply?'

It was barely mid-afternoon so there was always the possibility that the rider would wish to make the most of the remaining daylight.

She sat down to decipher her sister's message. For such tidy looking script, Lady Licanin's handwriting could be remarkably challenging to read. Her style was also politely remote. There was a full generation between Zurenne and Beresa; the oldest of her sisters, she had married Lord Licanin when Zurenne was younger than Neeny.

'Is it news of Baron Karpis?' Ilysh demanded.

The girl knew that the villain still coveted Halferan and moreover that Corrain had written to Lord Licanin ten days into For-Winter. Ilysh had been studying the manor's ledgers with Zurenne when Corrain had come to inform her that he had sought the older man's advice. He had been as perturbed as Zurenne by the letter she had received from Lady Diress, Baron Karpis's wife, mentioning that their neighbouring lord had no intention of travelling to Duryea for the solstice parliament.

Did Beresa have some reason to suspect that Baron Karpis was looking greedily across his borders towards Halferan again? Had he heard those rumours of corsair gold hidden in the manor's strong rooms which Corrain's courier dove message had relayed? Zurenne searched her sister's closely written missive for any such warning.

'Licanin's man says that he'll be grateful for dinner and a bed along with a night's rest for his horse.' Hosh couldn't hide his curiosity any better than Neeny. 'He's in no great hurry to return.'

'Lady Licanin writes of trouble in Relshaz during the festival.' Zurenne wondered what had actually happened as she tried to read between the lines of Beresa's vague and ominous account. 'Most particularly for the mages who live in the city.'

'Does she mention Madam Velindre?' Ilysh glanced at Hosh.

Zurenne had already noticed the boy stiffen. She still wondered what the daunting blonde magewoman had asked him when she had come to the manor with Jilseth during the last autumn solstice festival.

More than once she had bitten back questions about that ancient silver-gilt arm-ring Hosh had brought back from the Archipelago. Its magic had saved him from death amid the destruction of the corsair isle, after all. Each time Zurenne reminded herself that the poor boy would surely be as reluctant as Corrain to discuss his suffering amid the Aldabreshi, still less the horrors of captivity by the Mandarkin mage Anskal.

Besides, the arm-ring was gone. Hosh had been more than willing to hand it over to Velindre. More than that, wizardly affairs were no longer any of Halferan's concern, not now that Corrain and his fellow lords had secured the parliament's new law.

At least, that's what Zurenne had told herself. Beresa's letter suggested that the aftermath of the corsairs' defeat was still unfolding elsewhere.

'She says that the trouble started when a wizard died on Souls' Ease Night. He was a long-time resident of Relshaz who had been ailing since last year. He finally succumbed to injuries which he had suffered when he was attacked by some Aldabreshi after news of magic loose in the Archipelago reached the city last year.'

'We should ask the Archmage—' Ilysh was reaching for her rune sigil pendant.

'No.' Zurenne swiftly set the parchment down on the table, compelling her daughter's attention. 'This is wizards' business—'

She broke off as angry shouting outside in the manor's compound intruded through the baronial tower's open outer door.

'My lady.' Hosh was already on his way out of the audience chamber.

'Lysha!'

Her daughter didn't heed her, following close behind him. Zurenne hesitated for a moment before rising and holding out her hand. 'Neeny, come with me.'

Raselle was busy upstairs and leaving the little girl unsupervised with candles already lit and a fire smouldering in the hearth was out of the question, not to mention the temptation of an unguarded inkwell. Zurenne swiftly led Esnina out into the cold grey daylight, joining Ilysh and Hosh on the great hall's top step.

A double handful of youths hesitated between a knot of liveried Halferan troopers standing apart from their barrack mates. Even at this distance, Zurenne could see the loyal Halferans' unease as their eyes darted between Kusint and these dissenters. The captain stood, feet solidly planted and hands on his hips, challenge in the thrust of his jaw.

The newcomers wore undyed linen shirts and homespun tunics over buff breeches. They looked down at their boots, shuffling uneasy feet amid the windblown leaves that drifted inside every time the manor's double gates were opened. One youth stood alone, braced as though expecting attack.

Whatever had happened had already drawn lackeys and maids alike to doors and windows, curious to learn what was afoot. Even Mistress Rauffe waited expectant on the steward's lodging's doorstep rather than chasing everyone back to their duties.

'Lady Ilysh!' Zurenne hissed, low voiced, as her daughter took two steps down the stone flight.

Lysha looked back, her mouth set in a determined line achingly reminiscent of her dead father. She spoke briefly to Hosh before retreating to rejoin her mother. The boy hurried down the stair and across the courtyard to Kusint.

The newcomer standing alone heard Hosh approaching and looked around. He took a hasty step backwards, unable to hide his shock at Hosh's misshapen features. Zurenne winced as she saw Hosh's hand fly up to cover his disfigurement. Worse, half the manor's household had seen his humiliation.

Kusint's lip curled with contempt as he addressed the mutinous Halferan guardsmen, defying the gusting wind to be clearly heard from gatehouse to kitchen.

'I am your captain, appointed by your liege lord. It is my duty to recruit and train the best men to defend Halferan. It is your duty to obey me and to show common courtesy to each other.

'You.' Kusint's accusing finger jabbed at one of the dissenters. The rest hastily took a side-step to leave the man isolated. 'Pack your gear, surrender your swords and armour. Collect a day's meat and bread from the kitchen and start on your way home while the light lasts.'

The man must have provoked this trouble, though Zurenne was ashamed to realise she didn't know his name. Too many of her household were still unfamiliar faces. So many loyal servants who had survived the corsairs' attacks had chosen not to return to the rebuilt manor and the memories which could not be swept away. So Ilysh granted them leave to return to the villages where they had been born and Zurenne insisted that they accept a modest purse of coin to assure them that they were valued, to prove that they returned with honour.

She watched the disgraced guard trudging towards the barracks. At least he wouldn't warrant any payment to drain Halferan's modest reserves. Midwinter's tithes had indeed been as modest as Zurenne had feared.

Kusint clapped his gloved hands with a crack of leather. 'Weltray! Fetch blunted swords for these hopefuls. I want to test their mettle. The rest of you, get to your drills.'

Zurenne was relieved to see the dissenting troopers hurry, shame-faced, to rejoin their fellow guardsmen.

'Telore came with us from Taw Ricks.' Ilysh watched the man slam the barrack hall door. 'What burr got under his saddle?'

'I imagine the captain will tell us.' Zurenne nodded towards Kusint coming towards the hall with Hosh. 'And that stable-hand's expression is not fit for your lips, my lady.'

'Kusint,' she asked before Ilysh could offer some justification, 'what was amiss?'

The two men halted on the lowest step. Hosh didn't speak, turning to shield his injured face from view, his shoulder hunched.

Kusint shook his head. 'Telore said he won't have any dealings with mageborn. He wasn't going to back down.'

'Why would some mageborn lad seek to join Halferan's guard?' Zurenne tried to pick out the newcomer as the liveried troopers began testing the would-be recruits with thrusts and parries.

'If he's mageborn, he must go to Hadrumal.' Ilysh's hand already hovered over her silver pendant.

'Not this lad. It was his brother, a handful of years ago,' Kusint explained. 'From a village a day south of Taw Ricks. It was the talk of the barony's eastern march.'

'I had no idea.' Zurenne had rarely visited the Taw Ricks hunting lodge before it had become the household's refuge after the manor's destruction. She had certainly never known of mageborn among the barony's yeomen and tenantry in that district. Her husband would have dealt with such matters.

Breath caught in her throat. Had news of this mageborn lad sent away to Hadrumal first prompted her beloved's fatal ambition to have magic save Halferan?

'What is Telore's grudge?' Ilysh demanded.

Kusint shook his head. 'No grudge, but he said that having a mage's brother in the barracks would see Aldabreshin ships on our shores.' He looked at Zurenne. 'It's not just Telore. Half the household have heard the rumours coming up from Relshaz. They say that the Archipelagans have turned against all who have dealings with wizardry.'

Zurenne recalled Beresa's letter left lying on the table. Her sister begged her to cut Halferan's ties with Hadrumal. She insisted that merchants in Attar and Claithe would soon refuse to take Zurenne's coin if she didn't. Beresa was sorely afraid poor Ilysh would rue the day when her ill-advised proxy husband had accepted the Archmage's help to rebuild the manor. She could only lament Zurenne's folly in setting Licanin's honest and honourable guardianship aside.

'That's ridiculous,' Ilysh snapped. 'You were right to dismiss him.'

'I dismissed him for refusing to let the matter lie,' Kusint corrected her courteously, 'and arguing the rights and wrongs of my order. I will not have such ill-discipline in the barrack hall.'

Ilysh coloured as though he'd rebuked her as sternly as the trooper. Zurenne frowned.

Neeny tugged at her hand. 'Mama, I'm cold.'

Zurenne looked down to see the little girl's face was pinched against the chill. She ushered her down the steps.

'Hosh, please take Esnina to the kitchen and ask Doratine to find her some wafer cakes and warm milk.'

'My lady.' Hosh offered the little girl his hand.

Neeny giggled and Zurenne watched her skip happily across the courtyard at the boy's side. Granted, the child had been startled at first sight of the boy's disfigurement but Zurenne had explained how the poor boy had been badly hurt by the cruel corsairs and now they must be kind to him.

She nodded to Kusint. 'You may rejoin your men, Captain.'

'My lady, there is something—' Kusint hesitated. 'You saw how these recruits looked at Hosh—'

'Can you tell them that they must accept him without provoking their resentment?' Zurenne hugged herself against the winter wind, still watching Hosh and Neeny.

'I would like to see if we can see him healed,' Kusint said with a rush. 'I believe there is magic to do it. Those injuries still cause him a good deal of pain, my lady.'

Zurenne looked quickly at him. 'Do you think that he would agree?'

She had been contemplating that very question ever since Midwinter. Last Autumn Equinox, Madam Jilseth had said that Hadrumal knew a healer who might be able to mend Hosh's face. But Zurenne had never found the right moment to raise the matter with the boy.

Besides, she had told herself, surely Madam Velindre would have made such an offer when Hosh had surrendered that arm-ring which the mages had coveted. If he had turned the magewoman down, it was not for her to interfere.

Lately though, she had contemplated all that she and her children had suffered because those who could have helped them had chosen not to interfere when the renegade mage who had murdered her husband had claimed guardianship over them by means of forgery and lies. Moreover that villain Minelas would have never had that chance if the parliament's other barons hadn't refused to help the coastal lords against the corsairs.

Zurenne found herself wondering if Caladhria's traditions of deference were less courtesy and more cowardice.

'Madam Jilseth could cure Hosh's injuries?' Lysha stared at her mother. 'Why haven't we asked her long since?'

'I don't believe she can help him.' Kusint shook his head. 'But there is more magic than wizardry. At home—' he corrected himself '—in Solura, Houses of Sanctuary work the enchantments which you know as Artifice.'

'I believe that the wizards know them as aetheric magic.' Zurenne recalled Jilseth's words. 'She spoke of such a healer in the Suthyfer islands—'

'In the mid-ocean beyond Tormalin?' Ilysh looked askance at her. 'Abiath would find such a voyage a trial in the best of weather. We cannot ask her to endure such hardship in the depths of winter.'

Zurenne had only the vaguest idea where those islands were. In this instance she gladly deferred to

Lysha. The girl had taken possession of her dead father's surprisingly extensive collection of maps discovered at the Taw Ricks hunting lodge and evidently shared his fascination with places so far distant that she could never have cause to visit them.

'He might find aetheric healing in Col,' Kusint said unexpectedly. 'Solura's mages have ties to the university and the Houses of Sanctuary have always worked closely with the Orders of Wizardry. I know that aetheric adepts and mages have often travelled south together.'

'Col isn't so far.' Ilysh looked eagerly at Zurenne. 'It's not much further to Peorle than it is to Duryea and he could take a ship from there across the gulf to Col. Abiath could make that journey.'

'He would be better served finding a vessel in Claithe,' Kusint said thoughtfully. 'Even a winter voyage hopping from harbour to harbour up the coast would be quicker than risking the season's hazards on the road.'

'Such a passage would be costly,' Zurenne said reluctantly, 'all the more so for two. What would the price of such Artifice be?'

She couldn't help thinking of the diminishing coin in the strong room beneath this tower. But Halferan owed Hosh a debt beyond any repayment. This at least would be a reward which the boy would truly value, for his own sake and for loyal and devoted Abiath's.

'Soluran Houses of Sanctuary take no payment for their care of the infirm or for healing the sick,' Kusint assured her before hesitating. 'Things may be different in Col.'

Lysha waved that objection away. 'We have Hadrumal's gold.'

'There's precious little of the Archmage's coin left,' Zurenne reminded Lysha, 'and if Halferan is to stand on its own two feet, we must husband Midwinter's tithes.'

All the more so if Beresa's fears were proved right and the closest merchants and traders declined to deal with Halferan for fear of Aldabreshin displeasure. The further afield they had to send Master Rauffe, the more costly goods would be, necessities and luxuries alike.

'Have you asked this question of the runes?' Ilysh demanded of Kusint. 'Did you draw a single stick or cast a full foretelling with nine?'

'What?' Zurenne knew that the Forest-born captain sought such guidance in the manner of his people, but what did Lysha know of such things?

Kusint was colouring like a maidservant caught in mischief. The blush was all the more striking with his pale skin and coppery hair. He looked at Zurenne, his jaw set with the defiance which he'd shown facing down Telore.

'Hosh drew his own runes at Midwinter, my lady, to see what might lie in the year ahead. He drew the Eagle for a journey and hope, the Chime for a new beginning and the Wellspring—'

'—for healing,' Ilysh finished Kusint's explanation, turning triumphantly to her mother. 'Mama, don't you see?'

Zurenne wanted to know what Kusint had to blush for and just how much time he and Lysha had spent discussing Solura's customs over the five day festival. Regardless, Halferan's young lady would be far more closely chaperoned now that the manor's usual routine was restored.

She also wanted to see Hosh relieved of his pains, in

body and spirit. If his broken face could be mended, it was surely a simple decision. Zurenne nodded.

'When Baron Corrain returns, we will ask if he thinks the journey is best made by land or sea. Kusint, consider who you can spare to escort Hosh and Abiath. Though we will not mention this to either of them and raise false hopes,' she warned sternly. 'Not until I have spoken to the Archmage and asked that Madam Jilseth discover exactly what this healing Artifice might offer. Even then Baron Corrain may forbid this entirely. He wants nothing more to do with magic.'

'He won't deny Hosh,' Ilysh said firmly.

Zurenne saw that Kusint agreed with her daughter though he chose not to say so aloud.

She shivered. 'It's too cold to be discussing this out here. Captain Kusint, return to your men. Lady Ilysh, you and I must compose a reply to Lady Beresa's letter before Licanin's man leaves tomorrow.'

Once that was done, Zurenne would marshal her arguments to persuade Corrain to let Hosh seek this healing in Col. Before he returned from the parliament, she would have time to learn all she could from Madam Jilseth and most particularly from Kusint about these aetheric enchantments.

Artifice was different from wizardry. Corrain might want nothing more to do with the Archmage, and by and large, Zurenne agreed, but this was undoubtedly a special case. Once Hosh's face was restored, that could be the end of the barony's dealings with any and all magic.

— CHAPTER ELEVEN —

The Shield Wall Tavern, Ferl, Caladhria
9th of Aft-Winter

ANOTHER HANDFUL OF days and they would be home. The parliament had passed their new law so he had paid his last debt to the Archmage. With the new year now well begun, Corrain could look forward to securing Halferan's future for Lady Zurenne and his lost lord's daughters.

He scooped up the last remnants of fried onion and blood sausage with a crust of bread. The leisure for such a breakfast was one advantage of his proxy rank even if he still woke at first light with a captain's duties filling his thoughts.

Had Reven been out in the cold morning, ensuring that every man had checked his horse from hoof to every last buckle and strap of harness? Had the lad reminded the troopers to collect their damp clothing from the drying racks hauled up high above the kitchen hearth, every garment from a doublet to a darned stocking earning the smiling cook a copper penny?

This inn was well used to scores of horsemen arriving soaked to the skin. The Shield Wall was the tavern most favoured in Ferl by guardsmen travelling from the coast to the River Rel or up and down the length of Caladhria on the high roads which crossed here. So the kitchen served precisely what hungry swordsmen relished, to soak up their evening's ale and save the taproom from broken furniture and stubborn bloodstains on the floorboards or to set them up for a long day on horseback.

He looked though the window to assess the clouds; more white than grey and torn into rags scudding across the faded sky by the persistent wind. So there was every reason to hope they'd escape a soaking today. Better yet, this keen breeze would dry out the road under hoof and foot. Of course, that rune's reverse meant the wind's chill would leave men stiff in the saddle and slow to react by dusk when weary horses would be prone to perilous stumbles on frosted ground.

Corrain decided he would see how much ground they had covered by noon. Then he could choose an inn for the night ahead which they would be sure to reach in daylight. He swallowed the last of his breakfast small beer. This close to home he'd know which of the inns ahead would serve them a decent meal tonight, not just a ladleful from some stew pot which had been sitting in the hearth since Trimon was a lad, topped up daily with kitchen scraps by some scullery hand.

'Are you done with that?' the maidservant hovering by the taproom's kitchen door asked.

'I am.' Corrain offered her the plate and empty tankard. 'My thanks.'

As she took them and disappeared into the kitchen, the taproom door from the hallway opened. As Corrain turned, the newcomer laughed.

'My lord Baron. I heard you were in town.'

'Did you indeed?' Corrain cocked his head. 'How's merchant life?'

Had Vereor heard of the corsair gold supposedly filling Halferan's pockets? If anyone had picked up that rumour hereabouts, Corrain would wager honest coin on the former Ferl guard captain.

'Retirement has its entertainments.' The grey-bearded man's gaze drifted towards the hearth nevertheless.

The wall was hung with guard captains' shields, each one painted with the Ferl barony's colours. The oldest were so darkened with age and soot that their bronze chevrons could barely be distinguished from the blue ground. The most recent was still as vivid as it had been slung on Vereor's back or at his saddle bow before he had been honourably released from his oath three years ago.

'Are you just here to wish me a good day's journey?' Corrain's curiosity stirred.

Vereor pulled up a chair. 'You went north for the parliament. Did you spend any coin with Ensaimin merchants while you were there?'

'Not beyond buying my lady some kidskin gloves from a Friern trader. For my lady wife's mother, that is,' Corrain corrected himself. 'The Widow Zurenne.'

The kitchen door half opened and Corrain raised his voice. 'Some ale for my guest would be welcome, when you have a moment.'

The door opened more fully. 'Of course.' It wasn't the maidservant but the tavern keeper who looked around the taproom before retreating with a scowl boding ill for the absent girl.

'You didn't have business with anyone from Wrede?' Vereor raised a bristling eyebrow. 'Maybe you looked at some furs?'

'From Wrede? No.' Corrain couldn't recall ever having dealings with a trader from that distant city. Wrede was in northernmost Ensaimin, tucked into the pine-shrouded foothills where the mountains rose up to divide the lowlands from the wastes of Gidesta.

'So why would a Wrede man ask after you around Ferl's taverns last night?' Vereor leaned forward, his elbows on the table. 'Saying he owed you money after his fool apprentice overcharged you in Duryea's festival market.'

'Whoever he is, he's lying.' But Corrain wondered how many people would have pricked up their ears in hopes of doing the new Baron Halferan a good turn. It wasn't as though this stranger was making a claim on Corrain's purse, prompting his friends to say they hadn't seen him inside a year. He frowned. 'When did this suspiciously honest fellow arrive?'

'I've already asked at the gates.' Vereor's grin showed the chipped tooth which Corrain recalled him breaking when he'd tripped and hit himself in the mouth with that very shield hung on the wall.

'Your generous friend arrived a chime after you did, coming down the northern high road. Alas, the gate guards had no notion where you were lodging.'

'Remind me to leave you a purse to buy those lads a few flagons.' It was good to know he still had friends among Ferl's troopers. They would have readily guessed he would bring Halferan's men here but they would need a compelling reason to share any guard captain's business with a stranger.

Corrain chewed his lip as the tapster arrived with a jug and two pewter tankards. 'Your ale, Masters.'

'I never thought to look for anyone following us on the high road,' he admitted to Vereor as the kitchen door closed behind the man.

'Why should you, safe in Caladhria?' Vereor shrugged as he poured them each a drink.

Corrain glanced through the window to see that Reven had the Halferan troopers checking their horses' hooves one last time. 'What did this merchant from Wrede look like?'

'Middling tall, middling broad, dressed like any one of ten men on the road.' Vereor grimaced as he raised his tankard. 'Nothing to help us catch him if he stole a horse.'

'Just the man to send asking questions in a strange town.' Corrain took a thoughtful swallow of ale. 'Did he say where someone might leave answers?'

'At The Dapple Grey Mare.' Vereor grinned wolfishly. 'Shall we try to pick up his scent and ask a few questions of our own?'

Corrain rose to his feet. 'By all means.'

He was the baron. If he wasn't back by the time Reven had the troop ready to ride, they would just have to wait for him.

All the same, he tapped on the kitchen door. 'Tell my sergeant I have business in the market place. I'll be back soon.'

He didn't want Reven sending the whole troop out in search of him any more than he wanted the Halferan guardsmen hunting for this stranger before Corrain knew a little more himself.

'Of course, my lord.' The tapster acknowledged his request with a brief bow.

Leaving through the inn's wide front door, Corrain and Vereor strode purposefully through the busy streets. Ferl men and women were seizing this chance to run errands without risking a drenching. Corrain had no great concerns about heads turning to wonder why a nobleman was walking among them. He boasted none of the gold rings which the likes of Baron Karpis flaunted and his cloak was the same sturdy brown wool that kept the Halferan troopers warm.

He and Vereor soon reached the prosperous square overlooked by The Dapple Grey Mare.

'Shall we see how their cellar man keeps his ale?' the Ferl man suggested.

Corrain turned to hide his face from the inn across the square. 'Is that your man? Talking to the lass with the yellow braid around her hems.'

Vereor frowned. 'No. Who's the girl?'

'The maid who served my breakfast at The Shield Wall.' The one who had taken herself off without the innkeeper's permission. 'What's she doing?'

'Still talking to the man in the Tormalin top boots.' Vereor narrowed his eyes. 'I'd say he was born and raised in Imperial lands with those black curls and a bronzed cheek even in midwinter. Whoever he is, he's very interested in what she has to say,' he added.

'But this isn't the man from Wrede?' Corrain was growing more concerned. One curious traveller following him down the road could just be happenstance. Two hinted at conspiracy. Corrain didn't believe in coincidence.

'They're heading off.' Vereor stiffened. 'I don't think they're looking for a dry wall to rub up against. She's definitely leading the way.'

'Someone must have told her that news of me could be turned into coin.' Though Corrain couldn't imagine what knowing he'd had blood sausage for breakfast was worth. 'Let's follow them back to The Shield Wall and they can answer for themselves there.'

He didn't doubt that Reven would drive the Tormalin man off, with a whip if needs be, if he tried asking questions among the Halferan guardsmen. As long as he and Vereor were there to block the stranger's escape, the man in the topboots could pay for his freedom with some answers of his own.

Corrain raised his cloak's hood like any number of passers-by foiling the cold. 'You take the lead.'

If the girl recognised Vereor, she'd have no cause for concern. A retired guardsman had plenty of business around the town and the tavern.

'Keep your wits about you.' The older man sauntered across the square.

Corrain waited for a count of twenty before following. He frowned. They were taking the southerly lane where a cloth market's prudent awnings flapped in the breeze above trestles and boards piled with bolts of linen, fustian and calico. This wasn't the way back to The Shield Wall.

'Excuse me, ladies.' He slipped past a gaggle of women casting disparaging looks at wooden bowls of brass buttons and horn toggles.

Vereor was already a plough-length ahead. The maid and the man in the Tormalin boots were in some hurry and it wasn't lust spurring them on. They had already passed two accommodation houses which Corrain knew full well rented rooms by the chime.

As he reached the end of the cloth stalls, there was no sign of Vereor even though there were no crowds here to hide the old guardsman or his quarry. Corrain spotted a narrow lane cutting between a cobbler's workshop and a draper's warehouse. Turning into it, he was relieved to see Vereor striding purposefully towards the far end.

Corrain followed, pausing at the far end to get his bearings beside a shop selling crocks and pots. Vereor continued, leading him down the street, through another alley and along two further lanes raggedly pocked with puddles still frozen in the shadows.

The girl was taking the Tormalin man to a district of Ferl where a nicely-reared maid should hesitate to go even in broad daylight. Corrain adjusted his sword hilt. Never mind gold rings. Scoundrels here would happily rob him of his cloak. At least he'd have no one to answer to if he drew steel to kill a footpad. Only Baron Ferl could hold a fellow nobleman to account and he was still days behind on the high road, travelling at an easy pace.

Vereor halted beside a timber-framed building scabrous with flaking plaster. The gates to a down-at-heel tavern's dung-strewn yard hung askew on their hinges. Now Corrain knew where they were.

'Will you wait here while I waste some Halferan coin on undrinkable ale,' Vereor asked as Corrain joined him, 'to find out what they're doing in there?'

'No, I'll show my face and we'll see what they make of that.' Corrain settled his scabbard on his hip. 'How soon could you whistle up some swords if they choose to make trouble?'

Vereor sucked his teeth. 'Around here? Probably best if you keep it civil. I'll cut around to the front,' he offered. 'If you shout for Halferan, I'll kick in the door and we can both make a run for it?'

'That should be good enough. Let's roll these runes.' Corrain headed for the tavern's open back door.

The last time he'd been at this particular inn, he'd had the whole Halferan troop with him. It had been the only accommodation available when the parliament had been summoned out of season, meeting here in Ferl with the express intention of denouncing his marriage to Ilysh, to dishonour his claim to Halferan. Corrain hoped that whoever was in the taproom now remembered how emphatically he had won that battle.

He walked cautiously into a grimy kitchen. A small white dog with black ears was licking rancid dripping from a tray beneath the spit in the hearth. Corrain moved as quietly as he could to avoid attracting the beast's attention. That was easier said than done as his boots stuck unpleasantly to flagstones which hadn't seen a mop in years.

The door to the tap room was closed. Corrain opened it and stepped quickly through before the startled dog had offered a half-hearted bark.

The girl from The Shield Wall pressed guilty hands to her mouth. A second girl dropped a letter onto the frayed and filthy rushes covering the floor. The only other person in the tap room was the black-haired man.

He took a step back, shoving a purse back into his breeches' pocket. There was no doubt he was a Tormalin native, and a wealthy one judging by the cut of his long-sleeved velvet jerkin and the ornamentation on his slender sword's hilt.

Corrain wouldn't hesitate to fight him. The Tormalin man was fresh faced and slightly built, only a few years older than Kusint.

'I believe that's addressed to me.' Corrain nodded at the fallen letter.

'I was keeping it safe,' the resident maidservant wailed, 'against the day you returned, my lord.'

'I'm glad to hear it,' Corrain said with calculated menace. 'Otherwise you'll face the baron's assize for selling a nobleman's correspondence.'

'Could such a crime be proved,' the Tormalin man mused, 'while a letter's seal stays unbroken? Letters must pass from hand to hand if they're ever to reach their destination.'

The Shield Wall's maid seized that excuse. 'I came to collect the letter, my lord. I remembered—'

Corrain silenced her with a raised hand, looking at the Tormalin man. 'You kindly offered to escort her?' He didn't hide his disbelief.

The Tormalin's grin admitted his guilt even as he nodded. 'Quite so.'

'What brings a noble esquire to a humble Caladhrian town like Ferl?' Corrain demanded bluntly. Those finely honed accents meant this Tormalin was a true-born scion of some princely house.

Why was he so interested in Corrain? Where was his partner from Wrede? Why were two men from opposite ends of the long fallen Old Tormalin Empire working hand in glove?

'Shall we discuss both our travels over a glass of wine?' the young man suggested, guileless.

'No.' Uncompromising, Corrain nodded at the maidservant. 'I'll take that letter now.'

The nervous girl snatched up the grimy parchment. Corrain took it from her trembling hand and shoved it into the pocket inside his cloak's lining.

'Aren't you going to read that?' the Tormalin enquired.

'I can guess what it says.' The writing and the seal had confirmed Corrain's suspicions.

This particular letter had merely been an excuse for Baron Karpis's men to come here and provoke another scuffle with Halferan's guards. Karpis's sergeant had dropped it in some horseshit, hoping that Linset would throw the first punch. Corrain had ordered the boy to let it lie; letter and insult alike.

He waited for the Tormalin youth to make the next move. When it was clear he wouldn't, Corrain raised his voice. 'Captain Vereor, would you join us?'

The old guardsman entered so swiftly he must have been standing with his ear pressed against the door. 'My lord Halferan?'

'Take that one in hand to answer to Lord Ferl at the Spring Equinox assize.' Corrain jerked his head towards The Shield Wall's girl before glaring at the resident maid. 'You lose yourself before I change my mind.'

'My lord.' Vereor seized The Shield Wall girl's arm. She burst into noisy tears, wailing incoherent protests as the other maid fled though the kitchen door.

The young Tormalin noble winced. 'My lord Baron, there is no need to ruin a girl's prospects with a season spent in lock-up. Any fault here lies with me. Please let her go and we can share a glass of wine while I explain.'

Corrain shook his head. 'I don't drink with men I don't know. Vereor, have that slut put in irons.'

'My apologies, my lord Halferan.' The Tormalin offered him a bow fit for the Emperor's throne room. 'I am Yadres, Esquire Den Dalderin.'

The name meant nothing to Corrain, though he made sure to remember it. 'Good day to you, Esquire. Vereor, let her loose.'

Since the Tormalin had been the first to yield, Corrain would see what a gesture on his part might win him.

Vereor forced the grizzling maidservant out through the street door with a merciless shove which sent her sprawling into the gutter.

'My lord,' the Tormalin protested.

Corrain ignored that. 'Why were you so interested in buying a letter addressed to me?'

'To see if it held anything which you wouldn't want widely known.'

The young esquire's frank answer surprised Corrain almost as much as the glimpse of ruthlessness beneath his diffident manner.

He pulled the letter from his cloak pocket to win some time to think. Snapping the wax seal, he took petty pleasure in ruining Baron's Karpis's blazon. Unfolding the parchment, Corrain read the cursory blend of open insults and veiled threats, just as he had suspected.

He refolded the letter. 'What interest does Tormalin have in seeing Halferan's baron cast down?'

'You mistake me. You're welcome to your barony.' The Tormalin shook his head. 'We would have offered you a trade; our discretion for information.'

'Who is "we"?' Corrain demanded.

'My uncle the Sieur Den Dalderin has the Emperor's ear,' the Esquire said bluntly. 'Both are most interested to hear the full story of your return from the Archipelago. They're still more eager to learn the truth of the corsairs' fate and what became of their plunder.'

Corrain stared at the young man, incredulous. 'You think that their loot fills Halferan's strong rooms? Does the Tormalin Emperor claim it too?'

The corsairs had never raided so far east. The currents and storms around the Cape of Winds were notorious and besides, Tormalin's own pirates lurked in that headland's remote coves.

'What? No, neither my uncle nor the Emperor has any interest in whatever gold you might have recovered,' Den Dalderin assured him.

'What does interest them?' Corrain was growing impatient.

'Ensorcelled artefacts.' Den Dalderin looked at him keenly.

Corrain looked back mystified. 'What?'

Now Den Dalderin was wrong-footed. 'You agreed to support Planir with Caladhrian swords because the corsairs had discovered treasures imbued with magic among their loot.'

'What of it?' Corrain stared at him. 'You think we would bring such cursed things home to Halferan? When hoarding such magic is what finally persuaded the Archmage to attack the corsairs after all Caladhria's years of suffering had left him unmoved?'

'You never thought to claim a share, to secure an advantage in your own dealings with Planir?' Den Dalderin persisted. 'You don't know that Hadrumal's wizards covet such treasures?'

But Corrain heard the first hint of doubt in the esquire's words.

'The Archmage may have salvaged such artefacts but I know nothing of that,' he assured Den Dalderin. 'We want nothing more to do with Hadrumal, no more than any other Caladhrian barony. Hasn't your Ensaimin lackey told you that our parliament has just outlawed any suborning of wizardry in warfare? There are riders on the road carrying letters to your princes, recommending the self-same decree to your Emperor.'

Den Dalderin shook his head. 'The Convocation of Princes will never agree to forgo magical aid, not when we must rely on elemental spells to see our ships safely across the ocean to Kellarin.'

Corrain shrugged. 'That's no business of mine. If you want to know about these ensorcelled artefacts ask Archmage Planir.'

He nodded to Vereor and took a step towards the tavern's street door.

Den Dalderin moved into his path. 'You could ask Planir what he plans to do with these artefacts. You have a legitimate interest in knowing.'

He looked straight at Corrain. 'Tell me and the Emperor's gratitude could be worth more than gold to you. Halferan has precious few friends at present but while Caladhria's baronies find their wares and harvests shunned by Relshazri merchants fearing Archipelagan prejudice, you could earn even your enemies' acclaim if you could offer them introductions to Toremal's merchants instead.'

'No,' Corrain said shortly.

Den Dalderin folded his arms. 'My uncle would be most interested to learn of your dealings with Solura's wizards.'

'No,' Corrain said again.

'Forgive me, but we know that you visited Castle Pastamar and met with the Elders of the Order of Fornet.'

Corrain noted the reach of Tormalin's spies as well as the unyielding resolve in the esquire's eyes, so at odds with his inconsequential appearance.

'I don't deny my travels to Solura, nor who I met there. When I said no, I was answering your next question.'

'What's that?' Den Dalderin grinned despite himself.

Corrain wasn't amused. 'You want some introduction to Solura's wizards. Believe me, the Order of Fornet wants no more to do with me, and I want no more to do with them.'

'You underestimate Soluran interest in your most recent adventures,' Den Dalderin said firmly. 'You could trade what you know of the corsair isle's fate for considerable goodwill among Solura's wizards. Use that to serve Toremal and you'll have the Emperor's favour.'

So much for vowing to have nothing more to do with wizards, Corrain reflected. They seemed inconveniently determined to have more to do with him. What was his best course of action?

He folded his arms, challenging the young Tormalin noble. 'Answer me one question and I'll consider your offer. Who is this man from Wrede, if he's not your lackey?'

He'd seen the flicker of bemusement in Den Dalderin's eyes when he'd mentioned the Ensaimin sniffing after him.

'I don't know who you mean.' The Tormalin shook his head, apparently sincere. 'I swear it by Saedrin's keys.'

'Find out who he is and what his interest in Halferan might be. Then we can talk further.'

Corrain stepped around him. This time Den Dalderin let him go, as far as the door at least.

'I look forward to furthering our acquaintance, Lord Halferan.'

Corrain didn't look back, walking purposefully away. Vereor fell into step beside him.

'By all that's holy, what was that about?'

'I don't know.' Corrain ground his teeth. 'Trimon only knows what rumours will run round Ferl's taprooms after those two girls have wept on their friends' shoulders. Will you let me know the worst of it? Oh, and if you can turn this garbage into gold, do so and welcome.'

He proffered the letter which had started this. Let people hereabouts learn a little of Baron Karpis's true character.

'I'll write—' Vereor seized his arm. 'Over there. That's the man who was asking after you.'

'Where?' Corrain searched the crowded street for anyone matching the old guardsman's description of someone wholly unremarkable.

'On the bay colt.' Vereor nodded rather than alert the rider with a pointing hand.

Corrain wished he'd pulled his hood up as they had left the inn. He could only casually turn his back as the man passed by. Whoever he was, they couldn't follow him, not on foot. But Corrain would know him again, nonentity though he might be on that equally anonymous horse.

'I can ask around to see where he went this morning,' Vereor offered.

'Let me know what you learn. I want to be on the road as soon as my men are mounted.'

Corrain found this notion of Imperial interest in what he might know of wizardry in Hadrumal or Solura profoundly unsettling. Nearly as unsettling as discovering some unknown man from Wrede was dogging his footsteps from Duryea.

Well, for the moment at least, he could hope that he had set one spy chasing the other. If the Tormalin Den Dalderin could tell him who the man from Wrede was, perhaps he could see how best to defend Halferan's interests.

He picked up the pace. The sooner he got back to The Shield Wall, the sooner he'd be on his way to Halferan. Though he didn't relish trying to explain to Lady Zurenne that he had changed his mind about cutting all ties with the Archmage.

Doubtless Planir would be interested to know that this Esquire Den Dalderin had sought an introduction to Solura's wizards. In return, surely Corrain could ask Madam Jilseth to use her skills to discover if this man from Wrede was any threat to Lady Zurenne and her children.

Once he knew that Halferan was safe on that score, then Corrain could be done with wizardry.

— CHAPTER TWELVE —

Trydek's Hall, Hadrumal
16th of Aft-Winter

JILSETH ROUNDED THE turn of the spiral stair to see the door to the Archmage's sitting room standing open.

This chamber extended across the entire ancient tower. The broad table, usually accommodating some gathering of Planir's personal pupils or a more formal meeting of Hadrumal's eminent mages, was covered with books and scrolls. More were heaped on the window sills around the wide room. Some looked fresh from the bindery; others were so ancient that their dry calfskin was crumbling to powdery flakes. Some were tidily stacked while the rest sprawled open, piled on top of each other in haphazard fashion.

Velindre and Mellitha must have brought the last of Kerrit's personal library back from Relshaz while she was in Halferan. Though Jilseth wondered why the Archmage hadn't turned this archive over to those wizards who so diligently curated the irreplaceable records of Hadrumal's generations of learning.

Planir sat on one of the upholstered settles on the far side of the room, wholly absorbed in the book he was reading. Jilseth could only hope that his wizard senses would alert him if an unguarded ember sprang from the glowing hearth to ignite the curled parchments covering the hearth rug.

She cleared her throat. 'Archmage? You wished to see me as soon as I returned from Halferan?'

Marking his place with a ribbon, Planir closed his book. 'Good afternoon, and how are our friends in Caladhria?' He smiled. 'Was the trip a pleasant diversion from your current frustrations?'

'It was.' Jilseth saw no point in trying to deceive the Archmage, though she hoped Merenel, Tornauld or Nolyen hadn't seen how relieved she was to escape their nexus's futile labours, when Planir had asked her to answer Zurenne's unexpected summons on Corrain's behalf.

She crossed the room to sit opposite the Archmage. She was a little surprised to find this matching settle wasn't covered with reading matter. Even the white raven pieces which usually stood ready for play on Planir's gaming table had been stowed in their drawer, to clear the inlaid circle of the forest floor for a stack of ribbon-tied notes.

'What did the noble Baron Halferan wish to discuss?' Planir leaned back against his seat's high cushioned back, easing his stiffened shoulders. 'Have you learned why the delightful Widow Zurenne has been asking so many questions about Artifice?'

'Do you recall the guardsman Hosh, the lad with the injured face? Lady Zurenne has it in mind that Artifice could heal him.'

Planir rubbed the back of his neck. 'As you told her last autumn. What's prompted her to pursue the notion now?'

'It seems that Corrain's Forest-born ally, Kusint, has been telling her of Solura's Houses of Sanctuary and their aetheric healing.' Jilseth couldn't help a wry grimace. 'Now that Baron Halferan has returned and agreed, she wishes to seek healing for Hosh among any Soluran adepts who might be found in Col. She says

162

that the voyage to Suthyfer would be too arduous for Hosh's aged mother.'

'The obvious answer is for his mother to stay at home,' Planir remarked. 'But I take it she really wishes to limit any further obligation to Hadrumal.'

Jilseth nodded. 'She merely asks you to provide a letter of recommendation to a mentor at Col's university; someone suitably learned in Artifice who can introduce Hosh and his mother to a Soluran healer who will deal with them honestly.'

'That's easily done. Master Herion is best placed to help them. You could also offer to take the boy and his mother to Col.' Planir reached for his book with a rueful expression. 'Unless they insist on spending half a season travelling to prove to the Relshazri and Caladhria's barons that Halferan has no undue dealings with wizards.'

'I suspect that they will.'

Jilseth remained seated. Planir looked at her, closing his book on the ribbon once again.

'There is something more, Archmage. It seems that Corrain encountered a Tormalin nobleman on his journey back from Duryea. He is willing to relate the details in return for our assistance with another matter.'

Planir grinned. 'What can we do to reward him for telling us that the Sieur Den Dalderin has his minions trying to discover what we're doing with our hoard of ensorcelled treasures while His Exalted Grace, Emperor Tadriol the Provident, does his best to pretend not to covet such access to wizardry for himself, along with half the mainland's other nobles?'

Jilseth couldn't help a smile. She had half-expected that this would come as no news to Planir. But what of Corrain's other concern?

'Someone else is taking an undue interest in Halferan's affairs. A merchant from Wrede was claiming to owe him money, by way of starting conversations in Ferl about where Corrain might be found and what he might be doing. Corrain assures me that there's no such debt. He asks if we can find this man by magical means.'

'Find this unknown man or find out about him?' Planir queried.

'Corrain merely wishes to know where he's to be found. He intends making his own enquiries as to the man's master and motives.'

'By means of a fist to the face or something more subtle?' mused Planir. 'I wonder who this curious traveller is.'

As the Archmage paused to ponder, Jilseth wondered what to make of the fact that Planir had no notion why a man from Wrede might be so interested in Corrain.

'I believe—'

Before the Archmage could continue, they both heard footsteps. Jilseth turned to see Mellitha and Velindre enter the room.

'Good afternoon,' Planir welcomed the two magewomen. 'How is Master Resnada?'

'No one seems inclined to hold his association with Kerrit against him any longer.' Mellitha smoothed jade green skirts and sat down beside Jilseth.

'Not with temple guards still watching the house.' Velindre chose not to sit, surveying the archive spread across the table. Like Mellitha she wore a cobalt woollen gown of Tormalin cut and styling. Jilseth was struck by how different the blonde magewoman looked not wearing Aldabreshin garb.

'Not now that word has spread, reassuring the rabble that he has so bravely cleared the house of every last remnant of anything which could be considered tainted with wizardry,' Mellitha observed sardonically. 'I gather that such initiative has even won him congratulation in some quarters.'

Whereas, in keeping with the sealed testament which Brother Tinoan had produced, Kerrit had bequeathed his house to his friend on the strict condition that all his books and papers were safely delivered to Hadrumal.

Jilseth looked for Planir's response but the Archmage's thoughts had moved on. 'What news do you have from the Archipelago?'

'One of my few remaining friends was holding a letter from Kheda.' Velindre reached into the pouch she wore on her tooled leather belt. 'He's finally reached the Khusro domain and that was no easy journey. He's been looking since Solstice for someone with a Relshaz-hatched courier dove willing to let their bird carry an unknown cipher north to be passed on to my friend.'

She unrolled the paper, fine as onionskin; it was no wider than her smallest finger was long and covered in impossibly tiny script.

Jilseth was astonished. 'How—?'

'—could he write this without our spells?' Velindre passed her hand over the paper to summon a shimmering image of nonsensical words. 'You forget that the Aldabreshin have been stargazers for generations and their glassmakers are unmatched on the mainland. Their lenses for magnification are unequalled.'

'What does he have to say?' Planir demanded.

'The Nahik domain is no more,' Velindre said crisply. 'Those islands are nameless. No one knows what's become of Nahik Jarir himself but he's assumed to be dead, by his own hand or some other. His wives have returned to the domains of their birth and resumed their former names. They have each taken their own children with them and for the present, sons and daughters alike have abandoned their father's name.'

'All of them?' Mellitha queried. 'Even those of an age of discretion?'

'All of them,' Velindre confirmed.

Jilseth was curious to know the significance of this but concluded she could ask later.

'What of the islands' humbler inhabitants?' Planir asked.

Velindre read on. 'Those who could get onto a ship have sailed for neighbouring waters, north to Khusro and Jagai or south to Miris and beyond. Most are surrendering themselves into slavery—'

Jilseth couldn't help an exclamation at this. 'Why?'

Velindre answered as though such incomprehensible behaviour was entirely reasonable. 'It's the only way to free themselves of the misfortune which has overwhelmed the Nahik domain. Their warlord's errors of judgement have led every island and its inhabitants to disaster. Worse, the miasma of magic now hangs over them all. None of them can be trusted, or indeed, will trust themselves, to read even the simplest and most obvious omen aright, to guide their decisions from now on. Their only hope is to submit themselves to another's power, yielding wholly to someone else making their choices for them.'

'How are they being received?' Planir asked urgently.

'In kindly enough fashion in Khusro and Jagai. Miris Esul won't let them settle. He insists that they continue southward to seek sanctuary.'

Planir was cautiously relieved. 'At least he's not ordering their summary execution.'

Jilseth shivered despite the warm fire as she recalled the slaughter of those Archipelagans who had escaped imprisonment by the Mandarkin mage only to discover their fellow Aldabreshi now deemed them too contaminated by magic to live.

Mellitha gazed through one of the deep-silled windows as though she could see all the way to the Archipelago. 'Is there any hint which warlord will move first to claim those masterless islands and their sea lanes?'

'None of them, according to Kheda,' Velindre told her.

'They're shunning the entire domain? Not just the westerly reach where we destroyed the corsair island?' The Archmage's brow furrowed with fresh unease.

'What of trade northwards from the central Archipelago and the domains further south and west?' Mellitha demanded.

'Miris Esul is turning his back on everything north of his own waters.' Velindre contemplated the script hanging in the air. 'He argues that Archipelagans have no need of dealings with the mainland. That the Nahik domain's devastation is proof beyond all doubt, of the folly of having any contact with the northern barbarians so irretrievably stained by magic. He has reiterated the absolute prohibition on wizards anywhere in the Archipelago and has commanded the immediate execution of any mageborn within his own domain.'

'Has he closed his sea lanes to ships travelling north?' Mellitha was growing more alarmed.

'Not as yet.' Velindre's raised hand curbed the other magewoman's relief. 'It seems unlikely that he'll need to. Kheda says that almost no vessels have sought the warlord's permission to pass through the Miris domain and into formerly-Nahik waters. It took him six days to find a Khusro trader desperate enough to get home to risk it. Even then, the crew only agreed to sail the most perilous, easterly route and they carried no cargo, convinced that they would have to dump it overboard before being allowed into Jagai waters.'

'It is midwinter,' Mellitha countered. 'For the moment, caution will doubtless outweigh all but the most urgent need to reach the Khusro or Jagai trading beaches. No galleys would be crossing to the mainland at this season regardless.'

Planir leaned back, his eyes distant. 'Are any vessels heading southward from the northernmost domains?'

'No,' Velindre answered, 'though Kheda doesn't know if that's because Khusro Rina or Jagai Kalu have forbidden it, or because Miris Esul has sent word that they will be turned back as soon as they enter his waters.'

'What will Khusro and Jagai do, if they find themselves cut off from the rest of the Archipelago? When they have the added burden of feeding and sheltering those fleeing from the Nahik islands?' Planir shook his head, visibly perturbed. 'Do we have any hope of further letters from Kheda?'

'He may send them but I doubt I'll be able to collect them,' Velindre said curtly. 'My friend asks me not to call again. If I'm seen, he will be shunned.'

'It seems that wizardry is now wholly unwelcome in Relshaz,' Mellitha added. 'The Magistracy's undertaking to guard my house has proved entirely worthless. Everything which was left has been looted or despoiled.

'When I sought an explanation, I was told that I had no right to expect any protection after my treason in issuing commands to a Watch detachment. If I return to

Relshaz, I will be prosecuted for seeking to undermine the city's sworn guards' loyalty to the Magistracy. My voluntary exile has been taken for an admission of guilt. The Magistrates strongly recommend that I make my permanent exile public knowledge.'

Jilseth saw ominous anger burning through the magewoman's anguish.

Planir narrowed his eyes. 'Does the Magistracy imagine that I would see one of my most valued mages subject to their judgement?'

'I don't believe that they're thinking at all,' Velindre said frankly. 'They're running scared of Aldabreshi threats to their own livelihoods and to the city's trade which feeds the people whose votes give them their power.'

Planir looked at Mellitha. 'What of your household? Have those we sent back to Relshaz been harassed?'

'No, though of course, I have told them to say that they fled my service of their own free will.'

Jilseth saw that the magewoman's satisfaction at foiling such hostility was some slight balm for her wounded feelings.

Velindre looked dour. 'Every mage I knew in the city has left for Tormalin or Ensaimin or somewhere in between.'

'A good number have turned up here.' Planir nodded. 'Well now, what do we suppose the Relshazri Magistrates will do if the Archipelagan galleys they're so eager to appease don't actually appear on the spring horizon?'

'Do we think that's likely?' Mellitha clearly didn't want to believe it.

Velindre studied the ciphered message still floating in the air. 'Miris Esul commands considerable respect among the other warlords, all of whom are shocked by the corsair isle's destruction. As Kheda says, the

Archipelago doesn't need to trade with the mainland if they decide that living with their islands' limited seams of iron ore and other metals is the lesser evil, compared to engaging with magic even at second hand.'

Planir frowned. 'The realms and rulers of the mainland will be furious at the loss of Aldabreshin spices, gems and silks.'

'They will blame us,' Velindre predicted. 'They will know the corsairs' island's destruction has provoked this Aldabreshin withdrawal.'

Jilseth found her voice. 'Not if they know the threat which the Mandarkin Anskal posed to Caladhria. This tale of the corsairs wielding mysterious artefacts with magical properties is surely too vague to be convincing as a reason for Hadrumal's intervention.'

'Do you think you will convince them that Anskal was a threat to Tormalin, Lescar or Dalasor?' Velindre challenged her. 'Or to Ensaimin? If they cared about Caladhria's suffering, those nobles and guild masters would have offered armed support when the first coastal baronies were raided. As for Solura, that land is nothing to them but a remote kingdom with strange customs and stranger people.'

'That's hardly—' Jilseth began.

Planir intervened. 'Explaining that Anskal sought to menace the mainland with a cohort of mageborn taught to wield his own attacking spells will hardly reassure the populace or nobles—'

He broke off as footsteps echoed in the stairwell. Voices similarly overlapped, though these were more readily recognised.

'Our esteemed Flood Mistress.' Mellitha's sneer of dislike startled Jilseth.

'With Kalion.' Openly curious, Velindre waved away her spell and returned the tiny message slip to her belt pouch.

'Each with several companions. Who do you suppose they have brought to see me?'

Seeing the secretive curve to Planir's smile Jilseth suspected that he already knew.

'Archmage!' Kalion appeared first.

'Good afternoon.' Planir made no move to rise, merely nodding with amiable curiosity at the stranger escorted by the Hearth Master's chosen nexus; Ely, Galen and Canfor.

Jilseth looked keenly at Ely, wearing a moss green gown, and Galen in his dark brown wool doublet. They both followed Hearth Master Kalion in declaring their affinity in their clothing. Canfor scorned such convention in dun breeches and a lavender doublet.

She had seen precious little of any of them since the corsair isle's destruction. Rumour around Hadrumal's wine shops insisted that either Ely or Galen had suffered some unspecified disruption to their affinity while the other had won unsuspected insights into wizardry.

Opinion was divided as to which of them might have cause to lament or to celebrate. There was just as much speculation as to whether or not the couple's long-standing romance could withstand the resulting tensions.

Jilseth saw nothing in either of their faces to suggest any answers. She ignored Canfor's searching gaze. He was clearly speculating as to what these three wizards might be discussing with Planir.

Kalion's complacent smile multiplied his chins unbecomingly as he squared his shoulders to correct the drape of his rich red robes, disordered by hurrying up the stairs to be the first to speak to Planir. He laced his gold-ringed fingers together across his substantial paunch.

'May I make known to you Asetin Tref, Elder of the Fifth Order of Rapplen.'

'Good afternoon, Archmage.' The new arrival's low bow inadvertently revealed the balding spot amid his short-cropped mousy hair.

His flowing ochre mantle and the floor-length high-necked brown tunic beneath it marked him as Soluran as clearly as his accent and the carved wooden stave he carried. The four gems of wizardry were embedded in the brass band circling the top; sapphire, amber, ruby and emerald.

'Archmage?' Troanna followed Kalion's coterie into the sitting room, her annoyance as plain as her face. 'Please bespeak me when you're done with the Hearth Master and we will return.'

'Please.' Planir held up a hand to detain the Flood Mistress and her lone companion. 'Who is this visitor?'

This Soluran woman was another wizard with an earth affinity if the rich cinnamon hue of her cloak and the russet of her gown was any indication. Amber beads ringed her neck and wrists and shone amid her immaculately braided chestnut hair. Her jewel-studded stave was ebony ringed with silver.

Jilseth wondered if these visitors thought that Planir would be more amenable to mages who shared his birthright.

'May I make known to you Ifestal Sansem, Elder of the Third Order of Detich.'

The second newcomer spared Troanna the briefest glance of acknowledgement before challenging Planir with an openly appraising look.

Jilseth noted that this woman was a handful of years older than the first Soluran wizard, although Mellitha and Planir were at least ten years older than that while Kalion and Troanna were older still.

Soluran wizards rarely made old bones, so it was said around Hadrumal's wine shops, hence the insignificance of their scholarly traditions. What more could be expected from their multiplicity of rival Orders which so often rose and fell within a handful of generations?

'Enter and be welcome,' Planir invited. 'You can hear what Hearth Master Kalion has to say.'

'No thank you, Archmage.' Troanna's denial was firm. 'We will return later.'

'No, you will stay,' Planir commanded. 'So you won't be put to the trouble of scrying on us and denying it afterwards.'

Jilseth did her best to keep her face expressionless as she saw the shock on every Hadrumal mage's face. Every one of them apart from Kalion and Troanna. As for the Solurans, the man blushed with discomfort in sharp contrast to the woman's unguarded smirk of satisfaction.

Planir smiled at the Hearth Master. 'So, Kalion, what has your guest to say to me?'

Barely hiding his satisfaction at the Archmage's discourtesy to Troanna, Kalion turned to his companion. 'Master Tref?'

'Archmage.' The Soluran cleared his throat. 'My Order has considerable experience in crafting ensorcelled items—'

Planir raised an inquiring finger. 'Can your mages unravel the secrets of things already imbued with spells?'

The Soluran was clearly prepared for this question. 'We are confident that once we have established the nature of the spells within a given artefact, our own knowledge of the processes will offer us the key to fuller understanding. Naturally we will be delighted to share such understanding with you, in return for access to some of Hadrumal's lore—'

'Quintessential magic?' Troanna interrupted. 'The Council will never agree to that.'

Planir looked at Kalion. 'I take it you have some new argument to persuade the Council?'

Kalion glared at Troanna before answering the Archmage. 'The Council has always feared that such powerful magic would be used without restraint in Solura's ongoing skirmishes with Mandarkin. I agree these are valid objections—'

'—particularly when we've so recently seen the destructive potential of the highest wizardry,' Planir agreed amiably.

'So we propose,' Kalion continued resolutely, 'that only the Elders of Master Tref's Order are to be taught such lore—'

'—we will not share such magic with any wizard below highest rank,' Master Tref interjected with absolute sincerity. 'We will swear whatever oaths you wish and agree to any safeguards you may stipulate.'

As the Hearth Master nodded emphatically, Jilseth recalled an unguarded remark Planir had once made in her hearing. Kalion's own absolute and inflexible sense of honour could be more dangerous than any lesser mage's deceits. The Hearth Master believed that everyone whom he had chosen to trust would keep faith with him, just as he would uphold his agreements with them.

'Furthermore,' Kalion continued, 'the Order of Rapplen is sworn to the Duke of Ostern, in Solura's central provinces. Their Elders have not been embroiled in border strife for a generation.'

Planir looked at Master Tref. 'Your Order and your Duke don't see fit to help us simply by way of recompense for saving your realm from the Mandarkin Anskal? Wouldn't every wizard in Solura have been called upon if Anskal had returned to share his hoard of artefacts with the warrior-captains who serve this tyrant?'

Kalion spoke up quickly, seeing that the Soluran was at a loss for an answer. 'In the first instance, we can secure the Order of Rapplen's co-operation by sharing the bare techniques of establishing a nexus. As they repay us with insights into these artefacts, we can consider sharing more powerful quintessential spells.'

While he was unfailingly principled, the Hearth Master was no fool, Jilseth reflected. Meanwhile she was watching Troanna and the Soluran magewoman. Ifestal Sansem was growing increasingly impatient, her expression hardening as she saw the Flood Mistress allow Kalion and Master Tref to make their arguments.

Granted, if the Soluran was used to judging mages by appearances, Troanna wouldn't look very impressive in her faded moss green gown, with the faded hair and thickened waist of any humble grandmother, wearing no jewellery beyond a simple silver ring with a chipped beryl cabochon.

'The wizards of Rapplen have no more need for quintessential magic than the Duke of Ostern,' Ifestal Sansem interrupted, barely concealing her scorn for Asetin Tref. 'We of Detich have no interest in such bargaining, Archmage. We want those artefacts, no more, no less. Hadrumal has no need of them. You seek only to satisfy your curiosity.' She didn't hide her disdain for that.

'This is your argument? No more and no less?' Planir raised his eyebrows.

'We have need of such weapons and such defences,' she retorted. 'The Order of Detich is sworn to Lord Megriol. Megrilar is the province most frequently and viciously attacked by Mandarkin. We guard—'

'—the Gelakul Pass and the Ezin Gorge, yes, I know,' Planir informed her.

The magewoman was unabashed. 'Then you know if Megrilar falls, the way to Solith and the Lake of Kings will lie open to Mandarkin's invaders.'

Planir pursed his lips. 'Only if Lady Edath, Lord Safren, Lord Astrad and Lord Mafrid choose not to send their troops and mages into the fray while every House of Sanctuary between the northern forests and the lowlands chooses to stand on the sidelines. Even then I suspect King Solquen's own regiments would give a good account of themselves, backed by Trudenar and Vagisar forces.'

Planir raised a hand to silence Kalion's inarticulate outrage. 'But you have yet to explain what the Order of Detich offers Hadrumal in return for these artefacts.'

'We offer nothing,' Ifestal Sansem replied.

Planir steepled his fingers beneath his bearded chin. 'Then what will you do if we don't hand over the Mandarkin's loot?'

Ifestal Sansem didn't blink. 'You will come to regret such selfishness.'

Planir grinned. 'You will have to be more specific if you wish to threaten the Archmage of Hadrumal.'

'You have until the turn of For-Spring,' the Soluran magewoman retorted, 'to surrender the artefacts. If not, you will soon learn what it is to make enemies of mages who know how to fight. We do not forswear our wizardry's aid in warfare,' she sneered.

Hearth Master Kalion rounded on the Detich Elder, his voice shaking with fury. 'Does your king know that you are attempting to compel these artefacts' surrender with such menaces?'

'King Solquen is gravely concerned to see Hadrumal's unbridled power let loose in the Archipelago.' Ifestal Sansem answered in level tones. 'I understand that Emperor Tadriol is equally perturbed.'

'True.' Planir nodded as though they were having a perfectly amiable discussion.

'Hadrumal would do better to have the Order of Detich as allies rather than enemies.' Ifestal Sansem paused, her head angled. 'Archmage or not, do you have the right to make this decision for every man, woman and child living on Hadrumal's isle? Shouldn't your Council of Wizards decide such weighty matters?'

'That is none of your concern and I have heard enough of your demands.' Planir flicked a dismissive hand and the Soluran magewoman vanished. The great diamond in his ring of office burned with cold fire.

'Please believe me, Archmage—' Apprehension twisted the Rapplen mage's face.

'Thank you, Master Tref,' Planir said courteously. 'I will consider your proposal on its own merits. Do you require any assistance in returning to your own Order's tower?'

'No, thank you.' Tref fled in a blinding flash of magelight.

Kalion took a wrathful step towards Troanna. 'You dare to bring that woman here, to stand by while she threatens Hadrumal? You think that we should cravenly hand over these artefacts—?'

'No,' the Flood Mistress said scornfully before turning to Planir. 'But now you have heard that foolish magewoman's threats for yourself, believe me when I tell you that the Elders of Detich are not the only Soluran wizards contemplating such aggression to secure these artefacts.'

She glared at the Archmage. 'Your responsibility above all other is to safeguard Hadrumal and Trydek's legacy. We are making no progress in comprehending the magic underlying these cursed artefacts and what good would such understanding do us anyway? Any mage worth the name should be able to master such spells.'

'Then what do you propose?' Planir invited.

'Destroy these wretched artefacts,' Troanna said without hesitation. 'They are of no use and little interest to us. On the other side of the scales, they are assuredly far too dangerous for us to hand over to Solura's wizards or Mandarkin's tyrants or anyone else who would seek to make use of them.'

Planir raised his eyebrows. 'When your children or your grandchildren refuse to share a toy, do you end such bickering by simply taking it away?'

There was no mockery in the Archmage's words. Regardless Jilseth saw Ely, Galen and Canfor each catch their breath, dreading Troanna's reaction.

The Flood Mistress merely smiled with grim satisfaction. 'Yes, I do.'

'You would destroy such intricately magecrafted works of wizardry simply because you cannot fathom their secrets?' Kalion's anger turned to smouldering contempt.

'What would you do with them?' Troanna challenged him coldly. 'Curry favour with the mainland's realms and rulers from the Tormalin Emperor down by flattering them with such gifts? You have always advocated closer ties with noble and influential men. Is that your intent once you have the secrets of crafting such trinkets at your fingertips?'

'I believe that sharing these artefacts with a few carefully chosen and trustworthy friends would do a great deal to reassure those on the mainland now so nervous of wizardry,' Kalion said hotly. 'Such generosity would prove that we do not hoard such power for ourselves and equally that we are willing to offer our friends the means to defend themselves against renegade magecraft—'

'You think that those who receive your bounty will be so grateful when those Soluran mages arrive at their door to demand that they surrender such treasures?' Troanna challenged him. 'Not to mention sneak-thieves cracking their shutters to steal them away.'

She returned her attention to Planir. 'You have heard the mutterings from the mainland, Archmage. Those who've always envied the mageborn are eager to secure some such facsimile of wizardry now that they know ensorcelled artefacts truly exist outside tavern ballads and chimney-corner tales. How much strife would even one such trinket loose on the mainland prompt with so many of the mundane populace foolishly nervous of magecraft?'

The Archmage nodded. 'Please show me how to destroy these artefacts.'

Troanna narrowed her eyes. 'As yet—'

'Let's see.' Planir rose to his feet and took a red onyx ring from the fireplace's mantelshelf. 'Here's a curious piece. It confers the ability to climb without falling, whether up a sheer cliff or a branchless tree trunk, or indeed a windowless fortification of close-fitted stone free of handholds. What a gift for a Mandarkin tyrant's assassin, or a Soluran king's man or a Tormalin emperor's agent.'

He glanced at Kalion. 'I've no doubt that you wish to enlist Emperor Tadriol's assistance, to have him send word of his indignation to King Solquen, that Soluran mages have threatened Hadrumal. You don't think that the price of such a letter would be a trifle such as this?'

The Archmage laid the ring on his outstretched palm and the great ring of his office glowed. Magefire sprang up, around and within the onyx circle. It burned so viciously bright that Jilseth had to look away until the glow faded. She looked back to see the onyx ring unharmed.

Planir shrugged, and the ring was rimed with frost. An instant more and ice encased it. Green magelight shimmered as the Archmage's entire palm was covered with shattering cold. Planir shook his head and the ice vanished to reveal the ring still untouched by the magic.

Jilseth shivered as the air within the room crackled with blue magelight. Wizardry vivid as lightning wove a web around the Archmage's hand, darting at the onyx ring again and again to leave it entirely unaffected.

Planir sighed and released the elemental air to draw new wizardry from the stones which had built this ancient tower. Jilseth swallowed as she felt the Archmage subject the onyx to the inexorable pressures which would ordinarily turn wood to coal and thence to diamond through the natural passage of aeons and crushing depth. The paltry looking ring lay on his palm, unyielding.

'So.' Planir tossed the trinket into the air, startling them all. 'Do tell me, Flood Mistress, when you discover how to destroy these artefacts.'

Catching the ring, he set it back on the mantelshelf. The click of stone on wood sounded loud in the silent room.

'Meantime, thank you both for bringing these different Soluran proposals to me.' Planir resumed his seat by the fire.

Kalion rallied swiftly. 'These are matters for the whole Council to consider.'

'Quite so,' Planir agreed, 'and when we call such a Council, we can also call Despin to answer for his attempt to steal from a dying man. What do you consider a suitable punishment for your former pupil?'

'Despin bitterly regrets his impulsiveness. He will not be so foolish again,' Kalion said stiffly. 'Ever since his return, he has kept close to his rooms and Wellery's library, applying himself diligently to examining the dagger entrusted to the nexus he has now joined.'

'You are studying a blade which heats itself to furnace heat as soon as it clashes with any other steel, I believe?' Planir looked at Galen. 'Have you gained any insights as yet?'

'Alas, no, Archmage,' Galen said wearily.

Jilseth was watching Canfor. What did he think of Kalion's continued support for Despin? Surely he must hope that the offending mage's removal from the Council would see him voted into the now vacant seat?

'We should call a Council meeting to discuss how Master Kerrit's killers are to be held to account,' Troanna said. 'Such an insult to Hadrumal cannot go unpunished.'

'How do you suggest that we hold such an assize and pass judgement, let alone punish the guilty, without spreading the very alarm among the mundane populace which you so rightly wish to avoid? Ring the Council bell yourself, Flood Mistress, when you have a worthwhile proposal,' Planir invited.

'Now, by your leave, I will continue my own studies.' He gestured at the table. 'Some way to resolve our problems may yet lurk in Master Kerrit's library.'

'Let us hope so.' Mellitha rose from the settle beside Jilseth and headed for the door, acknowledging Kalion with a brief smile while ignoring Troanna entirely.

Velindre followed her. 'Thank you, Archmage. Good day to you, Hearth Master, Flood Mistress. That was most instructive.'

As Jilseth rose from her own seat, Kalion turned on his heel with a snort of frustration and led his trio down the spiral stair. Jilseth waited until Troanna had followed them, not wishing to irritate the Flood Mistress by preceding her.

'A moment if you please.' Planir leaned forward to take a log from the wood basket and toss it onto the fire. 'We were discussing Halferan's affairs before we were so interestingly diverted.'

Jilseth recalled his instructions. 'I will go to see Master Herion.'

Planir was looking thoughtful. 'I will have a letter of my own for Corrain, Baron Halferan. I am willing to help him find this man from Wrede but there's a service which he can do me in return.'

Jilseth wondered what the Archmage intended. 'How do you propose to scry for a man whom none of us have ever seen? We don't even have something belonging to this stranger to anchor a spell.'

'No indeed,' Planir agreed. 'But as Lady Zurenne and Baron Corrain have so usefully reminded us, there are more magics in this world than our own. Since using wizardry would indeed prove problematic, we can look elsewhere for assistance. Col's aetheric adepts may have

Artifice to help us find this curious stranger. They may also have other information useful for our purposes gleaned from their fellow healers in Solura. A good many Houses of Sanctuary work closely with their local wizardly Orders.'

'As you think best, Archmage.' Though Jilseth couldn't think what possible use Artifice might be in Hadrumal's current travails.

'Call back when you've spoken to Master Heriön. I'll have my letter ready for you.' Planir smiled and reached for the book he had been reading when she had first arrived.

After an irresolute moment, Jileth went on her way. She couldn't help feeling a little surprised. Shouldn't the Archmage be addressing the fresh challenges which this day had brought to Hadrumal rather than reading antique Relshazri books?

As she went down Trydek's tower's stairs, Jilseth wondered how even Planir's vaunted shrewdness was going to deal with dissent among Hadrumal's Council over how to counter these threats from Solura at the same time as rebuffing the Tormalin princes' uncompromising desire for a share in the corsairs' artefacts, never mind the mainland's other rulers' anger once they realised that Archipelagan hatred of magic now threatened to put an end to all trade with the Aldabreshi.

But at least that poor lad Hosh should find a cure for his own undeserved suffering in Col.

— CHAPTER THIRTEEN —

CORRAIN STIRRED IN his sleep. The heavy manacles dragged at his wrists. Sores where iron rubbing on bone had worn away his skin stung with the unceasing sweat prompted by the Archipelago's sultriness. Shifting his feet, he heard the faint clink of the chains linking the shackles around his ankles. Rolling over, he felt the tug of the crusted welts cut into his shoulders by the slaver's lash. As the scabs gave way, his skin crawled at the trickle of fresh blood.

'Captain?'

Hosh? Was some other oar-slave coming for the lad? The overseers could never be trusted to defend one rower from another's malice. Corrain struggled to wake, to throw off the weariness of propelling this corsair galley on from dawn to dusk. His heart was racing and breath rasped in his throat.

Opening his eyes, he saw the wooden planking above his head; this cabin's roof and the underside of the deck above. He felt the sailing ship roll; a different motion to a galley's wallowing. Rubbed a shaking hand over his stubbled face, he realised that his wrist was free of that broken slave chain.

'Captain?' Hosh ventured. 'You were dreaming.'

'What of it?' Corrain swung his legs over the side of the bunk, barely avoiding smacking his head on the cramped cabin's cross-beams. Space for cargo took precedence on this trading vessel. 'Where are we?'

'Coming into Col on the morning tide,' Hosh said promptly. 'We heard the city bells sound the day's second chime.'

'Why didn't you wake me?' Corrain scowled.

'You needed to sleep,' Hosh answered with unexpected firmness.

Corrain couldn't dispute it. He hadn't slept a whole night through since they'd set foot on this ship in Claithe. Even when exhaustion overwhelmed him, nightmares would besiege him. Twice, three times between dusk and dawn, he would wake to hear Hosh sleeping peacefully in the opposite bunk. As peacefully as the snores rasping through the lad's broken face allowed.

How did the boy escape such torment? Why had the peace of mind Corrain had enjoyed since ridding himself of that broken manacle deserted him? He didn't bother asking Hosh. Doubtless the lad would offer some trite tribute to Arrimelin and Corrain had no faith left in the goddess of dreams.

'Grab your gear.' Corrain slung his own shapeless leather travelling bag over his shoulder by its drawstring and took up his sword in his other hand, belt buckled tight around the scabbard.

Climbing up through the hatch, the cold sea air revived him a little. The chill was especially welcome, driving away lingering memories of oppressive Aldabreshin heat. He saw the harbour wall protecting a huddle of buildings approaching as the trader's ship rode the rising tide past a low expanse of mud flats tufted with stained reeds. Looking back he saw the creamy smear of the vessel's wake cutting across the mud-coloured waters of a broad shallow bay. Sea and sky alike were opaque with mist.

What was he doing here? He had sworn to defend Halferan, Lady Zurenne and her children for his dead lord's sake. Yet he was doing the Archmage's bidding once again.

Corrain pushed such treacherous thoughts away. This was the only way he could find out who that mysterious man from Wrede might be. He'd also wager good gold that his journey had been noticed by Den Dalderin spies. If Imperial eyes were following him, they wouldn't be contemplating Halferan too closely. Meantime, Kusint was more than capable of warning off any renewed Karpis ambitions to encroach on the barony.

Besides, whatever service he was doing the Archmage was incidental. He was here first and foremost to see Hosh healed; a fitting reward for all the lad had done for Halferan. Corrain could never redeem his failure to save the other loyal men who had died at the corsairs' hands but he could make good on this debt.

The ship rounded the watch tower at the end of the harbour wall and headed for the dockside's sodden and fraying wooden pilings, lapped by turbid water strewn with refuse.

'Mind your backs!' A sailor hurried past, a hempen cable slung over one shoulder.

Corrain grabbed for the ship's rail and straw-filled fenders crackled in protest as a large swell drove the vessel hard against the brick-built quay.

'Thank Dastennin for that,' Hosh said fervently.

A sailor sprang onto the rail, his salt-encrusted boot thudding beside Corrain's hand. Inside a breath, the mariner had leaped ashore, winding the sturdy rope around an iron bollard. All along the wharf, men were securing their vessel.

'You'd do better to thank Larasion in these waters.' His task done, the sailor pointed towards a statue some distance along the quayside. Twice life size, the Forest goddess was crowned with a wreath of blossom and a necklace of flowers defying the winter. Only the hems of her flowing gown gleamed bright, the bronze polished by countless grateful hands, while the rest of the metal figure was weathered to dull green by salt and mist. Her sandaled feet were surrounded by sodden silk blooms, earthenware leaves and glazed pottery fruits piled high on her plinth.

'I will make sure to leave an offering,' Hosh replied fervently.

Corrain kept his mouth shut. He would thank every last rat in the ship's bilge before he'd thank any deity for seeing them safely across the Gulf of Peorle. That said, he was grateful to be safely moored. This last leg of their journey, cutting across from the Caladhrian coast, meant a night at sea out of sight of land. That wasn't lightly undertaken at this season, even in these sheltered waters with the bulk of southern Ensaimin barring the path of winter storms sweeping in from the western sea.

'Where are you headed now?' The trader-captain paused on his way from his own cabin beneath the raised rear deck to the hold's hatches amidships.

'We have a letter of introduction to Mentor Garewin at the university.' Corrain buckled on his sword and picked up his bag from the deck. 'Where will we find that?'

'The university?' The trader laughed. 'Once you're away from the water, it's all around you, my friend.'

Corrain smiled as though he understood the man's joke. 'So where should we ask for this Garewin?'

'Try one of the inns by the carillon tower in the central square. The tapster will send a runner to find your mentor for a silver penny.' The captain continued on his way. Bales and crates were being hauled out of the depths of the ship and now they had made landfall, he was intent on turning as much profit as possible, to reward him and his crew for the risks of sailing the Caladhrian coast in winter.

His only interest in his passengers had been the coin they were willing to pay, which suited Corrain. He and Hosh had bought their passage in their own names, not claiming any rank for some sailor to carry ashore. Both wore plain and hardwearing clothes like any other winter traveller. Nothing marked them out as in any way noteworthy.

'A tower should be easy enough to find,' Hosh carefully wiped his face. Whether from the winter cold or the salt-laden breeze, his eye and broken nose had wept ceaselessly during their journey.

'Flat, isn't it?' A yawn cut short Corrain's agreement.

He walked to the gap in the rail where sailors were settling the gangplank to reach down to the quayside. Brick-built and steeply gabled warehouses were ranged along the dock, like nothing in Caladhria. Beyond the harbour, buildings sprawled in all directions; red-tiled roofs above walls patterned with every colour of brick to ever emerge from a kiln. Dull ochre was everywhere underfoot.

Hosh followed him ashore. 'How far do you suppose the walk is, to this central square?'

Corrain pointed to a trio of two-wheeled gigs drawn up beside another statue, this one honouring Trimon, the wandering god, who was striking his traveller's harp with a dramatic flourish. 'We'll hire one of those.'

As the horses chomped inside their nosebags, their drivers were passing a black glass bottle from hand to hand. The first to notice their approach turned ready to greet them. He took a half step back instead, gaping at Hosh's face. The boy quickly pulled up his cloak's hood to hide his disfigurement.

Corrain had grown used to the sailors ignoring Hosh's misshapen features. After a first day of frank appraisal, the merchant mariners had paid no more heed to Hosh's scars than they did to their own; deep gouges carved into their forearms by searing ropes or missing fingers wrenched from their sockets as errant winds yanked booms and sails.

'What's the rate for a ride to the carillon tower?' he asked curtly.

One man handed the black bottle to his neighbour. 'I'd say that would be a silver mark.'

Corrain looked the hireling driver straight in the eye. 'I'd say we'll walk instead then.'

Any guard captain worth his bread and beer knew Ensaimin arrogance always sought to take advantage of Caladhrian ignorance.

The hireling drivers laughed and the first man pressed a mock-repentant hand to his leather tunic's breast.

'I misspoke myself. That will be a silver penny for you and your companion.'

'For us both together?' Corrain queried.

'Of course. This way, if you please.' The man lowered the step to the seats at the rear of his gig before climbing up to his perch at the front.

Corrain shoved their belongings underneath the wooden seat as Hosh slid across to make space for him. They were barely seated before the black horse moved off. The ride was smooth across the ochre paviours as the driver headed for a broad thoroughfare running inland. Wagons, hireling carriages and private coaches trundled ahead, two abreast without impeding each other or hindering the vehicles coming the other way. With this wide, flat plain at their disposal, Col's builders had laid out impressively wide roads.

In the far distance, through the slowly dissipating mists, Corrain could just make out a great column of brick and stone looming over buildings themselves four and five storeys high.

'That must be the carillon tower.' He nudged Hosh but the lad was sitting hunched beneath his cloak hood. Corrain couldn't blame him. He wouldn't relish being stared at by so many passers-by.

Some were sauntering, some hurrying preoccupied. A few men and women were ostentatiously dressed in expensively dyed velvets and furs. Most wore workaday clothes in hardwearing colours. Corrain noted a good number of men wore swords, though a fair few of those blades looked more ornament than useful.

The horse trotted onwards past brick buildings painted in bright colours, vibrant even under the leaden sky. Trees separated the road from paved paths in front of the houses and shops. They must be bright with blossom in the spring, Corrain mused, shady with green leaves in summer and gaudy with autumn reds and golds. For the present, grey-barked boughs clawed at the cold air with barren twigs.

As they drew steadily nearer, he studied the carillon tower. The mighty edifice was evidently the work of more than one builder. Soaring up above the red-tiled roof of a broad building extending across the entire western side of the square, the tower's topmost two storeys were markedly different in style. Corrain was relieved to note that some of Col's fabled wealth had bought stone coigns to reinforce the patterned brickwork. Unbraced it could never have been raised so high without collapsing.

The tower overlooked a vast square lined with taverns and inns. An ornate fountain in the centre supported statues of Talagrin, Halcarion, Trimon and Larasion on a central pedestal. Their blind marble eyes stared north, east, south and westwards while water flowed around their heedless feet to fill the broad basin.

The gig drew to a halt and their driver turned around on his backless bench as the tower's bells began ringing. If there was a count of the day's chimes somewhere amid the clamour, Corrain couldn't make it out. The horse stood obediently still, so unbothered by the cacophony overhead that Corrain wondered if it was deaf.

He reached inside his doublet for his travelling purse and found a Tormalin minted silver penny within it. 'What's the best tavern for finding scholars in?' he shouted to the hireling driver.

'All of them.' The man laughed before indicating a yellow painted building with red varnished shutters. 'Try in there.'

'Many thanks.' Corrain dropped the coin into the man's leathery palm and jumped down from the gig. Hosh followed, silent as he retrieved their belongings from beneath the seat.

The tavern was called The Goose Hounds and the front wall boasted a lifelike painting of two well-muscled and shaggy-maned dogs splashing through a marsh. Despite the cold weather, the door stood hospitably open. Inside

Corrain found lanterns banishing the winter shadows while fireplaces at either side of the long tap room warmed the drinkers enough to discard cloaks. Corrain undid his brooch as he led Hosh towards a corner table.

'I'll ask about sending a message to this Mentor Garewin.'

As Hosh took a seat with his back to the room, Corrain reached out and pulled the lad's fur-trimmed cloak hood down. Hosh exclaimed before realising that would only draw attention to his injuries.

'Keep your face turned to the wall if you wish,' Corrain said quietly, 'but sitting hooded indoors will draw curious eyes. Do you want someone asking you your business?'

Mute, Hosh shook his head. Corrain headed for the counter running along the room's back wall.

'Ale?' The tapster gestured to barrels stacked to his off-hand. 'Or wine?' Bottles were racked twenty deep and twice as wide on his other side.

That was a lot of wine, even for a tavern in the middle of a trading city. Corrain wondered how ready the tapster would be to palm off some highly-priced vinegar on a couple of strangers.

'Ale if you please. Something to keep out the cold.' Corrain waited as the man drew two brimming tankards of an unexpectedly dark brew. 'I was told you could send a message for me, to one of the university's mentors?'

'Two silver pence for the ale.' The tapster held out a hand. 'Another to send a lad with your message.'

Corrain dropped a couple of coin into the man's palm and held up a third. 'Does that buy me paper and ink?'

The tapster grinned. 'Of course, Master.'

'Very well then.' Corrain let the coin fall to join the first two.

The man went to fetch some writing materials from a shelf beyond the racked wine. Corrain sipped cautiously at his tankard, mindful of the unpleasant surprises he'd encountered in taverns on his travels with Kusint. Solurans flavoured their ales with fruit and even spruce twigs. Thankfully this proved to be a rich winter brew, the hearty taste awakening his stomach to its emptiness.

He carried the second tankard over to Hosh. 'Are you hungry?'

'I am.' He sounded surprised.

Corrain nodded. 'I'll get something to eat.'

He went back to the counter as the tapster returned with paper, pen and ink. 'Could we have a bite or two of food? Our ship just came in with the tide.'

'Of course.'

As the man headed through the door to a busy kitchen, Corrain drew the sheet of chaff-flecked reed paper towards him and uncapped the inkwell. The quill would have benefited from trimming but it would suffice. However there was no sealing wax on offer or a candle within easy reach for him to at least make a gesture towards securing his letter. Corrain scratched out a brief note.

Master Scholar, I beg the favour of a conversation regarding an old injury to a loyal friend which has healed awry. Master Herion suggests you may be able to soothe his pain.
Corrain of Halferan

If this mentor was known as a healer, that shouldn't prompt too much curiosity, however many hands unfolded this note before passing along. His own name might prompt curiosity if anyone here knew of the guardsman returned from slavery to be raised to the rank of baron. Corrain wondered how readily news from Caladhria crossed the Gulf from Peorle. How interested were Col's merchants and scholars in such tales?

He folded the paper in two and scrawled a full direction on the outer side as the tapster returned with a broad wooden platter. Hunks of seed-crusted bread framed a fillet of some dark-fleshed fish soused in vinegar beside leathery rings of dried apple and slices of glistening beef sausage flecked with dull red spice.

Corrain hazarded a guess. 'A silver penny?'

'That's right,' the tapster grinned.

Corrain reached for his purse, wondering if anyone used copper pence in this city. 'This note is for Mentor Garewin, wherever he might be.'

The tapster snapped his fingers to summon a tousle-headed lad clearing empty tankards and plates from the tables. Corrain judged him around ten years old, maybe a summer either way. Lightly-built, bright-eyed and deft, if he was a handful of years older in Halferan, Corrain would have wanted him for the manor guard.

'Quick as you can.' The tapster handed over the folded paper.

'Mentor Garewin is sealed to the School of Rhetoric,' Corrain began. Madam Jilseth had explained that Col's mentors and students were divided into such schools rather than grouped into halls as they were in Vanam and indeed Hadrumal itself.

'I can read.' The lad thought for a moment. 'If he's not at the Red Library, I'll get word of him there at this time of day. I'll be back before you've drunk your ale, Master.'

'Good to know.'

Corrain watched the boy slide deftly between the tables, pausing only at the door to allow two newcomers to enter. The tapster was already walking along the counter as they approached, one with a silver mark held up between finger and thumb.

Corrain took the platter of food and his tankard over to Hosh at their corner table. The stool opposite the hunched lad gave him a clear view of tavern and Corrain was glad of that. Civilized though Col might seem, he was never going to sit with his back to any armed men.

'The pot boy seems to know where to pick up the mentor's trail.'

Hosh bit cautiously into a piece of apple, chewing on the uninjured side of his mouth. He didn't speak, his eyes distant. Corrain could guess what the lad was wondering. Would this mentor's Artifice, this aetheric magic, truly be able to mend Hosh's ruined face?

A loud voice rang through the taproom. 'You've heard the latest from Relshaz? They've driven the wizards out of their city, every last one. Found their cellars stuffed with gold and silver, so I heard.'

One of the newcomers was leaning on the counter, a goblet of wine in his hand.

'That's old news,' someone called out scornfully from over by the other fireplace.

'Or some tavern tarradiddle.' A second man's scepticism was plain. 'Why would the Relshazri do such a thing?'

The newcomer stared at him. 'You know that a whole warlord's domain was sunk beneath Aldabreshin seas on the Archmage's order? You've heard that the Archipelagans in Relshaz have sworn by the sun, both moons and all the stars that they won't trade with anyone doing business with wizards?'

Corrain laid a slice of the spiced sausage on some bread and took a bite. Dalasorian brass buttons fastened the man's doublet and beaver fur trimmed his cloak, while he spoke with the accents of northern Ensaimin. Why was he so concerned with Relshazri news?

'The Relshazri would bridge their canals with their own backs if some Aldabreshi asked to cross dry-shod,' the sceptical man opined. 'Why should we be concerned if the Archipelagans have run scared of wizardry?'

'The Aldabreshi kill mages on sight,' the newcomer retorted. 'Call that running scared and you'll live to regret it.'

'You still don't say what that has to do with the price of beans,' the first man retorted. 'Why should we care if the Relshazri want to do without wizards? More fool them, I say.'

The murmur around the room concurred and the newcomer bristled.

'What quarrel does Hadrumal have with the southern barbarians anyway, to set wizards sinking islands? The whole tale sounds like a fever dream.' The sceptical man waved a dismissive hand.

'I've heard from more than one trader that a nest of pirates was burned out of their lair in some northern Aldabreshin domain,' a woman swathed in plum coloured broadcloth said thoughtfully.

Hosh shifted on his stool and Corrain caught the lad's eye. He saw a faint smile twist Hosh's mouth and knew what he was thinking. Who would have imagined they would so easily be able to do as the Archmage had asked in return for the letter from Master Herion tucked safely in Corrain's pocket. To let Planir know what rumours and misapprehensions about last year's events were common currency in Col's taverns. As Jilseth had explained, no one would guard their tongues around two Caladhrian travellers as they would around visitors from Hadrumal, mage or mundane born.

'When would a wizard ever do something so useful?' A man by the window sneered.

'Whatever truly happened in the Archipelago, the Relshazri may be wise to distance themselves from magecraft,' a voice fresh to the conversation observed.

Corrain shifted on his seat to get a clearer view, instantly knowing this new speaker for a Soluran. He was sitting in the centre of the room, a bottle of wine and a pewter goblet on his table.

'I'll allow they'll pay heed if tales of magic in the northern domains are troubling the Aldabreshi.' The woman in the plum gown leaned back in her chair, hands folded on her prosperous belly. 'For the sake of their trade with Archipelago.'

The Soluran shook his head. 'That's not what I meant. Never underestimate wizards.'

The back of Corrain's neck prickled with suspicion. The Soluran had come into the tavern with that loud-mouthed Ensaimin youth, so why wasn't he drinking with him? So no one would think they were deliberately directing this conversation, as purposefully as hunting dogs driving their quarry?

'You've heard of Mandarkin's tyrants?' the Soluran enquired of no one in particular. 'You know that it's wizardly magic keeps their boots planted on their slaves' necks?'

'Mandarkin? We have nothing to do with that realm.' The woman in the plum gown was baffled.

'Consider yourselves fortunate,' the Soluran advised her. 'Mandarkin forces test Solura's mettle every spring, trying to slip through the mountain passes to plunder our lands and steal our children. I wonder that they have never sought a path through the forests and the lakes into northern Ensaimin. If they did, the men of Vanam and Wrede would find themselves hard pressed, I can swear to that.'

Corrain swallowed his mouthful of meat and bread. 'Don't Solura's mages drive off those Mandarkin attacks? Yet you say we should be wary of wizardry?'

The Soluran stared at Corrain with penetrating blue eyes. 'Caladhrian, by your speech. I heard tell of some manor along the Caladhrian coast which suffered most grievously when Hadrumal's wizards finally took on the corsairs.' The man shook his head slowly without his gaze ever leaving Corrain's face. 'When stags battle in the autumn rut, the grass is trampled underfoot, whichever beast wins.'

'Captain?' As Hosh leaned forward to lay an urgent hand on Corrain's forearm, his head blocked the Soluran stranger's view.

Corrain blinked and shuddered. Before Hosh could ask what the matter was, he saw the tavern's messenger boy appear in the doorway. A thoughtful looking man accompanied him, perhaps ten years Corrain's elder, with generous grey hair swept back from a high brow and boasting an ornately trimmed and pointed beard.

His high-collared, long-sleeved tunic was of excellent cut and tailoring, as was his old-fashioned midnight blue mantle. He carried no weapon, not even an everyday belt-knife. Gold gleamed on every finger of his sword hand but only a single broad silver seal ring adorned his other hand.

The potboy pointed to Corrain and Hosh. Corrain was about to rise when the mentor paused by the Soluran's chair, to greet the man with visible surprise.

The Soluran struggled to conceal his own shock as well as his displeasure. The two men exchanged a few brief words before the Soluran rose and departed with a brusque nod. Master Garewin arrived at their table frowning, somewhat indignant.

'Good day, Baron Halferan.'

Corrain stood and offered a courteous hand. 'Master is the only title I claim on this journey.'

'As you wish.' Garewin pulled up a stool to sit at their table. 'And your companion?'

'This is Hosh and here is our letter of introduction.' Corrain handed over the missive which Jilseth had given him 'What may I fetch you to drink, Master Mentor?'

'Wine, Kadras white, if you please,' the scholar said, intent on studying Hosh's face rather than cracking Hadrumal's seals.

As Corrain headed for the counter, he watched the Ensaimin man with the brass buttons and fur-collared cloak. The stranger hadn't followed the Soluran out of the tavern but he was as tense as a fox who'd heard a dog bark.

Corrain caught the potboy's eye. As the lad brought some tankards and an empty bottle to the counter, Corrain showed him a silver penny, pressed into his palm with his thumb so no one else could see it.

'Do you happen to know where that Soluran who mistrusts wizards is lodging?'

The boy's eyes flickered to the coin. 'Not yet, Master.'

'Let me know when you do.' Corrain waved to attract the tapster's attention. 'White Kadras wine, if you please, and do you have a room for me and my companion? We'll be in the city for a few days at least.'

'Of course, Master.' The tapster fetched a bottle of wine and set it down with an elegant Aldabreshin glass goblet. 'I'll send the girl to make a bedchamber ready and you can see if it suits you at your leisure.'

'Thank you.' Corrain took the wine and goblet back to the table where Mentor Garewin was still studying Hosh's disfigurement.

'If you could open your mouth?' he asked gently.

Hosh unhappily complied, revealing barren and shrunken gums on the injured side of his face. Corrain fixed his attention on the food, helping himself to a lump of pickled fish. Thankfully the pungent smell masked the rankness of Hosh's breath. The boy had run out of the herbs which Doratine gave him to chew halfway up the coast.

'Thank you.' The scholar poured himself a generous measure of the aromatic wine, opened Planir's letter and briefly scanned the contents. 'Well, my friend—' he smiled encouragingly at Hosh '—I believe we can indeed help you.'

Corrain seized his opportunity. 'We? You and the man you were just talking to?'

'What?' Garewin looked momentarily bemused. 'No, he is just a visitor who's had some dealings with our school.'

'Dealings in Artifice?' Corrain persisted. 'He's an adept?'

'Quite so,' Garewin nodded. 'But it is Col's scholars who will be helping you,' he assured Hosh. 'As far as we can,' he qualified. 'We will be able to reshape the bones of your face but we can do nothing to restore your lost teeth.'

'How soon?' Hosh asked warily.

Garewin sipped his wine. 'We can start tomorrow but it will be a lengthy process and painful, I am afraid.'

Hosh smiled crookedly. 'I'm well used to pain.'

'How lengthy?' Corrain reached for his ale. 'Just so I can send word home. We will stay for as long as it takes.'

'We should be done before the turn of For-Spring. You should come to the Red Library tomorrow, for the morning's second chime.'

As Garewin explained where Hosh was to go, Corrain watched the tavern's potboy busy about the taproom. How soon would the lad be free to go and find out where that Soluran was lodging? If Corrain had word by the following morning, he could quarter the city for the man's scent while Hosh was busy with Mentor Garewin.

Corrain had thought he had recognised the eerie sensation when that stranger had looked into his eyes. He had suffered the same intrusion when the Elders of Fornet, the wizardly Order sworn to Solura's Lord Pastiss, had turned an adept on him. The unnerving old woman had tested the truth of his words, when he had sworn that Hadrumal had no part in his folly, that he alone had offered the Mandarkin Anskal the pick of the corsairs' loot in return for driving them from Caladhria's shores.

What was this Soluran's business in Col? Why had he and his collaborator been stirring up mistrust of elemental magic? What secrets had he plucked from Corrain's head, when he'd looked straight into his memories and his intentions?

Corrain drank his fine dark ale and resolved to find out as much as he possibly could about the man. Then he would call on the Col wizard whom Jilseth had

— CHAPTER FOURTEEN —

Halferan Manor, Caladhria
29th of Aft-Winter

ZURENNE LOOKED UP as Reven knocked on the open audience chamber door. She and Ilysh were reconciling their personal expenditure; the first step in the full accounting of the manor's ledgers with Master Rauffe before the turn of the season eight days hence.

'There are riders at the gatehouse, my lady. They ask your permission to enter and speak with you.'

The young sergeant-at-arms looked from Zurenne to Ilysh, leaving Zurenne unsure whom he was addressing. She also noticed his fleeting smile when he saw that Lysha was using the fern stone which he'd given her for a paperweight but that was a concern for another time.

'Who exactly do they ask for?'

'For you, my lady. For the Widow Halferan. But one is Madam Jilseth.' Reven was baffled. 'Why should she ask for permission?'

'On a horse?' Esnina's astonishment spoke for her mother and older sister. 'The lady wizard?'

Zurenne knew that every mage had to travel by such mundane means from time to time; Archmage Planir had explained that a wizard's magic could only revisit a place. But Jilseth had often appeared within Halferan's walls.

She gathered her wrap around her shoulders. 'Stay here with Raselle, Neeny.'

Maid and child were both sewing quietly in the window seat, making the most of the day's unseasonal sunshine. Raselle hemmed new chemises while Neeny laboriously embroidered a linen runner for her new bedroom's dressing table.

Ilysh was donning the shawl she'd draped over the back of her own chair. 'Madam Jilseth must have news from Col. Corrain—' She corrected herself. 'My husband the baron calculated that their ship should arrive there today or tomorrow. He said so in his letter from Claithe.'

'Sergeant.' Zurenne gave Reven a commanding nod. 'Lead on.'

She and Ilysh followed the young guardsman outside and down the great hall's steps. As they approached the gatehouse's shadowed archway, she saw the iron-bound oak gates standing open. Two horses waited patiently on the road outside.

Madam Jilseth looked remarkably uneasy on her mount. The wizard woman's companion sat equally stiffly in the saddle, gloved hands clutching the reins so tightly that the horse shook its head fretfully from side to side.

'Let the mare have her head, friend. She's not going anywhere.' Kusint was standing just outside the entrance.

Was this second visitor a man or a woman? Despite the twin blessings of sunlight and a windless day, the magewoman's fellow traveller's hood was pulled up. Zurenne could only see a closely wound scarf within, as though the rider was forcing a path though a mid-winter blizzard.

This visitor was a man, she decided. The rider was significantly taller than Jilseth and Zurenne couldn't imagine any woman with the breadth of shoulder apparent beneath the newcomer's voluminous cloak.

'Madam Jilseth, you and your companion are most welcome to Halferan. Please, enter and share some refreshment with us.'

As Zurenne held out a graciously inviting hand, Ilysh copied her gesture.

'Good day, Lady Zurenne, Lady Ilysh.' Jilseth made no move to urge her horse forward. 'May I make known to you Kheda of the Southern Reaches.'

'Good day to you.' Zurenne wasn't sure she'd heard the name correctly through the rustle of feathers and indignant cooing from the cloth-swathed box which the rider was cherishing on his saddle bow.

That posed another question. Why would the magewoman bring courier doves when her wizardry could carry her words across hundreds of leagues in an instant?

The rider put back his hood. Awkwardly, with one hand clutching his reins as well as steadying the dove cage, he unwound his scarf.

Lysha gasped and took a step backwards. Kusint swore in the Forest tongue and moved in front of both women, his hand going to his sword hilt.

Zurenne heard Reven yell an urgent summons. 'Halferan! Guards to the gate! All of you curs!'

The newcomer's skin was the rich chestnut of his horse's flank. An Archipelagan or a man of mixed blood? His eyes were leaf green and his close-clipped hair and beard were dark and wiry brown rather than the inky black of the Aldabreshin corsairs who had ravaged Halferan.

'Mama?' Ilysh breathed, pressing close to her mother's side for reassurance.

'Good day.' Zurenne heard her voice rise perilously high and swallowed hard. 'You are from Relshaz?'

She managed to speak loudly enough to be heard by the troopers rallying behind her.

'No, my lady.' The man raised his voice to be clearly heard within the manor's gates, calm and sonorous and speaking in precise and courtly Tormalin. 'I was born in the Daish domain of the southernmost Archipelago. I bring you greetings and good wishes from the wives of Khusro Rina.'

Zurenne couldn't think what to say, distracted by ominous murmuring from Reven and the troopers behind her, by Ilysh's trembling presence at her side, by Kusint's ferocious scowl as he looked to her for guidance.

'Velindre of Hadrumal vouches for Kheda of the Southern Reaches and I am here to guarantee both his good conduct and his personal safety.'

Jilseth's pointed words silenced the muttering guardsmen. Zurenne breathed a little more easily. Hopefully no man with the wits that Saedrin gave a blackbeetle would risk wizardly ire by attacking this unforeseen visitor, who was after all, unarmed. She could see no sword or dagger at the tall man's belt as he shrugged his shoulders free of his flowing cape.

She hastily gathered her wits. 'Kusint, please see that our visitors' horses are stabled and tended. Ask Mistress Rauffe to prepare two guest chambers.'

For one heart-stopping moment, she feared that Kusint would defy her, still standing squarely in the entrance. After a long moment, the Forest-born captain stepped backwards. He still made sure that he stood in front of Halferan's ladies as the stranger rode past with Jilseth.

'Sergeant Reven!' Zurenne clapped her hands to demand the gaping youth's attention. 'Send word to the kitchens. Ask Mistress Doratine to send a tisane tray and food for our guests to the muniment room's audience chamber.'

Reven took to his heels like a startled hare. Trimon only knew what rumours would go racing around the manor, Zurenne reflected, once Reven had told Doratine who had just ridden though Halferan's gates.

'Lady Ilysh.' She slipped her arm through the crook of her daughter's elbow.

Lysha lifted her chin and squared her shoulders, her father's determination reflected in her eyes.

Kusint walked on her other side, hand still on his sword hilt, watching as Jilseth and the newcomer dismounted and their horses were led away towards the stables.

'Mama—' Ilysh murmured as Linset and Weltray escorted the visitors towards the baronial tower.

'I know.' Zurenne walked more quickly. They reached the steps first, hurrying inside to the audience chamber. 'Raselle, take Neeny upstairs.'

'Why was the lady wizard on a horse?' Esnina jumped down from the window seat, her embroidery abandoned.

'I don't know, Neeny. Raselle, as quick as you can, if you please,' Zurenne urged from the doorway.

'Of course, my lady.' Flustered, the maid gathered up pin cushion and scissors, folding fine white fabric into her work basket.

'Neeny, hurry up!' Lysha wrapped her sister's needle case and silks in the creased and grubby runner.

'I'll do it!' Indignant, Esnina snatched at the embroidery, spilling the multi-coloured silks everywhere.

'Girls!' Zurenne's exasperation silenced whatever retort had been on tip of Ilysh's tongue.

After one look at her mother's face, Esnina dropped to her knees and swept up the fallen silks. Ilysh crouched low to help before ushering the little girl past their mother and into the hallway after Raselle.

Too late. Zurenne saw the maid halt with a stifled squeak of surprise. Esnina yelped and fled for her mother's skirts.

'It's all right, Neeny, truly it is.' Zurenne gathered her younger daughter close.

Neeny's nightmares of bloody havoc and incomprehensible death surrounding her had been painfully slow to fade. Zurenne had begun to despair of the child sleeping the night through without waking in floods of tears and urine-soaked bedding.

The newcomer, Kheda, instantly dropped down into a low crouch. Now his green gaze was on a level with Esnina's white-rimmed eyes.

'Good day to you, my lady. May I ask, what is your name?'

'This is Esnina.' Zurenne tightened her comforting grasp on Neeny's trembling shoulders. At least astonishment at hearing the man's courtly Tormalin had kept the child from outright hysteria. 'And this is Kheda—' she hesitated over his appellation, as meaningless to Neeny as it was to her. 'He's Madam Jilseth's friend.'

She saw Neeny look at the magewoman. Jilseth answered her with a reassuring smile. Zurenne felt her little daughter's shudders ease to wary stillness.

The tall man removed the cloth from the wooden-slatted cage he carried. 'Perhaps you can answer my question, my lady. Are the birds in your dove loft as white as mine?'

Esnina was surprised into a whisper, looking upwards to Zurenne. 'They look just the same, Mama.'

'Raselle, take Neeny upstairs.' Zurenne stooped to kiss the top of her child's head. 'I'll send to the kitchen to see what Doratine has been baking, sweetling. Now, be a good girl.'

Raselle stepped forward to take the child's hand and led her away towards the staircase. Kheda watched them go, waiting until the pair were well past the turn of the stair before standing up again.

Zurenne realised that he was even taller than Kusint. The Forest youth was still standing by the tower's entrance, glowering at the Aldabreshin man's back.

'Please, come in.' She gestured towards the audience chamber door.

The Archipelagan smiled as he shed his cloak. He wore a plain black doublet and breeches, his clothes and boots as creased and grimy as Corrain's had been on his return from Duryea. Zurenne wondered how long he had been travelling.

He draped the heavy cloth over one arm. 'Your small daughter, she is six or seven summers old?'

'Six.' Reminiscence softening the man's eyes piqued Zurenne's curiosity. 'Do you have children?'

He nodded. 'I do.'

Zurenne waited for him to say something further but nothing was forthcoming. She turned hastily and led the way through the anteroom into the audience chamber.

Ilysh was standing behind the long table, hands folded at her waist. 'Please take a seat.'

Zurenne wondered if anyone else heard the infinitesimal tremor in Lysha's words. She offered what reassurance she could in her smile as she joined her daughter.

'Thank you, Lady Ilysh, for your welcome to Halferan.' Jilseth pulled out chairs for herself and the Aldabreshi.

'You are always welcome, Madam Mage.' Ilysh sat down and glanced at her mother, her eyes beseeching her help.

'You said that you had news for us?' Taking the chair beside Lysha, Zurenne saw Kusint standing stony faced by the door. His eyes were still fixed on the Archipelagan and his hand rested on his sword despite the visitor's lack of weapons. 'From Col?'

'Not as yet,' Jilseth apologised. 'I can scry for Baron Corrain if you wish, though I am sure one of my fellow mages in the city would have alerted us if anything had befallen his ship.'

'Then what are you doing here?' Ilysh managed to ask with reasonable courtesy.

Jilseth looked at the Archipelagan Kheda. As he explained, his resonant voice was as sombre as his expression.

'As I believe you know, Aldabreshin traders in Relshaz have gone from refusing to do business with mainland merchants who have any dealings with wizards to stirring up the city's riff-raff to attack the wizards themselves. There are those in the Archipelago who would go further still. Some propose ending trade with the mainland, to remove any possible risk of magical attack, for whatever reason.'

'Planir is most concerned by the hostility to wizards now spreading on the mainland beyond Relshaz,' Jilseth interjected. 'He knows this will only worsen if Hadrumal is blamed for the wholesale ruination of trade with the Archipelago.'

'What has this to do with us?' Zurenne was as bemused as Ilysh.

Kheda leaned forward, resting muscular forearms on the table. 'Khusro Rina is a stargazer, revered far and wide throughout the Archipelago's northern and western reaches. He has seen ominous omens, warning of disaster ahead if a schism becomes established between the mainland and the Aldabreshi. His wives have resolved to do all they can to mend matters. They have decided that they must act before the spring seasons open the sea lanes to travel between the mainland and the Archipelago.'

'The northernmost domains, Jagai and Khusro, are sustained by trade with the mainland,' Jilseth added. 'They also profit from their dealings with the rest of the Archipelago since every warlord's galleys and triremes must use their sea lanes to reach Caladhrian waters before sailing onward to Relshaz or Col.'

'The warlord's wives?' Ilysh asked, wide-eyed. 'How many does he have?'

Kheda answered her. 'Debis Khusro born Debis Ikadi, Katel Khusro born Katel Strei, Patri Khusro born Patri Miris and Quilar Khusro born Quilar Vuld.'

Zurenne looked helplessly at Jilseth.

'A warlord's wives manage a domain's trade between them,' the magewoman explained. 'They have considerable power and influence, all the more so when the warlord is a recluse like Khusro Rina. These particular women are very well connected with influential domains across the western reaches and down into the heart of the Archipelago, through their own previous marriages and through their sisters and daughters.'

'Oh,' Zurenne said faintly.

She had only ever thought that Aldabreshin wives were little more than slaves, albeit dressed in silks and jewels, lounging in barbarian luxury until their husbands demanded carnal use of their bodies.

Of course, she reminded herself, over this past couple of years, she had learned that a great many things which she had believed were as false as a peddler's lead pennies.

'What do they want with us?' Ilysh was still astonished.

'Halferan suffered most grievously of all Caladhrians from the corsair raids,' Kheda continued. 'If the Khusro wives can establish ties of friendship with you noble ladies, that will prove that you do not hold every Archipelagan responsible for the raiders' crimes. Just as their friendship with you will demonstrate their own confidence that such ties to the mainland will not bring down undeserved wizardly wrath on their own domain.'

'Do they know—?' Zurenne looked uncertainly at Jilseth. Did this Aldabreshin envoy know of Halferan's involvement in the destruction of the corsairs' isle?

'Everyone in the Archipelago believes that the Archmage alone ordered the corsairs' destruction,' Jilseth said promptly, 'in retaliation for their threats to attack the mainland with the mage-crafted artefacts which they had looted from the mainland. The use of such artefacts is, of course, anathema to the Aldabreshi.'

Kheda's sardonic smile told Zurenne that he knew far more of the truth of the matter. 'The Khusro wives know that Halferan has ties to wizardry. They wish to reaffirm the long-held belief among the Aldabreshi that having dealings with those who have dealings with wizards does not see magic's contamination passing from hand to hand like some spotted fever. That principle has always underpinned our trade with the mainland. Without it?' He shook his head. 'There can be no renewal of trade with Relshaz.'

'Is no one standing up for the wizards in Relshaz? The ones who have been attacked?' Ilysh demanded, abruptly indignant.

Zurenne wondered why those wizards hadn't defended themselves as ably as Jilseth had defended Halferan.

The magewoman sighed as she answered Ilysh. 'The Archmage knows how easily retaliation or revenge will merely beget more violence. He has advised the mageborn to leave the city, for the time being.'

'But you have come here with Madam Jilseth,' Zurenne interrupted, looking at the man Kheda, 'and you say that you're Madam Velindre's friend. Why have you involved yourself with wizardry when your people abominate it so? Why are you not deemed contaminated with magic and anathema yourself?'

Kheda leaned back in his chair, glancing at Jilseth. At her nod, he looked back at Zurenne.

'I was born Daish Kheda in the southernmost reaches of the Archipelago. I was my father's chosen heir and ruled as warlord with absolute power of life and death over all those born within my domain. Ultimate responsibility for their safety and well-being was my burden. A handful of years ago, my own islands and our neighbouring domains were attacked with wizardry—' He held up a hand to silence Ilysh's exclamation in unconsciously fatherly fashion.

'Not magic from Hadrumal, nor by any mage from the mainland. There are lands half a season's sailing beyond the western seas where the most savage wizardry lurks, born of dragons and those who worship them.

'We could not withstand their attacks,' he told Zurenne grimly. 'Islands burned and innocents died, men, women and children, in their tens and hundreds. I sought out magic to defeat them. There are times when one can only fight fire with fire. That's how I met Velindre. My exile from my home was the price which I must pay to secure my wives and children's safety along with the lives and livelihoods of those whom I had been raised to rule and to serve. I am more than willing to make that trade.'

Zurenne saw the light of truth in his green eyes. She still suspected this was far from the whole truth.

'I have seen more vile and destructive magic than you can ever imagine,' Kheda assured her, grim faced. 'Viciousness loosed on those who have done nothing to deserve such attack. Believe me, my lady, no matter how grievously your own lands and people may have suffered at the hands of that Mandarkin wizard, I have seen far worse.'

He leaned forward once again, looking across the table at Zurenne with frightening intensity.

'I will do all that I can to restore peaceful relations between the mainland and the Archipelago, in order that Hadrumal has no reason to turn the wrath that destroyed the corsairs on any other warlord's domain. More than that, I wish to keep Hadrumal in my debt, in case those savage mages who worship dragons beyond the western seas ever return. Then I will call on those wizards whom I trust to save my people, even if my fellow Aldabreshi would kill me for doing so.'

'But what has this to do with Halferan?' Zurenne persisted.

Jilseth hesitated before replying. 'You know of the ensorcelled artefacts which the Mandarkin mage Anskal uncovered among the corsairs' loot.'

'Of course.' Zurenne tried to shrug off the frightening memory of the repellent wizard's appearance in the manor's very hall, threatening her and Ilysh both if they didn't hand over their bespelled pendants.

Kheda nodded grimly. 'The Khusro wives are sorely distressed by the possibility that they may have such trinkets imbued with magic in their own strong rooms, unbeknownst to their lord. They seek to rid the Khusro domain of such perilous things as swiftly as they can, most especially under the current ominous stars. But they have no way of telling honest treasures from corrupt.'

Kusint broke his silence by the door with a muttered oath in the Forest tongue. Seeing Zurenne's displeasure, he ducked his head in mute apology.

Zurenne narrowed her eyes at Jilseth. 'What are you proposing?'

Now Hadrumal's involvement made sense. The Archmage couldn't possibly pass up an opportunity to get his hands on yet more of these magical treasures. Zurenne remembered what Corrain had told her of the assembled wizards' avid interest in the Mandarkin's discoveries, when he had been in Hadrumal watching the Archmage plan his attack on the corsairs.

'Kheda has promised the Khusro wives that you are entirely trustworthy.' Jilseth smiled confidingly. 'Just as Velindre has promised Kheda that she has every confidence in your discretion.'

'I'm honoured, I'm sure,' Zurenne said with growing apprehension.

'Kheda has assured the Khusro wives that you will deal honestly with them, if they bring their treasures here so that a mage such as myself can remove anything tainted by magic. No wizard can go to the Archipelago,' Jilseth pointed out. 'Magic and mageborn alike are forbidden there on pain of death.'

Besides, if this business is transacted here, Planir has every reason to believe that no one else will know of it, not mageborn or mainlander, Zurenne thought silently. This will be one more secret which I'm keeping to ensure that he keeps my beloved husband's fatal folly hidden, as well as Corrain's madness in bringing that Mandarkin mage to Halferan.

'The Khusro wives would far rather deal with another woman who will neither seek to overrule them nor cheat them,' Kheda added. 'They know full well that the mainlanders have no true understanding of Aldabreshin custom and law. If this were any other domain, the warlord himself would doubtless deal with the mainland's barons, man to man, in keeping with mainland practise.' He shrugged. 'But Khusro Rina is a recluse.'

Zurenne gave up trying to fathom the mysteries of Archipelagan thinking. Her attention had fastened on the most impossible aspect of Jilseth's proposal.

'The Khusro wives intend to bring their treasures here? They wish to come to Halferan?'

At her side, Ilysh gasped and over by the door, Kusint barely swallowed another Forest curse.

'Coming here demonstrates their trust in you,' Jilseth said quickly. 'At the same time, their presence will safeguard such wealth being carried back and forth.'

'They would be failing in their duty to Khusro domain to do otherwise,' Kheda agreed.

'So some great cavalcade of Archipelagan wagons and swordsmen would arrive at our gates?'

Zurenne didn't want to imagine it. She could all too readily imagine Baron Karpis and his troopers and any number of other brigands waylaying such travellers on their journey across Caladhria. Not to mention panic-stricken yeomen and villagers attacking them with mattocks and scythes and any other tools they had to hand. After the travails of recent years, anyone with skin as brown as this man Kheda's risked being cut down or strung up on sight.

'When Halferan would be responsible for their safety and their strong boxes?' She shook her head in absolute denial. 'No. We will not countenance it.'

Jilseth and Kheda exchanged a long, calculating look. Zurenne clenched her fists in her lap, hidden by the table top.

'We realise that we are asking a great deal of you,' Jilseth began carefully.

'You know that the Archipelagans do not use gold and silver coin as you do?' Kheda waited for Zurenne's reluctant nod before he continued.

'Instead we endeavour to trade something of equal value for goods or favours. The Khusro wives wish to offer you a service which they believe you will value sufficiently, to recompense you for this help which they seek.'

Once again, his intensity sent a shiver down Zurenne's spine. 'What could this offer possibly be?'

'The corsairs enslaved many more of Halferan's men than Captain Corrain and the boy Hosh.' Kheda looked steadily at her. 'The Khusro wives have been trading across the Archipelago to find them, or at least, to discover their fates. Help them rid their domain of these magically tainted treasures and they will restore those of your men who still live and offer what news they can find, to console the families of the ones who have died.'

'Oh!' Ilysh pressed shocked hands to her ashen cheeks.

Kusint was halfway across the room in three long strides.

Zurenne turned a searing look on Jilseth. Before she could utter the accusations boiling up in her throat, a devastating crash deafened them all.

Doratine stood in the antechamber doorway. A tray lay at her feet amid shining splinters of glass and the glazed shards of the manor's finest plates. Hot water puddled on the floorboards and steam rose from the cook's splashed apron, smudged with tisane herbs strewn far and wide. Pastries rich with precious honey and hoarded fruit were rolled across the floor.

If her ankles had been scalded, Doratine gave no sign of it. She was staring at Zurenne. 'Oh, my lady,' she gasped before looking down at the catastrophe around her feet. 'Oh, Saedrin save us!'

Before Zurenne could say anything to stop her, before Kusint could retrace his steps, Doratine had fled.

Now Zurenne pressed her hands to her face, eyes tight closed as Neeny's denying a nightmare. But here could be no denying what had just happened.

There could be no doubt that the cook had heard the Archipelagan's offer. Now there could be no possibility of Zurenne denying these Khusro wives the help which they asked for, once Doratine's news had spread around the manor, the village and the demesne beyond.

She opened her eyes and looked at Jilseth. She fought to look at the magewoman without trembling, stiff-backed as the chair she sat upon.

'I will require Baron Halferan's permission before I can agree to any such thing. I must speak to him, as you promised, through one of your fellow mages in Col.'

'Of course,' Jilseth assured her. 'As soon as he has arrived in the city and made himself known to my colleague.'

Zurenne nodded. Truth be told, she quaked at the thought of telling Corrain what the Archipelagan had just asked of Halferan.

Another suspicion chilled her. Was this why Planir had insisted that Corrain and no other must accompany Hosh to Col? To get him away from Halferan before this Aldabreshin Kheda arrived to make this offer which gave her no choice at all? Was this more of Planir's connivance?

She looked searchingly at Jilseth. When had a mage ever come to Halferan without some hidden purpose, serving the wizard isle's interests first and foremost?

— CHAPTER FIFTEEN —

Trydek's Hall, Hadrumal
30th of Aft-Winter

MAGELIGHT FADED AND Jilseth felt the flagstones of Trydek's Hall under her feet. The tolling of the tongueless Council bell shivered through her bones. She had heard that magewrought summons beginning when Planir had just bespoken her, to warn her that he was about to summon Hadrumal's eminent mages to an early morning gathering. Archmage Trydek's ancient spells ensured that no Council member could ignore the bell's voice, just as no lesser wizard could waken it.

Planir was on the lofty dais, standing beside the high table. The ancient hall was deserted but for the two of them. The portraits of long dead archmages gazed down on empty tables and benches; not even the hall's servants had risen yet, to serve their resident mages, pupils and apprentices breakfast.

Like the archmages of old, Planir wore a broad shouldered mantle over a long, high-collared tunic, all in unrelieved black save for the gems of wizardry surrounding the diamond in his ring of office. Every painted archmage wore the self-same ring.

'Has our friend Kheda passed his first night in Halferan without incident?'

'He has.' The Council bell tolled again, warning Jilseth to speak quickly even though the Council Chamber was close by, built alongside this oldest of Hadrumal's halls. 'He has sent a courier dove to the Khusro wives, telling them to take ship for Claithe.'

'Lady Zurenne agreed, even though Olved was unable to find Corrain in Col last night?' Planir looked impressed.

'She did.' Jilseth coloured. 'Though she made it clear that she suspected one of us was deceiving her. Was Olved lying to me?' she asked bluntly.

She hadn't particularly warmed to the Col mage, when she had gone to the city ten days ago to inform him of the Archmage's instructions and to scry out Corrain herself, to show Olved who he would be looking for.

Olved had assumed that she knew nothing of Col or its people or customs. He persisted, even after Jilseth had mentioned her previous visits to Col, to use its libraries or tracing rumours of renegade wizardry or untrained mageborn on the Archmage's behalf. How else did the wizard imagine that her magic had been able to carry her there?

'No,' Planir assured her. 'He scried out their ship's arrival and sent notes to the inn where he saw them take lodgings and to Mentor Garewin besides. It's Corrain who's chosen not to answer him.'

The Archmage shrugged. 'Let's see what lesson the noble Baron learns, when he hears the news we wished to give him from Halferan.'

The penetrating bell sounded again.

'Archmage?' Jilseth didn't move. 'Why summon the Council so early? Isn't every wizard in Hadrumal exhausted?'

Surely the ill-tempered mages would be more inclined to argue than to agree to anything?

Planir walked down the narrow steps at the side of

the dais. 'Have you ever had a mount bolt under you, when you've been travelling by horseback?'

'No.' Jilseth sincerely hoped she never would.

'Short of letting the beast carry you over a cliff, your best course will be to hold on tight and let it run itself out,' the Archmage advised as he continued towards the door at the far end of the hall. 'Then you'll find it much more amenable to doing as you wish.'

Jilseth followed and then waited at the top of the steps, the bulk of the hall behind her, between the Council Chamber and Hadrumal's high road. She studied the mages on their way to the Council Chamber in the cold, grey light.

Their faces were taut and weary. Jilseth also noted the silence as the first wizards to arrive went up the staircase to the Council Chamber's metal-bound door. Conversation and speculation usually echoed back from the ceiling's curved vault, whether whispered or incautiously, or perhaps deliberately, loud.

When a meeting had long been agreed, mages invariably sought their fellow councillors' opinions on the topic for debate. When they were summoned unexpectedly, speculation could reach the wildest surmise between the lowest step and the topmost. This morning it seemed that no one knew, or wished to guess, what this meeting was about.

Jilseth caught sight of Canfor's prematurely white hair heading up the stairs. He was as silent as the rest and looking straight ahead. She would have been expecting him to be glancing this way and that, noting which wizards were present and which Council members had sent a proxy. There were, she observed, very few proxies arriving this morning.

She joined the last of the mages answering the bell's

summons. As she reached the Council chamber, she saw that Canfor had claimed a visitors' seat to the offhand side of the door. Ely and Galen flanked him, both looking intently over towards Despin who was sitting hunched in his Council chair.

Hearth Master Kalion had already taken his own seat of honour in its ancient niche on the far side of the circular, high-vaulted room. His heavily jowled face sagged with weariness and dissatisfaction. So his chosen nexus had had no more success than anyone else in cracking an ensorcelled artefact's secrets.

Not that Jilseth was inclined to gloat. She had been forced to abandon her hopes of cracking that arm-ring's secrets as the Archmage had sent her to Relshaz, to deliver Velindre's letters, to follow the magewoman's subsequent instructions and to meet up with the Archipelagan Kheda, before escorting him to Halferan.

Nolyen, Tornauld and Merenel had continued without her. Gedart had taken her place and he had been studying in Suthyfer under Usara, a mage widely expected to succeed Planir as Stone Master. Regardless, the change in their nexus had won no tangible results.

'Jilseth.'

Velindre and Mellitha sat on the other side of the door, an empty chair between them. Both women looked even more short of sleep than the Archmage.

'Join us.'

Jilseth accepted the invitation, looking across the council chamber to Planir, now sitting silent in the Archmage's carved seat, his expression unreadable.

Almost all the seats were taken now. Cloud Master Rafrid was talking in a low tone to his neighbour. Troanna's chair remained vacant.

'What do you suppose has delayed the Flood Mistress?' she asked Mellitha discreetly.

The elegant magewoman snorted gracelessly. 'Yet another futile attempt to unmake some ensorcelled artefact?'

Nolyen had told Jilseth that Troanna made no secret of her intention to learn how to destroy such things. She had reminded the mages who shared her affinity of her authority over them, commanding that they reveal any insight or understanding which might further her endeavours.

What did Planir think of that? Jilseth's gaze circled back to the Archmage. He showed no sign of weariness, despite the spreading silver at the temples of his short cropped dark hair or the deepening lines at the corners of his eyes and his bearded mouth.

A frisson ran around the room as Planir gestured towards the entrance. The door's metal fittings flowed into an unyielding sheet of metal sealing everyone inside the chamber.

Jilseth breathed a little more easily. Equally impenetrable spells would protect the Council from any Soluran scrying. Like every pupil mage, she had tested her own skills against that challenge. She had failed, just like everyone else who admitted to doing the same in that first rush of arrogance which followed their elevation from mere apprenticeship.

Though scrying was water magic and Flood Mistress Troanna was the foremost practitioner of that affinity in the past handful of generations. Unlike the Solurans, she had quintessential magic within her grasp. Was she absent because she had found some way through the ancient, arcane wizardry, to learn what was said here this morning?

Jilseth slid a sideways glance at Mellitha. Given her abiding dislike of Troanna, Mellitha would surely be alert for such a possibility. Before she could whisper a question though, Planir stood up and strode to the round stone platform in the middle of the room.

'Good day to you all. Who would like to share some revelation as to the nature of the artefacts we are studying?'

No one spoke or raised a hand. Expressions around the room varied from veiled irritability to barely concealed anger.

Planir grimaced. 'My sympathies. I have nothing of any significance to report.'

Sannin raised her hand, sitting elegant and composed in her own council seat. If any shadows darkened the scarlet-gowned magewoman's eyes, her immaculate cosmetics concealed them. She rose gracefully as the Archmage acknowledged her.

'How much longer must we exert ourselves to so little purpose? We have other calls on our time, not least our responsibilities to our pupils.'

As Planir glanced around the chamber, Jilseth saw a growing number of mages inclined to agree.

'Please.' Planir's nod invited Nicasis to speak.

'We cannot expect our pupils to continue to instruct our halls' apprentices without our guidance,' he asserted with an emphatic shake of his head, 'still less to keep this recent influx of mageborn arrivals from the usual mischief or folly.'

'What of our obligations to future generations of mages? To bequeath them the secrets of this wizardry?' Vedral sprang to his feet. Always careless of his appearance, the wizard didn't look as though he had shaved or bathed since the bespelled artefacts had first come to Hadrumal.

'How can we turn away from such a challenge?' He appealed to the entire Council with outstretched hands. 'Never mind any significant discovery. Has anyone at least discerned something new, however trivial? Share it and perhaps that will be the spark to the tinder of someone else's insights?'

As Vedral's voice broke to betray his desperation, Jilseth noted that many other mages still found the notion of abandoning the challenge of the artefacts intolerable. She glanced upwards to the sphere of magelight hovering high in the windowless chamber's domed vault.

There would be protracted struggle when those in favour of giving up their current endeavours sought to dim the magelight while those opposed bolstered it. Each side's conviction would bolster their wizardry; Trydek had considered a mere show of hands insufficient for Hadrumal's purposes.

Everyone looked at the Archmage, waiting for his response. He turned slowly on the central platform, looking around the chamber.

'I am mindful of our obligation to wizards yet unborn, just as I am well aware that we cannot sustain our current commitment to the study of these artefacts. We risk failing in our duty to those who need our guidance through the hazards of their unsought, inborn affinity.' Planir paused, reflective. 'Perhaps it is time to look beyond our own shores.'

'To Solura?' Kalion couldn't help glancing triumphantly at Troanna's empty seat.

Planir shook his head. 'I was thinking more of Col.'

'Col?' The Hearth Master stared at him, astonished.

'I have had a good many enquiries from our fellow wizards, from as far afield as Selerima and Inglis.'

Addressing the whole Council, Planir smiled ruefully. 'News of the recent upheavals in the Archipelago hasn't only spread far and fast among those guild masters and petty lordlings who now long to get hold of a bespelled blade which can cut through steel or obtain a ring to allow them to pass unseen on their way to their lover's bed.'

The ripple of weary laughter around the chamber told Jilseth which mages had heard those same tavern ballads as she had and who, clearly bemused, had never encountered such mainland tales.

'Col?' Vedral was on his feet again, his voice ragged with anger. 'Any curiosity there is prompted by Solura's mages!'

Planir nodded. 'Various Soluran Orders of Wizardry have long-established ties with Col's university—'

'Always wheedling for Hadrumal's lore,' Vedral snarled. 'You may be willing to yield the secrets of quintessential magic in return for Soluran insights into magecrafting artefacts but this Council will never consent!' He sat down heavily, shaking his head in vehement denial.

Looking around the chamber Jilseth saw that opposition to sharing nexus magic with the Solurans would certainly prevail. Hearth Master Kalion's face sagged, betraying his disappointment.

'I have not made any such proposal, Master Vedral,' Planir pointed out with stern courtesy.

'We cannot contemplate any such trade.' Rafrid stood, shoving his hands in his breeches' pockets, cobalt tunic carelessly askew and unlaced at the neck. 'We know full well that the Solurans would use quintessential magic against their Mandarkin foes. Indeed, I would wager that they'd do so sooner rather than later. That renegade Anskal cannot have been the only wizard sent scouting south of the mountains with swordsmen at his side last autumn. As soon as the spring weather allows, I'll wager good gold that either the Mandarkin will attack in force or the Solurans will take the fight to them, in hopes of cutting their enemy down before they can draw their swords.

'If they have quintessential magic to use, once the summer sees traders coming through the Great Forest to Selerima, such news will follow their wagons and mules to every other town in Ensaimin.' The Cloud Master shook his head. 'The mainlanders are already fretting like hens who've caught the scent of a fox, for fear of unbridled wizardry let loose among them. I take it we've all heard of this recent law passed by Caladhria's parliament? The Lescari lawgivers are discussing much the same proposals, and of course we know of the antagonism towards mages in Relshaz.' He acknowledged Mellitha with a courteous bow.

'Antagonism? Antagonism wasn't the death of Kerrit Osier!' Okeal stood up without seeking any permission from Planir or her Cloud Master.

Jilseth couldn't remember when the reserved magewoman had last spoken in the Council chamber, despite the widespread respect she commanded, most particularly for her proficiencies with invisibility and concealment magics.

'He was murdered, plain and simple.' Okeal was enraged. 'When will the guilty of Relshaz answer for it, Archmage? We have let this offence go unpunished for too long!'

She shot a fulminating look of accusation at both Mellitha and Velindre. The blonde magewoman instantly stood to answer.

'What would you have had us do? Raze the city to rubble with hurricane winds? Summon a high tide to flood the ruins for good measure? How many innocents would you see killed alongside the guilty?'

'How many more enemies would that have won us on the mainland?' Still in her seat, Mellitha asked Okeal coldly, 'How many more of Hadrumal's innocents do you wish to see suffer the same undeserved fate as Kerrit? How—'

The sharp rap of an iron-shod walking stick on the flagstones cut her short.

Planir inclined his head. 'Master Massial, please remain seated.'

'Thank you, I will.' The venerable wizard clearly had no intention of troubling to stand. He narrowed his faded eyes as he looked at the Archmage before turning his scathing gaze on Kalion.

'You have, both of you, promoted Hadrumal's involvement with the mainland for nigh on half a generation. You, Hearth Master, have sought to ingratiate yourself with the noble born from the Tormalin Emperors down—' he switched his attention back from Kalion to Planir '—while you have encouraged those unfit for the rigours of a life of scholarship in Hadrumal to insinuate their trivial wizardry into the daily lives of the humble from east to west and north to south.'

He shook his white head in disgust. 'Now you have an innocent mage's blood on your hands, both of you. Yet you cannot make the guilty pay without provoking more violence. Hasn't the time now come to acknowledge your folly and withdraw from these pointless endeavours?' he demanded. 'Hadrumal is the only safe haven for wizardry, as Archmage Trydek knew full well thirty generations ago.'

'The mundane born have always feared us.' A

diminutive magewoman spoke up, older even than Massial and huddled in her chair, heavily cloaked against the winter's chilly fogs wreathing Hadrumal's towers.

'They know they are our inferiors. Once they acknowledge that fact, they can only live in terror of a day when we might choose to assert our authority. They are too ignorant of magecraft to realise that no wizard worth a seat in this council would ever waste their time seeking such trivial, transitory power.' Her reedy tones grew shrill with contempt. 'We would be better served to have nothing more to do with the mainland beyond the most trivial transactions.'

'Madam Shannet, with the sincerest respect—' keeping his tone civil visibly cost Kalion more effort than rising to his feet '—it has been ignorance of wizardry which has prompted violence against the innocent mageborn in past generations. The better understanding fostered by my own endeavours, and the Archmage's efforts,' he acknowledged tightly, 'has seen safe conduct to Hadrumal become accepted custom and practice for those caught unawares by their affinity's manifestation—'

'It was not ignorance of magecraft that saw Master Kerrit beaten so viciously,' Massial retorted scornfully. 'It was that Mandarkin renegade's display of unbridled magecraft wielded against the Archipelagans. Fear of that has infected Relshaz. How far will that contagion spread? Wizardry will be far better served by a period of complete withdrawal to our own shores.'

He emphasized his words with another rap of his walking stick on the floor, regarding Kalion with barely veiled disfavour. 'These whom you have so assiduously courted have grown accustomed to wizardry serving their interests. Let them discover how they fare without such conveniences. Perhaps if storms wreck enough Relshazri ships for lack of timely warning, the Magistrates will deliver up those who murdered Kerrit to Hadrumal's justice.'

'What of those mainland mageborn left to the dubious mercies of those encouraged to fear them by rumour and falsehood, while we stay safe on our island? No.' Kalion shook his head emphatically. 'Wizardry will be far better served by reminding the mainland's rulers, from the Emperor of Tormalin down, of the good which wizardry can offer them, not least to see their ships safely to Kellarin.'

Jilseth was relieved to see that a clear majority of the Council looked inclined to side with the Hearth Master rather than with the two venerable old wizards.

'I have had some other news from Col,' Planir said thoughtfully. 'It seems that some of Tormalin's princes have sought introductions to Solura's wizards.'

'What?' Kalion stared at Planir, aghast.

Jilseth saw equal disquiet all around the chamber.

'They believe they will soothe Aldabreshin outrage over the corsair island's fate if they distance themselves from Hadrumal,' the Archmage explained. 'Then Tormalin's noble houses believe that their merchants will be able to trade as usual when Archipelagan sailings resume with the spring. However, since they will still need magecraft to see their ships safely over the eastern ocean, they seek such aid from Solura.'

'Then they don't understand the Aldabreshi,' Velindre said crisply. 'Magic is an abomination in the Archipelago, whatever its origin.'

'But by the time Tormalin's princes discover their mistake, they will have forged ties with Soluran Orders.' Kalion's brow furrowed.

'Solura's wizards can have scant experience in guiding ships through ocean currents and storms,' Rafrid assured him. 'The eastern ocean is very different to the western coastal sea. Besides, I cannot see their Elders giving Soluran mages leave to travel so far from home, not with Mandarkin forces poised to renew their attacks. The lords to whom the Orders owe their fealty will forbid it, as will King Solquen.'

'What could the Tormalin princes have to offer the Soluran Orders?' Velindre interjected. 'They have no magical secrets to trade.'

'I cannot see the Tormalin Emperor permitting Soluran interests to secure any lasting stake in Kellarin,' Mellitha observed.

'No lasting stake perhaps, but faced with the immediate challenge of saving his noble princes' ships from sinking?' Sannin rose to her feet with a rustle of scarlet silk. 'I can see Tadriol the Provident coming to some agreement with the first Soluran Order able to offer at least some assistance. Then I would imagine Tadriol, or more likely his spymaster the Sieur Den Dalderin, will invite us to offer the Empire some inducement to prevent that arrangement becoming permanent.'

'You think this Council will go cap in hand to Tormalin's Emperor, begging to use Hadrumal's magic in his service?' Vedral sprang to his feet, furious.

'No,' Sannin retorted, scornful, 'but I think it highly likely that Emperor Tadriol and the Convocation of Princes will look long and hard for some way to secure their own advantage in this current crisis. We know how many noble Houses long to see Hadrumal yield to Imperial authority, just as Soluran wizards swear fealty to their liege lords.'

'This Council yields to no one,' Vedral snarled.

'Indeed,' Planir agreed. 'So shall we steer a middle course? We can let the Tormalin princes play out their game with the Solurans while we encourage the mainland's mages to withdraw to Hadrumal for the next season or so. That should be long enough for the mundane born, from humblest to most noble, to realise how inconvenient they would find a permanent lack of magecraft to call on. Meantime, the memory of the corsairs' fate should remain fresh enough in their minds to curb any brutality towards the innocent mageborn.'

'That would seem reasonable enough,' Cloud Master Rafrid said cautiously.

Massial's snort of disdain rose to the domed vault to meet Shannet's contemptuous cackle.

'Where are these mainland mages supposed to sleep, Archmage?' Okeal asked acidly. 'Hiwan's Hall is struggling to find room for our current apprentices and more mageborn wash up with every tide.'

'Wellery's Hall is similarly hard pressed,' Herion reluctantly agreed.

Planir nodded. 'As are we in Trydek's own hall.'

Weariness hung heavily in the air as the Council Chamber fell silent.

'Shall we seek assistance from our fellow wizards in Suthyfer?' the Archmage said a moment later. 'I can bespeak Master Usara and Master Shivvalan, to ask how many mainland mageborn might find a temporary home in their islands. Perhaps you could all consider which of your apprentices and pupils might benefit from a change of scene and fresh challenges? Some of Suthyfer's mages might wish to come and join us in unravelling the magecrafting of these artefacts.'

'Their studies have followed different paths to our

own for these past few years,' Sannin observed. 'They may even see some new route to understanding the Mandarkin's plunder.'

'No ensorcelled artefacts should be removed to Suthyfer,' Vedral said quickly, poised to rise to his feet once again. 'Let their mages come here to learn what we have already tried, to save them from treading the same fruitless paths.'

'Quite so,' Sannin smiled, agreed. 'We must safeguard such treasures. While I trust Master Usara implicitly, strangers and travellers constantly come and go in Suthyfer, crossing from Tormalin to Kellarin and back again. At very least, word of such studies among the islands' wizards would soon reach the Sieur Den Dalderin through one of his enquiry agents.'

Looking around the chamber, Jilseth saw that the Council was now united. Those wizards intent on studying the artefacts could hope for fresh perspectives to spur them on while those ready to abandon the quest could allow Suthyfer's wizards to take up the challenge with a clear conscience.

She made certain that her expression didn't betray the least amusement as she realised how skilfully the Archmage and his allies had brought the Council to the conclusion he had wanted from the start. No wonder Planir was such an expert player of white raven.

Even Kalion kept his peace, though he glowered darkly from his carved seat. The Hearth Master had never made any secret of his opposition to allowing those wizards who decided they were ill-suited to Hadrumal's disciplines to set up their own haven in the mid-ocean islands.

Then Rafrid rose to his feet, surprising everyone.

'Surely Suthyfer's mages should continue to assist any ships crossing the ocean. Those building a new life in

Kellarin hardly deserve being abandoned to their fate. While we can hope that no captain would be foolhardy enough to attempt a winter crossing without a wizard on board, some will assuredly attempt the journey once the spring equinox is past. In theory it's possible to cross the ocean without our help in favourable weather. I don't believe it will possibly help Hadrumal's cause if we are responsible, even indirectly, for innocents drowning for lack of our help.'

As the assembled mages nodded, Jilseth saw more than a few were ashamed to realise that such inevitable deaths hadn't occurred to them.

Kalion's expression lightened a little and he swiftly stood up. 'Such a gesture of goodwill should make restoring good relations with the mainland's rulers and lawmakers much easier, once they have come to fully appreciate the difficulties which they will face should wizardry withdraw to Hadrumal entirely.'

'Very well, then we will remind those responsible for justice and good order across Tormalin that we still look to them to safeguard the newly discovered mageborn and see them safely to Hadrumal,' the Archmage said sternly. 'We will make it clear that Suthyfer's mages' continued assistance depends on those seeking apprenticeship here arriving safely from Lescar, Dalasor and Gidesta, Caladhria and Ensaimin. Let those who might think otherwise argue with Emperor Tadriol and Toremal's legions.'

Planir looked around the chamber. 'Please indicate your accord or dissent with these proposals.'

As the wizards sent shafts of magelight soaring upwards, the hovering sphere of radiance swiftly brightened to unanimity.

'Very well, we are agreed.' Planir gestured at the door

and the magical wards enclosing the chamber melted away. The door swung open, with no sign that it was anything more than commonplace iron-bound wood.

Ely, Galen and Canfor hurried over to join Kalion, and the four of them left, deep in conversation. Despin trailed along behind, avoiding Jilseth's gaze.

She stayed seated, waiting for the chamber to empty and watching Mellitha talking to Herion while Velindre accosted Rafrid. Sannin was talking to the Archmage and Okeal.

Planir left the two magewomen to their conversation. Jilseth stood up as he approached the door.

'What do you want me to do now, Archmage?'

Planir halted, rubbing a hand over his bearded chin. Jilseth was surprised to see him looking suddenly exhausted.

'Do you have any notion how we might distract Emperor Tadriol and the Sieur Den Dalderin from courting Solura's mages? I—' Breaking off, the Archmage turned to look at Velindre and Mellitha. 'Never mind. I think I may have an idea.'

He looked back at Jilseth. 'It will be a day or so before Kheda returns to Halferan with the Khusro wives. Please could you visit Col, to see if Master Olved has heard any rumour of Tormalin visitors enquiring after Soluran wizards visiting the university?'

Now the Archmage betrayed his exasperation. 'You might also let me know if Captain Corrain has deigned to answer Olved's summons as yet, to tell us what he has heard around the taverns and taprooms.'

'Do you want me to go and find Corrain myself?' Jilseth offered.

'No.' Planir shook his head. 'The noble baron needs to learn the cost of ignoring my messages.'

— CHAPTER SIXTEEN —

The Red Library, Col
30th of Aft-Winter

'THERE'S MASTER GAREWIN,' Hosh stopped rubbing at the side of his face to look apprehensively at the mentor.

Now they were finally here, Corrain was beginning to fear that the boy was having second thoughts about submitting himself to this unknown aetheric magic. In his heart of hearts, he could hardly blame Hosh for being nervous. But it was his duty to see the lad healed despite himself.

'Excellent.' He raised his own hand to acknowledge the scholar strolling towards this imposing building across another of Col's broad squares.

The paved expanse was similarly ringed by taverns and inns. Here awnings outside each hostelry sheltered benches and tables where breakfasting students ate griddle-seared flatbreads, pale cheeses oozing out of floury rinds and the pungent fish that was so popular here, smoked or pickled. Potboys set down jugs of small beer and well-watered wine while kitchen maids brought out stacks of fresh horn beakers and carried away abandoned plates.

Corrain noticed several hopeful cats prowling the empty spaces dividing each tavern's territory from its neighbours. One ginger-striped opportunist darted forward as a careless elbow knocked scraps off a table.

The previous day Hosh had retreated to their bedchamber as soon as The Goose Hounds' maids had it ready. Corrain had lingered in the taproom, leaning on the bar counter and chatting to the tapster whenever the man had some leisure between customers. The tapster had obliged him with a great deal of information about Col, most particularly the university's libraries.

Corrain had been somewhat surprised to learn that the various schools of study to which the mentors swore their allegiance had no tangible presence in the city. There were no magnificent buildings with the various disciplines' names chiselled above a door for newly-arrived students to knock on. The mentors who made up the Schools taught their pupils in the various libraries as well as in the taverns and tisane houses. In the summer seasons, they gathered out in the open air in the city's pleasure gardens.

'Excuse me.' A student carrying books lashed together with a plaited leather thong hurried up the steep steps to the library door.

Corrain turned to watch the youth set down his burden and show a student's base-metal badge on the collar before shedding his cloak. After looking the boy up and down, the stern-faced and sword-belted door-ward gave him a grudging nod. Draping his cloak loosely around his shoulders, the youth joined the queue already lengthening by the doors.

'Good day to you.' Mentor Garewin reached them as the carillon's song announced the second chime of the day beneath the leaden sky. 'Larasion's still smiling, I see? Six days without rain at this season is truly an unlooked-for blessing.'

'Indeed.' Corrain managed a polite smile, though he found the Col populace's fascination with their weather as pointless as it was tedious. It would rain or it wouldn't and whichever way that rune rolled, he wouldn't thank any goddess.

'They said, in the tavern this morning, that this has been the mildest Aft-Winter in half a generation.' Hosh was rubbing at his face again, as unthinking as a man scratching a itch.

'Indeed?' Garewin drew his silvered beard to a point between fingers and thumb. 'I must ask my acquaintances in the School of Natural Philosophy.'

Corrain curbed an urge to demand some answers himself. How soon would Hosh see some visible improvement to his injuries?

But Hosh was more curious about the students, men and women, young and old, waiting by the library doors. 'Why are they searched like some assassin trying to smuggle in a dagger to kill the Tormalin Emperor?'

Mentor Garewin smiled, amused. 'The Prefects make certain that no student enters any of the city's libraries with something which might damage the books and the knowledge which they contain.'

'How many books are in there?' Hosh stared up at the red-brick building, five storeys tall not counting the garrets beneath the curly-gabled roof. Each floor was well lit by wide, stone-mullioned windows.

'I honestly couldn't guess,' Mentor Garewin admitted with refreshing candour. 'This is the oldest of Col's libraries, a hundred strides wide and two hundred long. Each floor has ten reading rooms, running the width of the building, each one furnished with reading desks. Then there are private studies flanking the staircases in each corner of the building, reserved for those of us with the rank of mentor.' He glanced with some pride at the solitary silver ring on his off hand. 'We'll have our pick of them, so early in the day.'

He glanced at Corrain to include him in this lesson. 'The Red Library was founded by the first avowed scholars who found common cause in this city. They were desperate to salvage what writings they could from the region's temple libraries and shrine family archives when the fall of the Old Tormalin Empire ushered in an age of mindless plundering and despoliation.

'But let us go in, before the rush,' the mentor hastily suggested to Hosh.

All around the square, wood scraped on brick paviours as the carillon's intricate song faded away across the city's rooftops. Students abandoned their meals, leaving tables and benches awry. A handful more black-liveried and white gloved door-wards emerged from the library to form a resolute line guarding the doors, even as those who had already submitted to the Prefects' scrutiny were allowed to enter.

'Mentor Undil will be joining us,' Garewin told Hosh. 'She is sealed to the School of Apothecaries.'

'Will you be here all day?' Corrain asked the mentor.

'We will,' Garewin answered before smiling at Hosh. 'Now let's make a start, shall we?'

Corrain clapped Hosh on the shoulder, to offer reassurance and encouragement. 'Then I'll see you this evening, back at the tavern.'

Hosh hesitated as Mentor Garewin headed up the steps. 'What will you do with the day?'

'Scout around the drapers' warehouses for gifts for Halferan's ladies.' If he said anything else, he guessed that the boy would try to insist that he needed his help. Corrain urged Hosh up the steps with a firm hand. 'On you go, before we're trampled by this mob of scholars. The sooner you're healed, the sooner we can go home.'

'Yes, Captain.' But Hosh only went up a few steps before halting and looking back. 'Will you look for some trifle I might buy for my mother?'

'I will.' Corrain noticed Garewin betraying some impatience. The mentor had reached the door-wards, showing them the silver seal-ring of his school and rank before looking around to see where Hosh had got to.

'Go on. We want some good news for your mother, don't we, when we find this wizard friend of Madam Jilseth's this evening?'

Corrain tapped the breast of his doublet to remind Hosh of the note in his inner pocket, from the wizard Master Olved, telling them to come and inform him what they had learned on Planir's behalf.

All in good time, as Corrain had told Hosh when the brusque summons had arrived the previous evening. They might be here at the Archmage's behest but they were at no wizard's beck and call. There was also no point in wasting this master mage's time and wizardry with messages for Halferan or Hadrumal, just telling Planir and Zurenne alike that they had nothing to tell.

'Go on.' Corrain turned on his heel and strode away, giving the lad no more excuse to tarry.

He headed to the south and east corner of the square. There were no drapers' warehouses in this direction, nor any emporium offering lace or ribbons for Lady Zurenne or silken flowers for Ilysh and Esnina. Corrain would make such frivolous purchases when he and Hosh were ready to leave this city. Meantime, he would find out something worthwhile to repay the Archmage for helping to heal Hosh.

The potboy from The Goose Hounds was waiting just around the corner.

'Estry.' Corrain nodded, not reaching for his purse until he knew if the lad could satisfy him this morning.

On the tavern's back stairs the night before, the lad had grudgingly admitted that he'd been unable to discover where the Soluran was currently lodging. It seemed the sly fox changed his accommodations as often as his drinking partners.

This morning though, the lad grinned, confident. 'He was waiting outside Casiter's Library. He met up with Mentor Lestuld from the School of History and Mentor Itselai from the School of Music and they went into The Black Donkey to share some breakfast.'

'Find out who else he's had business with lately.' Corrain flipped a silver penny through the air, both as reward and incentive for the boy. 'Tell me this evening.'

'Gladly, master.' The lad's fist closed around the coin, a glint in his eye. 'There's something else, Master.'

Corrain raised silent brows. He'd told Estry yesterday that he only paid for worthwhile information.

'There are Archipelagans in the harbour.' Estry smiled, confident that would earn him another silver penny.

'Aldabreshi? At this season? From what domain?' Corrain challenged.

'Jagai,' Estry said promptly. 'Not just one ship, neither. A great galley with three banks of oars and two lesser with a single tier, with two triremes flanking them. Come in on the dawn tide after rowing up the Caladhrian coast.'

'What do they want here at the tail end of winter?' Corrain wondered aloud before snapping peremptory fingers at Estry. 'Find out and you'll earn a silver mark, maybe more.'

'More, Master, for certain.' Estry grinned before turning away.

Corrain watched the lad lope down the street and wondered if he should head for the wharves himself. But what could he learn along a dockside where he knew no one and no one knew him? Worse, these unknown Archipelagans might set their own hounds on his scent, if word of some curious Caladhrian asking their business reached Aldabreshin ears.

Whereas the taverns would be buzzing with speculation for a sharp-eared potboy to catch. What could the Archipelagans want so desperately that they would risk such a voyage? The first Aldabreshin ships weren't expected until the Spring Equinox festival. Merchants' trains of wagons and loaded mules wouldn't arrive from northern Ensaimin until the last handful of days of For-Spring, bringing cloth of every weight and hue, wares in wood, brass and pewter, iron in raw ingots and every article which a smith's skill could shape, leather and fur from the most northerly reaches where oak groves yielded to the pine forests and the mountains.

For the moment, Corrain decided, he would stick to his original plan and pursue the Soluran adept. He began walking, turning up his cloak's collar against the wind pursuing him down the street. As he had learned quartering the district around the carillon tower the previous afternoon, there was always a wind blowing in Col from some direction or other, ready to catch people unawares whenever they left the shelter of a building to cross a broad street.

He scowled up at the unbroken grey clouds. This lull in the storms usually blown in from the western seas wasn't much of a blessing from the Col faithful's goddess if it allowed the Aldabreshi to arrive so unexpectedly.

He slowed as a new thought struck him. Aldabreshi had no more use for the mainland's deities than he did but they wouldn't risk this perilous voyage crossing the days of open water between the Archipelago and the mainland at the mercy of winter weather without favourable omens and the unequivocal urging of their stars.

Corrain began walking more swiftly, tallying up the days it must take to row from Jagai. That great galley would be their slowest vessel, making a mockery of the triremes' swiftness. These ships would be crewed by free oarsmen besides, insofar as any Aldabreshin was truly free with his life at the mercy of his warlord's whim. So they wouldn't be flogged into rowing to exhaustion as the corsairs had whipped their slaves. Corrain's shoulders tensed at the memory of the overseer's lash biting into his own flesh.

A great galley might make thirty leagues a day, he calculated, allowing for the need for halts and to take on water for the thirsty rowers while daylight lasted. He ground his teeth. When he visited this Master Olved to send word home to Halferan, he would ask Kusint to make it his business to find out which Caladhrian lords had chosen to profit by allowing this Aldabreshin flotilla to make landfall on their coasts and replenish its supplies. But that could wait for Caladhria's next parliament.

In the meantime, he guessed that these Jagai ships had left their home domain sixteen or so days ago. A moment's thought told Corrain that the Lesser Moon would have been waning and Greater waxing, both a couple of days from their half. Any guard captain worth his rank planned journeys, winter or summer, knowing if the nights ahead offered any chance of safe travel or if dusk must see travel curtailed.

That was all well and good but Corrain had no idea where the constellations which the Aldabreshi looked to for guidance might be amid their heavenly compass's precisely delineated arcs, still less the jewel-coloured wandering stars.

He would have to ask Hosh that evening. Corrain had never imagined he'd have cause to be grateful for the boy's fascination with Archipelagan superstition but he wouldn't scorn to make use of it now.

He frowned as he walked on. Omens would have told the Aldabreshi when to set sail but portents alone wouldn't have prompted this unseasonal voyage all the way to Col. Relshaz was the closest port with far longer-standing ties to the Archipelago if the Jagai warlord had some urgent business with the mainland.

What had the northernmost Aldabreshi made of the uproar in Relshaz over the winter festival? Corrain knew that Archipelagan merchants who over-wintered in the river-flanked city tended island-hatched courier doves to send news south. Information was traded and valued across the domains as readily as anything else.

Perhaps he could work backwards from whatever the lad Estry was able to tell him of the Archipelagans' purpose in Col, like a huntsman divining some pursuit and struggle from paw and hoof prints in the mud and tufts of fur caught on twigs and brambles.

Meantime, Corrain paused to take his bearings. How far was he from Casiter's Library and the tavern where this Soluran was breakfasting with these unknown mentors? He reminded himself to make sure that Hosh asked Master Garewin who the men were and what they might want with this traveller. Most particularly, what business would they have with an aetheric adept?

He gazed up at the building looming over him, its brickwork as black as the livery worn by the swordsmen and women guarding its gates. The masonry was banded with white bricks, reminiscent of their sashes and gloves. From The Goose Hounds' tapster's description, this must be this Court of the Prefecture.

As the amiable man had explained, as well as watching over the libraries, and enforcing good order and discipline among the students, the University Prefects safeguarded the ever-lengthening rolls of parchment recording the names of each mentor formally sealed to each school of study. Their ledgers recorded students' arrivals and departures of at each summer or winter solstice, and whether or not they had completed the requisite studies to satisfy their mentor's inquisition. Only then would that mentor press his or her seal ring in the wax on the bottom of the letter to the Prefecture which would win the student a silver ring of their own, identifying them lifelong as a scholar of Col.

So that meant Casiter's Library was only a short distance. Corrain curbed his pace and looked down the length of the broad street to see three taverns close at hand where students and mentors could work up a thirst debating or wash away the dust from pages of ancient learning. The furthest away was indeed The Black Donkey, according to the writing on the front wall and the carved and painted beast of burden up on the porch roof for those who couldn't read.

That's where Estry had told him the Soluran and his two companions should be settled. Corrain wasn't about to risk going inside and have the Soluran recognise him. He was still less prepared to have the man look into his innermost thoughts again. Now the man would learn of the wizard Olved's note and of this apothecary who was helping Hosh. Corrain didn't know what the Soluran might do with that information but as the tapster had said Col's scholars swore, all knowledge was power in the right place and at the right time.

So how could he find out what the Soluran and these mentors were discussing? Corrain walked slowly towards the tavern. Well short of the front windows overlooking the street, Corrain ducked down an alley way. As he'd surmised, it led to the back yard. Better yet, a sullen old man was winching a heavy bucket up from the well.

Corrain leaned on the gate post. 'Can I offer you a hand with that?'

The dotard glared suspiciously. 'Why would you be so helpful?'

Corrain showed him a copper penny. 'So you can be helpful to me.'

The old man rested his none-too-substantial weight on the winding handle to stop the bucket plunging back down into the water. 'If you want an arse for rent try closer to the docks.'

Corrain raised his eyebrows. 'You rent out your arse?'

'No, I do not!' The old man was so affronted he took a wavering stride, raising bony and age-spotted fists. Unfortunately that loosed the bucket to crash down the well.

'Good to know. Any fool can earn a few coppers dropping his breeches and bending over.' Corrain strode into the yard and began winching the bucket back up before the old man could finish his startled curses. 'I'm looking for someone with the wits to earn a few silver pennies with his eyes and ears.'

He soon had the full bucket winched back to the top

and pulled it safely onto the brick lip. The dotard reached for the rope handle. Corrain refused to relinquish it.

'There's a Soluran in your tavern this morning, a traveller who's met up with some scholars. I'd like to know what they're talking about.'

'That's worth a silver penny?' The old man eyed him, suspicious but equally coveting his coin.

'Copper for you to try.' Corrain set the bucket down on the paving. 'Silver depends on what you tell me.'

The old man snatched the copper penny and his wrinkled face broke into a toothless smile. 'Let's see.'

He disappeared through the tavern's back door. Corrain looked down at the bucket of water. Wasn't the old man supposed to be carrying that into the kitchen?

The dotard reappeared with a log basket. 'You wait there, Master.'

Chuckling with glee at his own cunning, the old man filled the basket with neatly split logs from the wood store.

Now Corrain was worried that the old fool would give the game away entirely, rousing the Soluran's suspicions. What would the adept see if he used his aetheric magic to look into the dotard's addled thoughts? Would he see Corrain as clearly as the old man had just seen him in the yard? Or would he only learn that some unknown man was unaccountably curious about what was being said in this taproom?

How did Artifice work? Would Mentor Garewin be willing to explain something of its mysteries? Would Corrain understand if he did, and anyway, would such understanding be of any practical use?

Corrain paced back and forth in the empty yard. When the tavern's back door opened again, he was ready to leave if some other lackey or maid appeared. To his relief, it was just the old man.

'Well?' Corrain slapped the purse hidden inside his doublet, to encourage the old man with the clink of coin.

The dotard squinted at Corrain. 'I don't know if it's worth coin to you, Master, but that Soluran, he doesn't like wizards.' He shook his balding head, puzzled. 'Though I don't see what Solura's troubles with Mandarkin have to do with us in Col.'

'Doesn't like wizards or doesn't trust them?' Corrain took the bucket from the old man and carried it to the kitchen door for him.

'Doesn't trust them, and doesn't reckon anyone else should either.' The dotard's frown deepened the wrinkles carved across his forehead. 'Where do you suppose mages get their coin? Can they truly draw silver and gold out of the ground with their magic and stamp out gold marks with their hands?'

'That sounds like a nursery tale to me. But your trouble's worth a silver penny—' though Corrain held the coin well out of the old man's reach for the moment '—as long as you don't tell anyone I was asking after that Soluran.'

'How could I tell anyone who you might be?' the dotard asked, guileless. 'I don't know your name and with my eyes so bad, I wouldn't know you again if we met on the street.'

'Quite so.' Corrain let him have the coin and walked briskly out of the yard.

Now he would find somewhere with a clear view of the tavern's frontage until the Soluran left. Then he would see where the man went next and who he met. If he could, he'd find out how the Soluran steered their conversation.

Corrain wasn't about to assume that the Soluran was only in Col to stir up mistrust of magecraft. As he'd told Reven more than once, one man's word was only as good as the second or third man or woman saying the same. More than that, Corrain wanted to know what the Soluran's purpose in spreading such unease might be.

There was no point in calling on the wizard Olved with only half a story. Corrain wanted to be able to tell the Archmage what the Soluran was up to as well as whatever Estry might have learned to explain the Archipelagan ships' unexpected arrival, as well as telling Abiath and Lady Zurenne how Mentor Garewin's healing efforts were progressing.

Though Corrain decided, he wouldn't trouble Lady Zurenne with any mention of the Aldabreshin ships. If they were already in Col, hopefully they had passed by the Caladhrian coast without raising undue alarm.

— CHAPTER SEVENTEEN —

Halferan Manor, Caladhria
31st of Aft-Winter

ZURENNE LOOKED UP from the great hall's steps as Linset shouted from his vantage point up in the gatehouse's turret. The gusting wind snatched away his words but his waving was clear enough. He had seen the Archipelagans approaching through the dusk.

'Mama?' Ilysh turned to her, shivering and not from the chill wind. 'When will Madam Jilseth arrive? Do you think she will bring news from Corrain today? Do you think anything has befallen him and Hosh in Col?'

'Jilseth assured us they had arrived safely,' Zurenne reminded her daughter. 'They must simply be busy. Mending poor Hosh's face cannot be a simple business.'

She smiled though truth be told, Zurenne was wracked with apprehension. Why hadn't Corrain visited the wizard whom Jilseth had promised would bespeak her and Ilysh by means of the Archmage's pendants? What would he say when she confessed to allowing Aldabreshi barbarians on Halferan land?

Now they were almost here. Zurenne trembled despite the warm embrace of her sable cloak, as black as her gown beneath it. She had not imagined that Aldabreshi travellers could reach the mainland so swiftly. Whenever anyone spoke of barbarians in the southern seas, she was used to picturing remote islands far beyond the most distant horizon.

Master Rauffe and Reven had agreed that the Archipelagans would arrive tomorrow, no sooner than midday, regardless of Kheda's assurances that the Khusro wives were awaiting his courier dove on their domain's closest island to the mainland, ready to head for the port of Attar on Caladhria's southernmost headland. They had laughed behind the Archipelagan's back when he had insisted on riding out yesterday. But Kheda had reappeared at their gates just after noon today to throw all Mistress Doratine and Mistress Rauffe's preparations into disarray.

The women's consternation had swiftly turned to indignation that Halferan's new lady and the last true baron's widow should be shown such a lack of consideration. That the manor should be expected to greet these visitors in such haste? Though what could they expect from shoeless barbarians, they had swiftly agreed. It had been the first time that Zurenne had seen the two of them so genuinely in accord.

Reven had ridden out with his liveried troopers to offer the Aldabreshi a belated escort. Zurenne had hurried to the shrine to beg that Saedrin had seen them safely through from Lord Tallat's lands. Though she wondered what good that might do, since any assault would already have happened before Kheda rode out. Then she offered the same prayer to Talagrin, Raeponin and any other deity who might possibly be well-disposed towards Halferan.

Lastly she had clutched frantically at her pendant until the magic had opened a ruby-rimmed void so she could tell the Archmage of the Aldabreshi's precipitate arrival. Like Jilseth, Planir had assured her that Corrain would surely commend what she was doing and promised that she and Ilysh would hear such approval from the baron's own lips as soon as he called on Hadrumal's wizard in Col.

Zurenne would be hard put not to rebuke him like some common trooper, when he did finally deign to let her and Ilysh know what was happening. Baron he may be but he was not Zurenne's husband, with a husband's right to expect her unquestioning deference.

At the foot of the steps Kusint stiffened. Zurenne followed his stern gaze to the knot of guardsmen standing in the pool of light beneath the barrack hall's lantern. From their gestures they were arguing with Master Rauffe.

'My lady.' Kusint growled an apology and headed across the cobbled expanse.

Ilysh followed, forcing Zurenne to do the same. This was hardly the time to publicly rebuke her daughter. Mistress Rauffe and Doratine had already informed her of uproar among the servants at the prospect of serving Aldabreshi noblewomen.

'Get to your posts!' Kusint shouted.

A trooper stepped forward to speak for the rest. At least Zurenne saw distress twisting his face rather than mutiny.

'Master Rauffe says that he must prepare the gatehouse apartments for these Aldabreshi and their swordsmen,' the man protested.

'Where else do Halferan's guests lodge?' Kusint retorted. 'You're so unmanned at the thought of a handful of Archipelagans above your guard chamber? You think they'll charge down the stairs to overwhelm you? What then? They'll hold the gate against the entire Halferan guard to pen up the household inside the wall?'

Master Rauffe cleared his throat. 'Setting aside the very good question as to why these visitors would start a skirmish, hundreds of leagues from their home and beyond any hope of assistance.'

'There's always the manor's side gate.' Ilysh turned to point towards the narrow doorway cut through the encircling wall, even though it was hidden from view by the great hall. 'Even if we lost the gatehouse, we could never be trapped.'

Zurenne was torn between a fervent wish to scold her daughter for such unseemly behaviour and relief that their lady's unexpected intervention had silenced the disgruntled troopers.

'Get to your posts,' Kusint snarled.

'Is all well?' The Aldabreshin Kheda appeared from the gatehouse's archway.

Zurenne wondered how long he had been standing there, hidden in the shadows. What had he heard? She swallowed as he approached to loom over her and Lysha.

He looked down, concerned. 'I thought you were to wait in your great hall.'

Zurenne lifted her chin. 'I have changed my mind.'

'Why have the Khusro ladies insisted on making such haste on the road?'

Ilysh seized her opportunity to ask the tall Aldabreshin the question which Zurenne had been unable to answer when the two of them had been so frantically dressing in their finest velvets and the pick of the barony's jewels.

'Truly, no insult is intended.' Kheda looked so intently at Zurenne that she knew for a certainty he must have heard the resentment ringing to the kitchen and the barrack hall's rafters.

'Indeed, their arrival today is testament to the importance of this journey, and to their trust in you. Khusro Rina himself advised waiting for another twenty days, until the Ruby would be in the heavenly arc of wealth and thus, set opposite the Emerald. Such stars would offer far more reassurance.'

'What else do the stars and skies tell you now?' Ilysh looked up at him, intrigued.

Before Zurenne could think how to curb her daughter's curiosity, Kheda answered with his customary courtesy.

'For the moment, the Emerald rides alone in that part of the sky where we look for omens of death.' He gestured towards a point somewhat westward of true north. 'That whole quarter of the sky is empty of jewels and the Emerald itself is encircled by those stars which we call the Winged Snake. Those stars offer encouragement for those showing bravery and also for those who seek unsuspected truth, to bring hidden things into the light. These are favourable omens for the Khusro wives as they arrive within your gates.'

At that moment, coach wheels rumbled and harness rattled beyond the manor's closed gates. Halferan's unwanted guests were here. Abruptly Zurenne's mouth was so dry that she found herself unable to speak.

'My lady.' With a curt nod, Kusint walked swiftly towards the gatehouse.

Kheda's hand cut across the circle of the sky to a point a little south of west. 'That is the heavenly arc of life and selfhood. The Ruby sits amid the stars of the Canthira Tree. That tree promises new life even after fire and disaster. That is most particularly significant just at the moment, opposite the Emerald in the arc of death. The Ruby is a talisman for strength and courage, offering hope for favourable outcomes. To have these portents aligned thus is most encouraging.'

His hand shifted. 'Better yet, the Diamond shines

alongside, where we look for omens for wealth. The Diamond is a gem for clarity of purpose and the most powerful of all talismans for rulers while the Mirror Bird's stars are a sign offering protection against magic.'

He pointed again and at least this time, Zurenne could see him indicating the two moons, Greater and Lesser, rising above the manor's encircling wall.

'The Opal is a powerful talisman against magic's malice and that shines in the heavenly arc of friendship where the Sailfish's stars offer hope of good luck. The Pearl is another talisman against magic and waxes in the arc of good health amid the stars of the Net which is an omen of unity and co-operation as well as of chaos and danger subdued.'

'You have a great many talismans against magic.' Ilysh looked thoughtful.

'The Aldabreshi consider it the most terrible of all dangers,' Kheda said soberly.

'The important thing is the Khusro ladies will be happy under these stars.' As Zurenne heard the manor's gates open and the rattle of wheels within the arch, she was pleased that she had chosen the diamond studded crescent from her jewel coffer to sweep back her hair. Let the Khusro ladies see her wearing a ruler's gems while she took comfort from this remembrance of her beloved husband; his gift to her after Ilysh's birth.

'I do not think that happy is the correct word.' Kheda hesitated. 'The Amethyst warns against over-confidence and rides in the arc of omens for children with the stars of the Sea Serpent which is a token of hidden dangers.'

'Do you truly believe that such guidance can be read in the skies?' Ilysh persisted.

'Do you truly believe that the gods and goddesses whom you honour in your shrine will hear your prayers?'

Kheda's half-smile and light tone reminded Zurenne of her lost husband turning aside questions which he didn't really wish to answer.

'What do you believe?' she asked him bluntly.

Kheda looked up at her for a long moment. 'I believe that life is full of uncertainties and that few things are ever as clear-cut as they might appear at first glance. I have learned that wizardry is both more terrible and more valuable than I was ever taught. I have seen my eldest daughter marry the son of an Aldabreshin warlord more vicious and treacherous than any shoeless savage wreaking havoc in your mainland tales of barbarian mayhem. The villain's son has long proved himself a brave and honourable man. I believe that the only certainty is that we must hold true to ourselves.'

'How old is your daughter?' Ilysh asked quickly. 'How many children do you have? How many wives?'

'Lysha, such things are none of our concern.' Zurenne silenced her daughter with a glare as three heavy coaches rumbled into the courtyard.

In all honesty, she was just as curious about this stranger and his unknown people's customs. But such questions must wait. Baron Corrain wasn't here so she and Ilysh must do their duty by Halferan.

The drivers hired with these vehicles in Attar had no trouble reining in their teams of four sturdy horses. The beasts' heads drooped with exhaustion after their long day's journey.

Reven's troopers followed, urging their mounts to either side and drawing up to a halt, precise as any Tormalin Emperor's guard of honour. Not that any Tormalin prince would ride in these old-fashioned, round-topped carriages. The thick-rimmed wheels at each corner wouldn't have looked out of place on an ox-cart but the Attar stable master had known that no elegantly-sprung coach riding high on spindly spokes would survive Caladhria's winter roads.

Zurenne wondered if the unseen Aldabreshi women believed that their escort was guarding the coach and their wealth from Caladhrian assault. Or were they defending the mainlanders from the Archipelagan swordsmen? Come to that, she wondered which of the two Reven considered to be his principal duty?

Kusint stepped forward to the foremost carriage. Before he could reach up to the handle, the door swung open. An Archipelagan swordsman jumped out, turning instantly to look forwards. A second followed, looking behind towards the second carriage. A third armoured man sprang down from the seat at the rear where a lackey or a groom would usually ride.

They wore chainmail more finely wrought than any Zurenne had ever seen. Their armour was patterned with swirls of bronze links amid the steel, fiery in the light of the barrack hall's lantern. Each wore more varied blades than she could imagine any swordsman using.

All three were bare-headed, which surprised her. Their faces were as dark-skinned as Kheda's, with black hair and beards trimmed close.Their expressions revealed nothing.

'You need not fear the Khusro wives' bodyslaves,' Kheda assured her. 'They would never disgrace their mistresses by laying hand on a weapon to insult your hospitality. See how they offer their unprotected heads and necks to Halferan's guards.'

Zurenne still wished that Madam Jilseth was beside her but the Archmage had insisted that no mage could be present when the Aldabreshi ladies arrived. Jilseth would send word as soon as she arrived in the village beyond the brook. Planir had promised.

Meantime, he had insisted, Zurenne must hide her ensorcelled pendant away. So as Lysha's fingertips strayed to her throat, she merely touched a necklace of linked gold filigree ovals set with aquamarines a shade paler than her green gown.

What omens might the Aldabreshi ladies read into those gems? Should she have asked Kheda? No, surely he would have spoken if the stones offered some incomprehensible ill omen.

'Let us welcome our guests.' Zurenne led Ilysh forward.

Kheda fell into step behind them. Doratine and Mistress Rauffe had emerged from the kitchen buildings leading a gaggle of wide-eyed maidservants. Master Rauffe had gathered a handful of dutiful lackeys between the gatehouse and the barrack hall, waiting to unload the visitors' luggage. Kusint was hesitating by the leading carriage, torn between standing his ground and striding over to displace Kheda at the Halferan ladies' side.

A woman stepped out of the carriage only to stumble over the hem of the homely grey blanket she was wrapped in. The second of the swordsmen sprang forward to catch her flailing hand. Two more women had hastily emerged, shedding similarly incongruous wrappings against the winter chill.

Kheda said something in the Aldabreshin tongue and all three women turned to Zurenne and Ilysh. The three swordsmen instantly dropped to one knee, their heads bowed.

The oldest of the women spoke in fluent Tormalin, sinking into a graceful obeisance first to Zurenne and then to Ilysh.

'Good day to you, my lady and my lady. We are most honoured to be welcomed into your home. I am Debis Khusro and may I humbly make known to you Patri Khusro and Quilar Khusro.'

As the second and third women did the same, Zurenne stifled an urge to beg them to stop. She couldn't bear to see the gorgeous silks of their flowing garments trailing in the courtyard's dust. They wore what at first seemed to be high-necked gowns with long sleeves and close-fitted bodices. As they sank into low curtseys, their skirts spread unfettered by seams at side, back or front, to reveal that they wore plain silk trews beneath and jewel studded sandals of fine gilded leather on their slender feet.

Zurenne guessed that the eldest woman was much the same age as her sister Beresa. Though she could never imagine Lady Licanin wearing lustrous garnet silk embroidered with sprigs of some unknown flower in shining silver thread. She couldn't picture any Caladhrian noblewoman's face painted with the vivid scarlet cosmetics colouring the woman's eyes and lips and the silver dusting her brow and cheekbones.

The Licanin and Halferan baronies together surely couldn't boast jewels to equal half the ornaments which these Aldabreshin women wore. Clearly, the strictures taught to Caladhria's ladies, frowning on wearing gold and silver together or combinations of different gems, were unknown in the Archipelago.

Debis Khusro's long black hair, threaded with copious grey, was piled high on her head and secured with silver combs studded with pearls. Three iridescent strands hung in a long twisted rope around her neck. She also wore a necklace of broad gold links, each lattice of metal studded with square cut diamonds. Diamonds for a ruler and pearls to ward against magic. Zurenne recalled Kheda's words.

But none of these women were the exotic beauties she had expected from the tales of barbarian warlords plucking the finest flowers of womanhood to be helpless slaves. None was ugly by any measure but they were unremarkable except for the colour of their skin among the winter-pale Caladhrians.

Then she realised that the Khusro ladies and everyone else in the manor's courtyard was looking expectantly at her.

'You are most welcome, truly.' Finding herself lost for further words, she resorted to the courtesies she would exchange with any other Caladhrian noblewoman. 'How was your journey?'

The second woman, Patri, said something rueful in her own tongue. She wore blue silk embroidered with tiny green feathers and a skein of silver necklaces in different styles, ornamented with finely carved turquoise. A single plain gold chain bore an ornate pendant jewel; a flower with carved emeralds for petals framed by white enamelled leaves. More such white enamelled flowers dotted her intricately interlaced black plaits.

The swordsman who had rushed to her aid looked up, his expression clearing.

Before Zurenne could ask Kheda what the Aldabreshi woman had said, Patri raised a chagrined hand to her mouth. Each of her fingers bore an ornately engraved silver ring linked by fine strands of pearls to a thick silver bracelet around her wrist. A gold-set ruby clasped the pearls together on the back of her hand.

'Forgive me,' Patri said carefully, looking from Zurenne to Ilysh.

She was clearly less fluent in the mainland language. How old was she? Zurenne guessed that Patri might be within a handful of years of her own age, perhaps a little younger, perhaps a little older though it was difficult to tell with the silver and blue cosmetics making a mask of her face.

'I have never travelled in such a fashion before. I found it most—' She looked at Debis Khusro for help.

The older woman smiled ruefully at Zurenne and Ilysh. 'We can spend days on end aboard ship in the roughest seas without feeling unwell. We had no idea that this new motion would prove so unsettling.'

'You've never ridden in a coach before?' Ilysh was surprised into speech.

'Have you ever sailed in a trireme?' the third woman, Quilar, countered with a smile.

Her garments were adorned with tiny golden glass beads sewn in leafy vines across pale grey silk. She wore heavy gold bracelets and thick gold rings on both hands, set with shimmering opals, and a collar of silver latticework enclosing plain-cut lumps of rock crystal. Her hair was a mass of tight midnight curls barely tamed with golden combs set with green agates. Zurenne guessed that she was somewhere in age between the other women.

Ilysh could only stare mutely at her. Zurenne quickly intervened, hoping that Lysha's silence would be taken for shyness, not wonder at the woman's complexion, as dark as polished ebony beneath her gold and silver paint.

'A great many people get coach sick,' she said firmly, 'even those who've spent half their lives travelling our roads. Now, my ladies, you are very welcome. Please join us for refreshments while your servants and ours see to your accommodations. The gatehouse apartments will be at your disposal.'

Master Rauffe and his lackeys promptly stepped forward to take charge of unloading the carriages. Horse Master Thuse and his stable lads went to help the Attar coachmen unharness their beasts while Doratine disappeared into the kitchen, ready to send trays of tisanes and dishes of sweetmeats to the private family sitting room up in the baronial tower.

Ilysh had pointed out how awkward it would be to sit in the audience chamber while the Aldabreshin swordsmen carried coffers of Khusro treasures through to be stowed in the iron-gated cellar beneath the muniment room.

'Our thanks,' Debis inclined her head gracefully, 'but first we have a gift for you and your people.'

'There is no need—' Zurenne protested.

Debis Khusro turned away, calling out sharply in the Aldabreshin tongue. Zurenne shot a searing look at the Archipelagan. Why had Kheda not warned her? Did the women expect some gift of equal worth in return?

The second carriage's door opened. A tall, raw-boned man, his head and jaw alike clean shaven, stepped down. He wore white cotton trews and tunic beneath an unmistakably Caladhrian sheepskin jerkin. He spoke in low, urgent tones to whoever was still inside the carriage. It belatedly occurred to Zurenne that Aldabreshi maidservants might be as apprehensive about this visit as their Caladhrian counterparts.

The man in white cotton retreated, the first of the passengers stepped down from the carriage.

'Saedrin save us!'

Zurenne didn't know who exclaimed first among

Halferan's household. Like everyone else, she stared open mouthed.

The man looked around as though he couldn't believe his eyes. Tears streamed down his gaunt face to be lost in his ragged beard. As he raised one bony hand to brush away the uncut hair blown across his face, his unbleached cotton cuff slipped down to reveal manacle scars on his wrist. Zurenne would recognise such marks anywhere after seeing Corrain's galls.

'My ladies of Halferan.' Debis Khusro curtseyed low to Zurenne and Ilysh. 'We return your own to you, as proof of our good faith.'

Two more men were hesitantly negotiating the carriage's step, both as roughly bearded and ragged-haired as Corrain, Kusint and Hosh had been on their return.

'Three of them? Is that all?' Zurenne didn't intend to sound churlish. She couldn't help speaking her first thoughts aloud.

'We sincerely hope not.' Debis earnestly addressed the entire household. 'There are merely the first of your people whom we could secure.'

'Oh, my boy! Oh, my boy!'

Ankelli, one of the laundry's older women, came rushing across the cobbles, her arms outstretched. The second man stared at her.

Two men from the guard troop broke ranks. Kusint took half a pace forward. Zurenne caught his eye and shook her head as discreetly as she could. Retreating, Kusint stood motionless as the two guards walked towards the carriage; one of the younger boys and one of the few remaining who was surely long overdue for release to go fishing alongside old Fitrel.

The lad broke into a run, not looking to embrace either of

the former captives. He ran straight through the gatehouse, his steps echoing beneath the archway. Zurenne hoped he wouldn't fall into the brook in his haste. She wondered how many of the villagers would follow him back, avid to see for themselves who had returned from the dead.

The older man silently approached the last of the three. Wordlessly he grasped the lost man's bony shoulders. The rescued slave hid his face in the old man's chest, silently shaking.

Ankelli sobbed incoherently as she wrapped her arms around her son so forcefully that he staggered backwards. Fortunately Mistress Rauffe and two other women had followed close behind. With inexorable kindness, they escorted the two of them away towards the sanctuary of the steward's house.

Quilar said something quietly in her own tongue. Zurenne saw Debis's painted face tighten, though she couldn't read either woman's thoughts through their cosmetics. That was doubtless the purpose of such paint, she concluded.

'We know we will never be able to return all your people to you,' the Aldabreshin noblewoman said sombrely. 'We know that your rites for the dead differ from our own but I believe that your custom is to cherish their burned remains in the place of their birth?'

For the first time, Debis's face betrayed uncertainty, glancing from Zurenne to Kheda. His unspoken answer must have reassured her. Debis gestured a second time to the tall clean-shaven man in white who was still standing with the first rescued Halferan, one reassuring hand on his shoulder.

Between them, they lifted a long plain box out of the carriage. The dull red wood gleamed with an oily sheen in the flickering torchlight from the gatehouse.

'We have brought you the bones of two of your dead.' As Quilar stepped forward, no amount of face paint could hide her anxiety. 'Together with written testimony from those who knew their names. If we cannot restore them to their kinsfolk, we can at least put their fate beyond doubt.'

'Thank you.' Zurenne bit her lip to compose herself. 'Kusint, if you please, take that box to the shrine. Now, ladies, please join me in my sitting room while your household and mine see to your luggage and your rooms.'

More than anything else, Zurenne wanted to get the Aldabreshin women into seclusion behind the baronial tower's doors before the manor was besieged by demesne folk desperate for answers. She managed a welcoming smile before indicating the great hall's steps.

Debis, Patri and Quilar exchanged a few words with their thus-far silent attendants. The two younger wives' bodyguards went to confer with the clean-shaven man in white while Debis's keen-eyed swordsman fell into step with Kheda, a few paces behind the women as they headed across the cobbles.

Zurenne offered Debis another meaninglessly amiable smile. She didn't start any conversation though. She desperately wanted a few moments of silence to think how she would explain all of this to Corrain. Though if he wanted to speak to her this evening, he would just have to wait.

She could only hope that this unknown wizard in Col would have the sense to scry first and see that she was occupied with the Aldabreshi women, and not mortally offend the Archipelagans by sending some magic into their midst.

⸺ CHAPTER EIGHTEEN ⸺

The Goose Hounds Tavern, Col
31st of Aft-Winter

CORRAIN SHIFTED AGAINST the end of the taproom's counter, as though to ease a cramp, in reality to be certain that no one was close enough to overhear them.

'All these mentors have shown an interest in Artifice? Most have been known to work some lesser aetheric enchantments?'

After another long morning following the Soluran, he had spent the afternoon retracing his steps and falling into conversation to learn the names of the scholars whom the adept had been courting with meat and drink, all the while slipping his poisonous doubts about wizardry into their ears.

Now Corrain had returned to The Goose Hounds to quiz Estry. So far he had established that those scholars whom the potboy knew of by reputation were all sworn to the study of Music, History and Rhetoric.

Corrain frowned. 'Are any of them friends with Mentor Garewin?'

Estry shrugged. 'I don't know.'

'Can you find out? For a silver penny?' Corrain prompted.

'I can try.' More curiosity than greed lit the boy's eyes. 'Is the master adept truly going to mend your friend's face?'

'Let's hope so,' Corrain said curtly.

There'd been no evidence of any aetheric healing after

Hosh's first day sequestered with the mentors in the library. Compared to the terrifying power of elemental spells, Artifice seemed paltry magic.

Over their evening meal of salt beef stew and peppery biscuits, Corrain had encouraged the lad to tell him what had transpired. Hosh had changed the subject every time, relating some snippet of Col's history in such uncharacteristic words that Corrain had heard the clear echo of Mentor Garewin's voice.

As long as Hosh showed no inclination to tell him, Corrain had sworn to himself that he would restrain his curiosity. Thus far he had kept his word, though this morning, he had found himself wondering if he had some unseen aetheric healing to thank for the lad's snoring not waking him five times in the night.

Or was that a consequence of the pungent herbal tisane which Mentor Undil had given Hosh? Either way, Corrain was encouraged to see that the bitter concoction had stemmed the weeping crusting his reddened eye and nose.

If there was some visible change when Hosh returned this evening, they could call on that wizard Olved, whose second peremptory summons was tucked in Corrain's pocket along with his first note.

Or perhaps he would wait till tomorrow, until he had some meaningful news for the Archmage. Corrain decided he would go with Hosh to the Red Library for the second bell of the morning. He would ask Garewin himself if he'd ever had dealings with those particular scholars. Perhaps the mentor would see some connection between them. At the moment, Corrain could no more understand the Soluran's aims than a dog could grasp criss-crossing strategies on a white raven board.

Then there was the other riddle he still had no answer

for. 'Any news of those Aldabreshin ships?' Corrain asked Estry.

'None as yet.' The pot boy scowled and went off to collect empty tankards and plates.

Corrain took another swallow of ale, listening to the carillon's bells marking the last hour of the day with its individual tune. Hosh would soon be making his way back here. He reached for the plate of food which the tapster had served him, to tide him over until the dinner chime. It seemed that Col's residents habitually ate a good deal later than Caladhrians, whatever the season.

He speared a slice of succulent pink mutton with his belt-knife and laid it on top of butter-rich bread flecked with shreds of dried onion. He was beginning to wonder if anyone raised pigs on this side of the Gulf of Peorle but the local mutton cured with salt and Aldabreshin spices was most palatable and he assuredly preferred it to the endless local variations on smoked and pickled fish.

Listening to the taproom chatter, he realised that those settled here for the evening were once again debating the wizardry underpinning Mandarkin's tyrannical rulers. More than that, they were musing on their own vulnerability to magecraft. Who had set that hare running through the conversation? Corrain looked around for Estry but the potboy was still busy.

'There's no denying it. There's nothing we could do, if some wizard took against us,' a man with a drinker's broken-veined nose declared.

'Why would such a thing happen?' a thin-faced woman demanded scornfully. 'Wizards come here to use our libraries and talk the nights through to guttered candles with alchemists and natural philosophers and the other scholars.'

'They spend their coin with a generous hand while they're at it,' her comfortably rounded companion added.

'True enough but a hundred Aldabreshi come to Col from equinox to equinox, for any one mage from Hadrumal year round,' a contemplative man with a merchant's manner countered. 'The Archipelagans turning against us would do as much harm to our trade as the corsairs ever did.'

'Is it even true that the Archmage cleared the seas of those corsairs?' a neatly-capped matron asked no one in particular. 'I heard that Hadrumal's Council rebuffed the Caladhrian parliament time and again. Wizards don't involve themselves in warfare, isn't that what they say?'

Corrain curbed an urge to answer for Planir, chewing on this puzzle along with his meat. This Soluran was spreading disquiet about magecraft through the city and most particularly, among those university mentors most deeply engaged in studying Artifice. But as Corrain had good reason to know, Solura's wizards and their aetheric adepts, of whom this man was undoubtedly one, worked hand in glove opposing Mandarkin's brutal wizards and warriors.

He was pleased to hear someone in the taproom was making that very point.

'Ah, but,' the ruddy-nosed man argued, 'Solura's wizards bow to their liege lords and those lords kneel to their king. Hadrumal's wizards answer to no one!'

'They answer to their Archmage.' Though the woman who doubted wizardry had driven off the corsairs didn't sound convinced.

'Who does Planir the Black answer to?' The merchant's question hung unanswered in the air.

'Who's to make him pay heed?' A new voice spoke

up. 'If his kind are no longer welcome in Col? If that's to be the price of doing business with the Aldabreshi? If we're not to lose all their trade to Relshaz?'

As Corrain looked up from his plate to try identifying that speaker, the ruddy-nosed drinker chuckled into his tankard.

'Ask these Archipelagans if they want our city rid of wizards.'

Along with everyone else in the tavern Corrain stared, open-mouthed, as three Aldabreshi entered and halted inside the door.

Two were swordsmen, clad in chainmail so finely wrought, each link so small, that the armour draped like cloth. Steel breastplates inlaid with curving bronze designs protected their vitals. Both wore round helms with chainmail veils to protect neck and face. For the moment, those veils hung loose and their helmets' sliding nasal bars were raised high on their foreheads to give them a clear view of the room. Both dark-eyed men surveyed the gathering with the calm gaze of untroubled killers.

Corrain sincerely hoped they had no intention of starting a fight. The corsairs who'd enslaved him had been brutally formidable in battle yet even those proficient and prolific murderers never dared to take on any warlord's chosen swordsmen. Corrain had seen such retainers practising their skills on the trading beaches where the corsairs had made landfall while he and Hosh were chained to their oar. Those deliberate displays made it clear that anyone hoping to rob a warlord's ships would end up hacked into carrion to feed the crabs which scavenged the sands.

So much for the two swordsmen. Was this third Archipelagan their master? Weren't warlords supposed to be redoubtable warriors in their own right? While this man might be taller than most, he didn't look as though he could lead a charge against anything more challenging than a dinner table. The diamonds and sapphires glittering on his rings almost disappeared amid his soft fingers while his broad smile added a third jowl to the rolls of fat blurring his clean-shaven jaw line. A gust of wind through the open door sweetened the taproom with the expensive scents perfuming his heavily brocaded azure silk robes .

'Good day.' He spoke in formal Tormalin, his voice more highly-pitched than Corrain had expected. 'I bring you greetings from my master Jagai Kalu, who has long traded with your city and has always valued your honesty and rigorousness in bargaining.'

His bland smile swept the room, encompassing everyone whether or not they deserved such compliments.

'My lord has determined that the skies to come offer the most propitious omens for the Jagai domain's continued trade with Col. Accordingly, we wish to retain men of this noble city to defend our interests—'

The merchant was on his feet, his smile eager. 'My lord, I would be willing—'

'Ah, forgive me.' Contrite, the plump Aldabreshin raised a beringed forefinger. 'We look for men able to defend our interests with sword and shield.'

He bowed again to the dumbfounded gathering.

'Please spread this word to any who will find this of interest. Our ships are anchored at the Spice Wharf. Those with skill at arms wishing to test their mettle against my lord's swordsmen are invited to present themselves at the first chime of the day, tomorrow and each morning following until the last night of the Greater Moon.'

He raised his forefinger once again. 'Warriors will be tested to the first, trivial scratch, not to any wound that might prove mortal. My lord has no wish to stain his new venture with ill omens of spilled lifeblood.'

With a final smile, he turned around with a dull rustle of heavy silk and left the tavern, his impassive swordsmen following.

Corrain's first impulse was to head out into the night, to hire a gig to go to the harbour and find out where the Spice Wharf might be. He could be first in the queue tomorrow. If the Archipelagans were looking for swordsmen, he could wield a blade with the best that Col could offer. Once he had proven himself, he could ask what this warlord Jagai Kalu wanted mainland men to defend. Why wasn't this Archipelagan trusting in his own loyal warriors?

All around him, the tavern's customers exchanged their own exclamations and questions.

'Does the Jagai warlord mean to build a permanent holding on Col's wharves?'

'To have his own men overwinter here, like the Archipelagans do in Relshaz?'

'The Elected would never allow it!'

Corrain raised his tankard for another swallow of ale and contemplated the slowly fading scars on his wrist. Strip off his shirt for a fight and he'd bare the whip marks on his back. Any Aldabreshin would know him for a former galley slave.

Corrain's heart pounded. Would the Archipelagans load him with chains and demand to know which warlord he had fled from? He knew full well how unforgiving the Aldabreshi were to absconding slaves.

Those accursed corsairs would go hunting through

the Nahik domain's outlying islands through the winter seasons when storms made venturing onto the open seas too hazardous. Prowling the backwaters and remote islets with their clubs and whips, they dragged fugitives from any number of domains back to the galley where Corrain and Hosh had toiled side by side on their bench. Most had been barely half-alive and half of those had died before they'd returned to the corsair island, to be penned like dumb animals until Nahik Jarir sent his own galleys to carry off the tribute which secured the raiders their anchorage.

Corrain forced himself to breathe slow and deep until the blood racing through his heart and head slowed. He was Baron Halferan, not some nameless slave. Even the Archipelagans would know him for a Caladhrian as soon as he opened his mouth. That Jagai warlord's underlings wouldn't risk offending Col's Elected by shackling Corrain without testing the truth of this claims.

Then of course, he would have to explain to everyone from the Elected downwards why a Caladhrian baron had been presenting himself as a sword for hire to these Aldabreshi and lying about his name and allegiance. No, Corrain concluded with a resentful sigh, there was nothing he could usefully do at the dockside.

'What omens could Jagai Kalu possibly have read in the heavenly compass?' The woman in the neat cap was perplexed. 'Aren't the skies ill-favoured above their islands now? On account of their Emerald star?'

Corrain looked at her. She was right. Hosh had said that only the Sapphire crept around the sky more slowly than the Emerald. Any shift of these slowest jewels was considered most significant.

Hosh had said that the Emerald would linger in the heavenly compass's arc of death until the third For-

Spring to come, as measured by mainland almanacs. The Archipelagans would read the most gloom-laden and ominous interpretations into the portents they saw around the earthly compass with this hanging over their heads. This Jagai warlord sending his envoys to Col became even more of a puzzle.

The tavern's front door opened. Hosh halted, aghast, on the threshold as every face turned towards him. The room fell silent but for the crackling fire. Hosh shied away, pulling his cloak hood across his maimed features as he fled into the night.

Corrain hastily wrapped the rest of his bread around the mutton and hurried out into the carillon square. To his relief, he saw Hosh hesitating halfway to the fountain. Where was the lad to go in this strange city with so few friends?

'Hosh,' he called out, low-voiced. The last thing the lad needed was more turning heads.

'Why must they stare so?' Hosh spun around and Corrain was relieved to see anger as well as humiliation burning in his eyes. He hid his disappointment at seeing no visible change in the boy's disfigured face.

'They were only wondering who was coming through the door next. Three Archipelagans had just been in to announce that they're looking for swords for hire.'

'What?' Hosh stood open-mouthed.

'Let's go and tell this mage Olved.' Corrain knew full well that The Goose Hounds' customers would subject Hosh to searching looks if he returned after he'd recoiled so publicly. Better to let a chime or so of the night pass before they came back to the inn.

'We'll see what the Archmage makes of that news. Then we can see what Madam Jilseth has to tell us of home. The blacksmith's pied bitch must have whelped since we took ship.'

As he walked across the square, Corrain held out the meat-stuffed roll. Hosh took it without a murmur.

'Did you have a wager on the litter? I put my coin on the pups being brindled. That black-eared hound from the village was always sniffing around the gatehouse.'

When Hosh didn't answer, Corrain moved on to speculating about the prospects for the year ahead's deer hunting around the Taw Ricks lodge.

They had walked down three of Col's long streets before Hosh spoke. 'Master Sirstin's pups will be pied. He put the bitch to Reeve Gartas's dog as soon as she came into season.'

'Care to wager a copper penny on that?' Corrain challenged.

'I'll bet you a silver mark.' Hosh halted and looked around. 'Where are we?'

'Looking to knock on this wizard's front door.' Corrain moved closer to the lantern hanging from a house frontage in accordance with the Elected's mandates, to check that he was following Master Olved's instructions correctly.

'This way.' He led Hosh to the fourth of the terraced houses, each one double-fronted with bay windows and three storeys tall over a basement level lit by half-windows at ankle height. It seemed that wizardry paid well in Col.

So it had in Relshaz until the Magistracy had decided that they needed Aldabreshin coin more than Hadrumal's friendship. Corrain reminded himself to tell the Archmage that some Soluran seemed intent on seeing Col go down that same path.

He walked up the steps and rapped on the varnished wood. A thin-faced man with receding black hair opened the door.

'Good evening to you. We'd like to see Master Olved.'

'Finally.' The thin-faced man said sourly. He turned around. 'Mentor Micaran! At least your evening hasn't been wasted this time.'

'Is this the wizard?' Hosh whispered uneasily on the step.

'If that sneer is any guide.' Add to that, the man's shabby maroon doublet and breeches were assuredly no servant's livery.

Corrain walked warily into the house, Hosh half-hiding a pace behind him.

'Come on, come on. You've wasted enough of our time.' Master Olved snapped impatient fingers and the hall's outer door slammed shut behind them.

He led the way into a book-lined study, Corrain offered a bow to the man in one of the chairs framing the fireplace. His straight dark hair and similar features suggested he had some blood tie to the wizard. He wore a dark grey scholarly mantle over a long brown tunic and the university's silver ring, though he looked at least a double handful of years younger than Mentor Garewin.

'Mentor Micaran, sealed to the School of Rhetoric and one of their most proficient aetheric adepts.' Master Olved snapped his fingers at a four-fingered candlestick on a table in the window bay. Flames blossomed on the wicks, bright crimson and then burning honest yellow.

'Baron Halferan, good evening.' The mentor rose to his feet and offered a welcoming hand.

Corrain shook it and noted the firmness of his palm as well as the breadth of the scholar's shoulders. This man didn't spend every waking moment hunched over old books.

'Master Hosh.' Micaran greeted him warmly. 'Mentor Garewin speaks highly of you.'

'He does?' Hosh was startled.

'Now you have finally deigned to come here, shall we pass on your news to Hadrumal?' Scowling, Olved took a silver mirror from a chest of drawers' cluttered top and sat at the head of the table.

'By all means.' Corrain curbed an urge to answer the wizard's sarcasm in similar fashion.

He and Hosh sat on either side of Olved. To Corrain's surprise, the mentor Micaran came to join them.

The wizard laid the mirror on the table. Corrain glimpsed the four candle flames reflected before a swirl of scarlet magic swept them away to leave an opaque grey mist rimmed with magefire.

'Master Olved?'

Corrain recognised the Archmage's voice.

'The Caladhrians have finally turned up,' the Col wizard answered, irascible.

'Have they indeed?'

Planir sounded amused. Corrain didn't imagine that would improve the wizard's mood.

'Good evening, Baron Halferan. What news do you have?'

'Some Soluran adept is spreading mistrust of wizardry in Col and some Aldabreshi have risked a winter voyage here on business I've yet to fathom.'

Corrain related what he'd learned these past few days with precise detail. Let this arrogant wizard accuse them of idle tarrying now.

'This is most interesting.'

Planir's approval rang through the spell.

'*The fat Archipelagan will be a eunuch, in their tongue, a zamorin. He will be a trusted advisor to Jagai Kalu and highly valued for his loyalty and learning. This business must be important for the warlord to risk the man's life on such a hazardous voyage.*'

'Perhaps that means—' Mentor Micaran looked eagerly across the candles and mirror to Olved.

'Later,' the wizard snapped.

Before Corrain could challenge them to explain, Planir spoke through the circling magic.

'*Let us make a start on repaying you for your efforts on our behalf. Mentor Micaran offers his Artifice to help us find this man from Wrede, so we can learn more of his interest in Halferan.*'

'Using Artifice?' Corrain looked at the mentor, startled. 'Not scrying?'

He had expected elemental magic would search for the man. Madam Jilseth's wizardry had found him in the far north and east of Solura, much further away than Ensaimin.

'No mage can scry for someone he doesn't know,' Olved said, exasperated, 'unless he has something which the quarry has handled.'

'The Archmage says that you saw the man's face clearly.' Micaran held Corrain's gaze. 'Once I have seen him through your recollections, I can use aetheric enchantment to search for him.'

'How long will that take?' Would this Artifice be as slow as whatever healing Mentor Garewin was working on Hosh? Corrain had been hoping for something with elemental magic's immediacy.

'It will take as long as it takes,' Olved cut in, 'and

if you had answered my first summons, such questing enchantment would already be two days in hand.'

The wizard stretched his hand over the mirror. 'Farewell, Archmage—'

'Master Mage, we were promised news from home.' Hosh insisted before looking anxiously at Corrain.

Planir answered through the spell.

'Quite so. Master Olved, please bespeak Madam Jilseth. She's lodging in Halferan village, Hosh, so she'll have more recent news for you than I do.'

'Thank you, my Lord Archmage.'

They heard Planir's chuckle.

'You are most welcome, and please tell her about these Archipelagans in Col and this Soluran adept. Let's see what Captain Kusint makes of that. Now, I won't delay you any longer. Good evening to you all.'

Olved reached forward but the Archmage had already swept away the spell to leave the silver mirror empty.

Micaran looked at Corrain. 'May I work my Artifice with you first? Then I can work further enchantments while you are bespeaking Madam Jilseth.'

Corrain squared his shoulders. 'Very well.'

Olved nodded and rose. 'I will fetch some wine.'

Corrain was startled to find Micaran taking his hand, interlacing their fingers.

'Look at me,' the mentor commanded. 'Recall where you were and who you were with when you saw this man's face, as clearly as you can.'

As Corrain closed his eyes, the better to concentrate, he heard Micaran muttering something under his breath. The words had the rhythm of music as well as a rising and falling lilt though he could make no sense of the language.

Micaran broke off. 'Concentrate on your memories, not my enchantment.'

Corrain nodded, doing his best to close his ears to the oddly seductive murmur.

A sensation of falling overwhelmed him. He gasped and tried to open his eyes only to find that he couldn't. He tried to pull his hand free but Mentor Micaran's grip tightened.

Corrain opened his mouth but before he could speak, he found himself in Ferl with Vereor by his side. He could see every detail of that street even though he knew for a certainty that he still hadn't opened his eyes. He could still feel the pressure of Mentor Micaran's fingers between his own even though he looked down to see that insulting letter from Baron Karpis in his hand.

He looked at the man on the horse as the mentor had asked. Vereor, motionless at his side, became as faint an outline as an inn sign's faded paint after a generation's wind and weather. The buildings around slowly vanished and Ferl's cobbles melted away into nothingness. Regardless, Corrain could still feel the floorboards under his boot soles.

Only the man on the bay horse remained. Who was this spy from Wrede and what did he want? As Corrain focused on the man's unremarkable face, he knew that he would now remember it until his own deathbed. Whatever enchantment was enabling Micaran to share his recollection was now engraving that visage indelibly into his mind.

'Very good!'

Mentor Micaran's congratulations broke through the Artifice holding Corrain in thrall.

Snatching back his hand, he opened his eyes to see Hosh staring across the table at him.

'Where did you go? Inside your head, where did you go?'

Corrain had more urgent questions for Mentor Micaran. 'I'm sure this Soluran has looked into my mind. Is that how he will see my memories, if he locks eyes with me again?' He looked around the room. 'Will he see this place and the two of you?'

'That will depend on the precise nature of his Artifice,' Micaran looked thoughtfully at Corrain, 'and on your will to resist him.'

'My will?' Corrain frowned. 'You mean I can simply guard my thoughts against him? How?'

'By thinking of something else with such single-minded intensity that there is no room in your thoughts for anything else,' Micaran explained. 'But please remember that something can be simple without being in the least easy.'

'Do you know who he is, this Soluran?' Corrain steeled himself for another intrusion into his mind, so that the mentor could see the unknown adept's face.

'No, but I can find out readily enough,' Mentor Micaran assured him. 'I may even contrive to fall into conversation with him, since he seems so interested in those sealed to my discipline.'

'Wine.' Olved arrived at Corrain's side with an inlaid rosewood tray carrying a crystal decanter and goblets of finest Archipelagan rainbow glass.

'Thank you.' Micaran rose and reached over to take the first golden glassful which the wizard poured. 'I will take this into the parlour, so I can work undisturbed and you can work your bespeaking. Good evening to you both.'

The mentor nodded to him and Hosh before departing.

'Wine, from Kadras.' Olved handed them both a

goblet before sitting down and passing his hand over the silver mirror a second time. 'Madam Jilseth?'

'*Olved?*'

The magewoman's voice was almost lost amid the babble surrounding her.

Hosh leaned forward, intrigued. 'Are you in the Halferan tavern, Madam Mage?' He leaned forward to peer into the mirror even though there was still nothing to be seen through the translucent grey mist.

'*I am.*'

The noise abruptly silenced. Corrain could only imagine the astonishment on people's faces as they saw the bespeaking spell's scarlet circle blossom in the empty air.

He sat back and sipped his wine as Master Olved told Jilseth about the Soluran adept spreading mistrust of wizardry and what little they had learned of the Jagai ships' purpose in Col.

Corrain no longer wondered why Hosh was so reluctant to relate his experiences. Aetheric magic's intrusion into his own thoughts had been profoundly unnerving and that must surely be a trivial enchantment compared to whatever Garewin and his fellow mentors were using to mend the lad's face.

Artifice might indeed seem paltry compared to elemental wizardry working such marvels as the bespeaking before them. Corrain reminded himself how often first impressions could lead a man fatally awry.

— CHAPTER NINETEEN —

Halferan Tavern, Caladhria
31st of Aft-Winter

'HOW IS MY *mother? How is the village faring?'*

'Halferan and its people prosper, Hosh.' Jilseth looked across the tavern to see the door still standing closed after whoever had hurried to fetch Abiath from her own fireside.

'Has Sirstin's bitch whelped yet?'

Jilseth had to stifle a laugh at the astonished expressions around her as Corrain's question rang through the floating magefire circle.

Old Fitrel was the first to answer. He had been regaling Jilseth with stories of better days in Halferan.

'Five healthy pups, two dogs, one pied and one black, three bitches, two pied and one white.'

'That's a silver mark I owe you.'

As the entire taproom laughed, the tavern door opened. Jilseth raised her hand.

'Abiath? Would you like to speak with your son?'

'Hosh? Are you truly there?' The old woman gazed in wonder at the spell, sinking into the seat which Fitrel vacated for her.

'Mother, I have met with the mentors for two days now—'

Jilseth watched the fascination on the Halferans' faces as Hosh related his experiences to his mother. After all, how many of them would ever have the chance to sail the length of the Caladhrian coast, let alone visit somewhere as distant and foreign as Col?

Then again, she reminded herself, no one here would ever have expected to see Aldabreshi noblewomen welcomed into the manor across the brook. The only sure thing in life was surprise.

She focused her attention on the bespeaking again as she realised that Hosh had finished detailing the Red Library's interior in exasperating detail. Now he was talking about Mentor Garewin's Artifice. Jilseth listened, intently curious.

'We go to a garden, only we don't, not really. That's just the enchantment woven around us. It's like a dream, except that we know that we're awake and truly somewhere else. But Mentor Garewin tells me to remember what my life was like before—before I was injured—'

Jilseth saw everyone listening in the tavern grimace and exchange sympathetic glances. Why did they find it so much easier to show their compassion when the boy wasn't here to see it?

'The whole day passes without it seeming like more than a chime. My pain is dulled already and I can breathe easier—'

'I can hear it in your voice.'

As Abiath beamed with joy, Jilseth realised that she was right. Hosh did indeed sound less congested. She wondered how long the whole healing process would take. Would he·let her explore the remade bones in his face with her own wizardry on his return?

Abiath had just asked that first question and Hosh was answering.

'*Mentor Garewin says it will take another ten days so we won't be home before the turn of the season.*'

'Will my lady's Archipelagan visitors be gone by then?' Abiath looked at Jilseth, along with everyone else in the tavern.

'I imagine so.' Jilseth couldn't think what else to say.

'*What did you say?*' Corrain's outrage rang through the spell.

Abiath answered him. 'I was just asking the lady wizard—'

'*There are Aldabreshi in Halferan? Jilseth! Why haven't you driven them back into the sea? What is Kusint thinking?*'

Jilseth was relieved not to be explaining this to Corrain's face, though on balance she would have preferred not to be answering him in front of this tavern gathering.

'Lady Zurenne and Lady Ilysh have graciously agreed to receive three of the warlord Khusro Rina's wives. They have agreed that Halferan's ladies will help cleanse the Khusro domain of any magically ensorcelled weapons or jewels lurking unsuspected in their treasury. I am to identify any such artefacts—'

'*You must come here to bring me back to Halferan at once. Hosh can remain until his face is healed—*'

'No.' Jilseth was pleased to find her flat refusal left Corrain speechless.

'Kusint has proved himself entirely capable of commanding Halferan's guard in your absence. Lady Zurenne is dealing with the Khusro wives with courtesy and good judgment and I believe I have proved beyond all doubt that I am capable of defending Zurenne and her daughters if needs be.'

The murmur of agreement around the taproom confirmed that these villagers remembered the magic which she had wielded in Halferan's defence.

'We have no need of you here and indeed, your precipitate return would do more harm than good, implying that we do not trust in Khusro's good faith. Whereas we assuredly have need of you in Col. You can determine what the Jagai *zamorin* is up to and find out more about this Soluran who's so keen to stir up mistrust of magecraft.'

'We? You mean Hadrumal has need of me here. This is no business of Halferan's. Nor is playing the go-between so that Planir can get his hands on more of those treasures which the Mandarkin coveted. How has he contrived this? Why have you dragged Lady Zurenne into such peril?'

Before Jilseth could reply, the scarlet-rimmed grey mist vanished. She saw everyone in the tavern gawping at the empty air.

'What happened?' Abiath quavered.

'The mage in Col ended his spell,' Jilseth said steadily.

She must remember to thank Olved, abrasive though she found the mage. She could only pity Hosh who must now be caught between Corrain's fury and Olved's scathing refusal to yield to the Caladhrian's demands that he renew the bespeaking.

'Some lamb's wool, Madam Mage.' The tavern keeper, Mistress Rotharle, appeared at Jilseth's elbow, setting down a tankard of spiced ale topped with a layer of apple pulp.

'Thank you.' Jilseth was still trying to accustom herself to this local winter favourite. It was at least undeniably warming.

She took a careful drink as Abiath yielded to the entreaties of her sewing circle and accompanied them to their preferred table by the tavern's fireplace.

The rest of the Halferan villagers withdrew into threes and fours, avid to speculate about what they had heard and what might happen the following day.

Jilseth was well content to be left alone. No, that wasn't true, she realised. She wanted to know what the Archipelagan Kheda would make of this unexpected news of Jagai ships in Col. Would he have any idea why Khusro's neighbouring warlord sought to hire Caladhrian swordsmen?

But she couldn't possibly go to the manor to find him tonight. Planir had made it clear beyond misunderstanding that she must not set foot within the gatehouse while the Aldabreshi women were inside the encircling wall. She would have to send a note to Kheda in the morning, asking for a few moments of his time.

She wanted to ask Kusint why some Soluran adept might be encouraging all and sundry to think ill of wizardry. Could this possibly have something to do with the arrogant aggression which that magewoman, the Elder of Detich, had shown towards Hadrumal? But Kusint could know nothing of that, surely?

Jilseth also doubted that she would be able to get Kusint to address such questions with anything more than brusque dismissal. His attention was focused, hostile and suspicious, on the Archipelagans.

She reminded herself that the Forest youth had been enslaved like Corrain and Hosh, even if he had not suffered as brutally or for as long as the Halferan men. The presence of the Aldabreshi must be awakening painful memories. Moreover she'd do well to remember that Kusint was of an age with Hosh while Corrain could be father to them both. It was too easy to think of Kusint as much the captain's own age, they had been so closely allied in escaping from the corsairs and searching for magic beyond the Great Forest to save Halferan.

Still, she would write Kusint a note in the morning as well, Jilseth decided. If he knew nothing, she could at least tell Planir that.

She had her own questions for the Archmage but she was still undecided about asking them, even in the privacy of the modest bedchamber Mistress Rotharle had prepared for her here in the tavern.

What was Planir doing, now that word of that dawn Council meeting was spreading through Hadrumal's halls and wine shops?

Jilseth would have asked her friends but bespeaking them had only left her with still more questions which only the Archmage could answer.

Merenel was in Suthyfer, far away in the eastern ocean. She had insisted that she was merely there to help Usara assess how many newfound mageborn the remote islands' wizards could take on as apprentices, in accordance with the Council's decision.

That was undoubtedly true but they were close enough friends for Jilseth to know that the Tormalin girl wasn't telling the whole truth. She must be laying the foundations for some scheme Planir had in mind while Jilseth was stuck here passing messages between Caladhria and Col.

Realising that her feelings were perilously close to envy, Jilseth rebuked herself. Merenel had travelled to Suthyfer the year before and she had made friends among the mages there. Add to that, she was Tormalin-born and those islands were the key stepping stones between the Imperial ocean ports and the untamed wilderness of Kellarin. So Merenel was ideally suited to serve as the Archmage's envoy. By contrast, as widely as Jilseth had travelled across the mainland on the Archmage's business these past couple of years, she had never had occasion to visit the islands.

What about Tornauld? Jilseth had been startled to find that he was now in Maubere Inlet, in Lescar's most easterly province of Parnilesse, along with Mellitha, while Velindre was apparently in the Carifate enclave further south on that coast. The Carifate had been a mercenary stronghold all through Lescar's festering strife while the now disgraced dukes fought for the mythical crown of high king. What were those sword companies doing now that Lescar's rebels and exiles had put an end to the fighting?

More particularly, what was Planir doing to encourage those mercenaries to draw the Tormalin Emperor's eye away from Hadrumal and its hoard of ensorcelled artefacts? To give the spymaster, the Sieur Den Dalderin, more urgent concerns closer to home than Solura? Jilseth hadn't forgotten her abruptly curtailed exchange with the Archmage after the Council meeting.

Nolyen was still in Hadrumal but he was working with Flood Mistress Troanna, who had summoned the most proficient water-born mages to join in her endeavours to destroy the ensorcelled items. Jilseth had no idea if the Seaward Hall was making any progress. The price of being admitted into Troanna's confidence had been Nolyen swearing a vow not to speak a word of their efforts beyond those walls.

All he had said was that Ely wasn't part of that coterie so at least Jilseth needn't fear the sly magewoman was learning some new and unprecedented wizardry to share with Galen and Canfor while Jilseth's own nexus had been scattered to the four winds.

Jilseth washed such sour thoughts away with a swallow of the spiced ale.

Why was she so out of sorts? She should be revelling in the prospect of searching through the Khusro wives' treasures the following day. If there were indeed ensorcelled artefacts in the numerous chests which had reportedly filled that third carriage, she would be the first mage to lay a hand on them, to see what her wizard senses could tell her. Perhaps she would find some insight to answer Hadrumal's questions?

Perhaps not. Jilseth ate a careful mouthful of the apple pulp. There might be nothing bespelled to find and she wasn't at all sure how the Archipelagans would greet that news. Would they be relieved, or accuse Lady Zurenne of some deceit, or at least, of being deceived? Wizardry was so abominated among the Aldabreshi because it turned every natural omen into lies.

She looked up as Fitrel's voice rang through the tavern.

'How do we know we can trust the barbarians?'

The former sergeant-at-arms was sharing a flagon of ale with Reeve Gartas. Realising that his passion had silenced the tavern, Fitrel addressed the whole room.

'They have offered affidavits swearing those are Bann and Damer Forey's last remains but how can their family know that for the truth? I don't say they are lying,' Fitrel said earnestly, 'but what about whoever gave them those bones? What better way to win favour with a warlord than give his men what they're searching for? Those barbarians could have dug up any old corpse and no one would be the wiser.'

She could be. Jilseth stared into her ale and contemplated answering the old man. His distress was genuine and she had the magic to put his mind at ease. Necromancy's arcane spells could reveal the unquestionable truth of the last living moments of those dead men whose bones the Archipelagans had returned.

She only had to offer. Moreover this would be her first opportunity to test her necromancy since the untamed magic surging through that all-embracing nexus had so expanded and extended her affinity. Jilseth longed to discover how much further and deeper her reach had become.

She sipped her ale, tallying up the arguments against making any such offer. Firstly, the dead men's families might simply refuse her and that could cause ill-feeling among their neighbours who still felt entitled to demand such answers.

Secondly her magic might reveal some truly appalling suffering and death to bring unwarranted distress to those already bereaved.

Third and perhaps worst, the visions which her spells revealed to those brave enough to stand witness might prove that these remains were indeed some stranger's bones. Giving the lie so publicly to the Archipelagans' promises of good faith might tip the villagers' anxiety over the barbarians' presence into open hostility.

Fourth, the Aldabreshi might hear some rumour of what she had done. Given their hatred of wizardry, that could provoke them into leaving Halferan immediately, ruining any hope of reconciliation between mainland and Archipelago.

The Archmage would hardly thank her for that, after Velindre's endeavours to make contact with Kheda and to help the Archipelagan devise the arguments which had persuaded the Khusro wives to make this unprecedented voyage.

Jilseth had far better leave those bones to burn on the pyre being prepared on the funerary ground beyond the brook, and no one would ever know the truth of those dead men's fates.

She looked around the tavern. She saw the covert glances of awe and admiration she had become used to in Halferan. These people couldn't imagine the power she had at her fingertips.

Did they ever imagine how often she was finding her magic of little use of late? Jilseth had never imagined that she would have such an opportunity to use her necromancy only to find so many compelling arguments against it.

She left the remains of her ale and went upstairs to write a comprehensive letter to Lady Zurenne giving every detail of Corrain's news from Col. She didn't hold back from mentioning the Jagai ships or the strange and suspicious behaviour of the unknown Soluran. She balanced that with Hosh's encouraging report of his dealing with the scholarly healers.

If Jilseth's own friends and allies were leaving her overlooked and half-informed amid so many uncertainties, she could at least ensure that she didn't do the same to Lady Zurenne.

— CHAPTER TWENTY —

Halferan Village, Caladhria
32nd of Aft-Winter

ZURENNE WONDERED WHO felt more ill at ease; herself or Mistress Rotharle. She smiled graciously, nodding with approval at the taproom. 'My thanks for making us so welcome.'

The tables were draped with white linen and every chair and bench gleamed with diligent polishing. There wasn't a speck of dust on the floor or a wisp of cobweb amid the rafters. The fire crackling in the hearth had been lit long enough before their arrival to fill the room with welcoming warmth. If time had allowed Zurenne imagined that the walls would have been freshly lime washed, even though the inn wasn't half a year rebuilt.

'You honour me, my lady.' Mistress Rotharle's eyes still kept darting to the doorway where Kusint and Reven stood.

'Shall we sit?' Zurenne tugged at Ilysh's elbow.

The girl was looking around, making no pretence of hiding her curiosity. In more normal times she would never have set foot inside a common tavern. More than that, as Halferan's heiress she would have not needed to go in search of a husband. Her visits to the luxurious inns accommodating the nobility on their travels would have been few and far between.

'Is this just as it was before?'

Zurenne couldn't tell her. In all her years living in the manor she had never stepped across the tavern's threshold. 'Lady Ilysh,' she said pointedly, 'we must sit to receive our guests.'

Kheda had been very clear about such etiquette, just as he had insisted that the Khusro wives could not possibly remain within the manor's encircling wall while Jilseth was examining the Archipelagans' treasures chests.

Zurenne had been thrown into utter confusion until Kušint had suggested that they commandeer the village tavern for the day. Even then she had been aghast at the notion, until Kheda had approved it, explaining that the brook's flowing water would be considered a safeguard against magic's inexplicable contamination.

'Here, my lady, my lady.' Mistress Rotharle pulled two chairs out from a table and dusted them with her apron though there was no possible need.

'Did Doratine did send word from the manor?' Zurenne was seized with sudden apprehension. 'You have the almond cup made ready?'

She didn't want a repeat of yesterday evening's embarrassment, when she had learned too late that the Aldabreshi shunned ale, wine and every other liquor. Zurenne had only been able to offer the Khusro wives well-boiled well water.

Thankfully Mistress Rauffe had recalled Lady Licanin's taste for the orgeat that was so commonly drunk in Relshaz and Doratine had remembered a recipe, hurrying to ransack her store rooms for ingredients. Though making the almond syrup was a lengthy process. Had there been sufficient time?

'Everything is prepared, my lady,' Mistress Rotharle assured her.

A shadow darkened the doorway and the alewife hurried away to her kitchen.

'My ladies of Halferan.' The tall Aldabreshin Kheda entered the tavern with the clean-shaven Archipelagan who was as ever, dressed in a plain, bleached cotton tunic and trews.

Though now he had swapped his sheepskin jerkin for a shapeless, knitted over-tunic such as the village craftsmen wore on cold days in their workshops. Zurenne wondered who he had got that from and for what price.

Master Rauffe had drily informed Zurenne that half the Halferan guard had found some reason to visit family and friends across the brook this morning. She would have to ask what he heard of the villagers' reactions, seeing the Khusro women and their bodyguards walk the length of their street.

At least Raselle had told her that most of the manor's household were reserving judgement, given the show of good faith by the Archipelagans in returning Ankelli's son, Reeve Gartin's nephew and Mundin's grandson. Opinion was more divided over the bones, supposedly those of Bann and Damer, cousins from the village. Though their families had declared themselves content to light a funeral pyre this very evening.

Kusint and Reven retreated from the doorway, as the first two Khusro wives' bodyguards followed Kheda into the taproom.

'My ladies of Halferan,' the first bodyguard said, his Tormalin speech heavily accented as he glanced between Zurenne and Ilysh. 'Debis Khusro, Patri Khusro and Quilar Khusro humbly request the honour of admittance to your presence.'

'We are most honoured to welcome Khusro Rina's noble wives,' Zurenne nudged Lysha's ankle with her toe under the table.

'We are—most honoured.' Ilysh hastily remembered Kheda's instructions.

As the armoured Aldabreshi turned back towards the door, Zurenne smiled encouragement at her daughter. Drianon bless them both, she knew how her daughter felt.

Zurenne still found the Archipelagan warriors fearsomely intimidating, even after Mistress Rauffe had told her, torn between astonishment and embarrassment, that the Khusro wives had brought no maidservants.

These warlike men were expected to wait on their mistresses hand and foot, doing every menial service from washing their most intimate garments to emptying their chamber pots. They even asked for blankets to sleep on the floors of their mistresses' bedchambers like faithful hounds. When Kheda had confirmed this was entirely as he expected, Zurenne could only insist that Mistress Rauffe respect the Archipelagans' mystifying customs, however disappointed Halferan's bravest maids might be. To her astonishment, a handful of the most insatiably curious had volunteered to serve the barbarian women.

The Khusro wives entered, wearing short tunics and loose silken trews beneath padded satin jerkins sumptuously embroidered with gold and silver flowers. As well as ropes of pearls, they wore bracelets and necklaces of twisted gold and rings of intricately braided silver framing gemstones to match their silks; opals for Debis, sapphires for Quilar and emeralds for Patri.

Debis's hair was woven into a towering coil of plaits secured with pearl-headed pins. Patri's gleaming midnight locks hung loose around her shoulders, held off her face by finely carved coral combs. Quilar's mass of tight black curls was threaded through with strips of gold, criss-crossing in a gleaming lattice. Each one was tipped with a trembling silver flower and twin leaves of gold, framing her strong features with musical whispers.

As before, exotic cosmetics made a mask of each woman's face. Nevertheless Zurenne believed that she was learning to read their expressions. Not Quilar's; the darkest-skinned woman remained as inscrutable as ever. Patri was looking around the tavern with as much frank curiosity as Lysha though, while Debis looked longingly at the fire. She had the fine Dalasorian shawl which Zurenne had given her at breakfast wrapped tight around her shoulders. Zurenne hadn't thought twice about doing so, seeing Debis shivering in the great hall's chill.

Now she looked down to see that the women were still wearing their sandals. Zurenne's own feet would have been blue with cold after walking from the manor to the tavern and she couldn't believe that Archipelagan women were so different, whatever the colour of their skin or the bright lacquer on their toe nails.

'Do warm yourself.' She rose, ready to fetch a chair for Debis, but the silent bodyguard was there before her.

'Thank you, Lafis.' Debis stretched her feet gratefully towards the hearth. 'And thank you, my lady, for this gift. It is so warm and yet the weave is so fine. May I ask where you find such cloth?'

Quilar gestured towards their clean-shaven attendant in his humble homespun. 'It is not from the same beast as that?'

'No, that is wool, from a sheep. The yarn which wove the shawl is spun from a goat's hair, from a land far to the north.' Zurenne saw the women looking at Kheda for explanation.

The tall Archipelagan sat at the next table with the three Archipelagan bodyguards while the white-clad servant perched on a stool beyond. Reven and Kusint remained standing either side of the doorway

'*Imkar.*' Kheda smiled at Zurenne. 'That is the word in our tongue for goat.'

Quilar was frowning. 'No goat—' she pronounced the new word with care '—in our islands has a pelt to make such yarn. They make indifferent leather though their meat is tasty.'

'Dalasorian goats live in the hills beyond the Dalas river. They grow thick fleecy coats against the winter cold. They're shorn, like sheep, at the turn of Aft-Spring and For-Autumn.' Ilysh coloured slightly as everyone looked at her. 'It says so in my father's book about the grassland nomads.'

'How far distant are these lands?' Patri leaned forward, her eyes keen.

Zurenne's interest in maps extended only as far as the routes from Halferan to Attar or Claithe and Pinerin where she visited favoured merchants. She was grateful to see Ilysh tallying on her fingers, concentration wrinkling the girl's forehead.

'Five hundred leagues as a courier dove might fly but it would be a journey of six to seven hundred leagues from here, depending on the route you took.'

'All on unbroken land?' Patri marvelled at the prospect.

'How far is it from the north of the Archipelago to the furthest south?' Ilysh asked shyly.

'Forgive me, I do not know how you count such things.' Patri said something to Kheda in her own tongue.

'Twelve hundred leagues, near enough,' he explained to Ilysh.

'And all islands?' She smiled at Patri as she echoed the young Khusro woman's fascination.

Debis turned to Zurenne as the conversation threatened to falter. 'Neeny is well, I hope?'

'Very well, thank you.' She sought some inoffensive excuse for her younger daughter's absence. 'She begged leave to spend the day with her dolls.'

'They are young for so short a time; we should let them enjoy such pleasures.' Debis's smile saved Zurenne from her sudden apprehension that Neeny's absence might seem discourteous.

'There is time enough for her to learn her duties once she's of an age of reason.' The glint in Quilar's eye suggested she knew full well that this was more motherly prudence than indulgence.

Raselle's reassuring presence and Zurenne's promises and pleading had seen Esnina join them for dinner in the great hall last night and for breakfast without incident but nothing could persuade the little girl to say a single word to these unnerving visitors. So Zurenne had told Neeny she could stay safe with Raselle in her bedchamber. This enforced sojourn in the Halferan tavern promised to be sufficient trial without fearing a childish tantrum.

'Your laws and customs reckon the age of reason to be seven summers?' Ilysh looked at Patri, curious.

The Archipelagan woman nodded. 'And the age of discretion is fourteen years.'

'When youths and maidens alike may assert their own judgement against their parents' advice,' Quilar added.

'While we parents can only look back on our own foolish certainty when we were so young,' Debis intervened with a wry laugh, 'and hope that we have earned our children's trust, so that they will still follow our guidance through the reefs and rocks ahead.'

'May I ask how old your own children are?' Zurenne enquired politely.

Debis smiled fondly. 'We have five sons and seven daughters.'

'Our sons are twenty-three years, nineteen, fourteen, eight and five years old,' Patri related. 'At the moment we believe that Khusro Rina will designate Khusro Anai as heir, our second son, but that may yet change.'

'We have one daughter of twenty-four years, two of twenty, one of thirteen and two of twelve, and one of three.' Quilar smiled with maternal pride. 'The eldest three have already made marriages useful for Khusro and now honour their new names with their trading successes.'

'You must be very proud.' Zurenne longed to ask which of these women was actually mother to each of these children but her nerve failed her.

'Trade that fine goat's hair fabric into the Archipelago and you would bring honour to Halferan,' Patri urged Ilysh.

Disconcerted, Ilysh looked at her mother. 'I wouldn't know how—'

'We would be delighted to offer you our assistance,' Patri assured her. 'Trading Khusro's embroidered silks is my particular responsibility so I have many good friends among the other domains' wives where textiles are highly valued.'

'Perhaps we can discuss it later.' Zurenne really didn't want to cause offence by explaining that no Caladhrian noblewoman would dream of engaging in commerce.

She looked towards the kitchen door. When would

Mistress Rotharle summon up her courage and serve the promised orgeat?

The clean-shaven Archipelagan rose and bowed low before speaking to Debis Khusro.

She turned to Zurenne. 'Soviro wishes to return to your home, to assist with the survey of our strong boxes. May I have your permission to send him back?'

'Of course, of course.'

Kheda had told Zurenne to expect this. The Khusro wives wouldn't insult her by insisting that one of their own watched over their treasures but it was hoped, he said delicately, that she would appreciate the value of an eye-witness account when the women returned home to tell their husband what had become of his possessions.

Having seen the quantity of locked and leather-strapped chests removed from that final carriage, and the quality and quantity of the women's jewellery, Zurenne wasn't in the least insulted. She was profoundly relieved that everyone would be safeguarded against accusations of dishonesty.

Now she only had to worry about word of such wealth within Halferan's walls spreading beyond the demesne, luring would-be bandits to lurk on the high roads in hopes of ambushing the Archipelagans on their way back to Attar. Whatever Kusint's objections, she would be sending every able-bodied Halferan trooper to guard them on that journey.

She looked over towards the door, her voice determinedly bright and courteous. 'Sergeant Reven, be so good as to escort our guest to—to the muniment room.' She remembered just in time how assiduously the Archipelagan women avoided making any mention of wizards.

Presumably Jilseth was already inside the manor, though Zurenne hadn't seen her since her arrival in Halferan. The lady mage's only communication had been this morning's letter posing all manner of unanswerable questions, though at least Hosh's news from Col seemed encouraging.

That would suffice for the moment. Better yet, since the magewoman couldn't work her bespeaking magic for Zurenne in person, she hadn't had to explain what was going on here to Corrain. Let the Archmage to do that since he had forced these Archipelagans on Halferan.

'My lady.' The young sergeant opened the door, looking expectantly at the white-clad Aldabreshin.

'Lady Patri,' Ilysh asked suddenly as the two men departed. 'How can Soviro be in the same room as—' Lysha flinched '—as your treasures without coming to harm?' She moved her foot out of Zurenne's reach. 'If there is any magic to be found?'

'That is a fair question.' Debis answered with a smile suggesting that she knew Zurenne had done her best to curb her daughter's curiosity. 'Soviro is *zamorin*.'

This time they all looked at Kheda for a translation, Khusro wives and Halferan's ladies alike. Zurenne was startled to see colour darkening on the Aldabreshin man's cheekbones as though he were blushing.

He cleared his throat. '*Zamorin* have been cut, as a horse master cuts a stallion to make a better workhorse of a gelding.'

It took Zurenne a moment to realise what he meant. Lost for words, she looked at Ilysh to see the same understanding dawn on her daughter's face.

'How—?'

Zurenne would have cuffed her around the ear and answered for it to Raeponin himself if Debis hadn't cut the girl's question short with a firm answer.

'Soviro may take some taint from whatever magic is discovered but he chooses to face that risk in our service.'

'*Zamorin* are among our most highly valued slaves,' Patri added, 'since their loyalty is never divided between a warlord's family and their own kin.'

'Freed from such distractions, they are often diligent scholars, highly prized,' Quilar observed. 'Soviro is both shrewd and erudite. We can hope that he learns something which will help him identify anything further which we may hold in our strong rooms, unaware that it is stained by magic.'

'Since *zamorin* can have no children and seldom take lovers, man or woman, they have no one to share such pollution through ties of blood or affection,' Patri explained to Ilysh.

Zurenne had thought she was beginning to understand these Archipelagan women, that they weren't so different. Now these gaping chasms of comprehension opened up between them.

To her inexpressible relief, the kitchen door opened to reveal Mistress Rotharle. She held a tray with a cloudy jug of orgeat and the brilliantly polished silver goblets which Doratine had sent over from the manor at dawn.

'May we offer you refreshment?' Zurenne managed a fair attempt at a smile.

'That will be most welcome,' Debis assured her.

Mistress Rotharle managed to set down the tray though the crystal wine jug rattled against the goblets.

'Thank you, we will serve our guests.' Zurenne didn't care if this was correct etiquette. She wasn't about to risk poor Mistress Rotharle staining those opulent silks with a shaking hand.

'May I?' Ilysh stood to pour drinks for them all.

'Thank you.' Debis took a sip of the almond drink and nodded with approval before looking around the tavern with open interest. 'Tell me,' she invited, 'what recreations do your people enjoy here?'

'Recreations?' Zurenne covered her hesitation with a swallow of orgeat. 'They sing songs, I believe, and tell tales to each other.'

She instantly regretted that answer. She knew no more of tavern ballads than she did of the Caladhrian parliament's debates and the only chimney-corner stories she knew were the ones she told to Neeny, as her own nurse had told them to her.

'They play games,' Ilysh ventured.

'Games of chance?' Patri's eyes brightened.

'Yes, with these.' Ilysh reached for her elegantly embroidered reticule. To Zurenne's mortification, her daughter produced a shabby leather pouch and undid its drawstring to tip a battered set of runes onto the spotless table cloth.

'What are these?' Patri picked up one of the stubby lengths of bone.

'What do these designs signify?' Quilar's quick fingers turned over the remaining eight to examine each different face.

'May I?' Ilysh took the first rune from Patri. 'This is the heavens rune. See, this is the sun—' she turned the length of bone to show them the radiant circle made up from eight lines pointing outwards to the points and half points of a compass circle '—and this is the greater moon, and the lesser moon.' She showed them the lozenge and the single broad dot carved lifetimes ago by some unknown knife.

'What of the rest?' Debis was studying each bone in turn, equally intrigued.

Zurenne swallowed the remonstrance on the tip of her tongue. The Khusro wives weren't to know such common pastimes were considered unsuitable for noble ladies. She could scold Lysha for such impropriety once the Archipelagans had gone home.

When she would also ask where Lysha had learned so much lore about these game pieces. Now the girl was explaining how the symbols covered every aspect of life. Zurenne had no idea what she was talking about but the Archipelagan women seemed to understand at once.

'The Wolf lives in the Mountains among the Pine trees?' Patri looked at the three faces of that particular bone.

'While the Salmon swims through the Reeds that fringe the Sea.' Debis examined the one with those three symbols.

'I can understand that the Sea Breeze travels over Water but what has that to do with the Harp?' Quilar wondered.

'We often talk of a harp's music rippling.' Lysha glanced towards the door and Kusint.

'Do you have such instruments in your islands?' Zurenne asked. 'A harp is a wooden frame, with strings—'

Debis nodded. 'We know of such things but alas, our wet season's dampness and the dry season's warmth alike are no friend to such frailty.'

'How are games played with these?' Patri demanded.

'You take three and roll them. I take three and roll them.' Ilysh threw trios of runes with either hand and far too much familiarity for Zurenne's peace of mind.

'See, you have the Harp and the Stag and the Mountain Wind.' She showed the Aldabreshin women the upright face of each rune as they had landed.

'I have the Salmon, the Wolf and the Chime. Oh, sorry, we should have rolled the Heavens rune first.'

Patri promptly did so. 'But these three, alone of the runes—' she pronounced the strange word with care '—look the same whichever way up they land.'

Ilysh nodded. 'So if the Sun shows, then the male runes will prevail but if both moons are showing then the female runes will win, with the stronger ones outweighing the weaker ones.'

'Which signs are male and which are female?' Quilar enquired.

'Wolf and Deer are both male, but since the Wolf is the hunter, that's the stronger of the pair. Eagle and Salmon are both female—'

'—but the bird eats the fish.' Quilar nodded.

As Ilysh began to explain the rest, Debis smiled at Zurenne. 'Our husband will be fascinated to explore the mathematics underpinning this.'

Zurenne could only smile with faint bemusement.

'The best way to learn a game is to play it,' Patri declared.

'But—' Ilysh looked at her mother, belatedly as apprehensive as Neeny caught in some mischief.

'Forgive me,' Zurenne said levelly. 'We do not carry coin for gambling.'

Patri laughed. 'All we need are some tokens. Saie!'

She snapped her fingers to summon her body servant and before Zurenne realised what she intended, the Aldabreshin woman plucked a lethal-looking dagger from the warrior's belt.

Patri lifted a rope of pearls over her head and sliced through its thread. Glistening pearls bounced and rolled over the table linen. Quilar gathered them up and Debis began counting out five separate quantities.

'I do not wish to play,' Zurenne said quickly. She had no wish to have her ignorance of this game exposed.

'My lady of Halferan.' Kheda spoke from the neighbouring table. 'Perhaps we could discuss what is to be done after today? We must establish how you will exchange letters with the Khusro domain, to receive news of those Halferan slaves whom Khusro Rina still hopes to return.'

Debis looked up. 'That would seem wise. Lafis, please remove this before something is spilled.'

Her body slave took the tray of orgeat to his table and poured drinks for himself and his two companions. Doratine had been scandalised when these men refused everything her kitchen could offer, only to eat and drink their mistress's leavings at last night's dinner and this morning's breakfasts. But once again, Kheda had explained this Archipelagan custom ensured that such bodyguards were always vigilant against poisoners.

'Ladies, excuse me.' Zurenne rose and took her goblet to the neighbouring table.

Kheda smiled. 'Your daughter is a credit to you. The Khusro women would be delighted to establish ties of trade with your barony.'

Zurenne shook her head. 'That is out of the question.'

'Why?' Kheda challenged her under cover of the laughter from the other table. 'Khusro Rina and his wives wish to restore trade with the mainland and Halferan could profit handsomely by leading the way. If Patri can offer the central domains such new luxury as that fine shawl, while Debis can swear by all the stars that they have rid their domain of magic, they may yet persuade Miris Esul's wives not to turn their faces southwards for good.'

Zurenne took refuge in the answer which her mother had always used to end any argument. 'The baron would never allow it.'

'Corrain is no true baron,' Kheda reflected. 'Ilysh is Halferan's heir. You could secure her position considerably if the mainland's merchants had to follow in Halferan's footsteps.'

Zurenne wasn't about to discuss such any such notion. 'Why is Khusro Rina's eldest son not his heir?' Let Kheda see how he liked impertinent questions.

The Archipelagan smiled. 'Because the warlord and his wives judge their second son to be more fitted to rule.'

'What does their eldest son think of that?' Belatedly, Zurenne realised how rude that sounded and blushed.

Kheda looked at her unblinking. 'I imagine he deems himself fortunate to have been born to Khusro where surplus sons are allowed to live. In some domains they are killed, before or after their father's death. In others they are made *zamorin* or blinded or maimed in some other way which leaves them unfit to rule. I have learned that the leader of the corsairs who plagued you was just such an unwanted son, deprived of his eyes and discarded.'

Zurenne couldn't believe how calmly the tall Archipelagan related such horrors.

Kheda smiled faintly. 'You think we are barbarians? But we are an island people. We cannot let rivals tear the domains apart, dividing each group of islands into ever smaller dominions. We cannot send surplus sons to seek their fortunes over the next hill or even far away over the ocean in this new land which your wizards and mariners have discovered.

'Consider this, my lady.' He glanced at Ilysh. 'No Aldabreshin warlord's daughter would be obliged to marry her guard captain to save herself from men and laws allowing her no voice in her own fate. No woman with the wits to enrich her household with trade would have her horizons limited to breeding children and tending a husband's whims. That would be considered barbaric from the northernmost Archipelago to the uttermost south.

'The Aldabreshi consider it arrant folly and an abject breach of faith to grant rule over countless subjects to a man whose only claim is the accident of birth. What if a first-born son lacks strength of character or the ready intelligence to defend his populace with just laws and if needs be, astute leadership in battle?'

Zurenne thought of some of the Caladhrian nobles whom her beloved husband had cursed as too foolish to come indoors out of the rain. 'But their own sons—'

Kheda laid his dark-skinned hand on hers. 'We are not all barbarians. Khusro Rina and his wives follow the custom of many in the western reaches. They simply do not teach their other sons to read or calculate beyond the most basic arithmetic. No man could take on a warlord's responsibilities without such skills.'

'Oh.' Zurenne couldn't imagine that solution ever occurring to a Caladhrian baron cursed with an excess of sons resenting the eldest born.

Kheda withdrew his hand. 'When Khusro Anai succeeds his father, his brothers will be allowed to join their married sisters' households. Of course, that could still lead to problems in years to come but I have travelled widely through the islands and across your mainland. I have learned that no one realm or race has any more infallible wisdom than any other. Any more than any man can build a roof guaranteed to never leak.'

Debis's thoughtful voice cut through the amusement at the other table. 'Surely the fall of these symbols could be read as omens in themselves, as well as taking the outcome of a game for a portent.'

'Oh, they are,' Ilysh said with a ready smile, 'among the Forest Folk and the Mountain Men. Cast one while you keep a question in mind. The upright rune suggests the answer, the reversed face offers a warning while the third which lands unseen reminds you of something you haven't considered.' As she spoke she rolled a bone onto the cloth.

Before Zurenne could see what the runes were, Kusint strode the length of the taproom.

'This is sacred lore and not to be shared with barbarians!'

The Aldabreshin bodyguards might not understand his words but they assuredly saw the anger in his face. Leaping to their feet, their hands went to their sword hilts. Kusint halted and reached for his own blade.

'Captain, do not dare draw steel in my presence!' Zurenne sprang up, terrified that Kusint would be gutted before their eyes.

On his feet beside her, Kheda spoke in the Archipelagan tongue, harsh and commanding. Debis instantly rebuked him, her eyes flashing with anger. Quilar rounded on the three swordsmen with some scathing reprimand of her own. The bodyslaves retreated, shamefaced, to sit down again at their table.

Kusint remained standing in the middle of the taproom although he held his hands prudently wide of his weapon.

'Forgive me, my lady Zurenne—' he didn't sound in the least contrite '—but the noble ladies of Khusro should be told that using the runes for foretelling is part of the ancient magic of the Forest and the Mountains which you call Artifice.'

'Magic?' Debis couldn't have been more horrified if she had found herself juggling snakes.

'Not wizard magic.' Ilysh was on the verge of tears.

'You have no knowledge of such Artifice, my lady Ilysh?' Kheda walked over to the table and gathered up the bones.

Mute with distress, Lysha nodded, handing him the leather bag which had held the runes.

Kheda said something in his own tongue and Zurenne saw the fear and anger on the Khusro wives' faces fade to wary relief. He gestured to the pearls scattered across the table and Debis Khusro forced a brittle smile, sweeping them into an iridescent heap with shaking hands.

'Lady Ilysh, we beg your forgiveness for this misunderstanding. Please accept my sister Patri's gift to your daughter as an apology from us all.'

'You honour my daughter with such generosity and truly, there is nothing to forgive,' Zurenne said quickly. 'Indeed, I beg your pardon, most humbly.'

Kheda tossed the bag of runes to Kusint. 'I believe these belong to you.'

The young captain plucked the bag out of the air and looked the Archipelagan straight in the eye. 'How can you have dealings with magic without being stained by it?'

'I killed a dragon.' Kheda stared him down. 'Its blood is the most powerful of all talismans against magic. The creatures will always shun any place where one of their own has died. They fear that whatever killed their kin still lies in wait for them. Since I was mired in such slaughter, that blood wards off contamination from any lesser sorcery.'

'How—?'

Ilysh bit back her question but the tall Archipelagan answered anyway.

'With ropes and nets and spears and swords wielded by brave men risking and losing their lives at my order, even though the beast was already half-dead from fighting one of its own kind.'

Zurenne couldn't decide what astonished her more; this tale of bravery fit for some minstrel's ballad or the self-loathing in Kheda's voice.

The bodyslave Lafis said something under his breath which prompted an unfriendly laugh from Saie. The previously impassive swordsmen looked at Kusint with scarcely veiled anger.

'Mama?'

Ilysh's frightened whisper spurred Zurenne to clap her hands.

'Captain Kusint. Return to the manor and ask— ask Sergeant Reven if Master Soviro has any news for Khusro's noble ladies. At once!' she added sharply as obstinacy flickered across the Forest youth's face.

After no more than an instant, though it felt like an aeon to Zurenne, he bowed his coppery head. 'My lady.'

He barely glanced at Ilysh but Zurenne saw his hectic flush of emotion as he turned for the door. So she and Corrain had missed the mark entirely, thinking that Lysha might be mooning after young Reven as the sergeant so visibly adored her. But that was a problem for another day.

She breathed a little easier as the door closed

behind the captain, only for her heart to pound with apprehension as the Khusro wives rose to their feet.

'We wish to see the view from that far window.'

'I'm sure you'll find it a very pleasant prospect.'

Zurenne saw the relief in Debis's eyes as she answered that transparent lie with one just as flimsy.

Sitting down, she reached for her goblet, barely managing to avoid pouring the almond dregs down her chin. She watched the Khusro wives stand close together in low-voiced conversation. Whatever they were discussing, Zurenne would wager all the gold in Halferan's strong room that it wasn't the view of the village market place.

Kheda produced a square of hemmed silk from a pocket and scooped up the pearls, securing them inside a lumpy bundle. 'These are yours, Lady Ilysh.'

'Mama, I can't.' Lysha looked apprehensively at Zurenne. 'That necklace was Lady Patri's. It's worth a prince's ransom.'

'You will accept her gift and thank her as courteously as you know how,' Zurenne told her daughter in a forceful undertone. 'I know you meant no harm, sweetheart, but the Khusro ladies are probably afraid that some magic has touched those pearls. Lady Debis as good as told Lady Patri that she must be rid of them.'

'Your mother is right,' Kheda confirmed. 'But remember that pearls are a talisman against magic. That will have protected the Khusro wives.'

'I don't understand.' Lysha's lip quivered.

Zurenne sighed. 'Nor do I, but we must do our duty to Halferan. Once Madam Jilseth has left with whatever she finds among the Khusro treasures, these ladies will return to their islands and search out our people still enslaved there.'

She must hold fast to that, Zurenne told herself, as the Aldabreshi women returned. She knotted her trembling hands in her lap. Knowing the fate of those lost guardsmen and saving those who still lived was her justification to Corrain or to Lord Licanin or any other baron who dared to chastise her or Ilysh for inviting these Archipelagans into Halferan.

'We were wondering—' Debis resumed her seat with a determined smile '—precisely what wares and materials your barony produces? Which merchants and markets do you favour?'

'We rear a great many sheep.' Zurenne began to elaborate, profoundly thankful for her unseemly knowledge of the demesne's ledgers.

If they could keep conversation limited to such innocuous topics, perhaps they could get through the rest of this perilous visit without further incident, or worse, bloodshed.

To make quite certain of that, Zurenne silently vowed not to ask these Khusro ladies anything about Jagai ships in Col or to question Kusint about Soluran Artifice. Madam Jilseth would just have to find some other, wizardly means to learn whatever she needed to know.

— CHAPTER TWENTY-ONE —

Halferan Manor, Caladhria
32nd of Aft-Winter

JILSETH RETURNED THE silver-gilt plate to the chest. It was embossed with a dramatic hunting scene where Archipelagans in small boats harried a monstrous sea serpent with spears and harpoons. It was no more imbued with magic than the table the chest stood on.

She closed the lid and rolled her head from side to side to ease her stiff shoulders. Her back ached from constantly stooping and standing up again. Though she was only physically weary; as far as wizardry went, the day's work had been more protracted than demanding. Her mage senses readily identified pieces with magic within them even if the precise nature of such spells was a more complex puzzle.

Twenty-seven strongboxes had been brought up from the iron-gated cellar to this narrow-windowed muniment room. They ranged from chests large enough to carry half an Aldabreshi noblewoman's wardrobe to nail-studded coffers with intricate locks, small enough to rest on two outstretched hands. Each one had been crammed with jewellery and ornaments though this could be barely a fraction of the Khusro domain's treasury.

Jilseth had diligently examined every piece. She turned to the white-clad Archipelagan standing silently inside the door opening from the barony's audience chamber. 'Do you know why these particular things were selected? Was there some reason to suspect magic's contamination?'

He didn't answer or even meet her gaze to acknowledge that she had spoken. As he stared intently at the array of items which she had set aside on the table Jilseth guessed that he was committing every one to memory, to tell his mistresses what this voyage had cost them, to free themselves from lurking sorcery.

A belt made up of four strands of plaited leather threaded through gold roundels, each one with a different bird's head in its centre. A long cylindrical whetstone with a silver finial shaped like a dolphin. Four narrow plaques of different lengths, cast in bronze and each one showing a violent battle scene. Jilseth guessed these were part of a swordsman's gear.

An alabaster statue of an eagle-headed woman holding a shallow dish. A bronze bowl engraved with ducks splashing among tufts of reeds. A gold cup embossed with enamelled feathers. Spoons, cast from bronze and copper or carved from horn or dense black wood and inlaid with chips of bone and coloured stone. A tall, narrow-necked ewer and a pair of enamelled copper candlesticks. Would these have spells imbued within them for unsuspected domestic purposes?

An array of silver and gold brooches shaped into flowers and sprigs of leaves, bright with precious stones. A pair of intricate ivory earrings studded with turquoise. Three anklets; one of braided copper, one of dull brown agates set in dark iron and one of silver bells.

Conferring some more personal magic, Jilseth guessed, but she hadn't tried any piece on to discover precisely what spells it held. Not with this daunting quantity of boxes to be opened and searched through, when Velindre and the Archmage had insisted that this task must be completed as swiftly as possible.

The blonde magewoman had warned that the Greater Moon, the Opal, would move from the region of the sky offering omens for friends into that arc offering omens of enemies this very evening. Sunset, not dawn, marked each passing day for the Archipelagans. The Lesser Moon, the Pearl, would pass into the arc of death to join the ill-omened heavenly Emerald in three days' time.

Planir had simply asked that she bring the artefacts to Hadrumal as soon as possible, so that the Aldabreshi women and their swordsmen would leave Halferan. Then the Archmage could reassure Corrain, still furious in Col, that Lady Zurenne and her daughters were unharmed.

Small figurines carved from soapstone; a kneeling child, two men wrestling, a reclining woman seemingly asleep. More ominously, a coiled snake, a crouching rat and what Jilseth had identified after a moment's thought as a scorpion. From the threat in its up-curved sting-tipped tail, she was glad she'd only ever encountered such a creature in books. A narrow bronze box as long as a large man's hand which had proved to contain reed pens although none of those had had the least hint of magic.

As far as Jilseth could see, there was no more commonality between these pieces than there was between the other Aldabreshin treasures. Some looked fresh from a craftsman's hands. Others were tarnished and neglected, evidently as long-lived as that arm-ring which Hosh had given to Velindre.

Reven was standing wide-eyed beside the silent Archipelagan. 'I suggest you send word to the tavern,' Jilseth told him, 'to tell Lady Zurenne that we're done here. I will remove myself and these offending articles before her guests return.'

She took care not to refer directly to the Khusro wives as Velindre had advised her. The white-clad Archipelagan in his incongruous woolly jerkin stiffened, making it perfectly plain that he understood what she had said. He still didn't look at Jilseth, only deigning to notice Reven addressing him.

'Please go to the village, Master Soviro and tell your mistresses and mine that the—that the work here is done.'

Jilseth saw that the young sergeant-at-arms was embarrassed by such discourtesy towards her. She waited until the Archipelagan had departed through the audience chamber and the anteroom beyond.

'It's difficult, isn't it, Sergeant, not to tread on their toes by saying the wrong thing.' She used a skein of air to lift the middling-sized coffer which she had earmarked for her own use onto the table.

'Saedrin save us, isn't it just?' Reven looked with wonder at the treasures on the muniment room table. 'These things all have some magic about them? What do they do?'

'They have had spells instilled within them,' Jilseth confirmed, 'though as yet, I can't say precisely what their magecrafting might entail. Some hold more than one spell.'

She realised that she had no idea how many chimes had passed her by, while she'd been so intent on examining the Archipelagan treasures. She hadn't even noticed the lamps being lit in the muniment room or the audience chamber beyond. 'How late in the day is it?'

'Coming up on the tenth chime.' Reven said promptly.

'When are the funeral pyres to be lit?'

'At the first chime of the night.'

Jilseth nodded. 'Then I need to be gone, so Lady Zurenne

and Lady Ilysh can bring the mourners to the shrine.'

Kheda had warned her this morning that the Aldabreshi women would wish to show their respects for Caladhrian funeral rites even though their own beliefs were so very different.

'Please convey the Archmage's thanks to your mistress. I will make sure that Master Olved bespeaks her with the latest news from Baron Halferan in Col as soon as we see that the Aldabreshi have left—' Jilseth broke off from putting the ensorcelled artefacts carefully in the coffer. 'Don't say that in the Archipelagan women's hearing or anywhere near their slaves. They mustn't know that they're being scried for.'

'They wouldn't like that,' Reven said fervently.

'Quite.' Jilseth gestured towards the strong boxes. 'I suggest you whistle up some help and get everything safely stowed in the cellar until the Aldabreshi take to the high road.' She closed the coffer's lid and pressed a finger to the lock.

'That'll be the day after tomorrow, most likely, according to Master Soviro. Saedrin save us,' the young Caladhrian said involuntarily, startled as the lock's tumblers turned and clicked.

Didn't he know that wizards had no need of keys?

'Farewell Sergeant, I hope to see you soon. Please convey my respects and my thanks to Lady Zurenne and Lady Ilysh.'

Jilseth laid a hand on the coffer to surround it with a dense ward woven of quadrate magic. Even with the spells quiescent in the artefacts, she didn't want to be surprised by some unsuspected clash of magecraft. The memory of her translocation colliding with Velindre's wizardry in Relshaz still unnerved her.

The lamp light mingled with the spell's strengthening glow. With Halferan's foundations rooted in the same bedrock underpinning the wizard isle, carrying herself and this booty back to Trydek's tower was the work of a moment.

There was no one in Planir's sitting room though lamps were lit here as well. Lowering the Archipelagan coffer to the floor, Jilseth looked around. The wide table was still piled high with poor Kerrit's books and papers. An untended fire in the hearth had died away to barely smouldering clinker.

Jilseth went to the mantelshelf to find a taper and mirror, about to bespeak the Archmage. She heard a door opening up above and footsteps descending the spiral stair leading down from the Archmage's private study beside his bedchamber.

'This is where I teach my pupils and receive more informal visitors to Hadrumal.'

Jilseth wondered who Planir's companion was, to be so unfamiliar with Trydek's tower.

Planir smiled as he saw her and that smile widened as he saw the Aldabreshin chest. 'Madam Jilseth, I'm delighted to see that your quest has prospered.'

'Archmage.' She answered him with equal formality and waited to be introduced to the tall, muscular man at his side.

Planir turned to him with an open hand. 'May I make known to you Mentor Micaran, sealed to the School of Rhetoric at the University of Col and an adept of aetheric magic.'

'Good evening, Madam Mage.' The dark haired man bowed politely.

'I am honoured to meet you, Master Scholar.' Jilseth

wondered what business he had here. She'd wager it had something to do with Corrain.

Planir rubbed his hands together and fresh flames kindled in the hearth despite the lack of coal for burning. 'Was there any word of strangers passing through the Halferan barony? Did you notice any unfamiliar faces in the village?'

'No.'

Jilseth saw that wasn't to be the end of it as Planir nodded.

'I would like Mentor Micaran to use his Artifice to show you this man supposedly from Wrede, who was dogging Corrain's footsteps in Ferl. It may be that you'll recognise him. You may easily have passed him in Halferan's village unawares.'

'I think it's unlikely that any stranger would have gone unnoticed, Archmage,' Jilseth said with careful respect. 'With Aldabreshi visitors within the manor, the demesne folk were as nervous as children watching shadows for the Eldritch Kin.'

'We have reason to suspect that this man from Wrede is also an aetheric adept.' Planir ushered Micaran towards the fire. 'He may have enchantments to convince everyone that he belongs wherever he happens to be.'

'Artifice can do that?' Jilseth realised too late how impolite her words must sound. She offered an apologetic glance to Mentor Micaran. 'Forgive me, I know little of your discipline.'

'Few people do, here or on the mainland.' He didn't seem perturbed. 'But there are many ways of going unseen using aetheric magic.'

'If you please?' Planir's nod indicated that Jilseth should sit beside the mentor adept on the settle opposite his own.

She complied, somewhat apprehensively. 'What should I do?'

'Clear your thoughts,' Micaran smiled. 'I often advise my subjects to stare into a candle flame but the Archmage tells me that would only focus a wizard's senses.'

'Indeed.' Jilseth glanced at the hearth, reminded that the Archmage's mastery now somehow allowed that fire to burn with no fuel. 'Oh!'

Two things caught her unawares. First, Mentor Micaran took her hand. Second, in the same instant, Jilseth found herself in a library, though it was assuredly not one in Hadrumal or any of those she knew in Col.

Sloped reading desks with comfortable chairs were set amid a labyrinth of waist-high book cases filled with neatly ranked tomes. Broad windows in all four walls as well as skylights in the roof allowed bright sunlight to illuminate long tables laid ready with every device and substance which a mage might need to test a theory.

'Forgive my stratagem.' Micaran was standing at her side. 'Turning your mind to wizardly matters makes it easier to weave my thoughts into your own.'

Jilseth studied her hands. How could she still feel the pressure of the scholar adept's fingers? How could it still be daylight when she had returned to Hadrumal at dusk? Those were the least of her concerns. She extended her wizardly senses and found nothing, not even the reassuring solidity of those stone walls. She reached further but there was still no hint of the elements which underpinned all things.

Jilseth felt wholly cast adrift. Worse, the sensation brought back the agonies of fear and uncertainty which she had suffered after exhausting her magic in Halferan's defence.

She reached out still more urgently with her affinity. The entire room shimmered like summer haze striking upwards from sun-scorched flagstones but she still couldn't find any elemental reality.

'Does the Archmage know where you have taken me?' She could barely stifle her growing alarm.

'I've taken you nowhere.' Micaran looked around with keen interest. 'This is a refuge within your own mind.'

At least his calm voice gave her something to concentrate on besides her burgeoning panic. Jilseth shook her head. 'I've never been here before.'

'It's not a memory; it's a refuge,' Micaran said patiently, 'wrought from some ideal which you cherish unawares. Please believe that this is an illusion. It is merely the simplest way for me to work the Artifice which Planir has requested. You are perfectly safe within the Archmage's tower. Your own imagination has made this place.'

Jilseth surveyed their surroundings, trying to ignore the vile absence numbing her wizardly senses. She had to agree that this library was perfectly suited to wizardly study. If she were ever to be Mistress of a newly founded Hall, she could commission just such a building.

'Good.' Micaran smiled. 'Now let's proceed before Planir tries shaking one of us back to awareness? He's as impatient as he is curious about Artifice.'

Jilseth turned back to Micaran. 'What manner of place do you find in Planir's thoughts?'

The adept didn't answer, looking instead at the far wall. Jilseth recoiled as a mounted man rode straight through the window's leaded glass and stone mullions, like some hunting shade in a tale of the Eldritch Kin.

But the wall wasn't truly there. Nothing here was real. Everything shimmered again.

'Please look at what I'm showing you.' Mentor Micaran gazed intently at the mounted man. 'The Archmage wishes you to know this man's face.'

Jilseth did her best to ignore the fact that the rider and his mount were now advancing through the book cases with no more concern than a horseman forcing a path through tall grass.

That became easier the more she concentrated on his face. The stranger's countenance was unremarkable, though she found she was curiously certain that she would be able to pick him out in a crowded marketplace any number of years from now.

Resisting the crawling dread now filling the void left by her absent wizard senses was becoming ever more difficult though.

'Madam Jilseth?' Micaran was behind her.

Turning, she saw him standing beside another man with sandy brown hair and hazel eyes. This new stranger sat at his ease in a leather upholstered chair which certainly hadn't been there before. The prosperous man had a glass of wine in his hand and his mouth moved as silently as a festival marionette. Was he talking to someone unseen?

'Thank you.'

As Micaran spoke, the library vanished and Jilseth found herself sitting beside the Archmage's fireplace. She seized on the elemental fire burning within the hearth, on the air swirling around the tower, moist with water drawn from the surrounding seas. Her affinity took hold of the ancient stones, rooting her in the present through their aeons of existence. She extended her wizard senses down through the tower's foundations and deep into the bedrock.

'Well?' Planir leaned forward, his eyes intent.

'That was—' Jilseth shuddered convulsively '—horrible.'

'I know,' Planir assured her, 'but you have passed a test which too many mages fail.'

'A test?' Jilseth stared at him. 'I didn't know.'

'My apologies.' The Archmage's eyes were opaque. 'If you knew, it couldn't be a fair outcome.'

'Have you ever seen the man on horseback?'

As Micaran released his hold Jilseth curbed an impulse to wipe her palm on her skirt. The adept's hands hadn't been in the least sweaty but she still felt an urge to cleanse herself of his touch.

If only she could wipe away her revulsion at being deprived of her elemental senses. As she thrust that repellent memory away, resentment surged up instead. How dare he intrude so completely into her thoughts that he could weave such illusions from hopes and dreams that she wasn't even conscious of herself?

'I don't know either man, Archmage.' She couldn't bring herself to look at Micaran for fear of berating him with undeserved hatred. He had only done Planir's bidding. She drew on all her wizardly training to get her emotions under control. 'Who was that second stranger?'

'The Soluran stirring up discontent in Col.' Planir leaned back in his seat. 'It may well prove useful if you can recognise him.'

'What do you want me to do? To help Corrain, that's to say, Baron Halferan?' Jilseth corrected herself hastily.

The Archmage shook his head. 'We'll take your spoils from Halferan to Suthyfer first, along with Mentor Micaran.' He acknowledged the scholarly adept with a courteous nod. 'Once his business there is concluded, please use your wizardry to return him home.'

'Suthyfer?' Jilseth hadn't expected that. 'Isn't Merenel already there?'

Planir nodded. 'She's also been shown how easily a skilled adept can invade a mage's mind. So she's been working with Suthyfer's Artificers, exploring why wizards are so vulnerable with their thoughts focused on elemental matters. As we of Hadrumal have learned to our cost, that can be the death of us even more swiftly than an adept's malice can overwhelm the mundane born.'

Planir's face hardened momentarily and Jilseth had to force herself not to look upwards, remembering the funeral urn in the Archmage's study.

It wasn't only Larissa who had died; Planir's beloved and a talented magewoman who would surely have earned high rank in Hadrumal in her own right. Jilseth had made her own discreet enquiries since Nolyen had told of the struggle some years before, between Hadrumal's wizards and unknown adepts from ocean islands even more remote than Suthyfer. She had been appalled to learn that little-known misadventure had seen the death of a handful of notable wizards including the redoubtable Otrick, Cloud Master before Rafrid and, it was rumoured, once Velindre's lover.

She wanted to steal a glance at Micaran. Did the scholarly adept know of these Elietimm who had challenged the Archmage? Barely any of Hadrumal's mages outside the Council were even aware of their islands in the icy northern waters, inhabited by this race akin to the Mountain Men and willing to use their knowledge of Artifice wholly without scruple, according to the whispers which Jilseth had heard behind cautious hands in the corners of Hadrumal's wine shops.

Why else had Planir been so willing to allow Col and

Vanam's scholars to explore the remnants of Imperial Artifice, pieced together from sources as disparate as folk songs and noble family archives? Why had the Archmage defied those Council members who so disparaged Artifice, insisting on allowing Usara, Shivvalan and the other mages interested in learning more of aetheric magic to establish their own hall on those mid-ocean islands? The Archmage wanted to understand the threat facing Hadrumal.

'Do Suthyfer's adepts have some insight to offer the mageborn, into warding our thoughts against such intrusion?'

'Insights, yes,' Planir agreed. 'Warding is proving considerably more complicated.'

Once again, Jilseth saw unexpected weariness on the Archmage's face. Before she could choose which of a handful of questions to ask, the sitting room vanished in a flash of blinding light.

— CHAPTER TWENTY-TWO —

The Island Hall, Suthyfer
32nd of Aft-Winter

EVEN BEFORE THE Archmage's spell released her, Jilseth's affinity told her that this translocation had carried her further than ever before. Her wizard senses reeled after crossing such a vast expanse of wind-tossed water. Then she felt solid ground beneath her feet and her wizardry reached deep into the rock below. She knew precisely how far she was from home.

The furthest Jilseth had travelled by means of her own magic had been to Inglis on the Gidestan ocean coast. This was the usual test to prove a would-be mage's skills in the final days of apprenticeship. Planir's wizardry had just taken the three of them half as far again.

A thousand leagues? That was her best guess and Jilseth seldom erred by more than one league in a hundred. She looked up at the ragged clouds scudding across the rain-washed sky and saw that they had travelled far enough east to outstrip the sunset.

On dry land this island would have been a mountain to fascinate wizards with earth and air affinities alike, with its peak soaring so high into the sky. Here in mid-ocean Jilseth could feel the plunging depths surrounding her as well as the fierce ocean currents surging through the channels between this island and its neighbours. A trailing line of such mountains had surged up from the ocean floor aeons before the molten rock's fires had been quenched in time out of mind.

As Planir's magic faded, Jilseth reached further through the turbulent ocean to realise that a great sweep of land lay somewhere to the east, far closer than Tormalin's ocean coast in the west. That must be the unknown expanse of Kellarin.

The Archmage grabbed her arm and pulled her sideways to save her skirts. Mentor Micaran collapsed onto his hands and knees to vomit copiously and helplessly onto the flagstones.

'Archmage?' Startled, Jilseth looked at Planir.

'The further our magic carries an Artificer, the worse their stomachs rebel,' he explained wryly. 'Those of a religious persuasion accuse Raeponin of a cruel sense of humour.'

Jilseth wasn't about to admit her own first mean-spirited thoughts. It was some comfort to see that adepts had their own vulnerabilities, after Micaran had so easily invaded her mind.

Rather than humiliate the stricken scholar by staring at his distress, she looked around. They had arrived beside a tall, high-windowed building of dark grey masonry rising to a shallow pitched roof of close fitted stone slates. It overlooked a gentle grass slope dotted with scrubby bushes and pocked with earthen scrapes suggesting burrowing animals.

There was no sign of anyone opening the door. From the savoury scents drifting from the high windows, Jilseth guessed at a kitchen within. Grease-flecked water filled the stone-lined gully running alongside this hardstanding to drain into a pit of gravel.

'Is this where you routinely arrive? Should I commit this place to memory?'

The Archmage summoned a surge of water to wash the consequences of Micaran's misery into the soakaway. 'If you are bringing an adept with you.'

'One moment.' Micaran managed to raise a hand as he took a shaky breath.

'Good afternoon, Archmage.'

A man and a woman appeared around the corner of the building. Both were within a handful of years of Jilseth's own age; the man older, the woman younger. Both were clothed in current Tormalin fashion, though in the broadcloth jerkin and breeches and calf-length gown of the merchant classes rather than nobility's full-skirted silks and frothing lace.

The man was lean-faced with a wiry build, with a fine sheen of sandy bristles on his head suggesting that he anticipated the untimely loss of his hair with a purposeful razor. His companion barely topped his shoulder, even allowing for the nut-brown braids coiled tidily on her head.

Jilseth noted the calm determination in her dark brown eyes. She had often seen such purpose in those who lacked the height to impose their will on others.

'Usara, Guinalle, may I introduce Jilseth, a mage of my own discipline, and Mentor Micaran, an adept from Col's university.'

'Master Usara.' Jilseth was taken aback by such informality. Many in Hadrumal's Council still hoped to see Usara acclaimed as Stone Master and his wife was a Tormalin noblewoman whose family had held the Imperial throne in antiquity. 'Lady Tor Priminale.'

'You are most welcome, Madam Mage.' Though Guinalle barely spared Jilseth and the Archipelagan coffer a glance as she went to help Micaran to his feet.

'My thanks.' Despite his greater height, the ashen-faced mentor leaned heavily on her. Fortunately the Tormalin woman was no frail reed.

'I have a restorative tisane brewing.' Guinalle ushered Micaran away.

'So what have you brought us?' Usara looked at the Archipelagan chest with keen interest.

'A baffling miscellany.' Jilseth couldn't think how else to describe the random collection of ensorcelled objects. 'I didn't have time to identify their spells.'

That was only the first of her concerns. Hadn't Hadrumal's Council insisted that no such artefacts be taken to Suthyfer?

'Let's go and see what we have.' Usara gestured and the chest rose to float a few paces ahead as he led them along the path skirting the kitchen building.

Jilseth saw that this practical range abutted what looked like a hall for gathering or dining, as in any Caladhrian manor or indeed Hadrumal's wizardly halls. On the hall's far side, a third building with windows indicating two storeys topped by garrets benefited from the south-facing aspect which Jilseth naturally associated with libraries.

A Caladhrian manor would be surrounded by barracks, servants' quarters and storehouses ringed with a high wall. Every wizardly hall in Hadrumal was hemmed in with quadrangles offering accommodation to mages, pupils and apprentices. Towers recalled past generations when such a defensible building was an essential refuge in time of trouble.

Suthyfer's mage hall stood without wall or watch tower in a wide hollow of short-cropped turf dotted with more stunted bushes. A deeply rutted gravelled road cut across the greensward from east to west, meandering to draw close to the kitchen though there was no immediate sign where any wagons delivering foodstuffs could have come from.

Jilseth could see a bare handful of modest houses, not one within easily hailing distance of a neighbour. Each had a garden large enough to be called a smallholding, with pigsties and chicken coops and vegetable patches roughly dug over for the winter. Such cultivation barely made a mark on the prevailing wilderness.

'This way.' Usara cut across the open court framed by the three buildings and gravelled like the road. 'You're welcome to use a study here whenever you're in Suthyfer—' he smiled at Jilseth as he opened the central door '—and if Guinalle and I already have guests, one of the other wizardly households across the islands will offer you a bedchamber.'

'Thank you.' Jilseth privately recoiled from the notion of finding herself wished on an unsuspecting family of strangers. Visitors to Hadrumal had their needs met by a wizard hall's impersonal servants.

She looked at the corridors of closed doors on either side and at the staircase ahead. 'Is your library up above?'

Usara shook his head. 'We've yet to amass enough books to warrant one. For the moment, this hall offers our mages and adepts peace and quiet for private study away from household distractions and somewhere for experimentation that might otherwise cause uproar. And of course, we meet with our apprentices and pupils to assess and guide their progress.'

He opened a door with a gesture and ushered the floating chest into a room overlooking another long sweep of turf bounded by trees, still densely leaved despite the winter season. 'Only Shiv and I have laid permanent claim to a room. He's just across the corridor, or at least, he will be when he gets back from the landing.'

Usara glanced at the Archmage. 'A ship arrived from Bremilayne with a cargo of Sitalacan wine. Livak sent a note on this morning's carrier's cart saying she's set a case aside for us, as long as she's paid by sunset tomorrow.'

'Then I will personally inform that ship's captain and whichever mage is aboard of the Council's decision to withdraw Hadrumal's magecraft from the mainland,' the Archmage said drily. 'One of your own mages can see the captain safely back to Bremilayne or Zyoutessela as he prefers, but make sure he understands that attempting to return here without wizardly assistance would be very ill-advised.'

Usara looked askance at the Archmage. 'What do we tell Temar D'Alsennin? He's not at all happy after hearing the rumours thus far.'

'I will visit Kellarin myself and explain to him and Captain Halice,' Planir assured the mage, 'as well as calling on Captain Ryshad while I'm here.'

He glanced at Jilseth. 'Please forgive our discourtesy, talking of people and places you don't know.'

'Please don't trouble yourselves on my account.' Privately though, Jilseth found herself uneasy.

How quickly and completely could the Archmage settle all Suthyfer and Kellarin's concerns? How many challenges could he deal with before he was caught looking in the wrong direction at some vital juncture?

The Archmage was already facing dissent in Hadrumal's Council, antagonism from Soluran wizards as well as this so far inexplicable hostility from Soluran adepts in

Col. Relshaz had expelled its wizards and Jilseth had no doubt that antagonism to the mageborn would soon spread more widely. Meantime the Tormalin Emperor's spymaster was seeking any way to compel Planir to deliver ensorcelled artefacts into his liege lord's hands.

Now Planir had chosen to defy the Council of Wizards by delivering this chest full of treasures to Suthyfer. When had he told Usara and Guinalle to expect these spoils from the Khusro treasury? Before or after the Council had forbidden the removal of any of Anskal's loot to Suthyfer?

Had Planir suspected that stricture would be laid on him? Had that prompted him to tell Velindre to persuade Kheda to advise the Khusro wives to cleanse their domain of such magic?

Was Jilseth supposed to keep this secret from her friends in Hadrumal? What would happen when the Council found out? She acknowledged the irony of her situation. She had been resenting not knowing what was going on. Now she would far rather be ignorant.

Rather than ask any such perilous questions, she contemplated the table under the study's window. It wasn't so different from her own in the Terrene Hall. Lumps of rock and ore were set beside worked stone and finished metal, along with robust dishes and crucibles should any of these things need reducing to powder or a molten state. Pen, ink and parchment lay ready for noting whatever insights such alteration might reveal.

What hitherto unsuspected understanding of elemental earth might Usara share with her, Jilseth wondered in passing, to inform and inspire her own studies? Or had his own vaunted prowess been blunted by more prosaic use of his talents in these islands?

Jilseth's shelves held her growing collection of journals, a new volume prepared by Hadrumal's bookbinders around the turn of each season as she wrote a concise summation of her thoughts and discoveries in accordance with Hadrumal's long-established custom. Usara had one small shelf stacked with haphazard sheaves of notes.

The rest of the walls were covered with maps; some finely delineated examples of the cartographer's craft, others sketches apparently drawn with a burnt stick on some scrap of sail cloth. Whether costly or crude, the maps were dotted with different coloured spots of paint and hasty notations.

A second table was covered with draftsman's tools, parchments with architectural designs, an Aldabreshin counting frame and a child's wooden-framed writing slate. Not that any child had worked those closely written equations. Previous calculations had been copied onto coarse paper before the slate was wiped clean and used again.

'Wizardry has to earn its own way in Suthyfer,' Usara was evidently amused by her frank curiosity. 'We don't have an island of farms and villages raising crops and beasts to feed us, nor a city of artisans and merchants paying us rents and dues. So we assist the islanders as best our affinity enables us. I help to build houses hereabouts and Shiv and I are improving the anchorage at the landing, above and below the tide line. I visit Kellarin from time to time, to lend a hand in the coastal settlements and to make sure the miners inland aren't digging a shaft that'll fall in on their heads.'

'The master mage is too modest,' Planir remarked. 'Usara and Shiv have also explored the ways in which wizards can blend their strength short of combining in a full nexus.'

'The Mandarkin Anskal could do that, whether or not the mageborn around him consented.' Jilseth would be very interested to know what these Suthyfer mages had discovered about such elemental thievery.

'Quite so.' The Archmage nodded. 'And wizards here also learn all they can from the aetheric adepts who study with Guinalle.'

'We know better than to scorn Artifice simply because we cannot use its enchantments.' Usara looked back through the door as a hand bell rang on the far side of the gravelled courtyard. 'Just as I know better than to keep my beloved wife waiting when dinner is ready.'

'Please make my excuses. I must visit Kellarin and the landing and then get back to Hadrumal.'

Planir vanished, catching Jilseth unawares and leaving her more than a little irritated. What was she supposed to do now? Beyond waiting to take Micaran back to Col, whenever he had concluded his mysterious aetheric business with Lady Guinalle. Was there any better use she could make of her time here?

'Master Usara, will Merenel be dining with us?'

Usara ushered her through the door and out into the fading daylight.

'No need to call me "Master." We're seldom so formal here.' The shaven-headed mage led her across the gravelled yard. 'No, she's in Kellarin. Do you know Allin Mere? They have become friends as well as collaborators.'

'Allin Mere is the magewoman who married Temar D'Alsennin?' Jilseth shook her head. 'We've never met.'

She only knew that the girl, mageborn from some Lescari family and barely out of her apprenticeship, had married the Tormalin nobleman who now ruled the settlements being hacked out of the wilds of Kellarin. The tale had been a ten day wonder around Hadrumal's wine shops but Jilseth couldn't recall any mention of her after that.

Usara glanced at her, his face unreadable in a way that reminded Jilseth uncomfortably of Planir. 'Don't dismiss Allin so readily. She's the fire mage who joined with Herion, Velindre and me to make up the fourth nexus, when Planir worked that ultimate magic against the Mandarkin.'

Before Jilseth could protest that she meant no disrespect, Usara continued, walking onwards.

'Temar D'Alsennin has some skills with Artifice, though he's very far from an adept. He and Allin work together, like Guinalle and I, to explore our vulnerabilities to each other's magic as well as wizardry's antipathy to Artifice.' He glanced at Jilseth. 'As you might imagine, such collaboration demands absolute trust.'

'Temar D'Alsennin is also—?' Jilseth couldn't find the right words to frame her next question.

Usara's thin smile suggested he was well used to confirming the rumours to the incredulous.

'He is one of the Old Empire's first colonists, who were bound in an enchanted sleep through Artifice and lost beyond the ocean for twenty-five generations. Along with my wife and a good many of those now living in Suthyfer and Kellarin. Very few have chosen to return to Tormalin, with everything they once knew so utterly changed and everyone known to them so long dead.'

He paused to look intently at Jilseth. 'Here and in Kellarin, we have drawn one lesson above all else from that. Just because something can be done with magic, elemental or aetheric, that's no recommendation to actually do it.'

'Surely the colonists cannot regret that their lives were saved?' Jilseth ventured.

'No, they don't regret it but equally, they live every day with the knowledge of what such salvation has cost them.' He shook his head. 'Perhaps Hadrumal's mages will learn a little humility, as they consider what destroying the corsair island will cost wizardry, now that the mainlanders and Archipelagans alike have learned how truly fearsome elemental magic can be.'

'Planir had no alternative.' Jilseth protested.

'No, indeed,' Usara agreed, halting to open the kitchen door. 'The price remains to be paid regardless. Let us hope that some of our insights help you limit the cost.'

He smiled encouragingly, though Jilseth found that cold comfort as they entered the kitchen.

'—since I was not mageborn myself, I never had any hope of wielding elemental magic like my uncle,' Micaran explained. 'When I was old enough to study at the university, I heard rumour of Artifice and sought out those mentors studying to become adept. I proved to have some aptitude—'

He broke off to rise politely from his stool. 'Master Usara, Mistress Jilseth.'

'Please, sit.' Usara waved him back down. 'We don't stand on ceremony here.'

So Jilseth was coming to realise. Guinalle and Micaran were alone in the kitchen, sitting at the long scrubbed wooden table beneath hanging lanterns.

Beyond the table, a substantial cooking range occupied the end wall. Shelves on one side were filled with stores and foodstuffs while a copper for boiling linens and deep sinks along the opposite wall drained into the stone-lined gully leading to the soakaway beyond the far door.

'We have no cooks or laundry maids here. We all lend a hand.' Guinalle Tor Priminale rose to stir a bubbling pot on the range, evidently the source of the aroma which Jilseth had savoured on her arrival.

Had the Tormalin adept read Jilseth's surprise in her face or plucked that from her thoughts?

'We use our magecraft to lighten the load wherever we can, however reprehensible some Council members consider abusing the privilege of wizardry for such trivial purposes.' Usara's smile widened. 'You would be surprised how many of our visitors cannot use their magic to do something as trivial as cooking an egg without showering themselves with yolk and shell, seeing the water turn instantly to steam or melting the cooking pot in their hand.'

'Most find that the first of many salutary lessons here,' Guinalle remarked as she tended to her pottage.

Jilseth turned her attention to Mentor Micaran. 'Are you feeling better?'

'Fully restored, thank you.' His colour was indeed far healthier. He raised a glazed earthenware beaker. 'Have you encountered this remarkable black tisane?'

'I have.' Planir had served it to her after an exhausting night scrying on the Archipelagans' first attempt to attack the renegade Mandarkin mage on the corsair isle. The Aldabreshi might loathe wizardry but they didn't lack courage when it threatened them.

Jilseth wondered how much the Archmage was relying on the bitter black brew in lieu of sleep as he tackled his myriad concerns. She took a stool beside the Col adept, leaving Usara to sit beside his wife.

'I will brew a fresh jugful.' Guinalle moved a kettle from the back of the range to a grill over smouldering coals.

'May I ask what you intend to do with the Archipelagan artefacts?' Micaran asked the Tormalin noblewoman. 'Surely if they are wizard-crafted items, you cannot fathom their secrets through aetheric means?'

'I cannot penetrate their mysteries with Artifice,' Guinalle agreed as she sat down, 'but I can use the spells instilled within them just as their maker intended, like any other mundane born. Then I can use my own enchantments to convey every sensation, every unexpected tie to some magical element, to my husband.'

Usara laid his freckled hand over hers on the table top. 'No description, however detailed, can possibly equal the understanding which Artifice conveys.'

'This is an endeavour requiring absolute trust and the closest of bonds between mage and adept,' Guinalle warned.

Jilseth caught Micaran's uncertain glance in her direction. She didn't need Artifice to see that he was no more prepared to attempt such a thing than she was. That was a relief.

'What have you learned from such insights?' she asked Usara. 'What are you hoping to learn?'

'First and foremost, how to unmake such things,' he said bluntly.

'You don't agree that the mundane born would find magic less daunting if they had the limited experience of wizardry that these artefacts can confer?' Jilseth might not agree with Kalion's wish to make such gifts to noble or powerful men on the mainland, but she was obscurely disappointed to find this unconventional mage sharing Troanna's prejudices.

'That's certainly possible.' Usara rose to tend the singing kettle. 'But those of Solura's Orders who have threatened Planir in hopes of getting hold of these artefacts may pause for further thought if we can destroy what they covet.'

'Unless such a demonstration provokes them into still more reckless action.' Guinalle fetched two more earthenware beakers glazed like the one Micaran cupped in his strong hands. Usara poured boiling water into a tall jug of similar design.

'How are your attempts progressing?' Despite herself, Jilseth was curious.

Usara grimaced. 'They're not, but hopefully we'll understand more of such magecraft now that we have a wider range of artefacts to study.'

'Where do you feel your knowledge is lacking?' Jilseth wondered if Hadrumal's wizards might be better advised to broaden their own focus, exchanging artefacts as well as members of each nexus, rather than continuing to hammer on the same locked door.

'You'd be better off asking Shiv,' Usara apologised as he brought the jug of tisane to the table. 'He has been drawing our notes together as well as working with his own beloved's insights.'

'Pered is one of my most apt pupils in Artifice,' Guinalle added, 'and his own skills as an artist mean he sees the colours of wizardry within these artefacts with remarkable clarity.'

Now Jilseth was tempted to wish that she might share in such study. Though she still couldn't help wondering if Suthyfer's mages would be able to offer anything of immediate use to the Archmage with Hadrumal beset by so many pressing problems.

She looked around as the kitchen door opened. Had Planir returned?

A woman of Jilseth's own height entered, her blonde braids pale in the gloom. She held a small child's hand. The red-headed lad pulled free to run to Usara, scrambling onto the wizard's lap. 'Papa—'

'A moment, Darni,' he chided. 'We have guests.'

'Say good day to Madam Jilseth and Mentor Micaran.' Guinalle moved the hot jug of steeping tisane well beyond the child's reach.

'Good day, Madam Mage and Master Mentor.' The child obeyed with more composure than Jilseth expected. Then again, she seldom had anything to do with children. Those wizards who chose to marry in Hadrumal invariably raised their families well away from the scholarly halls. She guessed that Usara's son was a couple of years younger than Esnina of Halferan but she couldn't be certain.

Guinalle introduced the newcomer with unexpected formality. 'Mentor Micaran, Madam Jilseth, may I make known to you Aritane, formerly of the *sheltya*.'

'Good day to you.' Jilseth had already guessed that this must be the woman whom Nolyen had once told her about; an aetheric adept of the Mountain race. Her twilight blue eyes and corn-coloured hair reminded Jilseth of two Mountain Men she had previously encountered. She had the same sensuous full lips and sharp cheekbones though Sorgrad and his brother had obstinately firm jaws, unlike Aritane's narrow face.

Consulting her must be Micaran's business in Suthyfer. How would he fare? Jilseth wondered if this Mountain woman would prove as devious and self-willed as those infernal brothers, though she must have learned more self-discipline to master Artifice's mysteries.

'Madam.' Micaran rose to offer the Mountain woman his hand. 'I am honoured.'

'Thank you for answering our summons so promptly,' Guinalle said with more deference that Jilseth had seen her show to anyone else including Archmage Planir. 'We expected you after dinner. Please, will you eat with us?'

'I felt the strength of your concerns warranted immediate answers.' Aritane regarded the Col mentor with a sardonic eye before taking a seat at the table. 'You are seeking some stranger whose Artifice is foiling your own questing enchantments, I believe?'

Her Tormalin was entirely fluent though strongly accented with something akin to the harshness which Jilseth had encountered in wizards from northernmost Ensaimin.

'What enchantments have you woven so far?' Guinalle asked Micaran as she poured fresh beakers of the darkly glistening tisane.

'Would you like some honey?' Usara asked Jilseth.

'I will, thank you.' Jilseth remembered how bitter she had found this particular brew. She also recalled Planir explaining that Aritane had found the holly trees needed to make this Mountain infusion in Kellarin after the *sheltya* woman had been exiled from her homeland for some unspecified crime.

The child Darni was already hurrying to a cupboard, returning with a wooden canister holding a ceramic jar and a dipper.

'I take it dinner will be somewhat delayed?' Usara asked his wife with a wry grin.

She answered him with a smile. 'It's pottage and bread. It can wait.'

'I suggest we leave them to it.' Usara held two tisane

beakers steady so that the child could drizzle honey into each one. 'Let's go and open that chest before we eat.'

'As you wish,' Jilseth rose and followed as the mage unhooked a candle lantern from the doorpost and lit the wick with a whisper of fire.

Outside, dusk was deepening and clouds obscured the quartered moons. As they walked across the gravelled yard, lamplight in the kitchen windows was the only sign of life as far as Jilseth could see. She lifted the cup to her lips, grateful for the black tisane's warmth. Honey definitely soothed its bite and as she sipped her weariness begin to recede.

'Darni, go and open the doors.' Usara handed the child the candle lantern and watched his son scamper across the gravel before glancing at Jilseth. 'If Aritane is sufficiently concerned to want to talk to Micaran immediately, it's best to accommodate her. Even in exile she holds true to her *sheltya* oaths and most of those revolve around keeping their lore a closely guarded secret. When she chooses to talk, Guinalle has always learned something new and valuable and Aritane will assuredly talk more freely if only aetheric adepts are present.'

'I understand,' Jilseth assured him.

She did, and moreover, she wasn't particularly interested in sitting and listening to the adepts' discussion. Anything she learned of Artifice could only ever be theoretical knowledge. She would much rather survey the Khusro artefacts alongside Usara and see if he could offer any insight or observation which might have evaded Hadrumal's mages.

If the opportunity presented itself, she might ask what he had discovered about drawing on another wizard's mage strength. That was a skill she would never learn in Hadrumal.

First though, she remembered her other responsibilities. If Planir was moving so many people about like pieces on a game board, she should play her part, even if she couldn't see his strategy.

'Do you have a bowl I can use for scrying?'

Until Mentor Micaran was ready to return to Col, she should make sure that all was well in Halferan and that Baron Corrain wasn't doing anything ill-advised in Col. The Caladhrian's rashness in single-minded pursuit of his goals had been the cause of so many of Hadrumal's current difficulties. No manner of magic seemed able to counter that.

— CHAPTER TWENTY-THREE —

THE CARILLON TOWER'S musical notes heralded the day's second chime. Corrain pushed Hosh up the Red Library's steps. 'Master Garewin's waiting.'

'Shouldn't I help you today?' Hosh looked apprehensively at Corrain.

Too late, Corrain realised that he shouldn't have poured out his frustrations the night before, along with one too many glasses of white brandy. But by all that was sacred and profane, he had spent a wearisome and exasperating day learning the same limited information over and over again.

That Soluran assuredly had no interest in honest scholarship. The man had met with more of the university's mentors, in twos and threes, outside three further libraries, Revesk's, Manser's and the Pawnbrokers'. Each time he had taken his new friends to a tavern close by.

Again, Corrain didn't risk following them inside, retracing his steps later in the day after the Soluran had returned to the inn where Estry had finally discovered he was lodging.

The first time Corrain fell into casual conversation with a merchant well satisfied after sharing a bottle of wine with a trading partner as the city slowed from its daily bustle. The second time he had no such luck. At the third hostelry, he'd been able to accost a student reeling amiably out into the street, on his way to meet more diligent scholars released from the libraries by the day's last chime. Both merchant and errant pupil had told the same tale.

But Corrain still didn't know what the Soluran hoped to achieve by badmouthing wizardry the length and breadth of Col. Perhaps Micaran would have learned something by now, gleaned from those scholars whom Corrain had already told him about. If the adept hadn't, Corrain had a handful of new names to tell him and perhaps there might be some significance to those particular libraries.

'Are you sure you don't need my help?' Hosh persisted.

'I'm certain,' Corrain said firmly. 'Your business is getting yourself healed. The sooner that's done, the sooner we can head for home and find out what the Archmage has cozened Lady Zurenne into doing for these Aldabreshi.'

'As you command, Captain, I mean, my lord Baron.' Hosh's smile betrayed his relief as he turned and ran up the steps.

Corrain wondered if it was his imagination or had that smile tugged a little less cruelly at Hosh's face? Was that brutal dent in the lad's cheekbone shallower?

Doubtless time would tell and meanwhile, time was something he didn't have to waste. The thought of Archipelagans inside the manor's wall made his skin crawl. Had they come to Halferan to discover what weaknesses remained after the corsairs' attacks, to plan their own assault?

A few things puzzled Corrain. Why had the Khusro warlord sent his wives to the mainland? Presumably pretty slaves could be replaced easily enough if Halferan proved hostile but what man took a pampered songbird from its gilded cage to do a courier dove's work?

Beyond that, he had seen for himself how truly and earnestly the Archipelagans hated and feared magic. Would that keep them honest, if they really believed that Lady Zurenne could rid them of treasures with wizardry bound into them?

Perhaps, perhaps not. He could trust Kusint to sleep with one eye open, not giving these unwelcome visitors the least benefit of any doubt. He could only hope that Lady Zurenne had her wits about her in her dealings with these Aldabreshi and with Hadrumal's wizards alike.

Dealings which should now be concluded. Corrain's first business today was ensuring that was the case. He walked across the square and whistled up a hireling gig.

'Tolekan Street.' He climbed up into the rear seat and drew his cloak around him to ward off the ever-present chill wind. At least that meant the gig's horse was willing to trot on to keep itself warm. They reached the wizard Olved's house in good time.

'Do you want me to wait?' The driver accepted the silver penny which Corrain had learned was the standard fare for any journey within sound of the carillon's bells, however long or short.

'Yes, thank you.' Corrain jumped down and hurried up Master Olved's steps. Since the door showed no inclination to open by way of wizardry, he rapped a brisk summons with the brass knocker.

A flustered maidservant appeared, barely opening the door wide enough for Corrain to see her face.

He offered her his most charming smile. 'Please present my compliments to your master and tell him that Corrain of Halferan needs to see him.'

The girl looked at him as though he'd just asked her to hand him one or other moon. 'The master mage never rises from his bed before the day's third chime.'

'He will today.' Corrain pushed at the door. As he anticipated, the maid was too browbeaten by Olved to defy such inexorable courtesy.

As she scurried up the stairs, Corrain found his purse and a silver penny for the lass by way of recompense for the scolding she'd doubtless receive.

He soon heard the wizard's voice upstairs, acid with outrage. A door's petulant slam echoed through the house and Master Olved appeared at the top of the stairs, wrapped in a tattered night robe, tousled and foul-tempered.

'What do you want? I told you to call in the evenings between the night's second and third chimes. Where were you yesterday?'

'I was otherwise engaged.' Corrain replied with the bland politeness he offered to the likes of Baron Karpis. 'I will call back later. Meantime, can you bespeak Madam Jilseth and confirm that the Khusro Archipelagans have indeed left Halferan?'

He could see that he would get nowhere asking Olved to work such magic here and now. Never mind; any swordsman worth his salt was always ready to adapt to some change of circumstances. Corrain would move on to his next plan for the day. He'd had enough of trying to scavenge hearsay. The time had come to go hunting the truth and Corrain had realised how he could do that.

'I need to speak to Mentor Micaran. Can you tell me where he lives, please?'

'Micaran? He's—' Olved stared at Corrain before

cutting himself short. 'He'll be here this evening. You may talk to him then.'

'You know that I'm in Col at the Archmage's request? If I'm to do Planir's bidding, I need Master Micaran's help,' Corrain said firmly. 'Where can I find him? Or would you rather I tell Madam Jilseth why I've had to waste this whole day?'

Olved narrowed red-rimmed eyes. 'Mentor Micaran's house is on Audoen's Row. The fourth from the corner with Muras Square, the door with the reed mace lamp.'

Without another word he turned around and disappeared into the gloom of the upper landing. The maidservant hurried down the stairs to shoo Corrain towards the door.

'Thank you.' He managed to press a silver mark into her hand before she closed the door on him.

'Where to, master?' the gig driver called out.

'Audoen's Row by way of Muras Square.'

This proved to be a longer journey. The carillon tower's bells sounded out their jaunty tune for the day's third chime before the driver reined in his bay gelding.

'This is Muras Square—' he jerked his head '—and that's Audoen's Row. Do you want me to wait?' he asked hopefully.

'My thanks and no, you can be on your way.' Corrain paid the man his second penny and walked briskly down the street.

The fourth door from the corner did indeed have a lantern with each iron corner strut crafted like a stalk of reed mace framed with leaves. Beyond that, the house looked distinctly unpromising. Every window was shuttered and knocking on the door got Corrain no answer.

He looked across the street. The fourth house opposite had no door lantern at all. Was the missing lamp another one from the same craftsman? Was Master Olved having some joke at his expense?

As he wondered, he saw a servant woman glaring suspiciously through a window on the ground floor of the next house along. Corrain wasn't surprised. These quietly elegant residences wouldn't look favourably on even respectably dressed loiterers.

He peered over the railing edging the steps to look at the basement entrance. There was no sight or sound of anyone down there. Should he go and knock on the kitchen door or would disappearing from view convince the watching woman that he was intent on housebreaking?

If she sent some lackey hot-foot to summon the Watch, or whoever enforced the Elected of Col's ordinances, Corrain foresaw an awkward conversation. He could claim to be Baron Halferan of Caladhria, undertaking a commission on behalf of Hadrumal's Archmage, but he carried nothing to support his word and as long as Mentor Micaran was absent, there was no one to vouch for him here.

Hooves echoed down the street. To his relief, he saw Mentor Micaran in the hireling gig's back seat. To his surprise and displeasure Jilseth sat beside the adept.

'What are you doing here?' The magewoman spoke first, as Micaran paid off the gig's driver.

Corrain replied with equal asperity. 'Why aren't you in Halferan keeping Lady Zurenne and her daughters safe?'

'I have other responsibilities, not least to the Archmage,' she said curtly.

'Shall we go inside?' Micaran politely offered Jilseth his hand to help her down. 'Rather than tell the whole neighbourhood our business?'

As Corrain and Jilseth nodded in mute agreement, the

mentor unlocked the door and led them into a dusty tiled hall.

'One moment.' Opening an inner door, Micaran skirted familiar furniture in the gloom to reach the shutters and admit the daylight into a shabby sitting room. He evidently didn't have any servants.

The mentor looked eagerly at Corrain as he dropped into a leather-upholstered chair in sore need of oiling. 'After consulting with those far more adept than myself, I have made some significant progress in understanding how the man from Wrede is hiding from my questing Artifice. Better yet, I have woven a new enchantment to further our search. I hope to learn where this man may be within a couple of days, three at the most. Then you should be able to scry for him,' he told Jilseth with a broad smile.

'I can scry for someone I've only seen through your Artifice?' Jilseth said warily.

Micaran nodded, frowning faintly. 'Didn't I say? Do you know so little of working with adepts in Hadrumal?' He looked suddenly contrite. 'Forgive my discourtesy.'

'No,' Jilseth replied stiffly. 'Forgive me.'

Corrain interrupted to forestall some tedious exchange of rival apologies. 'Can you use your magic for a different purpose today,' he asked Micaran, 'to help me on the Archmage's behalf?'

'What do you need Artifice for?' Jilseth demanded.

Corrain took a seat, leaning forward with his elbows on his knees. 'The Archipelagans are hiring mercenaries, sword by sword. They will only say that they seek mainland warriors to defend Jagai's interests. They're paying handsomely though, with good gold coin to keep their chosen men in bread and beer until more Jagai ships arrive just after the turn of For-Spring. Once those galleys have taken on supplies and water, these mercenaries will embark on a voyage which will see them return richer than their most extravagant imaginings.'

Once Corrain had decided there was nothing more to be learned about the Soluran's scheming, he'd made a brief circuit of Col's more insalubrious taverns. He hadn't needed any subterfuge to learn what the Archipelagans were doing but as with the puzzle of the Soluran's motives, he left with no answers as to why.

'Without knowing where these ships are taking them? Without knowing who they're going to fight?' Jilseth perched on the edge of a high-back settle.

Corrain shrugged. 'A good few will doubtless swear allegiance and fill their bellies at Jagai's expense before vanishing like mist in the morning when the day comes to board those galleys. But I reckon most will hold true to their word, at least until they learn the full story. Archipelagan plunder is a powerful lure.'

Jilseth stiffened. 'That's what they're being offered? A chance to loot some Aldabreshin island?'

Corrain shrugged. 'That's what they're assuming.'

Jilseth frowned. 'Why would Jagai hire mainland swords to fight their battles instead of the warlord's own warriors?'

'We must warn the Elected and the Prefecture to be ready for trouble.' Micaran had more immediate concerns. 'Mercenaries have long been used to wintering in Col and in the towns and villages from here to Kadras between the fighting seasons in Lescar. Ever since the dukes have been overthrown, those who can't get work with some Ensaimin town guard or watching over a merchant's wagons have lingered idle and hungry.'

He shook his head, uneasy. 'Word will be spreading, drawing them to the city like rats to a market midden.'

'Don't expect the city's authorities to put a stop to this,' Corrain warned. 'The Archipelagans are promising to bring all their trade here from Relshaz in return for loyal service from these new hirelings.'

He had some reassurance to offer. 'Apparently these Archipelagans say that anyone causing trouble in Col between taking their coin and taking ship will be dismissed out of hand. They believe that the heavenly Topaz's shift in the sky will see the start of a new era of trade between the Aldabreshi and Col so keeping the peace here is crucial.'

Seeing Jilseth looking bemused, he suggested the explanation which Hosh had offered when Corrain had expressed his own exasperated bafflement over dinner at The Goose Hounds tavern.

'This shift in the night sky will happen around the sixteenth day of For-Spring. Apparently the Topaz strengthens omens for home and family after that and it's also a talisman for creativity and friendship, prized for promoting new ideas and paths.'

Micaran nodded. 'That star's shift marks the start of each new year according to Aldabreshi calculations. We should see where the other heavenly gems will be and look for significant conjunctions.'

'Hosh said—' Corrain paused to be certain he was remembering correctly '—the Diamond and the Pearl will linger where the Topaz has been, offering omens for brothers and sisters and anyone as close as such kin, along with the Mirror Bird's stars and the heavenly Sapphire. Those are powerful portents guarding against magic's malice as well as promoting wisdom and clear thinking.'

Micaran nodded. 'That would be considered very influential.'

'That's not all,' Corrain assured him. 'Another shift further round their heavenly compass and the Ruby offers portents for wealth, directly opposite this Emerald and its omens for death and ill-fortune.'

'What about—' Jilseth hesitated '—the Amethyst and the Opal?'

'They'll be bracketing the Emerald, so Hosh says. The Opal will offer good omens for travel along with the Winged Snake which encourages boldness, with the Amethyst for new ideas on the far side.'

Corrain saw the magewoman's brow furrow.

'I suspect that any Aldabreshi would see more complex meanings,' Jilseth remarked.

'Maybe so, but what of it?' Corrain was more than satisfied with Hosh's view of these coming skies. 'What we need to know is why these Archipelagans need boatloads of mercenary swordsmen from the mainland at this turn of their year.'

'How far could they row those swordsmen by the shift of the Topaz,' Micaran wondered aloud, 'if they take ship here just after the turn of For-Spring?'

Corrain rose and walked to the table beside the fireplace where the dust was thick enough for him to draw a swift map with a forefinger.

'Could they reach Nahik waters?' Jilseth asked suddenly.

'Perhaps, if they weighed anchor on the very first of For-Spring.' Corrain was doubtful.

'Why do you ask that?' Micaran looked at the magewoman.

'The Nahik domain has been wholly abandoned,' Jilseth said slowly, 'for fear of lingering magic staining those islands along with anyone still left there. From what we hear, no galleys are using the sea lanes to head north or south, leaving the Jagai domain cut off from the rest of the Archipelago. But the Aldabreshi don't believe that mainlanders suffer from magic's taint, since we're not guided by the omens of earthly and heavenly compasses. And they believe that shedding blood washes away such corruption.'

Corrain saw the apprehension in the magewoman's face. 'You think that they want to put everyone still living on those islands to the sword?'

Jilseth was pale with dread. 'What else?'

'But the Khusro domain is similarly cut off,' Micaran objected, 'and they're seeking to cleanse themselves of magic by far less drastic means. That's why they came to Halferan.'

'Let's try calculating rather than guessing.' Corrain studied the lines on the dusty tabletop with growing unease. 'These galleys supposedly coming to carry these mercenaries off to earn their fortunes wouldn't have left Jagai before that fat *zamorin* sent a courier dove or two home to say he had good reason to hope he could hire the swords which his master wants.'

Micaran nodded agreement. 'That was only the day before yesterday—'

'—so those doves would have reached Jagai today, most likely.' Jilseth interjected.

'Those galleys won't arrive here until at least a handful of days into For-Spring.' Corrain looked at Jilseth. 'If they load up their mercenaries and catch the very next tide, the furthest they could hope to reach by the shift of this heavenly Topaz is somewhere around Halferan.'

She stared at him, aghast. 'Why would Jagai Kalu send mercenaries against a Caladhrian barony?'

Perhaps because the Archipelagan warlord knew who

was truly to blame for the Mandarkin Anskal arriving to wreak havoc in the Nahik islands? Would shedding the blood of those responsible somehow make amends? Would the Archipelagans to the south look northward again if Jagai Kalu could put Baron Halferan's head on a stake?

Corrain might have asked Jilseth if he and the magewoman had been alone but he had no idea whether or not Mentor Micaran knew of Halferan's guilt; of his dead lord's desperation or his equal folly, both of them trusting a renegade mage loyal only to his own purse.

Micaran was still searching for an explanation. 'Could Jagai wish to challenge the Khusro wives as they're ridding themselves of ensorcelled artefacts? Surely both domains will wish to be the first to re-establish trade between the mainland and the rest of the Archipelago.'

'There's no point in ifs and buts and guesses.' Corrain obliterated the dust-drawn map with a sweep of his hand. If only he could wipe away these new fears now filling his mind. He looked straight at Micaran.

'You can pluck the answers out of that Jagai *zamorin*'s head with your Artifice.'

Micaran recoiled from the idea. 'We should pursue other avenues first.'

'I did that yesterday,' Corrain assured him. 'Trust me, there's nothing more to be learned by loosening tavern tongues with coin or ale. You're not forbidden to read a man's thoughts in such dire need, are you?'

'Not forbidden, precisely.' Micaran was still reluctant. 'But I should be searching for this man from Wrede.'

'You can still do both, can't you? The Archmage will definitely want to know what Jagai Kalu's men are plotting.' Jilseth had no doubt of that.

Corrain hadn't expected to find the magewoman

allying herself with him but he'd take every advantage he was offered. 'If you come with me to find this *zamorin* now, you'll be back home and working your enchantments well before Master Olved is ready to bespeak the Archmage this evening.'

'I suppose so.' The mentor's expression lightened. 'I confess, it will be an interesting challenge to read an Archipelagan's thoughts.'

'Good.' Corrain turned to Jilseth. Whatever her concerns for the Archmage's interests, his loyalties lay first and foremost with Lady Zurenne and her daughters. 'You must go to Halferan. Warn Kusint and Reven to prepare the manor's defences, just in case your scrying magic shows us the Jagai galleys heading for our shore.'

If they did, Corrain vowed silently to himself, he would have a wizard carry him back to lead Halferan's defence if that meant holding a dagger to one of their throats.

To his relief, Jilseth nodded. 'As soon as Kheda's seen the Khusro wives on board their ship, I can ask what he thinks. He can set further enquiries in hand through his own Aldabreshi contacts. I'll see you at Master Olved's house this evening.' She rose and vanished in a shimmer of white magelight.

Micaran shuddered. 'I don't believe I will ever get used to that.'

Too late, Corrain realised that he should have asked the magewoman to save them a journey with such a spell. No matter.

He gestured towards the mentor's scholarly mantle and long tunic. 'I'll go and hire a gig while you change into some clothes that won't tell everyone and the tavern dog that you're a university mentor. These aren't the places where your kind go to drink.'

— CHAPTER TWENTY-FOUR —

'I DON'T BELIEVE I've ever been to this part of the city before.' Micaran looked around as their driver pulled up his horse.

Corrain was relieved to see the scholar was sufficiently circumspect not to draw hostile attention their way. His height and heft should also deter anyone thinking of trying to cut his purse or steal his silver ring. Micaran had refused to leave off that sign of his calling.

He paid off the gig driver who whipped up his horse as soon as they got down; so eager to leave that Corrain wondered how easily they would get a ride back to more central districts. Well, they would solve that puzzle in due course.

'The Jagai *zamorin* will most likely be hunting hereabouts, according to what I heard yesterday.'

Learning which districts the Aldabreshi had already visited had shown Corrain a steadily uncoiling spiral path. He had no reason to think they would have abandoned that course.

'The Elected will be only too happy to see the Archipelagans taking these ruffians away,' Micaran observed in an undertone.

Corrain nodded. This particular brick-paved square only had buildings along two faces. The open ground on the far side was cluttered with makeshift shacks hammered together by destitute mercenaries. He wouldn't give a copper-cut piece for the local weavers' chances of reclaiming these grounds for hanging the cloth they produced from the wool shorn from those sheep which ended up as mutton on Col's plates. The hooked tenter frames had long since been smashed for firewood.

'Mind you, the word around the beer barrels is that the Jagai swordsmen are turning away all but the quickest and strongest turning up at the docks to try their luck. The ones who can take a bruising from a blunted sword without flinching.'

Corrain had heard a good deal of sour grousing from those who'd merely earned a silver mark as recompense for their trouble instead of gold to buy their loyalty.

'That's still good for Col.' Micaran pursed his lips. 'Men used to commanding respect, the ones able to rally a scattered company in battle and fight on, are the ones most likely to cause trouble for the city.'

Corrain had come to the same conclusion. 'The Archmage will need some powerful arguments to weigh against Col's interests, if he wants the Elected to put a stop to Jagai hiring these men. Let's see what this *zamorin* can tell us. This is the biggest tavern in the district and that's where he usually starts.'

Micaran braced himself as Corrain led the way to the tavern. It wasn't the filthiest taproom he had ever been in but it had doubtless been a good deal cleaner when the locals had been quenching their thirst after a long day's work at their looms.

'If he's already been in here today, we'll have to start quartering the side streets.' He looked around for someone to fall into conversation with, to learn if they had seen or heard of the *zamorin*.

'Caladhrian!' An unwashed Ensaimin vagabond hailed him from a corner table.

Corrain had spoken to the man the day before in a different tavern. The Ensaimin claimed to have signed on a mercenary company's muster roll in his youth. Now he scratched out a living running errands for those still fit to hire out their swords.

Raising his own hand in acknowledgement, Corrain glanced at Micaran. 'Do you want something to drink?'

'Hardly,' Micaran said, startled. 'I need to keep a clear head.'

'You and me both.' Corrain headed to the counter regardless. Nothing drew curious eyes in a drinking den more than two men not drinking.

'A jug of ale, sweetheart.' He smiled at the drab serving the indifferent brew and picked up a couple of horn cups. Laying down two copper pennies, he took the jug over to the Ensaimin's table and topped up the ragged man's drink.

'Any word of that Aldabreshin in the fancy silks hereabouts today?'

'You fancy chancing your arm against his swordsmen, longshanks?' The Ensaimin looked at Micaran, mildly curious. 'You'll need more than a longer reach against those fine fellows.'

Corrain nodded at the men sat around the taproom's tables in threes and fours looking expectant. 'They're waiting for him as well?' He sat down and poured a mouthful of ale into his and Micaran's horn cups to pass for dregs.

The Ensaimin took a long swallow from his refreshed drink. 'So they say.'

Corrain looked at Micaran. 'We'll wait and see, shall we?'

The Ensaimin man's bleary eyes brightened and he reached for the jug of ale to help himself. 'If you're looking for an adventure, longshanks, by way of spitting in your father's eye, I hear they're hiring in Oakmont, for guards to ride the wagons taking the Dalasor road to Inglis.'

Corrain let the man ramble on, nodding as required. A chance shift in the wind brought the faint sound of the fourth chime's bells some while later and he started to feel a little uneasy. Would they still be waiting when the carillon tower sounded midday? Should they try another lesser inn or would malign luck see the *zamorin* walk through these doors as they walked out?

He spared Micaran a glance. The mentor had leaned back and closed his eyes, as though he was taking a nap. Corrain was close enough to see the tension in his body and the subtle flexing of his hands though. Was the scholar working some unseen Artifice?

As that thought crossed Corrain's mind, Micaran opened one eye and looked at him with the faintest of smiles.

Yes, and your friend there is telling you a tale concocted from rumour and optimism, even if he's convinced himself he's telling no lies.

Corrain managed a slow nod as well suited to the Ensaimin's gossip as it was to Micaran's words echoing eerily inside his head. It was a challenge not to shudder at that unnerving sensation.

Since we have a moment to ourselves, may I offer you my help as well as my friendship, when we're done with this particular business? I swear I haven't sought to pry but it's plain to see that you're plagued by distressing dreams. Mentor Garewin says the same of your friend Hosh. There are enchantments to dull the sting of such recollection.

Corrain shifted uneasily on the bench. If anyone else had made him such an offer, if Micaran had spoken aloud rather than use his Artifice, he would have given them a warning glare at best and most likely the threat of a fist to shut their mouth, if not an actual blow.

'Well, now, don't you find that this conversation gives you a thirst?' The Ensaimin man poured himself the last drops from the jug and looked hopefully at Corrain.

'True enough.' He was about to rise when Micaran's hand on his forearm held him back.

The tavern door opened and the plump *zamorin* entered, as sumptuously dressed as before, though in red-shot blue silk today and escorted by two different swordsmen. He looked as out of place as an Archipelagan glory bird among moulting farmyard fowl.

Corrain feigned mild interest as the *zamorin* made his offer, word for word the same as his speech in The Goose Hounds' taproom. Micaran still appeared to be asleep, though Corrain noted his hands were now clenched into white-knuckled fists.

'—tested to first blood, to the first, trivial scratch, assuredly not to any wound that might prove mortal,' the *zamorin* concluded in his curiously soft voice. 'My lord has no wish to stain his new venture with ill omens of spilled lifeblood.'

The *zamorin* offered the silent taproom one last bow. As he turned to leave, one of his guards went ahead to open the door while the other walked backwards, keeping watch on everyone in the tavern until the door swung closed.

Now Corrain could tell the tavern's regular drinkers from the men who'd followed the rumours of Archipelagan gold. The latter were on their feet, gathering cloaks and settling their debts with the slattern at the counter, doubtless before heading straight to the Spice Wharf.

We should go.

Micaran opened his eyes and rose to his feet.

Juliet E. McKenna

Corrain would rather have waited for a count of a hundred to make sure the Archipelagans were long gone but he could hardly say that aloud. He dropped a silver penny in front of the Ensaimin as he stood up.

'Buy yourself a pie to go with your ale.' He didn't hold out much hope though, not for a man living so deep in drink.

'I will, Caladhrian,' the vagabond assured him with a stained grin.

Corrain followed Micaran to the door, content to see that the only one watching them go was the sagging maidservant behind the counter. The regulars were amusing themselves by mocking anyone fool enough to take an Archipelagan's coin. Anyone taking ship with the *zamorin* would doubtless find they'd sold themselves into chains and slavery, so the old men assured each other.

'That was definitely a lie,' Micaran said ruefully as they left the tavern. 'Our smelly friend plans on buying himself a bottle of Forest berry liquor.'

'He's welcome to it.' Corrain ushered the mentor further from the door. 'What was our fat friend leaving unsaid?'

Micaran looked around the paved square, twisting his scholar's ring around his middle finger. 'We must hire a gig and get to my uncle's house as quickly as we can.'

'Master Olved?' Corrain resisted the temptation to shake an answer out of the scholar. 'Very well.'

But by the time they'd walked through three squares without seeing so much as a pile of dung on the paviours, the midday bells were ringing in the heart of the city. They crossed another two streets before Corrain was able to wave down a gig trotting briskly back towards the more lucrative central districts.

'Where to, good sirs?' The driver halted with a broad smile.

'Tolekan Street,' Micaran said curtly, climbing into the back seat with one long-limbed stride.

'You want to send word to—' Corrain looked at the back of the driver's head. Could the man possibly turn a coin by selling what he might overhear?

—to Archmage Planir. Yes, at once. That zamorin *is recruiting men for Jagai ships to deliver to Hadrumal, to tear down the wizard city.*

'What?' Corrain didn't care that he'd spoken aloud.

His next breath froze in his throat. He was no longer sitting in the gig. Micaran stood with him in the carillon square, with the tower's shadow indicating early morning rather than midday. The sun shone from a cloudless spring sky and yet the square was entirely deserted. There were no people to be seen, no horses, no movement at any door or window in the surrounding buildings.

'This isn't real.' Corrain turned in a slow circle. 'Where am I?'

'Still in the gig, and no, you won't fall out.' Micaran was apparently clothed in his scholarly tunic and mantle again. 'We can talk privately here.'

Corrain wasn't amused. The notion of riding senseless through the city appalled him. They had best deal with the matter in hand and be done with this Artifice as swiftly as possible.

'What exactly did you pull out of the *zamorin*'s head?'

'He knows how to find Hadrumal.' Micaran couldn't hide his own disbelief. 'Him and Jagai Kalu's most trusted shipmasters.'

'No one can find Hadrumal.' Corrain insisted, obstinate. 'The whole island is hidden with magic. I've travelled there myself. Only the captains whom Planir trusts can find a way through the rocks and fogs and they have to follow magical guidance. No one can see the sun anywhere close to the island and no mariner can use a compass or take a bearing to find his way back.'

'Nevertheless, Jagai's shipmasters know exactly where to sail to find the wizard city.'

Somehow Micaran's certainty resounded through Corrain's thoughts.

'How?' he demanded.

'Someone,' Micaran said grimly, 'has put that knowledge into their heads. More than that, this unknown adept has done it in so subtle a fashion that the Jagai mariners and this *zamorin* don't think to question it, any more than Jagai Kalu himself does. This is something they have always known, as far as their memories tell them.'

'Has this same Artifice somehow done away with their fear of wizards?' Whether in reality or this waking dream, Corrain's throat was dry as dust.

'No, that would be a folly too far. Such a suggestion would surely fail when anyone of Jagai was challenged by an Aldabreshi from another domain reiterating the Archipelago's reasons for detesting magic.'

Micaran shook his head before Corrain could express any relief.

'This unknown adept need not attempt anything so risky. The Aldabreshi have always hated wizards but they've always known that even the most powerful mage can be overwhelmed,' the mentor pointed out. 'Jagai, Khusro and Miris were prepared to send hundreds of men to their deaths when they first attacked the Mandarkin, all for the sake of seeing one warrior live long enough to put a sword through Anskal's head.'

Corrain gasped, floundering neck deep in salt water. The waves burned with magefire as the corsair island ripped itself apart underfoot. Bodies and broken lumber thumped him from all sides. His men's terrified yells filled his ears. He felt the sinking ground beneath his feet shift, unseen fissures opening to swallow him as the waters closed over his head—

In the next instant, he was standing in the deserted carillon square, bone dry and unbruised.

'That's it!' Micaran snapped his fingers like a gambler rolling the winning rune. 'The Aldabreshi know that any wizard's strength has its limits. They believe that the Archmage and his cohorts have exhausted themselves destroying the Mandarkin and his apprentices. So they're confident that Hadrumal lies undefended against these mercenaries.'

Corrain shook his head. 'Mainlanders will never attack the wizard isle.'

'No?' Micaran challenged him. 'Not mercenaries from Col whose heads are full of tavern gossip insisting no mage can be trusted? When they've heard tell of the riches which the Relshazri found when the wizards fled their city? Why would they leave such wealth behind? Because they have no need of it in Hadrumal when the Archmage can pluck coin out of the air to fill his purse.'

The empty air of the paved square filled with the clamour of voices, echoing every sly criticism and sneer which Corrain had heard in the taverns through these past few days.

'The Soluran's done this.' He was certain of it.

'Complex enchantments are spreading through the city.' Micaran couldn't hide his reluctant admiration, 'I've never encountered such Artifice before.'

'Can it be undone?' Corrain leaned back against the tree, grateful for its shade.

Micaran bit his lip. 'I will ask—'

'Not such a pair of lackwits, are you?' the Soluran said ruefully.

'What are you doing here?' Corrain reached for his sword only to find himself stripped to the tattered breeches he'd worn as a corsair slave. Heavy fetters linked by a rusting chain hobbled his bare feet.

'Where is this?' Micaran looked around the dusky woodland apprehensively. He was also barefoot, wearing only threadbare breeches and a ragged shirt. He stared at the Soluran. 'Who are you? This is no memory of mine.'

The Soluran smiled with malicious satisfaction. 'You are lost, my friend.'

Corrain lunged for the man. Before he could lay a hand on him, the Soluran vanished. He swallowed a vile oath. 'Take us back, Micaran.'

The mentor didn't seem to hear him. He was pressing his hands to the side of his head, eyes tight closed as he muttered something under his breath.

Corrain recognised the lyrical flow of Artifice even if the words were meaningless to him. He waited for the carillon square to reappear. Meantime, he looked warily for any movement in the shadows beneath the oak trees. Somehow this unreal day had shifted from mid-morning to late evening.

Nothing changed.

'Come on, Micaran!' he demanded curtly.

With no sign that the scholarly adept had heard him, Corrain took a swift step towards him. The clanking chain between his feet pulled him up short, forcing him into the loathsome slave shuffle of the Archipelago. Anger rising to match his growing fear, Corrain shoved Micaran's shoulder to compel his attention.

Corrain's hand passed straight through the adept's shirt and the flesh and bone beneath. Worse than that, as Micaran opened his eyes and looked fearfully around, his gaze swept straight past Corrain.

Had he somehow become a shade himself? Despite himself, Corrain tried to grab the scholar's arm. Once more, his fingers found only empty air.

'Micaran!' He yelled so loudly that his throat burned.

The scholar backed away. Corrain's instant of relief died as he realised Micaran wasn't looking at him. The adept's eyes were fixed on something behind him, white-rimmed with terror.

Corrain heard a footfall and whirled around. He took a startled step backwards, initially unable to believe what he was seeing.

A handful of Eldritch Kin, blue-skinned, wearing loin cloths and scanty wraps of black fabric as insubstantial as shadow. Man-shaped but subtly different. Subtly wrong, with their limbs too long and their bodies unnaturally thin. Their black hair was more like a cat's pelt and their eyes were featureless pools of darkness without white, iris or pupil.

Eldritch Kin. As the thought formed in Corrain's mind, the closest turned its inky gaze on him. Its smile widened to reveal teeth as wickedly pointed as the sharks which had followed the corsair slavers, ready to eat those thrown overboard, dead or alive.

Breaking off from its companions, it stalked towards him. As its form shifted eerily with every stride, Corrain couldn't help thinking of a man's shadow on a sunny day; rising and falling, now tall and thin, now short and squat as he passed by walls and alley ways.

Corrain clenched his fists. Eldritch Kin were children's

tales, phantoms born of grandmothers' warnings to frighten children away from hot hearths and to curb any wish to stray from their skirts.

The creature's smile widened and it shook its head as though chiding him. Corrain took a hasty step backwards, only to find himself hampered once again by that cursed chain. The Eldritch Kinsman matched him pace for pace while the others advanced, intent on Micaran.

The mentor had his back pressed hard against an oak tree but he was no longer standing tall. Micaran cowered like a child, hiding his face in his hands.

One of the Eldritch Kin lashed out with a talon-tipped hand. The filthy claws ripped five deep gouges in Micaran's shoulder. Blood soaked torn, grubby linen as the adept screamed.

Corrain took a step towards him but the smiling Eldritch Kinsman swiftly blocked his path. Corrain snarled wordlessly and threw a brutal punch at its skinny midriff. His fist passed straight through its shadowy form and he sprawled headlong, to land flat on his belly.

He heard Micaran scream for a second time before choking on a sob of agony. The Eldritch Kin were laughing; a hateful, whispering cackle. Micaran screamed again.

Corrain planted his hands in the leaf litter, ready to spring up. Before he could move, the Eldritch Kinsman landed on his back, knocking the wind out of him. The creature leaned forward, its face close to his ear, hissing with wordless malice. Corrain felt its cold breath on his cheek and terror threatened to unman him utterly.

Shame was more lacerating than the creature's talons now digging into his shoulders. He was no warrior when he couldn't even safeguard this defenceless scholar. He was failing Micaran just as he had failed every last one of those Halferan men enslaved alongside him. He was truly only fit for chains.

Chains. Corrain swung his feet upwards and forwards with all his might, arching his back so violently that his knees left the ground. If it could claw him then he could surely hit back and that heavy loop of chain striking the Kinsman's back should give it something to think about.

The creature sprang away with a venomous gasp. As soon as he he was relieved of its weight, Corrain rolled over, his fists ready.

The Kinsman crouched like a wrestler, its unnatural mouth wide in a menacing snarl. Corrain got slowly to his feet as he waited for the creature to make the first move. He was more concerned with assessing Micaran's plight.

He could see the adept huddled on the ground with his knees drawn up and his arms wrapped around his head. Micaran was doing nothing to fight off the Eldritch Kin. His shirt was a bloodstained mess of rags and Corrain could see bright lifeblood pumping from a rip in his breeches to stain the dry turf.

'Micaran!'

As he yelled, the Kinsman leaped forward, clawed hands spread and fangs bared. Corrain dived straight at it, ready to wrestle it to the ground and snap its neck if he could.

Instead, he felt a paralysing chill as he passed straight through its shadowy body once again. The only constant in this fight seemed to be inconsistency. No matter. Only the remaining four stood between him and Micaran. He just had to get the scholar away before the murderous creatures ripped the fool to shreds—

'You can strike them when you're angry enough but you can't hurt them,' the Soluran observed, leaning against an oak tree. 'They're not your fear.'

Corrain halted. 'Who are you? Why are you doing this?'

The Soluran smiled with malice to equal any of the Eldritch Kin. 'I'm the man who knows what you fear most.'

The Kinsmen now looming over Micaran tore at his quivering flesh. Their taloned hands were bloodied to the elbow, wet stains dark on their dusky blue skin.

But Corrain had seen the evil creatures standing immobile while the Soluran was speaking. His silence had loosed them to renew their attack.

'What do you think you know about me?' he challenged him.

In the next instant, the Soluran was at his side, whispering into his ear. 'I know that you fear losing those who look to you to defend them. I know that you fear seeing them die while you look on, unable to do anything to save them. I know that you fear dying alone, so far from home that no one ever knows what has become of you, only wondering if you failed or you fled to live out your days in disgrace.'

Corrain couldn't help shuddering. The Eldritch Kinsman at his other shoulder hissed with satisfaction. Its spittle stung his cheek, sharp as frost. The Soluran chuckled and Micaran screamed.

Corrain couldn't look away. Micaran wept, his defiance weakening. His arms sagged to leave his head unprotected. His eyes were screwed tight closed as his mouth gaped in a silent scream of terror.

One of the Eldritch Kin clawed at his head, ripping locks of hair from his scalp. The pale bone of Micaran's skull showed through the bloody gashes. Another stabbed at his hand, time and again until the scholar struck out, flailing wildly in vain hope of evading such torment.

The Eldritch Kinsman thrust its talons deep into his

forearm. Micaran couldn't shake off its grip so the creature wrenched his arm wide. The third creature sprang forward to rake at his face. Micaran barely managed to block its blow with his free hand.

Corrain's warning died in his throat, bitter as ashes. That was just the move his attackers had wanted the scholar to make. The third Kinsman dug its claws deep into Micaran's wrist, securing a firm hold. The two creatures pinioning him cackled with terrible glee as they dragged his arms wide.

The last Kinsman advanced, hissing with delight. It drew one talon delicately down the side of Micaran's face. Blood gushed from the wound, oozing down his neck.

The mentor suddenly thrashed in his captors' grip. Where he had been weeping in utter despair, now he bellowed with furious defiance.

Corrain's heart soared. 'Fight back! You know they're not real!'

What did this Soluran know? He was right about Corrain hating the memory of chains and being stripped of his weapons but he hadn't been most afraid of dying in this northern forest. This was where he'd come in hopes of finding a wizard, only to secure the Mandarkin Anskal's services and to double and redouble Halferan's misfortunes.

True enough, Corrain was terrified of his guilt being revealed and he had buried that dread deep in his innermost heart. But such fear still came second to the nightmare of finding himself back on the corsair island. If the Soluran knew that, surely this forest would have been fringe trees and ironwoods, not oak and hazel thickets?

In the blink of an eye, the Soluran was on the far side of the clearing. The Eldritch Kinsman hissing at his side was nowhere to be seen. Corrain took a long stride forward, free of his fetters. He took another step, ready to drag the vile creatures off Micaran.

Too late. Even as the scholar fought to free himself from the two holding down his arms, the third slashed at his face and neck in sudden frenzy. Blood sprayed high into the air and Micaran slumped insensible between the Eldritch Kinsmen. The creatures crowed with exultation as they ripped into his chest and stomach to eviscerate him.

A horse whickered irritably at the rankness of murder tainting the sweet woodland air.

Corrain spun around to see the man from Wrede, dressed as he had been in Ferl, riding the same bay colt.

The man pursed his lips. 'This hardly seems fair.'

'Who are you?' Corrain was ready to pull the man clean from his saddle. He wanted to get his hands around someone's neck today.

'That doesn't matter.' The man smiled. 'What matters is what you believe.' He jerked his head beyond Corrain. 'Do you believe you can kill him? If so, you can avenge your friend.'

Corrain heard a twig snap behind him, as though someone had taken an incautious step. Turning as quickly as he could, he saw the Soluran barely a pace away, staring with horror at his own foot.

The Eldritch Kin had disappeared. Micaran lay limp in a welter of blood.

The Soluran looked at Corrain, aghast.

The Soluran ran. Corrain chased him. Without any clear path, the undergrowth was thick enough to hamper the desperate Soluran. Not thick enough to slow Corrain with the prospect of vengeance before him.

Birds flew up from the thickets, calling loudly, harsh

with fright. Corrain ignored them along with the thorns raking his bare arms and the brambles tearing his unprotected shins. If such discomfort was real then so was the Soluran.

He was gaining with every step. Now the man was almost within reach. With a sudden lunge, Corrain seized hold of his cloak. He hauled on the cloth, twisting to use his body weight to bring the Soluran down.

The clasp at the cloak's collar gave way with an audible snap. No matter. The man was staggering sideways in a vain attempt to regain his balance.

Corrain was on him, wrapping his arms around him and bearing him down to the ground. As the Soluran writhed, Corrain twisted to get on top of him. He drove his knee into the man's groin to cut his struggles short with a shrill yelp of pain.

The Soluran doubled up around his agony. Corrain got one hand around his throat and forced his head backwards, driving his other fist deep into the man's midriff just for good measure. The Soluran retched, about to vomit.

Corrain clamped the hand he'd just used to punch him over the man's face, to hold his nose and mouth closed. Drowning on his own spew would kill the bastard just as surely as a blade and Corrain had nothing to cut his thrice-cursed throat.

The Soluran tried to dig his nails into Corrain's hands. His fingertips slipped on the sweat and muck coating the Caladhrian's skin. Corrain tightened his grip around the man's throat, feeling for the vessels carrying blood to Micaran's murderer's brain.

The Soluran struggled more frantically. Corrain pinned him with a brutal knee just below his ribs. As he brought all his weight to bear, the man's thrashing weakened. Corrain didn't yield, not about to be caught out by that brawler's trick.

The hired gig swayed as they rounded a corner. Corrain grabbed frantically for the rail. Micaran's body slid across the seat and the adept's dead weight almost tipped them both out onto the cobbles.

The driver glanced over his shoulder as he felt his vehicle so perilously unbalanced. 'Is your friend all right?'

Corrain searched desperately for any sign of life; the faintest breath or the slightest hint of Micaran's heart still beating to be found at wrist or neck.

'Get us to Tolekan Street,' he yelled. 'As quick as you can!'

Or should he direct the gig to the Red Library? Could Master Garewin and one of his fellow adepts work some marvel? If Micaran wasn't truly lost but somehow held at Saedrin's threshold? For an endless moment, Corrain clung to that frailest of hopes; that Micaran's undeserved fate wouldn't be another death to be laid to his account.

Then brutal reason reasserted itself. Corrain had seen enough dead men to know that he held Micaran's corpse in his arms.

Tears trickled down his cheeks even as he felt rage burning beneath his breastbone.

What of the Soluran? He could only hope that somewhere in this city, the bastard's body lay just as lifeless.

Though that wouldn't be the end of it, not by a long measure. Not once Corrain called down Hadrumal's vengeance on whoever was behind the murderous adept. As long as some wizardry could find out who that might be. Despite himself, doubt closed cold fingers around Corrain's heart.

— CHAPTER TWENTY-FIVE —

'THEN I PLACED the artefacts in the Archmage's keeping.' Jilseth couldn't recall when she'd last picked her way through a conversation so carefully but satisfying the Col mage's curiosity about events in Halferan was the price of him telling her whatever he knew or suspected of Jagai dealings in Col.

So far she was telling the truth as long as Olved didn't ask her what Planir had done with the Khusro treasures after that. She still hoped to avoid telling him a bare-faced lie, not least because she had got the worst of this deal. Olved could only tell her that the Jagai domain's shipmasters traded with this city's merchants with no more and no less duplicity on either side than occurred in any port from here to Zyoutessela.

Olved leaned forward in his chair on the other side of the fireplace with its merrily dancing fire. 'Has Khusro Rina told the other warlords what his wives are doing?'

'Not as far as we know.' Jilseth explained before Olved could press her in his tiresomely impatient fashion. 'The Archipelagan Kheda tells us that their voyage hasn't been kept a sworn secret since that would suggest they had something underhand to hide when this finally comes to light.'

She shrugged. 'On the other hand, the only people

who know of this trip are those directly involved, such as the crew of the galley which brought them to Attar. As far as their visit to Halferan itself is concerned, only their personal bodyslaves accompanied the women and by all Aldabreshin custom and practise, no one can demand that those men reveal their mistresses' business, not even Khusro Rina himself.'

Jilseth had been surprised to learn from Kheda how much of her supposed knowledge of Archipelagan life was inaccurate. When she got back to Hadrumal, she had vowed to learn the truth of Aldabreshi law from Velindre and never mind if that revealed her own ignorance.

Olved was already waving her words away. 'A bodyslave will cut his own tongue out before he betrays his mistress. Can you ask this Archipelagan what he thinks Jagai Kalu will do when he hears of the Khusro domain approaching mainlanders for such aid?'

Reaching for the kettle keeping warm within the fireplace's fender, the mage halted, his eyes brightening. 'Do you suppose that Jagai wishes to recruit these mainland swordsmen to defend a similar ship full of treasure? Might he send the pick of his strong rooms to Col, in order that anything touched by magic might be identified and removed?'

'Perhaps.' Jilseth would rather hope for that than see Corrain's forebodings proved right as Jagai Kalu attacked Halferan. Could the warlord have learned how enmeshed the manor was in the Archmage's schemes? But even if he had, what could the Aldabreshi hope to gain by renewing hostility between the Archipelago and the mainland?

She offered Olved her tisane glass in its silver holder so that the mage could add hot water from the kettle.

Jilseth would rather have had a fresh cup complete with unsteeped herbs in the pierced silver ball, but she would settle for diluting this cool and bitter drink since that was clearly all Olved was going to offer her.

A horse's galloping hooves and the rattle of wheels prompted sudden uproar outside the sitting room window. A woman screamed, startling Olved into pouring scalding water over Jilseth's hand.

'Forgive—' Almost before he had spoken, his fire magic had drawn off the wounding heat.

Before Jilseth could reassure him, urgent fists hammered on the house's front door. Olved's maid ran through the hall. As Jilseth and the mage reached the sitting room's threshold, the girl threw open the door to cry out, appalled.

'What is it?' Olved seized the maid and thrust her aside.

Jilseth was about to try and calm the girl's hysterics when she saw Corrain struggling up the steps burdened by Micaran's limp body slung over his shoulder.

Though there wasn't a mark on him, her necromancy told her instantly that the young mentor was dead. Corrain stumbled and Jilseth flung out a hand. As her air magic lightened his load, the Caladhrian looked straight at her. She recoiled from the murderous rage in his eyes.

'Oh, my boy,' Olved whispered hoarsely as he stared at the corpse.

Jilseth grabbed the cowering maid's arm so hard that the poor girl yelped. 'Mentor Micaran was his son?'

She hadn't thought to ask if the Col mage had a family. There had been no sign in this house and Olved hadn't mentioned any such thing.

'His sister's eldest child,' the girl quavered before looking past Jilseth's shoulder and screaming yet again.

Jilseth felt elemental fire roaring out of control as Olved's grief overwhelmed his hold on his affinity. The sitting room hearth was an inferno. The kettle lay in the fender, a molten pool of metal. The wooden mantle was ablaze and the chairs on either side of the fireplace were filling the hallway with the stink of burning horsehair.

She sought to wring elemental water from the air to quench the flames to no avail. Summoning dust imbued with her earth affinity to smother the blaze would mean bringing down the ceiling. Stopping short of that, Jilseth drove the air feeding the fire from the room, to gain a few moments for thought.

She seized Olved by the shoulders and shook him. He was still staring at Corrain and his burden. "Mica..."

Jilseth hauled the stricken mage around so he could see nothing but her face. 'Do you want this whole house to become his funeral pyre?'

To her relief, Olved focused on her. His eyes filled with tears, spilling down his thin cheeks.

'Master Mage,' Jilseth said forcefully. 'You must secure your affinity.'

'Saedrin save us.' Olved turned his head, horrified to see what had become of his sitting room.

To Jilseth's intense relief, she felt the elemental fury fuelling the blaze cool. She could relax her warding driving away the air. As she did so, she realised that Corrain was now staggering under Micaran's dead weight, bereft of the support which her magic had given him.

She threw open the opposite door with a thrust of elemental air before sending that same wizardry to help Corrain once again. 'Carry him in there.'

Jilseth wanted to get everyone out of the hall. Avidly curious neighbours were gathering in the street outside. Gawkers peered up the steps in hopes of seeing something through the open entrance. Jilseth stole a momentary eddy from the ensorcelled air surrounding Corrain to slam the front door closed.

'I must tell my sister.' Before anyone could speak, Olved vanished in a surge of ominously red-tinted magelight.

Corrain muttered something under his breath. Going into the dining room, he set Micaran's body on the long polished table, as gently as he might lay down a sleeping child.

'You, girl.' The Caladhrian turned on the maid who was starting to grizzle for want of knowing what else to do. 'Who else is in the house?'

The girl flinched. 'Mistress Galle.'

'Go and tell her what's happened,' Corrain ordered, 'and then send word to whichever shrine prepares bodies for their pyres hereabouts.'

Jilseth stood silent until the girl had vanished through the door beyond the stairs at the end of the hall. Then she walked into the dining room. 'What happened?'

Corrain had dragged a chair away from the table, to sit with his head in his hands. 'The Soluran.'

'How?' Jilseth demanded.

'Artifice,' Corrain retorted.

Jilseth wanted far more from him than that but could see that asking wouldn't be wise. Besides, what could the Caladhrian possibly know of such lethal aetheric magic? Not that she had any reason to feel superior. She couldn't hope to understand even if Corrain could tell her every detail of this deadly enchantment.

'We have to find him.' Corrain got to his feet.

'The Soluran? Surely he'll be long gone. He must know that he's forfeited his own life with this murder.'

Even as she spoke, she wondered how such a crime might be proved. Would the Elected's courts accept Corrain's sworn word as proof of whatever tale he might have to tell? She looked at Micaran and shied away from the thought of using her necromancy to learn how Artifice had killed him. How dangerous could that prove for her?

'If there's any luck or justice in this world, that bastard's as dead as mutton,' Corrain growled. 'I think I killed him. I hope I did. Even if I didn't, we can beat some answers out of him,' he concluded with vicious determination. 'So scry for him, Madam Mage. What do you need? A bowl and some water?'

'Not until I know how Micaran died. I'm sorry, truly, but if this adept isn't dead, he might be able to strike at me in some similar fashion.' She didn't want to anger Corrain with her refusal but Usara's warnings of wizardly vulnerability to Artifice rang ominously in her memory.

Corrain stared at her for a moment. 'Let's ask Mentor Garewin. He'll still be in the Red Library with Hosh and those other adepts.'

Jilseth moved to bar his path to the door. 'You won't be allowed into the library without someone to vouch for you. I can do that, if we go together. Tell me what has happened first. Why did this Soluran kill Micaran?'

Corrain drew a deep breath. 'Micaran learned that this Soluran hasn't only been spreading ill will towards wizardry through Col.' He looked straight at Jilseth. 'And he's been using some Artifice to spread that mistrust, not just a generous purse and a glib tongue.'

'What else was he doing?' Apprehension knotted Jilseth's innards.

'He's putting wild ideas into that Jagai *zamorin*'s head,' Corrain said savagely. 'Along with everyone else in that domain from the warlord down.'

Jilseth listened with growing astonishment as Corrain told her what Micaran had died to learn.

'You truly believe that these Archipelagans will find mercenaries willing to attack Hadrumal? That these mainlanders will somehow become convinced that they're not simply sailing to their deaths?'

'Does it matter what I believe,' Corrain challenged her, 'when this Soluran can twist anyone's mind to believe whatever his Artifice wishes?'

'One adept couldn't do all this on his own.' Though Jilseth recalled how little she truly knew of Artifice. 'We must tell Planir.' She looked around the room for something to kindle magefire and something to reflect it for a bespeaking spell.

'We need to find this Soluran's lair,' Corrain insisted. 'Whether he's dead or fled, there should be some hints to give us a scent, to offer a trail back to whoever he's working with. You said it yourself; one man wouldn't do this alone—'

As Corrain broke off, Jilseth looked more closely at him.

'What is it?'

Corrain swallowed. 'The Soluran killed Micaran by using his own fears against him. He sent some nightmare of the Eldritch Kin to tear him to pieces. I couldn't lay a finger on the bastard. He was no more solid than smoke. Not until the man from Wrede appeared. He trapped the Soluran inside his own imagining—' Corrain struggled for words.

'Micaran said that Artifice offered a refuge—' Jilseth

thrust away the pain of recalling the cheerful mentor's explanations.

'This was no refuge. It was a trap and then the man from Wrede trapped the Soluran inside it. That meant I could get hold of him and I choked the life out of the bastard. At least, I think I did.' He glanced at the table where Micaran lay. 'How else would I have found myself back in the gig we were riding?'

'I don't know.' Jilseth saw no point in hiding her own ignorance. 'But why did the man from Wrede help you?'

Corrain gestured towards the door. 'Let's ask Master Garewin to find him and we'll ask. Maybe the mentor can use the same questing Artifice as Micaran. Now, can you take us to the Red Library with your wizardry or must I find a gig?'

'Mistress?' A female voice hesitated behind her.

Jilseth turned to see a grey-haired woman. She was carrying a bowl of water, her sturdy arms draped with shrouding cloth. Her face was pale with shock and grief and the tear-stained maid cowered behind her.

'Mistress Galle?' As the woman nodded, Jilseth stepped aside. 'We will leave Mentor Micaran in your care.'

There was clearly no stopping Corrain and she dared not contemplate what havoc he might wreak let loose in the city on his own. He looked capable of cutting down the Prefecture's librarians on their very steps if they tried to bar his path to Mentor Garewin. She would have to find time to bespeak Planir later. At least she should have a fuller tale to tell him.

She laid a hand on Corrain's arm and with the Red Library so close, the white magelight of translocation came and went in the blink of an eye.

They arrived at the corner of the steps. Corrain was already striding upwards, taking two treads at a time, one hand on his sword hilt. One of the Prefecture's men moved to intercept him.

'One moment, if you please.' Jilseth summoned a surge of air to carry her forward swiftly enough to arrive in front of the black-liveried librarian. She smiled politely at the man. 'I have the Archmage's authority to enter, as sanctioned by the Elected.'

Holding out her hand, palm upwards, she wrought a shimmering illusion of Col's standard rippling in an unseen wind.

The library's white-gloved guardian bowed. 'Madam Mage.'

He still eyed Corrain with some misgiving. 'You're usually with that lad who's seeking healing from Mentor Garewin.'

'We have urgent business with Mentor Garewin,' Jilseth spoke before Corrain could reply. 'Of concern to the Archmage and the city alike. I will vouch for my companion.'

The librarian looked sternly at Corrain. 'Do you swear by Arrimelin that you will not deface any book in our care or cause any flame to be kindled within the library?'

If this day wasn't so dire, Jilseth would have been amused to see the Caladhrian taken so thoroughly aback.

'I swear it,' Corrain said with gritted teeth.

'This way, Madam Mage.' The man led them through the entrance and into the vestibule where the panelling was hidden by countless cloaks heaped on broad hooks. He opened a corner door to a stair spiralling upwards. 'Mentor Garewin is on the third floor, in the north-eastern study.'

'I know the way,' Jilseth assured him, 'and my thanks.'

Corrain pressed hard on her heels. She was somewhat surprised that he didn't simply push past her.

They reached the third floor and Jilseth reached for the study door handle. Now Corrain's impatience did get the better of him. He turned the handle and pushed. The door pushed back and locked itself.

Jilseth chose to knock rather than use her own magic, leaning close to the crack to speak. 'Mentor Garewin, we have grave news of Mentor Micaran.'

A woman opened the door. Garewin and two other men sat around the small room's table with Hosh on the far side by the window. The table was heaped with books but beyond that, the panelled room was bare.

'Good day to you, Hosh.' Jilseth was startled into a smile. 'My compliments, Mentor Garewin. I see you still have a long way to go but this progress is most encouraging.'

Hosh's hand flew to his damaged cheek. 'Progress?'

Jilseth looked quizzically at him. 'Don't you use a mirror for shaving?'

'I'm pleased that you see the improvement, Madam Mage.' Mentor Garewin smiled. 'Each day's changes are very subtle and the boy guards his hopes so fiercely against any hint of wishful thinking.'

'Captain?' Hosh looked desperately at Corrain.

'I did wonder,' he admitted haltingly. 'I didn't want to say until I was certain—'

'Mentor Undil, sealed to the School of Apothecaries.' The woman offered Jilseth the briefest of bows. 'You said you had grave news of Micaran?'

'The gravest, alas.' Jilseth wove a brief cantrip from water magic to dry her clammy palms. 'He has been killed by some aetheric means—'

'—by the Soluran adept you saw that first day in The Goose Hounds.' Corrain couldn't restrain his anger. 'Who is he, Master Garewin? Where can we find his lodging?'

'If he's guilty of such an unconscionable crime, he's surely fled,' one of the other men objected.

'Not as long as I truly managed to kill him,' Corrain countered with bitter satisfaction.

Mentor Garewin raised a hand. 'Please, tell us all that's happened. And forgive my ill-manners. May I make known to you Mentor Parovil and Mentor Lusken.'

Both men were in their middle years, robed and beringed as befitted mentors sealed to Col's university. If Jilseth had not known, she would never have guessed that they were aetheric adepts.

'Masters,' Corrain acknowledged them grimly. 'You should know that I am responsible for this tragedy. I asked for Micaran's help in searching this Jagai *zamorin*'s thoughts.'

Jilseth listened with half an ear as the Caladhrian told his wretched tale a second time. She looked around the room for anything which she might use to cast a bespeaking to Hadrumal, though she would need to go outside to do that. The Prefecture's librarians would consider a mage-kindled flame a breach of her own sworn oath to equal anything struck with flint and steel. Where might she find sufficient privacy close by to work her spell?

She realised that Corrain had fallen silent. Hosh gazed at him with more sympathy and understanding than Jilseth might have expected in such a young man's eyes.

'You all know this Soluran?' Mentor Garewin

demanded of his fellow adepts, his face taut with grief and outrage.

'I do.' The woman, Mentor Undil, nodded and the other two men did the same.

'Remec Estinesh of Trudenar,' Mentor Parovil growled.

Jilseth frowned as she recalled the map of Solura. What business did a House of Sanctuary from a central and southerly province have killing Col's scholars? Why was this adept helping to turn Col's residents and Archipelagans alike against the wizard isle? As she wondered, suspicion stirred in the back of her mind. But suspicion was no use without proof.

'Let us find him, whether he is living or dead.' Garewin sat and reached out to the adepts on either side.

Hosh shoved his stool back, getting out of the way as the four linked hands to form a circle.

'*Aderumai ar sesfital dar orida nal Estinesh.*'

The four mentors sat motionless, their eyes closed, intoning their incomprehensible enchantment.

'*Aderumai ar sesfital. Aderumai ar sesfital.*'

The woman and the older of the two men began repeating the first phrase while Mentor Garewin and the other continued with the full chant.

'*Aderumai ar sesfital dar orida nal Estinesh.*'

Mentor Undil's voice rose to harmonise with the baritones on either side while Garewin's resonant bass underpinned the whole.

Jilseth's fists clenched with frustration. When a wizard worked a scrying, the results were there for all to see. What was this Artifice showing the mentors? Were they searching the city with their mind's eye or were they sharing some vision of the Soluran, trying to see some clue to tell them where he cowered or lay dead?

At some unspoken signal, the four adepts released their hold on each other's hands and opened their eyes.

Mentor Undil spoke first. 'He's in an accommodation house, a respectable one, in Blackpits Lane.'

'With a green-painted door—'

'—and cream awnings over its windows.' The other mentors said in swift succession.

'Where is that?' Hosh asked meekly.

'Close by,' Corrain assured him before Jilseth could reveal her own knowledge of the city.

'He is dead.' Mentor Garewin's vicious satisfaction sat oddly on the mentor's well-groomed face.

Jilseth breathed a little more easily.

Corrain grunted. 'We'd best not delay. We don't want anyone else finding the body and raising a hue and cry to summon the Elected's men. Not before we've searched his room and his effects for some clue as to his partners in this crime.'

'We should inform the authorities of such malice at work in our city.' The older mentor looked affronted.

'Naturally, and now that we know where to find him, you can do that,' Jilseth said quickly. 'I'm sure we can learn what we need before the Elected's men arrive.'

Corrain scowled. 'We can deal with the carrion, Masters and Mistress, but we must ask more of your Artifice. We still have no idea who this man from Wrede might be. After today, I don't believe he's an enemy but I would hesitate to call him a friend. Regardless, we need to know who he is.'

Jilseth nodded. 'Mentor Micaran was searching for this stranger with a questing enchantment which he'd learned from Guinalle Tor Priminale in Suthyfer—'

She was encouraged to see the adepts keenly interested in this revelation.

'—but now that he is dead, his endeavours will be lost—'

Mentor Lusken, the younger man, raised an assertive finger. 'Not necessarily, if we can pick up the thread of that enchantment swiftly enough.'

'We need to know the specifics of this Artifice.' Undil looked around the table. 'Do any of us know Lady Tor Priminale sufficiently well to reach her thoughts over such a distance?'

'I believe that I may.' Mentor Parovil's confidence encouraged Jilseth.

Garewin looked apologetically at Hosh. 'I fear this would be the end of our work with you today.'

'This is more important.' Hosh was already on his feet. 'I can help my captain and the lady mage.'

Though he looked at Jilseth with a wariness which surprised her. Regardless, she spoke up before Corrain could offer some objection or send the lad back to kick his heels in their tavern room.

'We'll be glad of your assistance.' Whether or not Hosh could help was of little actual concern. After what had befallen Mentor Micaran, Jilseth wasn't letting anyone with detailed knowledge of Archmage Planir's concerns out of her sight. She could only hope that the Soluran had died before he could tell anyone what he had learned with his insidious Artifice.

Corrain's nod of accord suggested that he knew precisely what she was thinking. He bowed to the assembled mentors. 'We'll bid you good day, Masters, Mistress.'

Garewin held up a hand to stop him leaving. 'Where and when shall we meet to share what we have learned? We can hardly gather at Master Olved's home, now that it's a house of mourning.'

'We will meet at the Prefecture,' Mentor Parovil declared with absolute authority. 'We will share what we learn and then the Prefects and the Elected must be informed, before day's end. A mentor of this university lies dead.'

Jilseth could see this was not negotiable. She would have to find time before they met later to bespeak Planir and let him know what had happened as well as asking what he wanted her to do next.

'Very well, provided you have Artifice to foil any attempt to eavesdrop on our conversation through aetheric magic?' She looked around the adepts. 'I can baffle mundane eyes and ears with elemental wards against sight and sound.'

Mentor Lusken nodded. 'We can do the rest.'

'Then we will leave you to your magic.' Corrain jerked his head towards the door in unmistakable command.

Jilseth was torn between the need for haste and her disinclination to let him think that she was his to instruct. She compromised by having the final word, letting both Caladhrians precede her out of the room.

'Let's meet at the Prefecture at the last chime of the day. That should give us sufficient time to learn what we can.'

With a final bow, she hurried after Hosh and Corrain who were already halfway down the stairs to the floor below. She had barely caught up with them before they were making their excuses to the liveried door ward.

'You won't be admitted without a mentor or the lady mage,' the black-liveried man warned them as he opened the outer door.

'Of course.' Jilseth smiled at him as she followed them out onto the steps.

'Halferan!' she called sharply to halt Corrain's swift descent. 'A moment!'

'Why?' He stood ready to challenge her.

Jilseth chose her words carefully. 'Now that I know the Soluran is dead, there is some particular wizardry which I can work to learn exactly who he had dealings with before he came to Col. That will be the quickest and most certain route to knowing who's behind this plot against Hadrumal. But I must have certain things if I am to work this spell. I need oil and a vessel sturdy enough to hold it when it's heated.'

She expected the Caladhrian to demand some explanation and braced herself for his revulsion at the notion of necromancy.

Instead he unbuckled his sword belt and handed the weapon to Hosh. 'Go to Blackpits Lane and start knocking on doors if there's more than one house matching the mentors' description. You go—'

'I know where it is,' Jilseth assured him.

Corrain nodded. 'Then I'll see you there as quickly as I can.'

'Yes, Captain.' Hosh quickly secured the blade at his own hip.

'Baron.' Jilseth wasn't finished with Corrain yet. 'I must have oil pressed from nuts or seeds or olives, nothing that's come from an animal. I cannot use dripping or lard.'

'Very well.' Corrain nodded impatiently and strode away.

Jilseth watched him go, still surprised that he hadn't insisted on knowing why this might be essential for her wizardry.

'This way.' She turned to Hosh and led him westwards across the square. As they rounded the corner, she offered him a friendly smile. 'You are looking well, truly.'

'Thank you, Madam Mage,' he said guardedly.

She waited for him to say something further, to ask some question. When neither was forthcoming, she concentrated on finding the lane they were seeking by the most efficient path which she could recall through Col's byways.

It should hardly come as a surprise, Jilseth reflected, that Hosh would be chary around mages. Like Corrain, he had seen the corsair island destroyed at first hand, caught between Hadrumal's vengeance and the Mandarkin's savagery. The lad hadn't been anywhere near a wizard since he'd returned to Halferan and handed that arm-ring to Velindre. Since coming to Col, he'd only met Master Olved and he was hardly the warmest of mages.

— CHAPTER TWENTY-SIX —

HOSH WAS GLAD the captain had given him his sword. Keeping one hand on the hilt and using the other to stop his hood falling victim to the gusting wind meant that he couldn't succumb to temptation and explore his broken face with curious fingertips.

Had the magewoman truly noticed a difference? Was there an improvement beyond the easing of his pain? Surely Jilseth had nothing to gain by a kindly untruth. Besides, in Hosh's experience, wizards didn't deal much in kindness.

He stole sideways glances whenever they slowed for Jilseth to make certain of her bearings. Hosh still struggled to reconcile her modest height and unremarkable appearance with his mum's tale of the magewoman's astonishing spells wielded in Halferan's defence in that last stand against the corsairs, before her magic had concealed their escape.

'This way.' Jilseth led him down a lane of shoemakers' workshops.

Then again, Hosh reflected, Anskal the Mandarkin had looked like some pathetic beggar; stunted, starveling and filthy. His savage, selfish magic had been as astounding as it had proved appalling. The wizard had held life as cheap as any of the corsairs. More cheaply.

Even corsairs as vicious as Ducah with his murderous sword, or as crafty as Nifai with his overseer's whip, had been loyal to their allies. Time and again, Anskal had let one of the mageborn Archipelagans whom he had enslaved die an agonized death simply to see the survivors learn a brutal lesson.

What magic was Jilseth planning to work with a corpse? Hosh didn't even want to speculate, thrusting ghastly imaginings away. As he followed her dutifully across another brick-paved square, he wished, now that he could be sure of privacy in his own thoughts, that Mentor Garewin or one of the other Col adepts knew some Artifice to uncover this dead Soluran's secrets.

Artifice's softly spoken enchantments were so quietly reassuring. Over these past few days in the Red Library, there had been no garish, eerie magelight crackling out of nowhere in harsh, unnatural colours, or blinding whiteness as menacing as lightning from a storm cloud and disappearing just as swiftly.

Adepts were no different to anyone else. That was to say, Hosh allowed, these mentors who were healing him had a marked aptitude for scholarship which few folk would share, as well as sharper wits than any five in a hundred met in a marketplace.

But they hadn't been born with arcane abilities to steal away the air that a man needed to breathe, to summon up water to drown someone where they stood or fire to burn them alive. Artificers couldn't open up a gaping chasm to swallow someone whole, closing up the earth again to leave no sign that someone had been murdered.

Hosh had heard any number of such stories in Halferan's tavern, tantalizingly terrifying as well as comfortably set in long-lost days of old. But now he had seen such magic for himself, along with the guardsmen from Halferan, Antathele, Licanin and Tallat. The tales now spreading like fear of spotted fever along Caladhria's highways and byways were rooted in reality with dates and places and names.

'That must be the rooming house.' Jilseth halted at the end of a short lane curving down a shallow slope.

There was only one building matching the mentors' description; four storeys with a row of seven windows on the upper floors and a wide double door in the middle at street level. Though Hosh reckoned his mum would quibble over calling this respectable accommodation. The green door was in sore need of new paint and the cream awnings over the windows were stained with soot and weighed down with dead leaves.

'How will we know which room he's in?'

Jilseth waved that away. 'I'll know, unless there's more than one corpse under that roof, but I'm sure that's unlikely.'

Hosh fervently hoped so. 'Should we wait for the— for the baron?'

'Let's see if we can get inside first.' The magewoman started walking towards the green door so Hosh was forced to fall into step behind her, one hand on the captain's sword.

As Jilseth knocked on the door Hosh peered through the grimy glass pane beside the weathered wood. Seeing the rooming house's keeper bustling down the tiled hall, he hastily retreated.

The housekeeper opened the door in an apron so stained that Hosh's mum would long since have given up hope of boiling it white and cut it up for rags.

'Good day to you?' The woman's greeting clearly included a demand that they explain themselves.

'Good day.' Jilseth inclined her head politely. 'We are here to see Master Estinesh, a Soluran residing here.'

Hosh stood behind the magewoman, doing his best to keep his face obscured. For a change, he was more concerned that the housekeeper would see his apprehension rather than gawp at his injuries. If this woman escorted them to the Soluran's door, surely she would find his dead body? What would the magewoman do about that?

He had no chance to ask as the housekeeper led them along the mud-smeared hall and up the scuffed and dusty stairs. When they reached the second floor the slatternly woman knocked on the third door facing the front. 'Master Estinesh?'

'Enter!'

Hosh couldn't conceal his start of surprise at hearing that peremptory bark from within. Thankfully the housekeeper had her back to him.

Jilseth shot a warning glance over her shoulder, one finger raised to her lips as she gestured with her other hand towards the room's closed door. As the housekeeper turned the knob, the door opened.

'Oh!' Jilseth dropped a handful of coins.

Even allowing for the bare floorboards, the noise was so loud that Hosh was sure some magic was doubling their clatter.

'Let me help you.' The housekeeper stooped low, sharp-eyed and scooping up fallen silver like a hen pecking corn.

'Thank you.' Jilseth fluttered helpless hands at the same time as giving Hosh a meaningful glare and jerking her head towards the half-open door.

He quickly went to stand blocking the housekeeper's

view as the woman straightened up to hand Jilseth her money. Though Hosh didn't dare turn to see what might lie behind him.

'Thank you, and please, take something for your trouble.' Jilseth pressed a coin into the woman's hand. At the same time, the magewoman pushed Hosh into the room and closed the door so deftly that she cut off the housekeeper's thanks in mid-sentence.

Hosh stared at the table beneath the window where the Soluran sat in a chair, as motionless as any shrine statue.

'It's an illusion, like his voice.' As Jilseth looked up from counting her coin, the unmoving figure vanished.

Hosh looked around the meagre lodging. Plastered walls were bare of decoration and no rug softened the floorboards. Apart from the table and chair, only a small clothes press stood beside the door and the narrow bed which would preclude a couple sleeping together in any comfort, whatever else they might do on the lumpy mattress.

A dead body appeared amid the rumpled sheets and blankets although the Soluran wore breeches and shirt rather than night clothes. Hosh became aware of an unpleasant odour, something between a sick room and an infant's soiled swaddling. He recalled how slaves had lost control of bladder and bowels when he'd seen them flogged to death on the galleys.

'He lay down to work his Artifice in comfort,' Jilseth observed. 'That is fortunate. If he had fallen to thrash on these floorboards someone could well have complained about the commotion and discovered him. It seems he died hard,' she added with some satisfaction.

Hosh looked at the man's bitten lip, blood clotting on

his chin. What would the housekeeper have thought if she had discovered the Soluran's corpse? That he had suffered some seizure as he slept?

Perhaps Artifice wasn't so kindly a magic. Could anyone tell if some murderous adept was responsible for an unexpected death? At least it was plain to see when wizardry killed someone.

'Good.' Jilseth was by the window, looking into the street. She gestured at the door and Hosh heard the solid click of the lock securing itself. 'Wait here.'

Before Hosh could ask what she intended, the magewoman vanished. He had barely blinked in astonishment before she reappeared with Corrain at her side, her hand on his shoulder. The captain was cradling a battered cooking pot with a broad-necked flagon inside it, its stopper secured with a lumpy smear of wax.

The captain acknowledged Hosh with a nod and jerked his head towards the door. 'Don't let anyone in.'

'I don't imagine we'll be disturbed,' Jilseth said drily. 'Mistress Housekeeper won't wish to account for the silver she pocketed from the floor.'

'What—? Never mind.' Corrain abandoned his own question, contemplating the dead Soluran on the bed, his expression bleak.

'At least you won some justice for Master Micaran,' Hosh ventured.

'Much good that'll do his family. He's still dead,' Corrain said harshly.

Shrugging that off, he turned to Hosh and pointed to the clothes press. 'Search that while I search the body and the bed. Madam Mage, see what's in his cloak pockets if you please?'

He jerked his head towards the Soluran's cloak lying

draped over the chair before he stooped over the corpse
and ripped the dead man's shirt open.

Hosh opened the clothes press and pulled out clean
shirts and under linen. He shook the garments but
there was nothing hidden within their folds. He did the
same with the man's breeches, searching their pockets
for good measure. Nothing. Hosh examined the two
jerkins hung on the back of the door inside and out,
running the seams and hems through his fingers.

'Madam Mage—' He turned to Jilseth, similarly
checking the cloak for anything stitched within the cloth.

Corrain knelt on the floor, one hand pushing the dead
Soluran towards the wall as he thrust his other arm
between the flock-filled mattress and the bed boards. A
travelling bag hauled out from beneath the bed already
lay open, revealing the dead man's razor, strop and
mirror and a few pots of medicaments.

He grimaced at the sordid smell. 'Nothing. What now?'

'I work some necromancy.' Dropping the cloak onto
the chair, the magewoman contemplated the corpse.

Corrain couldn't hide his instant of revulsion.
'Necromancy?'

'It will show us his life before he travelled here.'
Jilseth looked at Corrain and Hosh. 'You need not stay
if it distresses you.'

Before Hosh could answer, Corrain squared his
shoulders. 'What are you going to do?'

Jilseth studied the corpse with a faint crease between
her brows. 'I normally work this spell with some
salvaged bone or other fragment to discover how
someone died. I wonder if I should cut off his hand.'

Hosh couldn't decide which was more unnerving; the
thought of the lady wizard handling such carrion or her

matter-of-fact tone, as composed as his mum discussing cutting up a woollen dress length to sew a new gown.

'Which one?' Corrain drew his belt-knife, his face twisted with distaste.

'Let's try something else first.' Jilseth went over to the cooking pot. As she lifted out the glazed flagon, the wax melted away and she poured the contents into the pot, stopper and all. 'Open the window, if you please.'

Hosh watched with growing unease as she carried the pot carefully across to the bed. He breathed a little more easily as Col's incessant breezes scoured the oppressive smell from the room, though as he caught Corrain's eye, they shared a silent moment of mutual queasiness.

Jilseth tugged the Soluran's limp hand free of the tangling blankets, to let it dangle over the side to hang inside the cooking pot. She nodded with satisfaction. 'Good. His fingertips just reach the oil.'

She settled herself on the floorboards, sitting cross-legged in a most unladylike fashion with her skirts tucked around her.

'Madam Mage, what wizardry—' But as Hosh summoned up the courage to ask what she was doing, he couldn't frame a question.

Jilseth leaned forward and cupped her hands around the battered pot. 'I will search out his most significant recent encounters.'

Barely a handful of moments later, Hosh's eyes began to water. He coughed as the acrid bite of burning oil seared the back of his throat and nose, most of all on the injured side of his face. This was worse than the stink of soiled bed linen.

Smoke and steam rose from the cooking pot. Even without amber threads of magelight weaving through the vapour, this could only be wizardry with no fire beneath the pot. The oil bubbled softly within yet Jilseth pressed her hands against the sides. If she hadn't been mageborn she would be weeping over agonising blistered palms.

A swirl of steam, smoke and dull gold magelight drifted to float above the dead Soluran's face. The haze spread but rather than dissipating like a natural mist, it thickened. Soon the cloud was so opaque that Hosh couldn't see the pale wall behind it.

Deep within the darkness, golden magelight coalesced into a shining sphere no bigger than an apple. It swelled into a globe which would have filled both Hosh's hands. Colour and movement appeared; tiny figures veiled by swirling mist, a flickering succession of indistinct glimpses. Then the grey haze thinned to no more than the glistening sheen on dirty glass.

Hosh studied the vision of some distant room. It was night; unshuttered windows were black mirrors reflecting the candle-filled sconces around the circle of the unpainted stone wall. The single narrow door was barred from inside.

Eight chairs surrounded a round table of polished, honey-coloured wood. Five of the seated figures were dressed as richly as barons and their ladies at a wedding. The three remaining wore plain robes with hooded surcoats; a man in pale grey over black, a thin-faced woman in cream wool over dark brown, and a black-bearded man favouring tan over charcoal. Each one wore a different pewter ornament on a leather thong around their neck.

Hosh blinked and looked more closely to see that the man in grey and black was the dead Soluran.

'Where is that? Who are they?' Corrain demanded.

Jilseth shook her head, slowly and carefully, her unblinking eyes never leaving the vision. 'I cannot say where they are but that woman in the russet gown is a mage from the Order of Detich.'

Jilseth's tone told Hosh that this was ominous news.

'What are they saying?' Corrain narrowed his eyes as though that might help him hear the faint voices floating through the smoke.

Hosh concentrated and found he could just make out their conversation.

'*Then Detich, Noerut, Ontesk, Ancorr and Temosul are agreed.*'

The woman's satisfaction was vindictive in its intensity.

'*Does Remulde of Solith know of this?*'

This speaker was far from sharing her confidence.

'*As yet the Order of the Lake of Kings has no reason to know anything which might perturb them.*'

Hosh instantly mistrusted such slyness.

'What does this mean?' Corrain demanded, frustrated.

'What—' Hosh would have drawn the captain's sword except that swift reason told him that at least one of these two people appearing in the room must be a wizard to step out of the empty air in such a startling fashion.

The man was of middling height and wiry build with an amiable face and the merest fuzz of hair softening his balding scalp. His companion was no taller than Hosh's mum, though her figure was womanly and curved rather than girlishly slender like Lady Ilysh.

'Usara?' Jilseth still didn't look away from her spell. 'This necromancy will be lost entirely if I break off now.'

'Forgive me. We came here as quickly as we could.' The man turned to answer the question on Corrain's lips. 'I am Usara, a mage of Suthyfer in Archmage Planir's confidence. This is my wife, Guinalle Tor Priminale, an aetheric adept of advanced skills.'

'Why are you here?' Jilseth's tone was clipped with concentration.

'May I show you rather than try to explain?' the woman said in strangely accented Tormalin.

She knelt beside Jilseth and laid her silver-ringed hand on the magewoman's forearm. Jilseth flinched as though she had been stabbed with a pin and the amber magelight around the necromancy flared bright as sunlight.

Corrain stifled an oath and would have stepped forward. The Suthyfer mage barred his way with an outstretched arm. From the surprise on the captain's face, Hosh guessed that the wizard was stronger than Corrain expected.

'What is that?' Jilseth demanded harshly.

'I will explain, but let me work,' the Tormalin woman replied with equal intensity.

The golden light faded to a web of amber threads amid the smoke and steam framing the vision somehow drawn from the dead man's flesh.

Do we have sufficient allies among the Houses of Sanctuary?

The dead Soluran answered the russet-clad magewoman emphatically.

We do.

Hosh was repelled and fascinated in equal measure. He had never imagined that the dead could be subjected to such wizardry. Was this why even those with scant faith in the gods sought a funeral pyre to burn their bodies to ashes?

'I'm sorry.' The Tormalin lady adept withdrew her hand.

Her husband helped her to her feet. 'We couldn't know.'

'A moment, if you please.' Still seated on the floor, Jilseth leaned forward, her breathing harsh in the abrupt silence.

Hosh could see that the meeting in the vision had drawn to a close. The conspirators were rising to their feet and making brief farewells.

'Master Usara, shall I return this spell to its beginning or shall we see where the Soluran goes next?'

As Hosh heard the tremor in Jilseth's voice and noted the strain on her face, he recalled his mum saying that the magewoman had collapsed with exhaustion during their flight from Halferan. The manor's folk had agreed that the only thing more terrifying than seeing a wizard's power unleashed was being deprived of such aid.

'Will you be able to work a second necromancy on this body?' Usara asked, concerned.

'I believe so.' Jilseth didn't sound as certain as Hosh would have expected.

'Then I suggest you halt and tell us what you've learned so far.' The Suthyfer mage looked for his wife's nod of agreement.

'Very well.' The sag of Jilseth's shoulders betrayed her relief as she removed her hands from the pot. Her palms weren't even reddened.

Acrid smoke surged upwards from the bubbling oil. Steam laced with golden magelight spread throughout the room. Before they all choked, a cold gust surged through the window, too purposeful to be anything other than wizardry. Hosh drew a deep, appreciative breath of clean air.

Jilseth tried to stand but her strength failed her. Corrain went to offer his assistance.

'Thank you.' As soon as she was on her feet, the

magewoman held out her hand to the captain. 'May I have your knife?'

Hosh wondered queasily what she intended as she stooped over the corpse.

Jilseth sliced open the Soluran's shirt sleeve and prodded his dead flesh with the knife's tip, fingerwidth by fingerwidth to a point just above his elbow. Standing upright, she looked at Usara.

'Once we remove this arm, I believe I can repeat the necromancy.' She offered Corrain his knife back, only for the captain to hand her the leather scabbard instead. 'Keep it, please.'

Jilseth shrugged and sheathed the blade, tucking it into a pocket in the seam of her skirt as she looked intently at the Tormalin woman.

'What were you doing?'

The Tormalin Artificer raised her hand to display the silver ring which Hosh had noted earlier. 'Have you heard tell of an ensorcelled ring which Cloud Master Otrick had from a mage called Azazir? The ring Planir gave to Larissa?'

Hosh wondered who these people were and what this ring's significance might be.

'We don't know if Azazir crafted the magic in this ring or if he had it from somewhere else,' the Tormalin noblewoman went on, 'but the first and most potent spell instilled within it is scrying, to enable someone mundane born to search for a person known to them with a bowl of water and ink.'

Usara continued the explanation. 'We have discovered that an adept can work certain enchantments through another mage's scrying while wearing this ring. We wondered if Artifice could reach through your necromancy.'

'That explains the surge of water magic.' Jilseth looked thoughtfully at the ring on Guinalle Tor Priminale's finger.

Hosh had always known that wizards' concerns were far removed from ordinary people's lives but now he was caught in the midst of this, seeing Madam Jilseth's spells and listening to this incomprehensible conversation, magecraft seemed more unnatural and inexplicable than ever. To witness this in Col was still more unnerving. The renegade Anskal's magic might have been more dramatic and deadly but the Mandarkin had menaced Hosh far away amid all the dangers and mysteries of the Archipelago. Col was far too close to home.

He looked at the Tormalin noblewoman with well-hidden misgiving. Her Artifice seemed far more powerful than Mentor Garewin's benign charms. More powerful and much more daunting, if aetheric magic had truly held hundreds of people in enchanted sleep in some Kellarin cave. Hosh had heard that story along with everyone else. Like everyone else, he'd had his doubts. Seeing Lady Tor Priminale and hearing her archaic speech, he found he could believe it and that was more unsettling still. Kusint had told him stories of the Mountain *sheltya*'s ominous and eerie powers but like the Archipelago, the Gidestan peaks were safely far away.

Guinalle looked at him, her eyes narrowing. Hosh took a step back only to find his shoulders pressing hard against the door. Was she reading his thoughts?

'What did you learn from your necromancy?' Usara asked Jilseth.

'That the Orders of Detich, Noerut, Ontesk, Ancorr and Temosul are conspiring with at least three Houses of Sanctuary,' she answered crisply, 'to provoke an Archipelagan attack on Hadrumal.'

'To take on the Archmage?' Usara shook his head in grim wonder. 'How do they propose to foil Hadrumal's defences?'

'Some adept, here or in Suthyfer, may well be able to tell us.' Guinalle Tor Priminale smiled thinly. 'Whether he or she wishes to or not.'

Jilseth contemplated the dead Soluran. 'He came from Trudenar so I imagine that's where we'll find the House favouring those grey and black robes.'

'We can thrust a spoke in their wheels by telling these mercenaries they're being duped,' Corrain said forcefully. 'Hirelings or not, they don't deserve to be sent to certain deaths against Hadrumal's wizards. Hosh and I will take care of that while you get rid of this body.'

He raised a hand as Jilseth would have spoken. 'Do whatever you like with the corpse, just as long as it's not found anywhere in Col. I want his friends to have to go asking, not searching for him with magics. Tracing word of that hunt back could well lead us to some of his allies.'

'Perhaps—' Hosh ventured but before could explain his own idea to give the Archipelagans pause for thought rather than trying to persuade fighting men not to pocket ready gold, Guinalle Tor Priminale interrupted.

'I require your assistance first, my lord Baron.'

'With what?' Corrain asked warily. 'My lady.'

'We share Archmage Planir's concerns about this man from Wrede. He is clearly a proficient adept, able to evade even the ancient questing enchantments which I taught Micaran. I wish to direct such enchantment through a scrying. I don't believe he will expect to be sought through a union of magics, so we can hope that he won't guard against it.'

'How can I help?' Corrain was baffled.

Hosh noticed Jilseth looking intently at the Tormalin woman's silver ring as Lady Guinalle explained.

'You are the only person to have actually seen this man. I believe that Micaran working my Artifice through second-hand recollection materially weakened the enchantments.'

Hosh wondered why Jilseth looked fleetingly relieved before she addressed Corrain with what was surely calculated challenge.

'If you're afraid, I can assure you that Lady Tor Priminale's proficiency outstrips any adept in Col or Vanam. Master Usara's expertise in his own magic is second only to the Archmage.'

'I'm not afraid,' Corrain said scathingly. 'How do we do this?'

All the same, he shivered and Hosh didn't think the cold breeze through the open window was wholly to blame.

'First, we scry.' Usara gestured and the rank oil rose up from the cooking pot to pour itself back into the flagon. As soon as the oil was gone, the cooking pot began softly ringing as though rain were falling inside it.

'Here and now?' Corrain queried.

'There's nothing to be gained by delay.' Guinalle stooped to lift the pot and carry it over to the table. 'This man intervened in your struggles, so he must know this Soluran is dead. Perhaps what he is doing now will give us some hint as to whether he's friend or foe.'

'My lady?' Usara offered Guinalle the single chair.

'If you could stand beside me, my lord Halferan?' Guinalle's open hand demanded Corrain's own as he did as she asked.

Usara glanced at Jilseth. 'You can come closer, if you wish.'

'Thank you.' She went quickly to the far side of the table.

Unregarded by the door, Hosh realised that the magewoman's expression reminded him of something. When he realised what it was, an involuntary shudder twisted his shoulders.

Those unsuspected mageborn whom Anskal had discovered among the corsairs and their slaves had watched him work his wizardry with that same avid interest. Hosh recalled how magic's fascination had tangled those captives so thoroughly in the Mandarkin's snares until there had been no escape but death.

These mages and the lady adept could doubtless defend themselves but was the captain about to risk some fatal magic? Master Micaran had already died today.

Corrain looked at Hosh as though feeling his gaze. 'Come and see. I want you to recognise this man if you see him anywhere.'

Hosh walked forward reluctantly.

'How can you scry if you don't know this man?' Jilseth asked Usara, perplexed.

'Guinalle will find Corrain's memory and pass it straight to me.' The Suthyfer mage took his wife's free hand and laid his other on the battered cooking pot.

Hosh saw that it was now full of glowing green water. An image floated on the surface an instant later.

He saw a man of middling height, neither particularly handsome or ill-favoured with neatly cropped brown hair. He wore riding boots, buff breeches and a long sleeved jerkin of dun broadcloth, a brown cloak slung over one arm. There was nothing else to see. The man might as well be standing in front of a green velvet curtain.

Guinalle sat with her eyes closed, clasping Corrain and Usara's hands. The Suthyfer mage stared into the green glow of his magecraft. A deep frown of concentration drew Jilseth's brows together.

'Where is he?'

As Hosh wondered aloud, the mossy haze thinned. Now they could see the man standing with a handful of others in an unfurnished room with windowless walls of plain, dressed stone.

All the rest wore plain grey robes. Their hoods were thrown back to reveal three men with shaven heads and two women whose blonde hair was cropped so close that they might just as well have taken a razor to their scalps.

The distant strangers turned, along with the man from Wrede, and looked through the circle of the cooking pot's rim.

'How very enterprising.'

Hosh heard a man's voice inside his head, just as he did when Mentor Garewin encouraged him to revisit his childhood memories of home.

Usara snatched his hand back as though the metal had burned him. 'Saedrin's stones!'

The vision blinked into nothingness. Not even the green magelight remained in the water.

Guinalle opened her eyes. 'Your friend from Wrede is *sheltya*.'

'From the Mountain Men?' Hosh remembered what Kusint had told him of those mysterious adepts.

'What is their interest in this?' Usara blew on his sore fingertips.

'I suggest you ask Aritane,' Jilseth said swiftly, 'while I tell Planir.'

Usara looked at Guinalle. 'Do you suppose she will tell us what she might suspect?'

The Tormalin lady adept hesitated. 'We can ask but

I don't suppose she will say very much.' She looked at Jilseth. 'You must understand. Aritane has shared healing and other lore which the *sheltya* teach Solura's adepts and the Forest's wise folk and she has offered her insights into my own Artifice but she has never told us anything of the *sheltya*'s inner counsels or secrets.'

'So what do we do now?' Corrain demanded.

'You two see if you can hobble the Archipelagans,' Usara said decisively. 'Guinalle and I will see what we can learn from our friend while you let Planir know everything that's happened today.' He looked at Jilseth. 'Then we will meet at the Prefecture. Mentor Garewin told us what you agreed with him and his colleagues.'

'Very well.' Jilseth nodded and vanished.

Hosh looked at the bed. He was relieved beyond measure to see that the dead Soluran had disappeared along with the magewoman.

Usara looked at Corrain. 'Do you want us to take you to the Spice Wharf?'

The captain shook his head. 'We'll find our own way there.'

As the Suthyfer mage and his lady adept disappeared, Hosh unbuckled Corrain's sword and offered it back.

'We do still have to get out of here unseen,' he pointed out. 'A little magic might prove useful there.'

He was secretly satisfied to see a moment of chagrin on Corrain's face. He was even more pleased when the two of them managed to leave the rooming house without encountering the slatternly housekeeper.

— CHAPTER TWENTY-SEVEN —

As JILSETH'S STUDY appeared around her, she reflected that working necromancy with splintered bones or a withered scrap of flesh was a good deal more convenient than being burdened with an entire Soluran corpse.

It was also far less offensive. She looked at the limp body on the floor. The charnel stink was repellently strong. How much worse would the smell become if she left this carrion here with doors and windows closed? Even allowing for the chill weather Jilseth would wager good gold that the spreading reek would attract notice sooner rather than later. The hall's servants would investigate such a stench as readily as the city's rats, hungry in the depths of winter.

She stooped to lay a hand on the Soluran's cold forehead. Resolute, she thrust all emotion away; her fear of this man and his allies, wizardly and adept alike. Otherwise her magic risked going awry and Jilseth didn't wish to contemplate any unpredictable consequences with a dead man sprawled on her carpet.

Achieving such composure had been a great deal easier back in Col. She had been so focused on testing her newfound strengths through this unforeseen opportunity for necromancy. She had been so exultant at the far greater depth and breadth of her insights into the dead man's life.

But what had her magic achieved? They had seen who conspired against Hadrumal but beyond the Detich magewoman and the Soluran, they didn't know who those guilty men and women were. They couldn't lay an accusation before the Elected in Col, to comfort Micaran's grieving family. Would the city's lawmakers even trust a wizard's word with the dead Soluran's lingering enchantments still poisoning their thoughts?

Would the Archmage deliver justice on Micaran's behalf, when she told Planir what she had learned? What of the other questions that nagged at her? Did she have the right to demand answers of the Archmage?

First things first. Jilseth drew a deep breath and focused her mage senses on the body. She reached through her innate affinity to her command of all the elements and sought cold. Not the slow cooling of mortal flesh, not merely winter's seasonal chill but the enduring, unchanging frost of the remote and frigid north.

Jilseth drove every last lingering glimmer of elemental fire from the man's flesh, blood and bones. She warded his substance against the equilibrium of elemental earth which sought to bring every unliving thing to the same level temperature. She wove air and water deftly together to leave the corpse frozen as solid as the stone floor beneath it.

Finally she wove a shroud of quadrate magic to baffle any Soluran scrying. Doubtless they knew that their man was dead but let them wonder where his remains had disappeared to. Of course, Artifice might have some means of finding the dead but Jilseth could do nothing about that. She decided to bespeak Usara and ask if Guinalle could conceal the corpse from questing aetheric magic, once she had spoken to the Archmage.

If Planir wanted her to work any further necromancy, Jilseth knew that this wizardly cold would prove no hindrance. She'd worked such spells on pathetic remnants from the depths of Relshaz's harbour and heads recovered from an executioner's spikes in Parnilesse.

She still shuddered at the thought of the corpse on her floor as she locked the door behind her and hurried across the quadrangle. If Planir committed the Soluran to a funeral pyre, Jilseth would gladly fling her rug into the same flames.

She walked quickly to Trydek's Hall. The door to the tower was closed, which was unusual. However as Jilseth raised her hand to knock, the ancient oak swung open. She climbed quickly up the stairs. The door to Planir's sitting room opened with similar swiftness.

The Archmage was reading by his fireside. At first glance it looked as if he hadn't moved since she'd last been here. Then Jilseth noted that the stacks of books and papers from Relshaz were markedly reduced.

She also feared that the Archmage looked correspondingly weary. Was there no one who could help him with this research? Or was he refusing to allow anyone to help, for fear of some discovery being used against him in a Council meeting?

A tisane glass stood within the fender, half full of black dregs. How long could that sustain him before he was forced to take some proper rest? What would happen then, Jilseth wondered with growing misgiving. What mischief could the Flood Mistress and the Hearth Master contrive while their Archmage was sleeping, oblivious, high in his tower?

Planir smiled and set his book aside. 'Usara has told me what happened in Col.'

'Good.' Jilseth spared a moment to admire the mild faced mage's swift presence of mind. Most wizards would have allowed themselves a little respite after carrying two people as far as Suthyfer and back again, never mind working another demanding spell like that scrying.

'I hadn't expected to find the *sheltya* so interested in lowland affairs,' Planir remarked. 'I will be very interested to learn what Aritane thinks might have prompted them to send an enquiry agent south from Wrede.'

'The *sheltya* are no great friends to wizardry.' Jilseth recalled that those Mountain brothers she'd encountered in Lescar had been exiled on account of Sorgrad's magebirth, long before embarking on their notorious careers as scoundrels and thieves.

Planir considered this. 'I would say rather that they're no great friends to any arrogant or unrestrained magic, aetheric or elemental. That's why they drove the Elietimm into the eastern ocean, refusing to let them rule the Gidestan mountains through Artifice. They hold the mountain passes against Mandarkin attacks whether the skirmishers' efforts are bolstered by the tyrants' wizards or by adepts.'

'But they don't generally involve themselves with affairs beyond their own mountains.' Jilseth knew that exiles such as Sorgrad and his brother, and Aritane, had the *sheltya*'s self-imposed boundary to thank for their lives and liberties.

'That we know of,' Planir pointed out. 'Who's to say what this man from Wrede has done before now with none of us the wiser?'

He waved that away. 'For the present I've seen no evidence he's done anything more than gather information, beyond levelling the scales for Corrain when the Soluran would have killed him. Let's see what Aritane thinks the *sheltya* will make of that intervention.'

Jilseth was more concerned with adepts and wizards closer to hand. 'What should we do about this Soluran conspiracy between these Orders and the Houses?'

Planir looked thoughtful. 'We may well be best advised to do nothing.'

'But he wasn't working alone, Archmage. Shouldn't we track down his allies in Col? I caught glimpses of his drinking companions' faces as I searched back through the echoes of his life. If I work some further necromancy to uncover his more recent endeavours, I can show Lady Guinalle by means of her Artifice—'

'To what purpose?' Planir queried. 'To publicly accuse university mentors of malice towards Hadrumal, when they are merely this Soluran's dupes? That will hardly put a shine on wizardry's already tarnished reputation in Col. Besides, even with Lady Guinalle's aid, it would simply be our word against theirs.'

He raised a hand before Jilseth could object. 'Lady Guinalle has already set her own enchantments searching out the Soluran's malevolence. I'll make sure she knows of your offer as she devises some Artifice to draw the sting of his venom. It may help her to see the faces of those he's subjected to aetheric influence.'

'How long will that take, Archmage?' Jilseth quickly related what Corrain had learned before Micaran had died. 'We can expect to see Archipelagan ships in Hadrumal's waters in under twenty-five days.'

'What do the Solurans hope to see then?' Planir mused. 'Our island's warding magics driving these ships onto the rocks or out into the western ocean for their hapless crews to die of hunger and thirst? Or do they imagine that Hadrumal's mages will start slaughtering the Aldabreshi? Do they hope to turn still more of the Archipelago's warlords against us, whenever word reaches them of Jagai dead washing up on Caladhria's beaches? Perhaps they will try warping the western sea's currents to wash the broken remnants of their triremes and galleys all the way back to the islands.'

The Archmage pressed his palms together, fingertips to his bearded lips, lost in contemplation for a long moment.

'Wizardry has precious few friends among the realms and rulers from Ensaimin to Tormalin at present. We'll have fewer still once bodies begin drifting ashore. The noble lords and guild masters will hardly thank us for wrecking whatever faint hope they cherish of restoring trade with the Archipelago.'

He shook his head slowly. 'Do you suppose that they imagine fear of these consequences will have us trembling so cravenly in our shoes that we will hand over these artefacts which they covet, simply to put an end to their scheming against us?'

'Are you still determined that the Soluran Orders shan't have those artefacts?' Jilseth decided that she might as well ask the questions which were plaguing her. 'Is that because you don't want them discovering how to use Artifice through such instilled elemental spells, as Usara and Guinalle have done in Suthyfer?'

Planir lowered his hands and leaned back, smiling. 'I will certainly make that argument, most forcefully, if the Council does contemplate giving in to Soluran menaces.'

'Meantime, Suthyfer will still have that coffer of Khusro artefacts which I don't suppose you've seen fit to mention to the Council,' Jilseth observed.

Planir spread innocent hands. 'There has been no Council meeting where I could have told our fellow eminent mages of these fresh discoveries. Besides, were anyone to call us together, I am sure they would wish to discuss far more urgent matters. I hear that Flood Mistress Troanna is currently seeking allies for the day when she finally proposes a vote demanding that I surrender the Archmage's ring. I've yet to learn if she also intends seeing me stripped of the rank of Stone Master.'

He didn't sound overly concerned. Jilseth could only hope he had good reason for such confidence.

'Are any Council members giving the Flood Mistress a hearing?'

'They're mostly too busy to listen.' Planir smiled wryly. 'Those who haven't already worked themselves to a standstill are still intent on cracking the mysteries of the artefacts they already hold. Even those who talked of abandoning the challenge for the sake of their other duties keep finding reasons to hope that a few more days will bring success.

'I don't propose to bother about Troanna until she approaches Kalion, since she must know that she cannot succeed without the Hearth Master's support.' He shrugged. 'Sannin is now working in a nexus with Ely, Galen and Canfor so I'm hopeful she'll be one of the first to hear when that happens. Then I will consider how best to respond.'

Jilseth didn't find that as reassuring as she would like. 'Are your supporters countering Troanna? Velindre and Mellitha must surely command a hearing in any hall?'

Planir's face hardened. 'Velindre and Mellitha are helping the mercenary shipmasters of the Carifate who have made common cause with the mariners of

Maubere Inlet who used to serve the Dukes of Parnilesse. Magecraft will shape their rough harbour into a safe haven where Archipelagan traders can offer their goods to Tormalin merchants and both sides will profit from not having to deal with intermediaries.

'In the fullness of time, I'm confident that ports such as Attar and Claithe will welcome wizardly help to improve their anchorages and approaches to accommodate Aldabreshin galleys. With this recent peace in Lescar looking ever more likely to hold, there's also every chance that more new ports will flourish at the mouths of the Dyal and Annock rivers.'

So the Relshazri were going to rue the day when they decided to turn on wizardry for the sake of their ties to the Archipelagans. Though Jilseth wondered how many of the Council would consider seeing that city beggared was sufficient retribution for Kerrit's death. More urgently, what good was such long-term scheming when this far more immediate threat hung over the wizard isle?

'When will you warn the Council that Hadrumal is likely to be attacked? At the moment, barely a double handful of us know that Jagai Kalu intends to send shiploads of mercenaries against us, still less that these Soluran Orders who covet Anskal's loot are behind such scheming. Surely there are other wizards in Solura who owe favours to Hadrumal and its halls? The Flood Mistress and the Hearth Master have acquaintances among eminent Elders who could command King Solquen's attention. Couldn't they help us put a stop to this?'

'Perhaps, but doubtless their price would be either the ensorcelled artefacts or the secrets of quintessential magic. I am in no mood to surrender any such thing through gratitude, any more than I will yield them to threats. But

I will tell the Council and all Hadrumal,' Planir assured her with a glint in his eye, 'when I am quite certain that such an attack will actually happen. Usara tells me that Baron Halferan intends to undermine the Solurans' plans by turning these mercenaries against the Aldabreshi.'

Jilseth looked askance at him. 'Do you really believe that Corrain can somehow disrupt an entire Archipelagan domain's plans for an assault?'

The Archmage shrugged. 'Surely we have learned not to underestimate the good captain? He has a remarkable capacity to do something so wholly unexpected that it forces those around him into actions they would never have contemplated. A year ago, would you have imagined that you would have helped wizardry to demolish an entire Aldabreshin island?'

Jilseth had no answer to that. Planir reached for the book which he had been reading and opened it.

'We also need to know if it is merely Jagai Kalu and his shipmasters and swordsmen who have been shown the way to our waters and convinced to attack us. If this malice has spread more widely through the Archipelago, we will find ourselves playing a very different game of white raven. Once we know how our enemies are arrayed against us, we will be able to see what stratagems lie open.'

'How do you propose to find that out?' Jilseth asked.

'By waiting to see.' Planir looked up from his page, mildly surprised.

Once again, Jilseth found herself with more urgent concerns. 'We agreed to meet this evening, the Col mentors, the Caladhrians and I, at the Prefecture, to share what we've discovered and to inform the city's authorities of the Soluran's connivance. What shall I tell them?'

'Whatever you think they need to know. I trust your judgement.' Planir shifted to ease stiff shoulders. 'See what else you can learn from your dead Soluran in the meantime and share your discoveries with Mentor Garewin and his adepts in return for whatever they can tell us.'

The Archmage settled to his reading once again. 'Please close the doors on your way out.'

Jilseth stared at him for a long moment before rising to depart. Planir surprised her by looking up with a smile.

'I look forward to learning if Corrain has indeed contrived some useful mayhem among the mercenaries and the Archipelagans.'

— CHAPTER TWENTY-EIGHT —

Red Library Square, Col
33rd of Aft-Winter

CORRAIN DRUMMED THOUGHTFUL fingers on the rail around the gig's seat. Would he fare better challenging the mercenaries who had already taken Archipelagan gold with the truth or should he warn off those still waiting to test their mettle against the Aldabreshi swordsmen?

He decided to confront those who'd already taken the *zamorin*'s coin, catching them before they left the Spice Wharf to enjoy their windfall. Dissuading some hopeful who didn't pass muster would be wasted effort. Convincing swordsmen who'd just been hired would most likely repay him and Hosh twice or thrice. Each mercenary would surely tell his trusted friends how he had been duped. No warrior worth the name would let his allies stick their heads into a hangman's noose.

However greedy or desperate these mercenaries might be, surely they would have lingering doubts about taking Archipelagan coin to voyage into the unknown? Even if they didn't believe Corrain today, they'd have a double handful of days to kick their heels in idleness and reflect on his warnings. Surely a good number would think better of turning up when the Jagai galleys arrived? Especially now that the Soluran adept was dead. As long as the Col mentors could scupper his malicious enchantments.

The gig halted, taking Corrain completely by surprise. He leaned forward to poke the driver in the back only to see Hosh had a silver penny ready in his hand.

'I told him to stop here.'

'Why?'

But Hosh was already climbing down from the gig, forcing Corrain to follow. The lad waited for the grey mare to pull the gig and its driver out of earshot.

'If we're going to persuade these swordsmen that aetheric magic has deceived them, we need more than just our word. We need a mentor to prove that Artifice is real.'

'That's a good point.' Corrain's thoughts had already gone a step beyond Hosh.

If they couldn't convince the mercenaries that this attack on the wizard isle was folly with reasoned argument, perhaps Artifice could do their work for them. Corrain was fully prepared to use the Solurans' own weapons against them.

He looked up the steps. 'How do you suggest we get in without a scholar or a wizard to vouch for us?'

The black-liveried guard by the library's door wasn't the man who'd escorted them out. Would he carry a note to Mentor Garewin? Perhaps but that meant finding paper and pen in one of these taverns. Corrain didn't begrudge spending the Archmage's money but he didn't want to waste the time.

'This way.' Hosh headed around to the side of the building. 'That's the study window.' He threw a coin at it, only for them both to see it fall short and roll away unseen to delight some beggar or street-sweeper.

'Watch your head.' Corrain reached for his purse, letting coins trickle through his fingers until he felt a copper penny's smooth edges. Only Col's silver coins were milled to foil clippers. Now all he had to worry about was breaking the glass instead of merely getting the mentors' attention.

His aim was true. Unfortunately there was no response.

'They might not even still be in there,' he warned Hosh.

His second copper struck the window so hard that he did fear he'd cracked the pane. No matter, the casement was opening and a cautious head peered out.

'Mentor Lusken!' Hosh shouted and waved a hand. 'We need your help.'

'Wait there,' the scholar called.

'Well done.' Corrain led Hosh back to the front steps, trying to curb his growing impatience as they waited for Lusken to appear.

The mentor hitched up his long scholarly gown as he hurried down the steps from the doorway. 'We thought we were to meet at the Prefecture this evening,' he said apprehensively. 'What's happened?'

'Nothing untoward,' Hosh assured him.

'No more untoward than the two dead men we already have on our hands,' Corrain said bluntly. 'The lady wizard has used her magic to learn this is part of a plot contrived by the Archmage's enemies beyond Col. She's gone back to Hadrumal to tell Planir. Lady Guinalle helped devise an enchanted scrying to show us this man from Wrede with his allies. You mentors can put your skills to better use now.'

Lusken's face cleared. 'That is good to know. We were having no success finding him even after following Lady Guinalle's advice. That's to say, we could pick up the echoes of Micaran's questing enchantments but—'

'Perhaps you should tell Mentor Garewin?' Corrain interrupted as politely as he could. 'And please tell him that while we wait to learn what the Archmage advises, we want to dissuade at least some of these mercenaries who are taking Aldabreshin coin. Will you help us with your Artifice?'

'I will not use my skills to warp anyone's thoughts.' The young scholar looked deeply insulted.

'That's not what we ask,' Hosh said quickly before Corrain could speak. 'We simply ask if you can show these men the reality of Artifice, so that they can ask themselves if these new thoughts are really their own.'

'I will ask Mentor Garewin.' Still scowling, Lusken hitched up his robe again, ready to run back up the library's steps without tripping on the hem.

Hosh laid a hand on his arm. 'Ask if he wishes Col to be seen as Hadrumal's foe.'

Lusken stared at him, indignant. 'Planir knows that Col is no enemy to wizardry.'

'What the Archmage knows and what folk across Ensaimin think will be very different,' Hosh countered, 'once word spreads that these mercenaries boarded Jagai ships here before attacking the wizard isle. As long as that Soluran adept's spite is still tainting talk in the taprooms and stables, travellers will believe that this city scorns wizardry and carry that lie home with them.'

'Our Artifice will soon nail that falsehood to the floor,' Lusken insisted.

All the same, now he was dubiously biting his lip as he hurried back to the door.

Corrain handed a silver penny to Hosh. 'Go and find us a gig.'

He found he couldn't stand still to wait. Pacing back and forth, he ignored the watchful librarian. How long would the other mentors delay Lusken with questions and arguments? What would they do if Master Garewin forbade him to come with them? Try to beat some sense into these mercenaries? How long would that take?

How long before the Elected's watchmen turned up to throw everyone into their lock-up? That might stop a few mercenaries from taking the *zamorin*'s coin but Corrain couldn't afford to spend a night in a cell.

He paused to look up at the clouded sky. Both moons would be at their quarter tonight if they were ever able to show themselves. Beyond that he had no notion what their place in the heavens might signify to the Archipelagans.

He must ask Hosh. He watched the lad hurry across the square to offer an immediate new hire to a driver letting a passenger descend from his gig. Corrain approved. More than that, he reminded himself that Hosh had survived, alone with no hope of rescue amid the corsairs and later when Anskal had enslaved him.

Not that Corrain knew much of Hosh's sufferings. They'd spent little time together since the corsair isle's destruction with Corrain so busy about a baron's duties and Hosh finding tasks around the manor that kept him out of view. Even if they had found themselves alone, Corrain would have been as reluctant to ask the lad about his trials, as he was to answer such intrusive curiosity about his own tribulations.

For the moment, it was enough to remind himself that just because Hosh was quiet, that didn't mean he was dull-witted. This detour to ally themselves with a mentor proved that.

Lamplight caught his eye and he saw the library door open to allow Lusken to leave. Corrain whistled for Hosh. The young mentor began talking before he was within ten paces.

'Now that they can stop hunting the man from Wrede, Mentor Garewin and the others will work an enchantment to counter the Soluran's lies.'

'To renew trust in wizardry?' Corrain was relieved. That proved short-lived.

Lusken shook his head. 'To remove the doubts which Soluran Artifice makes so unnaturally compelling. Then the populace will be free to make up their own minds.'

That was better than nothing, Corrain supposed, as long as this enchantment could move as swiftly as the Soluran's malice. Otherwise it would prove as useful as a man on foot chasing a horse thief.

'You will come with us to the Spice Wharf,' he persisted, 'to help stop the Archipelagans recruiting mercenaries?'

Lusken nodded. 'I will see what Artifice is at work and what may be done to counter it.'

Hooves clattered on the paviours as Hosh arrived in the gig. Corrain urged Lusken up and climbed after him. The driver whipped up his horse, already told where to go.

'Word of Mentor Micaran's death is spreading through the university,' Lusken said sombrely as the vehicle left the square. 'Our adepts are most disturbed to think that aetheric magic can be used with such deadly intent. Soluran Artificers will find scant welcome in our libraries now.'

'Good.' Though Corrain would wager good gold that at least one or two Col scholars would be secretly wondering how they might learn those particular enchantments for their own use. Regardless, scholars giving the cold shoulder to Solurans visiting the city for the rest of the year would do nothing to stop the Archipelagans intent on putting Hadrumal to the sword in twenty days or so.

Hosh had different concerns. 'Not all Soluran adepts are to blame. We saw only three of them meeting the wizards opposed to Hadrumal.'

'Which Houses of Sanctuary are they sworn to?' Lusken demanded.

Hosh could only shake his head. 'I don't know.'

'How can we find out?' Lusken scowled.

'Perhaps Madam Jilseth can offer you some clues when we meet at the Prefecture,' Hosh suggested, 'or Lady Guinalle might know some enchantment?'

'Perhaps.' Lusken lapsed into brooding thought.

Corrain was more than content to ride the rest of the way to the docks in silence. He rested one hand on his sword's scabbard to stop the hilt digging into Mentor Lusken's ribs. Mentally, he rehearsed every thrust, every parry, every guarding stroke which old Fitrel had ever taught him.

If even a handful of the mercenaries could be dissuaded from this fools' quest, Corrain could hope that word would spread through the rest like a rumour of pox in a popular whorehouse. How long before the *zamorin* or his lackeys saw those who'd been waiting to try their luck drifting away? Would they realise who was responsible? Perhaps Corrain would get a chance to test his sword skills against one of these fabled Aldabreshin warriors.

That prospect didn't thrill him nearly as much as it would have done once. Life as a baron required little by way of sword play. Mostly it demanded talking and reading and writing letters. True, Corrain kept promising himself he would find time to drill Reven with blunted blades, to improve the young sergeant's skills. He still intended to hone his own expertise against whatever tricks and ripostes Kusint had learned in the mercenary company which he'd joined looking for riches in Lescar's civil wars. It wasn't the Forest youth's fault that a swift defeat in battle had seen them captured and sold to Relshazri slavers who'd sold them on to the corsairs.

If plans were pans there'd be no need of coppersmiths. That was one of old Fitrel's favourite sayings. Corrain realised, with painful clarity, that he hadn't wielded a sword in practice, much less in anger, since he'd led the attack on the corsairs' island. Even then, he hadn't bloodied his blade. Hosh had killed the blind corsair leader and the black-bearded brute who had murdered the true Lord Halferan. He would do well to remember that as well.

'Spice Wharf.' The driver reined in his horse.

'There's the Jagai great galley.' Hosh choked on his words as he pointed to a wide-bellied vessel with capacious holds below its rowing deck and generous accommodation in the cabins above. Ropes as thick as a man's wrist secured it to dockside bollards, stern on so that ladders on either side of the tiller rested on the stone quay.

Two triremes were anchored further out in the harbour; lean and watchful with their vicious rams cleaving the slowly drifting water. Aldabreshin archers patrolled the narrow decks raised above the tiered rowers' seats.

Corrain's own hands clenched around the memory of an oar shaft first slick with sweat and then with fluid from burst blisters and finally with blood as overseers' whips allowed his raw palms no respite.

'Where are they going?' Lusken wondered.

Corrain blinked and saw that the half-circle of armed and armoured men gathered around the galley was breaking up. Some turned away disgruntled, some resigned, a few with contented grins or clapping each other on the shoulder in congratulation.

'Pay me your penny, if you please, Masters,' the gig driver prompted. 'This is where you told me to come. It'll be another fare if you want to go further.'

'Thank you.' Corrain gathered his wits and found the driver's coin.

He jumped down. Lusken and Hosh quickly followed.

'Is this Mentor Garewin's doing?' Hosh asked the Col adept hopefully.

Corrain didn't wait to hear the answer. He hurried forward to accost one of the departing mercenaries. 'I heard these Archipelagans were hiring? They can't have filled their roster?'

'Come back tomorrow morning,' the man advised. 'They say there's not enough daylight left to test a man's skills and they won't risk an accident sparring by torchlight or lanterns.' He jerked his head towards the fat *zamorin* conferring on the quayside with a trio of dark-skinned swordsmen in Archipelagan armour. 'Our man in the silks insists that they cannot risk blood being shed.'

'Why?' Corrain demanded.

'Who knows?' The mercenary shrugged. 'I won't argue and risk going home needing an apothecary to stitch a wound.'

Hosh stepped forward. 'Has the man in the silks told you where the Jagai galleys will take the men he hires?'

'Not as yet.' The man was unconcerned.

With some effort, Corrain held his tongue, waiting to see where Hosh intended to lead this conversation.

'You know he hasn't even told the swordsmen who've taken his gold,' the lad persisted.

The mercenary shrugged again. 'They swear that we'll be told once the galleys are underway.'

'When it's too late for you to jump ship.' Corrain couldn't help himself.

'I know where they're going.' Hosh looked the man in the eye. 'They plan on attacking Hadrumal. They'll send you fools ashore to try killing the wizards. How many do you think will even get off the dock before you're turned to stone or blowing away as ash on the wind?'

The mercenary stared at Hosh before bursting into a guffaw. 'I don't know who sold you that story, but he saw you for a fool.'

'I swear—'

'Enough, Hosh.' Corrain gripped his elbow and drew him aside to let the laughing man pass.

'Captain—' Hosh protested.

'A moment of your time, friend.' Corrain held up a silver penny as he stepped into another mercenary's path.

'Just one.' The man took the coin with a wary glance at Lusken waiting a few paces behind them.

Corrain could see the man judging where the real threat lay. Put the Caladhrian with the sword on the ground and the man was confident that Hosh and Lusken would lose their nerve.

'Friend!' He challenged the mercenary to reclaim his attention. 'Do you know that these Aldabreshi are hiring swords to send against Hadrumal? The Jagai warlord wants to take on the Archmage.'

'Does he now?' Disbelief rang through the mercenary's words.

'My oath on it,' Corrain insisted, 'or Saedrin throw me to Poldrion's demons.'

'And you're so keen to save my skin,' the man sneered, 'when you don't know me from a beggar in the gutter?'

'I wouldn't leave a beggar in the gutter to have his

throat cut if I could raise a shout to stop it.' Corrain spread empty, placating hands.

The mercenary stepped forward to shove Corrain's shoulder, belligerent. 'Liar. You just want to thin tomorrow morning's line; to get yourself tested all the sooner.'

Sorely though it galled him, Corrain retreated with his hands still raised. 'I'm only telling you what I heard.'

'Liar.' The mercenary spat contemptuously on the brick paving before going on his way.

Hosh looked askance at Corrain. 'It must sound like a tavern tale.'

'I suppose so.' Whatever else he had expected, Corrain hadn't anticipated outright disbelief.

'It's more than that,' Lusken said soberly. 'There's Artifice at work, setting these men against anyone who might try to turn them against the Archipelagans.'

'The Soluran?' Corrain shook his head. 'How long can a dead man's Artifice plague us?'

'How soon can Mentor Garewin put paid to his enchantments' echoes?' Hosh demanded.

To Corrain's dismay Lusken shook his head. 'The mistrust of wizardry that's spread through the city is the dead Soluran's work. Such readiness to trust the Archipelagans, this eagerness to fill their pockets with Aldabreshin gold and to dismiss anyone who would gainsay them is some different Artifice entirely.'

'So the bastard does have allies lurking somewhere,' Corrain growled.

'Unless they're already riding a fast horse north after learning that he's dead,' Lusken pointed out. 'Leaving such delusion to be passed from hand to hand through the stables and taprooms.'

'Can Mentor Garewin silence this enchantment too?' Corrain demanded.

Lusken nodded but Corrain's relief died an early death as the adept spoke.

'We can, once we have divined the precise nature of the aetheric magic underpinning it and composed our own counter-charm.'

'How long will that take?'

Lusken bit his lip. 'A handful of days.'

'When they're on board the Jagai galleys and away from Col, can this aetheric magic remain strong enough to persuade them that attacking Hadrumal isn't the shortest way to Saedrin's threshold?' Hosh shook his head in disbelief.

'Perhaps, perhaps not,' Lusken allowed, 'but who's to say there won't be another enchantment at work to wipe away all doubts?'

'Micaran said that this *zamorin* was already convinced that Hadrumal's wizards had exhausted themselves destroying the corsairs,' Corrain remembered. 'Can you and your fellow adepts keep watch for such an enchantment beguiling the mercenaries when the Jagai ships arrive?'

'We can try.' Lusken didn't sound overly confident.

'We must talk to the Archipelagans.' Hosh started walking towards the moored galley.

'The Archipelagans?' After an instant of astonishment, Corrain hurried after Hosh. He caught his arm and forced him to a halt. 'We cannot—'

'They're the ones sending the mercenaries to Hadrumal. They're the ones intent on attacking the Archmage. They're the ones we need to stop.' Hosh matched Corrain stare for stare. 'Cut off the snake's tail and it'll bite you twice to pay you back. Cut off its head and it's dead before it can open its mouth. We learned that on the corsair island.'

Corrain shivered at an abrupt recollection of the furtive, dull brown snakes whose bite left men thrashing in agony for a day and a night before they invariably died.

Hosh pressed home his point. 'I speak their tongue, Captain, and I can read their stars. I will find something in the heavens to convince them I'm telling the truth.'

And the lad wouldn't even be lying, Corrain realised, even if the Archipelagans had no Artifice to tell them so. The fool boy was as ready to give credence to the islanders' heavenly compass as he was to Kusint's runes or to the blind and voiceless statues back in the Halferan Manor shrine.

'They say they don't want any bloodshed,' Hosh shook off Corrain's hand. 'I'll stay out of reach of their swords regardless.'

He continued walking and Lusken followed. Corrain could only fall into step behind the pair of them.

Hosh shouted out something in the Archipelagan tongue. The *zamorin* had been about to ascend the galley's stern ladder. Startled, he stopped and turned back, saying something to Hosh.

Corrain had no notion what he meant but the *zamorin*'s combative tone was clear enough. So was the Archipelagan swordsmen's challenge as they moved to stand between their silk-clad master and this unknown Caladhrian.

Hosh's tone turned pleading as he undertook a lengthy explanation. Corrain watched the three swordsmen warily. He didn't move his hand anywhere near his own hilt for fear of provoking them but he mentally measured the paces it would take for him to meet them before they could cut Hosh down.

Meet them, parry and surrender. That's what he would have to do, however distasteful he found it. Not for fear of Caladhria's Baron Halferan being disgraced by a dockside brawl. For fear of failing in his duty to his dead lord by leaving Ilysh a widow. If he fell, Zurenne and her children would be prey to those who would already have laid claim to them without the shield of his sham marriage.

The *zamorin* was talking to Hosh, fast and fluent. Hosh raised his hands and said something humbly apologetic. The *zamorin* scowled before continuing in the Tormalin tongue.

'I asked how you know so much of Jagai Kalu's purpose?' His glance included Lusken and Corrain in his question.

'As I have said,' Hosh bowed humbly, 'through this magic of the mind. Through Artifice's enchantments.'

'There are no such enchantments,' the *zamorin* said unequivocally. 'Wizardry is the evil we must counter and that is what we will do.'

'Let us show you that Artifice is real.' Corrain looked warily at the Aldabreshi swordsmen before returning his attention to the *zamorin*. 'Let us prove the truth of what we're saying.'

'No!'

Hosh and Lusken spoke in the same breath.

'What?' Corrain saw that the *zamorin* was almost as startled as he was by their denials.

'Excuse us.' Hosh bowed low before turning to hurry back to Corrain.

'I have already told you.' Lusken's amiable face was

annoyed. 'I will not work Artifice on anyone without their consent.'

'I'm only asking you to prove to him that aetheric magic exists,' Corrain protested before turning on Hosh. 'That was why you wanted a mentor with us in the first place.'

'To convince the mainland mercenaries who've already heard of aetheric magic,' Hosh retorted.

'How do you propose I do such a thing,' Lusken interrupted, 'without working some enchantment to make him see or hear something that his companions do not? Besides, who's to say that whoever has already subjected him to aetheric influence hasn't also warded him against anyone attempting to do such a thing? That's what I would do, if I were so lost to honour to corrupt someone's mind.'

Corrain glared at the young adept. 'Then why did you come with us, if you're not willing to use your magic?'

'To learn more of this unsanctioned Artifice at work in our city,' Lusken replied, undaunted. 'I can tell you that there's been a third adept at work. Convincing the Aldabreshi that they know how to find Hadrumal stems from a different enchantment to the two charms turning the common folk against wizardry and convincing these mercenaries to trust the Archipelagans.'

So those who used aetheric magic weren't so different from those who used elemental wizardry, Corrain concluded. They were concerned, first and foremost, with their own interests and if they didn't tell outright lies, they would readily hide the whole truth.

'Using an enchantment to convince this *zamorin* that aetheric magic exists would be utter folly.' Hosh stumbled over his words in his haste. 'If Lusken did such a thing, the man would simply believe that he's been contaminated by magic and he wouldn't thank us for that. Either he'll order those swordsmen to cut our throats in hopes that will cleanse him or he'll kneel so one of them can take his head off.'

'Would that shed enough blood to curse this whole endeavour with an ill omen?' Though even he saw the shock in Hosh and Lusken's eyes, Corrain knew that they couldn't risk it. He couldn't risk his own neck for Halferan's sake and he had never been a captain to order other men to do what he wouldn't.

He managed to curb an urge to shake the young adept by his shoulders. 'Is there truly no way to use aetheric magic to do something, anything, which doesn't involve touching his mind? Can't you make something fly through the air?'

'Then they'll just think he's a wizard,' Hosh pointed out.

'And hack my head from my shoulders,' Lusken said forcefully.

'Then this whole excursion has been a waste of time.' Corrain wished he could deny what the two younger men were telling him but he couldn't. All he could do was refrain from lashing them with his fury.

'Not wholly,' Lusken insisted. 'I have a far clearer understanding of the Artifice woven by our enemies. I can help Mentor Garewin and the other adepts weave enchantments to counter it.'

'Now we know that there's scant chance of foiling the Solurans by depriving the Archipelagans of their mercenaries.' Hosh shook his head, frustrated.

Corrain looked warily at the Aldabreshi still standing by the galley's stern ladders. The swordsmen were watchful as ever. The *zamorin* merely looked irritated.

He forced himself to bend his neck in something approaching a respectful bow to placate the barbarian. Looking upwards he saw the sky darkening rapidly to winter's early dusk. Were night's bells already nearly here? On the other hand, this day felt as though it had lasted half a lifetime.

'So we have something to tell the wizards and the mentors when we meet at the Prefecture. We had better find a gig to take us there.'

Corrain sighed heavily as he walked away, flanked by the other two. He strained his ears for any sound of the Aldabreshi swordsmen pursuing them.

Some small rebellious part of him wished that they would, so he could relieve his anger and frustration by cutting them down. The wiser part of him recounted all the reasons why even such a victory would be no victory at all, and why, moreover, any such victory was vanishingly unlikely.

As they left the docks, new fears crowded around him. If they couldn't foil the Solurans' malice or the Archipelagans' plans, it was up to Jilseth, the Archmage and all the other wizards of Hadrumal to drive off this Aldabreshi attack.

After what Corrain had seen wizardry do to the corsair island, that was a fearful prospect. What unspeakable havoc might these mages wreak in defence of their homes and families?

— CHAPTER TWENTY-NINE —

The Prefecture of Col
33rd of Aft-Winter

JILSETH WALKED TOWARDS the tall gates in the iron railings which barred access to the courtyard surrounded by the black brick building.

'Good evening.' A white-gloved black-liveried guardian approached.

'I am here to meet with Mentor Garewin, Mentor Undil—' Jilseth desperately searched her recollections for the other two adepts' names. Fretting over what little she had to tell this gathering seemed to have wiped such details from her memory. Worrying about what she must conceal was still more distracting.

'You're expected, Madam Mage.' The Prefect smiled and unlatched the gate. 'This way, if you please.'

Once she had entered and he had carefully secured the gate behind her, the Prefect led Jilseth to a door in the off-hand angle of the hollow square. It opened onto a stairway and he preceded her up to the second floor. A long corridor flanked with closed doors ran the length of this northern wing of the building, ending in a window shrouded with dusk.

The Prefect opened the closest door into a room overlooking the central courtyard. Plain chairs crowded around a bare table. The four mentors were already present along with the two Caladhrians and Usara and

Guinalle. Jilseth was startled to see the last but one chair occupied by Aritane, the Mountain woman from Suthyfer.

'We had no success turning the mercenaries against the Jagai *zamorin*,' Corrain growled without preamble. 'Artifice has convinced them that whatever the Archipelagans wish them to do, this voyage will be a certain route to riches.' The youngest mentor shook his head.

Lusken; that was his name, Jilseth was relieved to recall as she took the vacant seat opposite Aritane.

That relief was a pennyweight in the scales against her disappointment. So much for Planir's confidence in Corrain's ability to provoke unexpected disruption.

'Thus far we have divined three distinct and complex enchantments contrived against the wizards of Hadrumal,' Lusken continued, dividing his attention between Guinalle and his fellow scholars of Col. 'One is stirring contempt and mistrust of magecraft among the populace. That was the work of the Soluran adept whom Corrain of Halferan killed. Without him to sustain it, we can hope that this Artifice will soon fade.'

'All the sooner now that we have devised our own aetheric working to stifle it,' Mentor Garewin said with satisfaction. 'We have done just that this afternoon.'

'My thanks, Master Adept, on behalf of Hadrumal and the Archmage. Planir will be very pleased to know that.' Jilseth was glad to congratulate the scholar and the other two mentors but she still wanted to know what else they had to contend with.

'Then there is the enchantment luring the mercenaries to take the Archipelagans' coin. I truly believe that this will prove strong enough to convince these men that this proposed attack on Hadrumal stands at least some chance of success.'

As he ticked off the different workings of Artifice on his fingers, Lusken's eyes flickered nervously to Aritane who was looking at him, expressionless, not offering any comment even when he paused after some speculation, looking hopefully at the Mountain woman.

'Believing they have two chances out of three of living through a venture will be good enough odds for most hirelings to roll those runes,' Corrain growled.

'Especially since the survivors will share out the loot which the dead men can't claim,' Hosh added.

'Lastly there is this enchantment telling the Archipelagans where to sail to find Hadrumal.' Lusken looked apprehensively at Jilseth. 'That spell is also convincing them that the wizard isle lies open and undefended now that the Archmage has exhausted every mage's strength by unleashing such cataclysmic magic against the corsairs.'

She found her mouth was dry as she recalled Planir's final question; the one he said needed an answer before he could devise any plan to safeguard the wizard isle. 'Have you seen any indication that this Artifice has spread beyond the Jagai domain? Can we expect any other warlords to send their triremes and battle galleys?'

Lusken spread apologetic hands. 'I have no way of knowing, Madam Mage.'

'Would these Archipelagans who've visited Halferan have heard anything of such plans?' Corrain scowled at Jilseth as though he knew of Planir's hand in prompting the Khusro wives' visit. 'Can you ask Lady Zurenne by means of your magic?'

'I can,' she answered him coolly. More than that, she would ask Zurenne to ask the Archipelagan Kheda who was doubtless far better informed. Jilseth also decided to bespeak Velindre and Mellitha as soon as she got the chance. Even if they were so inconveniently pre-occupied in Parnilesse, she could hope they might still be able to make their own enquiries.

'I believe we can devise some Artifice to pursue this malice which will show us how far it has reached.' The eldest mentor looked hopefully at Guinalle. 'With your assistance, Madam Adept?'

She nodded.

Usara spoke for the first time. 'As yet we've seen no indications of preparations for warfare among the Khusro islands or in Miris or any domain south of that. The Archmage asked us to scry from Suthyfer in hopes of such concerns going unnoticed by these Soluran Orders who may well be spying on Hadrumal to see what magic is being worked there.'

He shook his head, his expression grim.

'That's scant comfort. The Jagai domain is readying a substantial fleet. They have bought up shiploads of slaves from Relshaz, just as they did when they sought to attack Anskal on the corsair island. They have also sent other *zamorin* to recruit mercenaries in Relshaz and from as far afield as the Carifate, according to our friends there. Hadrumal's mages and Kellarin's adepts have done what they can to hobble their plans but with limited success. They still expect to see a fleet of galleys depart at the turn of the season with a substantial mercenary force aboard.'

What was it the Caladhrians said, Jilseth mused; that every upright rune had one upside down on its reverse side. Just as she was relieved to think that Velindre and Mellitha were doing more in Parnilesse than remaking the Maubere inlet and its people for a profitable future, she learned that even those redoubtable magewomen were finding themselves outfaced.

'Jagai plans on attacking Hadrumal from north and south,' Corrain said suddenly. 'One fleet will come from Col, the other will come from the Archipelago. They may even divide their ships and launch an assault on the island's eastern and western flanks at the same time.'

He looked at Jilseth. 'Can you defend Hadrumal on all quarters?'

'I'm sure that the Archmage will make his plans accordingly.' Jilseth had no doubt of that. A far more worrying question was how would the Council of Mages react? Was there the slightest chance that the most self-absorbed and contentious mages could set aside their fixations and simply do as Planir asked without arguing for so long that only a mercenary sword cutting their throats would finally silence them?

What of Hadrumal's halls and those wizards who would at least be free of the Council's rivalries and preoccupation with those thrice-cursed artefacts? Were there enough journeyman mages to watch every league of the island's coastline? To sustain the magical misdirections that had defended their sanctuary since Trydek had first brought his followers there?

Despite the warmth in this small room, Jilseth felt cold. Had that ancient warding magecraft ever truly been tested or had awe of the Archmage and the rumour of the wizard isle's unknown wizardry simply been sufficient to deter the curious and adventurous?

'We must watch for further Artifice,' she said abruptly. 'There must be something more yet to come. I cannot believe that the Solurans would contrive this Archipelagan attack if they knew full well that these ships will simply become lost in Hadrumal's mists or be blown back out to sea.'

'Quite so,' Usara agreed soberly.

'However vigilant we may be for aetheric malice, and we will be,' Guinalle promised, 'the most certain way to be forewarned of their precise plan of elemental attack would be to search out these wizards whom we know wish Hadrumal ill and to look into their innermost thoughts.'

The Col adepts looked at her, affronted.

'That would be—' Mentor Garewin's face twisted with distaste '—an unconscionable abuse of our Artifice.'

Guinalle gazed levelly at him. 'I do not say that we should, merely that we could.'

'They've shown themselves more than willing to plant their lies in countless unwitting minds,' Corrain interjected. 'Why should we cripple ourselves with such scruples? Forewarned is forearmed.'

'If we lower ourselves to their level, we are no better than they are,' Mentor Parovil said sternly.

'If a man goes into a tavern brawl expecting festival fisticuffs, he'll be lowered soon enough by a boot in his stones,' Corrain retorted.

'That Soluran invaded Mentor Micaran's thoughts,' Lusken said abruptly. 'Surely there can be no greater abuse of Artifice than using it to kill?'

'Your point?' Mentor Undil asked coldly. 'Do you propose that we murder the Soluran adept's allies in retaliation?'

'Enough.' Mentor Garewin raised a hand before the young adept could answer. The bearded scholar was sorely troubled. 'I could not in good conscience sanction such unwarranted intrusion into anyone's mind purely at a venture. We could perhaps reconsider, if we were to learn anything as we keep watch over these Soluran adepts which convinces us that some outright elemental assault on Hadrumal is truly intended. Then, and only then, we could brush against these wizards' thoughts, to learn whatever might be most urgently preoccupying them. Only these wizards whom we know to be directly involved in this conspiracy.'

He raised his hand again to anticipate Mentor Parovil's protests. 'I know and I share your reservations, Master Scholar. I would not even contemplate such a thing if it weren't for Micaran's death. But Lusken is right. These people have abandoned all decency in their own use of Artifice.'

'If we are to be on our guard against these other Soluran adepts, we need to know who they are,' Madam Undil pointed out. 'At the moment, we only know the fading echo of their enchantments through the aether.'

Jilseth stiffened, realising Aritane was looking straight at her.

The Mountain woman spoke, her upland accents stark in this gathering. 'Madam Mage, Guinalle tells me that you used your necromancy to see this dead Soluran meeting with a handful of wizards and two other adepts. May we see them for ourselves through your memories of your spell?'

Her gesture took in the other adepts in the room who at least looked as startled as Jilseth felt. She baulked, regardless.

'Surely Lady Guinalle can share her own recollections.' Jilseth had no wish to repeat the experience of Micaran's Artifice deceiving her wizard senses in Planir's study. That had been bad enough and she had been safe in Hadrumal, only facing one adept.

Guinalle shook her head with sincere regret. 'I was

concentrating entirely on trying to work my own Artifice through your spell. That will blur and distort any attempt to share my memories.'

'I can tell you what I have learned—' Jilseth began.

'Forgive me,' Master Garewin apologised, 'but you cannot know which details might tell us something of particular significance. It would be far better if we could see this meeting for ourselves, albeit through your eyes.'

'Even if we were to ask you for every detail, that risks inadvertently overlooking something vital,' Undil added, 'something we won't recognise until we see it.'

'We must know which Houses of Sanctuary these adepts are sworn to,' Usara urged Jilseth.

Guinalle nodded. 'Then we can use our own Artifice to find out if these Soluran Orders are merely working with a few men and women who've turned traitor to their vows or if this corruption has polluted the entire House.'

'Or if it stems from their teachers,' Aritane said coldly. 'Fish rot from the head.'

Planir would want to know precisely these things. Jilseth had no doubt of that, however fervently she might wish to deny it.

'How—'

Aritane reached across the table and took firm hold of her hand.

Jilseth didn't find herself in that peaceful library she had dreamed of more than once since Micaran had first shown it to her. Instead she was in the very chamber where the Soluran wizards and adepts were meeting. It was as though she had stepped into the vision summoned by her own necromancy. But this was undoubtedly Artifice. As before, Jilseth could not feel the least hint of any element through her wizard senses.

Once again, she had to fight the compulsion to search, panic-stricken, for some reassuring reality. Instead she forced herself to concentrate on what she could see before her, as if her eyes and ears weren't deceiving her in this repellent manner.

She and the Mountain woman were not alone. Guinalle stood over by the window and the four Col mentors were huddled by the resolutely barred door.

The five wizards and the three Soluran adepts were seated around the table, though they were not talking as they had been in Jilseth's necromantic vision. Each one sat unmoving, though not with their faces and hands at rest as though someone had called their meeting to order before plotting further treachery. Each one was frozen in mid-gesture or with unguarded expressions on their faces, as if momentarily startled by some loud noise outside this room.

'This is truly remarkable.' Master Garewin looked around, astonished.

'This is *sheltya* Artifice,' Aritane said without emotion. 'Used to search a witness's recollections when some crime has been committed or grave accusations are made.'

Was she accused or suspected of some offence? Jilseth wanted an explanation if not an outright apology for the woman inflicting such precipitate enchantment on her. She had been about to ask how Aritane proposed to proceed. She hadn't agreed to anything. But when she attempted to speak, Jilseth found that she couldn't even open her mouth.

'Do the *sheltya* pay any particular heed to Soluran Artifice?' Mentor Undil asked hesitantly. 'Might they be able to tell us more of these particular Houses?'

'They keep watch over any adepts who encroach on

the uplands,' Aritane replied. 'If these are Houses in any of Solura's northern border provinces, the *sheltya* may well know of them and their concerns.'

'How can we see such every detail so clearly?' Mentor Lusken was peering at the amulets hung around each of the seated adept's necks. All three of them wore different patterns of interlinked and concentric circles.

'You will have to ask Madam Jilseth to explain the secrets of her necromancy.' Guinalle came to look as well. 'Do any of you recognise these particular devices?'

Jilseth tried to take a step forward so that she could commit them to her own memory. She couldn't move her foot.

'Do we know where this room is?' Mentor Parovil advanced cautiously to one of the four windows, as though his silent footsteps might somehow rouse the motionless wizards and adepts. 'Does Madam Jilseth?'

Why were they speaking as though she wasn't even there? Jilseth looked down. She could see her hands, her skirts, even the toes of her boots as clear as day.

'Surely this is a tower.' Madam Undil studied the curving masonry and the exposed rafters supporting the floorboards of the room above. 'But is it in one of these wizardly Orders' retreats or part of some Soluran noble's castle?'

Jilseth's fury choked her. She could tell them precisely where they were if this cursed Artifice wasn't gagging her. Not that she had her affinity to thank for that knowledge, severed as she was from elemental sensation. She had spent the afternoon wringing all the information she could from the Soluran adept's corpse before consigning it to the deepest and coldest cellar beneath the Terrene Hall to await Planir's decision on its fate.

She had seen the Soluran adept arrive along the road skirting the edge of farmland as Megrilar province's northern forests thinned towards the border with Astrad to the east. This tower was at the heart of the Order of Detich's compound; a daunting fortification in its own right.

'If this conspiracy extends to any of Solura's nobles, matters become considerably more grave.' Mentor Garewin's expression was as dour as his words.

'This is the Detich wizards' tower.' Aritane looked directly at Jilseth. 'The necromancy worked since this spell has not shown the Soluran adept meeting with any nobleman or woman, at least not with anyone who could be known to hold such a rank from their clothing or their manner.'

So the Mountain woman could assuredly see her standing here, imprisoned within her own necromantic vision. Worse, Jilseth realised with a chill that would have been a shudder if she could have moved a single muscle, Aritane was reading her thoughts as each question the Col mentors asked prompted Jilseth's memory of the information which the Soluran corpse had yielded.

She stared back at the Mountain woman. Now it was Aritane's turn to be disappointed by the meagre return on Jilseth's endeavours. Without knowing the man's purpose, seeing where the Soluran had gone was of limited value.

Memory of the irritation and frustration which Jilseth had felt shifted into fierce anger at now finding herself so invisible, so wholly ignored, entirely subject to this Mountain woman's Artifice. Jilseth glared at Aritane. Let this arrogant adept read the depth of her outrage if she dared.

'Have we seen enough?' Garewin had drawn closer to the table to contemplate the thin-faced woman with a cream surcoat over her brown robe.

Guinalle raised a silent hand. She was intent on surveying the fifth wizard from head to toe.

Jilseth found herself wondering if the Tormalin adept was contemplating some Artifice. Was Guinalle somehow working in harness with Usara's wizardry beyond the confines of this enchantment? She strained to feel some touch of his earth affinity to no avail. Jilseth strove to quell the gnawing, irrational fear that she would never feel any element again.

In the next instant the tower room disappeared and they were safely within the Prefecture once more.

Jilseth snatched her hand out of Aritane's grasp. She shoved her chair backwards, rising to her feet. Even with the table between them, she couldn't bear to be so close to the Mountain woman.

'How dare you?' Though inconvenient relief blunted her fury. At least she could now speak and be heard. At least she could feel the elements around her.

Aritane gazed at her, unrepentant. 'It was of the utmost importance that we saw your memories before you had any chance to twist what you recalled. I don't say you would have done so deliberately but remembrance is a fragile thing easily warped by hopes or fears. We could not risk you unwittingly changing some detail.'

Guinalle looked at Aritane, making no attempt to conceal her displeasure. 'I have taught you gentler methods of learning unsuspected truths from willing witnesses.'

'Forgive me.' Aritane didn't sound in the least contrite and worse still, as far as Jilseth was concerned, her half-hearted apology was solely for Guinalle. 'The *sheltya* will demand that any evidence I lay before them passes the measure of their own Artifice. They will accept no other.'

'The *sheltya*?' Usara asked carefully.

'They do not concern themselves with lowland affairs.' Aritane looked around the table to address everyone in the room. 'However, it is evident that their attention has been drawn to this alliance between Soluran wizardry and the Artifice which is now turned against Hadrumal. I do not know where their interests lie but they sent this man from Wrede to make enquiries on their behalf.'

'Do you think that they will object to the abuses of Artifice which we have uncovered?' Guinalle asked with ill-concealed hope. 'Will they help us unravel these malicious enchantments?'

'If we don't have to worry about some aetheric assault, Hadrumal's wizards can withstand anything these Soluran Orders might hope to threaten us with,' Jilseth assured everyone. With or without Planir's help if he was still so absorbed in reading through Kerrit's archive. She hastily crushed that disloyal thought.

Aritane continued as though the magewoman hadn't spoken. 'I do not know what the *sheltya* will do but I am willing to lay all this before them, to add to whatever they have learned from the man from Wrede. I am willing to do this to repay the debts which I owe to Suthyfer. But I will not risk my life and sanity by encroaching on *sheltya* business without invitation.'

'How do you propose to let them know that you want such an invitation?' Corrain demanded.

'I will approach the valleys north of Wrede where my people still live untroubled on foot and as a suppliant. The *sheltya* will know I am there so they may greet me as they see fit.' She shrugged. 'Or not. I offer no guarantees.'

'Then to take such a risk—' Guinalle protested.

'It is my risk to take.' Aritane looked at her. 'I do not only owe debts to Suthyfer.'

'You can take her to the mountains today.' Corrain looked hopefully at Usara and Jilseth. 'Through your wizardry?'

Aritane shook her blonde head. 'I cannot arrive unsummoned within the *sheltya*'s purview by such means.'

Jilseth was sorry to hear that. Seeing Aritane's icy composure cracked by the nausea which had wracked Micaran would be some recompense for the distress the Mountain woman's Artifice had inflicted.

'Then there's nothing more to be said.' Corrain shook his head, aggravated. 'You could not walk from here to Wrede in less than fifty days, never mind venture further north into the mountains. These Jagai ships will attack Hadrumal in less than half that time.'

'You should learn to listen and make fewer assumptions,' Aritane said coldly. 'I will not travel north through elemental magic but I can use my own Artifice to carry me to Wrede.'

'You can?' Lusken gaped, astonished.

Aritane ignored him and the other dumbfounded Col adepts, still addressing Corrain. 'If the *sheltya* are willing to receive me, I will know within a few days.'

'By the turn of For-Spring.' Corrain considered this. 'The Jagai galleys won't arrive until a handful of days after that and then they have to load men and stores before heading southwards.'

'Could the *sheltya* help put an end to Jagai's madness before those galleys weigh anchor?' Garewin asked tentatively.

'I cannot say.' Now Aritane looked around the room. 'Nor can I say what will happen to me if I am called to account for my offences. One of you will need to come with me, to return with news of their decisions.'

'I will,' Guinalle said instantly. 'I can tell the *sheltya* the good which you've done in Suthyfer—'

'I need no such witness.' Aritane shook her head, perfectly calm. '*Sheltya* will learn everything which I have done through their own Artifice. Besides, you are needed here. There can be no hope of devising enchantments to counter the Solurans' malice without your skills.'

She looked at the Col adepts. Jilseth saw their expressions betray uneasy knowledge that the Mountain woman was right. She also saw the unguarded relief on Usara's face. He definitely didn't want his wife venturing into the mountains to face these unknown adepts. Then she realised that Aritane was looking straight at Corrain.

'Me? Why me? No.' He shook his head before Aritane could answer. 'I must return home. My responsibilities are there—as soon as Hosh's face is mended.' He shot a guilty look of apology at the disfigured boy before challenging Mentor Garewin. 'You will keep your promises to the lad, even amid all this?'

'Of course—'

The Mentor would have continued but Aritane addressed Corrain, as implacable as before.

'You started this.'

'What do you mean?' Mentor Garewin demanded.

'Baron Halferan cannot be held accountable,' Usara said firmly. 'He could have had no notion that the corsairs would be so reckless to try using the ensorcelled artefacts which they had plundered, in hopes of retaliating against the wizardry which they discovered defending the Caladhrian coast.'

Jilseth didn't need any Artifice to see that the Suthyfer

mage was as determined as Planir to stop these Col scholars learning the full story of Anskal's arrival in the Archipelago. Did Aritane know the truth? The Mountain woman's face was unreadable.

'He is still the best placed to bear witness to all that has happened.'

'I can go.' Hosh spoke up, surprising everyone. 'I was on the corsair island longer than anyone and the baron is right. His place is back in Halferan.'

Jilseth steeled herself to speak. 'That is true.'

She had no wish to see Hosh sent on such an uncertain journey after the sufferings he had endured but she remembered Planir's reasons for sending Corrain to the Solurans the year before. Their adepts could only learn what the Caladhrian knew. They could not steal the secrets of quintessential magic as they might from a wizardly envoy. But if the *sheltya* searched Corrain's memories, they would learn the whole sorry story of his misadventures and their unforeseen consequences.

Aritane shook her head. 'I will not go without Baron Corrain.'

'That might be for the best. You can use your skills at least as usefully here.' Jilseth was also wondering apprehensively what these mysterious *sheltya* might learn from Aritane to Hadrumal's discredit. What would they make of the way in which Suthyfer had obtained the Khusro artefacts? Of Usara and Guinalle using wizardry alongside the Artifice which these Mountain adepts reputedly guarded so jealously?

'I'm sure we can discover these Soluran adepts' Houses without sending Baron Halferan three hundred leagues north.' Jilseth found a handful of silver pennies in her pocket and she tossed them onto the table.

The devices stamped by Col's mint shimmered and blurred to leave blank discs rimmed with amber magelight. Jilseth concentrated and the metal flowed as though it was fresh from a silversmith's crucible.

The corpse had worn an amulet of five overlapping circles; two placed edge to edge north and south, with two more crossways on top, to east and west. The last circled the amulet's centre, overlaying the other rings.

The black-bearded man's device had a central circle surrounded by eight smaller ones, all framed within a larger ring. The unknown woman had worn ten concentric rings joined by a single vertical bar.

'These are their devices.' Jilseth contemplated her handiwork with satisfaction. 'Cast as many copies as you need from these exemplars. Send them far and wide and someone is sure to recognise at least one.'

'How long will that take? How soon before our enemies hear that someone in Col is asking after them?' Corrain contemplated the silver amulets before looking at Aritane. 'If these *sheltya* hold you to account, can you promise some Artifice will send me back here before the Jagai ships arrive?'

'I cannot promise but I give you my oath that I will do all in my power to achieve it.' She looked steadily back at him.

'I have travelled in the mountains' southern fringes,' Usara said suddenly. 'I can use my wizardry to retrieve you, if needs be.'

'I can guide you to a place he knows through my own Artifice,' Guinalle added.

Jilseth wished furiously for aetheric magic of her own, to speak unheard to Usara, to tell him to stop furthering this plan, surely so detrimental to Hadrumal's interests.

Corrain crossed his arms and looked across the table at Aritane. 'I'll give you ten days. I want your oath that you'll see me back here after that.'

The Mountain woman said something in her own tongue. Jilseth assumed it was just such an oath until Aritane and Corrain both vanished from their seats.

The Col adepts stared in open-mouthed astonishment, though Jilseth noted that Guinalle showed no such surprise. Did she have similar enchantments to call on?

'Let us hope we soon get word from them with information that helps us.' Usara clapped his hands to command everyone's attention. 'Meantime, we can't put our feet up by our firesides. 'Madam Mentor, Masters—' he looked to the four Col scholars '—please do whatever you can to devise enchantments to counter the malicious Artifice at work in your city.'

'I can help,' Guinalle added quickly.

Usara looked at Jilseth. 'We will go to Hadrumal and tell Planir what's happened.'

Jilseth nodded. At least she wouldn't face the Archmage's anger alone when he learned where Corrain and the Mountain woman had gone.

'What can I do?'

Hosh's offer surprised everyone. As they turned to him, the boy's blush cruelly emphasized his injuries.

'You can keep watch as the mentors work,' Usara said slowly. 'Our enemies will doubtless be on their guard against artifice and wizardry alike. Perhaps they won't notice a humble Caladhrian in the shadows.'

'Very well.' Hosh folded his bony arms across his skinny chest in unconscious imitation of Corrain. 'I won't go home until the captain's back regardless.'

— CHAPTER THIRTY —

Halferan Manor, Caladhria
1st of For-Spring

ZURENNE WATCHED ILYSH lift the white jug of elderflower
cordial from the shrine table. It had stood overnight
before Halcarion's alabaster statue and now the sunrise
proclaimed the goddess of love and luck's sacred season.
Halcarion's carved diadem of stars between twin crescent
moons was hidden beneath a garland of sunspeed with
white frostbells nodding among the golden blooms.

Ilysh wore a similar garland along with Neeny and
Raselle and every other maiden gathered outside on the
courtyard's cobbles. Every roadside bank throughout
Halferan was glorious with these flowers as the mildest
winter in living memory turned to a hopeful spring.

'Both moons are waxing. That'll see the goddess
favour our lady in the season to come.'

Zurenne could hear the matrons honoured to join
the Halferan noblewomen for these rites whispering
behind her. She gave no sign that she had heard as Ilysh
curtseyed to the goddess and carried the heavy ewer
through the open shrine door out into the courtyard.

Applause and cheers greeted her, slender in a white
silk gown with bodice and skirt overlaid with fine lace.
Even the humblest of the village girls wore lace this
morning; a collar carefully sewn to their finest dress or
a tippet draped around their shoulders to be admired

by friends and would-be swains before it was carefully wrapped in calico until next festival-tide. Ilysh was also adorned with her rope of pearls, carefully threaded and knotted on white horsehair. She had insisted it was fitting to wear these symbols of the Lesser Moon.

The brightness of true sunrise was strengthening in the east beyond the manor's wall. As Ilysh carried the cordial to the great hall, Zurenne followed with Neeny and Raselle and the women who had joined them in the shrine while the crowd followed after at a respectful distance.

No one was in the least concerned about Corrain's absence, Zurenne reflected as she followed her daughter up the stone stair. The demesne folk wanted to see their true-born lady celebrate these rites.

Zurenne wanted to know where Corrain was. She was absurdly conscious of her silver pendant's trifling weight on the breast of her gold velvet gown. Should she bespeak the Archmage this morning? She could wish him good fortune at this turn of the season by way of an excuse. But Planir had nothing to tell her when she had last stirred the pendant's wizardry three days ago. Corrain was travelling north in hopes of finding allies for Hadrumal. He was expected to return to Col within a handful of days.

She wanted to ask what need could the wizards have of allies and besides, why must Corrain go in search of them? Was Halferan to be bound to the wizard city's concerns for ever and a day in return for the magic which had saved and restored the manor? She hadn't dared to challenge the Archmage. Besides, Zurenne had no doubt that Corrain had his own reasons to go on this journey. She could only trust that his loyalty to Halferan remained his lodestone, first and last.

She would leave her pendant untouched for another three days, Zurenne decided as she followed Ilysh into the hall. Then she could reasonably request some answers from Planir.

Doratine stood beside the long tables where dishes were piled high with sweet cakes. Mistress Rauffe waited to receive the cordial from Ilysh. Jugs of water drawn fresh from the well stood ready to dilute the overpowering sweetness into scented refreshment. Every cupful would offer the promise of lengthening days for those now breaking their night's fast and sharing their hopes for the spring seasons. Laughter and chatter swiftly put the shrine's reverent silence to flight.

Zurenne watched Ilysh help Mistress Rauffe distribute white cups of cordial, exchanging nods and greetings with the manor's yeomen and tenantry.

'She looks so like her father, Saedrin bless his memory.'

'Halcarion and Drianon bless her and send her a true husband when she's of an age to warrant one.'

Two village women passed behind Zurenne.

'You believe that the captain-as-was will step aside, when she asks him to?'

'If he doesn't, he'll find every man loyal to Halferan ready to thrash him like he'd slighted their own daughter.' From the woman's chuckle she didn't expect to see it.

No, no one was missing Corrain today. It wasn't even as if he had any family still living to think of him. Though Zurenne guessed that old Fitrel would spare a passing thought for the orphaned youth he'd once sheltered.

Before she could reflect on that, she noticed Doratine counting heads as men, women and children continued to file through the open door. The cook swiftly despatched her most trusted kitchen maids to reheat their griddles and cook more sweet cakes. It seemed that everyone in the household, from the village and manor's demesne beyond, had decided to celebrate For-Spring's first sunrise here today.

'Thank you.' Zurenne accepted a cup of cordial from Raselle and a cake from Neeny. The little girl had crumbs around her mouth to suggest she had already eaten her own.

'Halcarion's blessings, Mama.' Neeny smiled sunnily before scampering off to join a gaggle of little girls around the table where the cakes were laid.

Zurenne smiled. She didn't begrudge this demand on the manor's stores or the coin she'd had to spend to buy the elderflower cordial. If she must go another season without wine for the high table, that would be her penance to Halcarion for her hopeless helplessness last year, prisoner to her own fears.

After Lord Licanin's troopers had put the renegade Minelas's henchmen to flight, there had been nothing to stop her harvesting elder blossoms from the demesne's coppices with her daughters before directing Doratine to make the manor's own cordial. But Zurenne had been too overwhelmed with grief, too terrified of corsairs, too fearful of Baron Karpis's predatory ambitions.

This year would be different. She and Ilysh and Neeny would gather the household's women and honour the moon maiden as they prepared the cordial for the following year in token of their faith that they and their loved ones would see another spring.

The shattering crash of a cup on the flagstones momentarily silenced the merry conversation.

'Oh my boy!' Abiath's quavering delight turned every head towards the great hall's door.

Hosh stood on the threshold, Kusint at his shoulder. For a moment, Zurenne thought that the lad would turn and flee. Not as he had done before, shamed by his disfigurement, but overwhelmed by the shouts of welcome and congratulation.

He didn't get the chance. Kusint urged him on just as Abiath's sewing circle bustled her forward. Zurenne expected the old woman to gather her son in a close embrace. Instead Abiath framed his face in her wrinkled hands and gazed, smiling, at his face no longer dragged askew by the broken bones beneath. Hosh smiled back, tears of joy filling his eyes.

Village and manor folk alike voiced their awe as readily as they besieged the lad with questions. Kusint clapped Hosh on the shoulder and left him to his kith and kin. He cut through the throng to reach Zurenne as quickly as he could. 'My lady.'

'What is it?' Zurenne's heart beat a little faster. She could see that Kusint had more on his mind than his friend's return.

'Hosh wasn't the only one knocking at the gates with the sunrise. We have another visitor. You should speak to him first, before we let him loose around the manor or the village.'

'Who is he?' Zurenne followed the young captain out of the great hall. 'Where is he?'

'In the gatehouse guard room.' As they emerged into the daylight Kusint answered her questions in turn. 'His name is Yadres Den Dalderin and he wishes to offer his best wishes for the new season's blessings to Baron Halferan and his family.'

Zurenne remembered that name. 'He's the Tormalin who was spying on Corrain in Ferl.'

Kusint nodded. 'Just so, my lady.'

For a moment Zurenne's pleasure in this spring day was curdled by resentment. Why couldn't Halferan be left alone to celebrate these gentle rites in peace? Why must the barony be perpetually besieged by other people's intrigues and scheming? Tormalin concerns were none of Halferan's.

Though of course such selfishness among the neighbouring barons had left Halferan alone and undefended when her beloved husband's desperation had led them to disaster. Such blinkered thinking had seen the parliament's inland lords refuse to join forces against the raiders, leaving Corrain with no choice but to pursue the perilous course which had brought catastrophe to the corsairs, followed by the unease and upheaval which was still spreading like ripples from a stone thrown into a pond.

More immediately, whatever Corrain was doing now, he wasn't here. Zurenne couldn't simply close her sitting room door and address herself to her needlework trusting in wiser, male minds to deal with such visitors.

'Where did he spend last night?' Zurenne walked as swiftly as she could towards the gatehouse, though that still inevitably meant Kusint curbing his far longer stride. 'In the village?'

'He arrived on horseback but I would guess so,' Kusint said thoughtfully. 'He doesn't look as if he slept under a hedgerow.'

'Send Linset to ask Mistress Rotharle.' Zurenne was sure she had seen the tavern mistress among the throng in the great hall. 'Tell him to ask what questions this visitor was asking and what answers he may have gleaned.'

She was pleased to find Reven sitting with the visitor at the guard room table. The young sergeant would have offered this stranger nothing beyond the festival cakes on the plate before him and his choice of elderflower cordial or ale.

Reven rose and bowed before retreating to stand by the door with Kusint.

Zurenne took the seat which the sergeant had vacated.

'Good day to you, Esquire.' She extended her hand according to what she knew of Tormalin custom. 'May the new season bless you.'

The young nobleman sprang to his feet, abashed and hastily brushing crumbs from his excellently tailored coat and subtly scented linen shirt. He gently brushed his lips against Zurenne's knuckles before releasing her hand. 'May Halcarion bless you and your household, my lady.'

'Please be seated,' she urged him when he remained standing, 'and do take another cake.'

'My thanks, my lady.' He grinned, boyish, as he did both.

Zurenne contemplated the young Tormalin, as tall as Kusint and somewhat stooped as though through self-effacing habit. While he was slightly built, his hands and the breadth of his shoulders suggested that he would grow into a more impressive physique. Whether he would have a similarly commanding personality was less certain. His fresh-complexioned face was amiable without being handsome and his soft brown eyes looked more honest than forceful.

If Zurenne had met him while she was visiting a neighbouring baron's house, she wouldn't have given the esquire a second glance beyond wondering if he knew the steps to Caladhria's dances and hoping that he paid at least some heed to the latest fashions in Tormalin's court.

So she offered him a polite and meaningless smile

befitting a meek Caladhrian widow. Let him wonder if Corrain had told her of their earlier encounter.

Den Dalderin smiled back with charming entreaty. 'I was hoping to offer my good wishes to the baron himself but your sergeant tells me he is away from home.'

'He is in Col.' Zurenne had no doubt that the esquire already knew that so admitting it cost her nothing.

'What takes him there?' Den Dalderin wondered with apparent surprise.

'Matters of trade,' Zurenne said vaguely.

'Trade with the Archipelago?' The young Tormalin sat a little straighter in his chair. 'Further to your visit from Khusro Rina's wives? I was in Attar,' he explained with ready candour. 'An Aldabreshin galley in the harbour at this season was the talk of the town.'

'I'm sure,' Zurenne agreed.

'But surely Baron Halferan had already left for Col, before these Archipelagans arrived?'

Den Dalderin's seemingly belated recollection was extremely convincing but Zurenne had seen the gleam in the young man's eye.

'Quite so.' She left him to continue the conversation again. After a fleeting hesitation he obliged.

'So you played hostess to these ladies alone? I confess I am surprised, given what I know of Caladhrian custom. Though it would hardly seem remarkable at home,' he confided. 'From the Emperor down, Tormalin menfolk have the highest respect and regard for our mothers and wives and daughters. The princely houses are very well served by their insights in many areas beyond marriage and child-rearing.'

Zurenne smiled agreeably. 'As a mother of daughters, I find that most pleasing.'

There was another pause before Yadres spoke more bluntly.

'My own House of Den Dalderin has an interest in seeing trade with the Archipelago restored. Should I advise my uncle the Sieur of our Name to open negotiations with Baron Corrain since Halferan is taking this initiative with the Khusro domain?'

Zurenne fluttered startled hands. 'I couldn't say, truly.'

'Truly?' Den Dalderin looked just a trifle sceptical.

'I would not presume to advise your uncle, nor to predict what the baron might wish to do once he learns of the Khusro ladies' visit on his return,' Zurenne assured him earnestly.

'What did you discuss?' Den Dalderin asked quickly.

'Besides child-rearing and gowns and jewellery?' Zurenne leaned forward, her face serious. 'They wished to return the bones of some Halferan men enslaved by the corsairs. They hope to return more remains as the seasons turn, as evidence of their good faith towards Caladhria. They wish us to know that they do not hold us responsible for whatever Hadrumal's wizards have done in Archipelagan waters any more than we should blame them for the corsairs' crimes against us.'

Den Dalderin would have learned this already in the village tavern or on the road through the barony. Those funeral pyres had been the talk of the demesne and beyond.

'What do they ask in return?' Yadres leaned forward in like fashion, inviting her confidences.

'Our goodwill, as I said.' Zurenne looked at him, puzzled. 'Our oath that we don't blame them for the corsairs' crimes.'

'Quite so.' Den Dalderin stood up and bowed low to Zurenne before acknowledging Reven and Kusint with a brief nod. 'I hope that you will both prosper in the season to come.'

Reven opened the door to the archway through to the gatehouse. 'Shall I fetch you your horse, Esquire?'

'You are welcome to stay for cakes and cordial with the household this holiday morning.' Let him try flirting with Ilysh, if that was his intention, so youthful and handsome in such fine clothes, with Reven and Kusint at his side. 'If you leave by mid-morning, you will still make a good day's journey—' Zurenne broke off, innocently confused. 'To where? Are you returning to Attar?'

'No, I am heading north.' Now there was the faintest challenge in Den Dalderin's eye. 'I am to deliver my uncle's compliments to Baron Karpis, among others.'

Zurenne smiled. 'Please offer his lady wife my best wishes for the season.'

And she would write to Lady Diress within the day, to learn what the detestable baron's admirable wife might tell her about their visitor.

'I will be sure to do that.' Den Dalderin nodded at Reven. 'Please do fetch my horse and I will be on my way.'

Zurenne remained seated at the two men left for the manor courtyard. 'Tell Master Kheda to stay out of sight until he has gone,' she told Kusint quickly. 'Then I will wish to speak to him.'

'Very good, my lady.' Kusint's face hardened slightly. 'When will he be on his way, might I ask?'

'Very soon,' Zurenne assured the Forest-born captain.

She left the gatehouse for the courtyard and watched a groom bring Den Dalderin his horse. She noted the Tormalin spy noticing that she hadn't stayed closeted with Kusint to discuss their recent conversation.

Going to stand by the manor's shrine door, Zurenne

waved to the young nobleman as he mounted and rode away. As soon as Den Dalderin was out of sight and unable to glance over his shoulder to see her fail to return to the great hall, she hurried back to the gatehouse and up the stairs leading to the guest apartments.

She knocked on the door to the largest bedchamber and Kheda promptly opened it.

'Your guard captain told me about your inquisitive visitor.' He grinned. 'He said that you were the embodiment of a Caladhrian lady, oblivious to anything beyond her household's concerns.'

Zurenne reflected how recently that would have been an entirely accurate description of her. 'I don't like to think of the Tormalin Emperor's spymaster looking so closely at Halferan. I would far rather he looked elsewhere.'

She walked to the window overlooking the road to the bridge crossing the brook and leading to the village beyond. Yadres Den Dalderin hadn't yet reached the fork where he must choose to return to the village or to head for the high road.

'Where would you like to draw Tormalin eyes?' Kheda enquired as she turned away from the window.

'Do you think that there are other Archipelagan warlords who might wish to follow Khusro's example and rid their treasure houses of magic? Do you think that such Aldabreshi would be prepared to deal with the lords of Antathele, Licanin or Tallat? All those baronies sent their swordsmen to attack the corsairs and their forbidden magic.'

Zurenne had been pondering this for some days now, concerned that Halferan would draw jealous Caladhrian eyes if the barony became the only apparent conduit for renewed trade with the Archipelago. She had no more wish for such scrutiny and the parliamentary debate which would surely follow, than she did for Imperial Tormalin attention.

Kheda nodded slowly. 'Miris Esul might be persuaded to consider dealing with a Caladhrian baron of proven good character. He would have grave doubts about involving any of his wives in such perilous matters. Were he to lead, other warlords might well follow.'

'Then would you go with Reven and a company of Halferan guardsmen, to take letters to these lords, asking if they would be willing to receive envoys from the Archipelago?'

Zurenne had already been considering how best to phrase such letters; allowing these noble lords to believe that they were doing Halferan a favour while hinting plainly at the benefits which their baronies would accrue from taking the lead in restoration of trade with the southern islands.

She would be happy to see these lords profit. Halferan owed Licanin more than she could possibly repay, and Antathele had proved an unexpectedly loyal ally while Lord Tallat deserved some recompense for being an unwitting pawn in Corrain and the Archmage's schemes.

Would Yadres Den Dalderin get wind of this? Zurenne could only hope so. Surely he must be an efficient spy if he was serving the Emperor's chief intelligencer.

'Then will you carry word to these warlords,' she asked Kheda, 'offering to help rid them of lurking magic?'

She didn't imagine Den Dalderin would follow Kheda into the Archipelago but that didn't matter as long as the Tormalin spy was occupied dogging his trail around Caladhria until Corrain returned to Halferan and whatever he had been doing for the Archmage could be concealed behind some further veil of half-truth and misdirection.

'I would be willing to do all this and more in hopes of ending this hostility.' Kheda pursed his lips. 'Have you discussed your scheme with Madam Jilseth?'

The magewoman? Zurenne hadn't seen her since her brief visit a handful of days ago, and they had barely exchanged ten words. Jilseth had come to tell Kheda that another Aldabreshin domain was threatening the wizard isle, incredible though that might seem. She had asked if he had any means to send messages or receive replies from any other domains beyond Khusro. Kheda had said that he would exchange courier doves with the Khusro wives, to inform them and see what he could learn, but there was little more that he could do. Jilseth had left in a seething fury which Zurenne had found profoundly unnerving.

'I will tell the Archmage himself this very afternoon,' Zurenne said resolutely.

'Very well.' Kheda went to open his travelling bag.

He took out an Aldabreshin compass, no larger than the palm of his hand. The round brass base was engraved with arcing lines and mysterious symbols, overlaid with a further intricate plate pierced and shaped into interlocking circles and arcs studded with tiny gems.

'The Ruby will stand in the arc of wealth at the start of the new year and beyond, offering forty days of its influence to counter the Emerald in the arc of death.' Kheda pushed the brass bar revolving around the central pivot with a thoughtful finger. 'Let me consider which will be the most auspicious days for these warlords to send their envoys to the noble barons, and when the heavens would be most favourable for them to submit their treasures for scrutiny once they have arrived on the mainland.'

'Let me know by the end of the day and I will advise our allies accordingly in my letters.' Zurenne's spirits rose, emboldened by Kheda's ready co-operation. 'Now, if you will excuse me, I will return to my people and their celebrations.'

She went down the stairs to the guardroom and opened the door. 'Captain Kusint, tell Reven to pick a troop and make ready to travel tomorrow—'

Zurenne halted on the threshold, surprised to see Ilysh and Hosh sat at the table. Kusint stood between them, contemplating a spread of runes. She realised that those bones were laid out for some Forest foretelling, not merely cast in a game of chance.

'What did the Tormalin spy want?' Ilysh asked quickly. 'What were you talking to Master Kheda about?'

'We can discuss that in due course.' Zurenne had already realised that she would have to include Ilysh in her plans. Letters to Licanin, Antathele and Tallat would have to go out under the barony's seal and over the acknowledged Lady Halferan's signature.

Well, since she commanded the yeomanry and tenantry's true loyalty, Ilysh would need to learn far more of the intricacies of life than more sheltered Caladhrian noble maidens.

So much for the future. Zurenne had more immediate concerns. 'What are you doing?'

Ilysh bit her lip. 'Hosh has been telling us what Corrain is doing.'

As the young man looked at Zurenne, she was struck anew by the marvel of his healed face. Then she saw the depth of apprehension in his eyes.

'The captain has gone north to find the *sheltya*, those who use aetheric magic in the mountains,'

Hosh explained. 'The Archmage hopes that they will have some Artifice to counter the Soluran adepts who threaten Hadrumal.'

'Soluran adepts?' Zurenne didn't understand. 'I thought it was some other Aldabreshi who were plotting against the wizard isle?'

Hosh looked guiltily at her. 'The captain helped to uncover a Soluran conspiracy while we were in Col.'

'I see.' Zurenne found that didn't come as a surprise particularly; any more than the news that Corrain was now somehow hip-deep in whatever had followed. If ripples of unease had reached as far as Tormalin to stir the Imperial spymaster to send out his minions, why shouldn't the consequences of the corsair island's destruction have reached beyond the Great Forest?

'I asked Kusint to see if the runes offered any guidance as to whether or not he will succeed,' Ilysh explained.

'Do you see any such indication?' Zurenne looked at the Forest youth.

He shook his head slowly. 'Forgive me but I cannot tell.'

'May I sit?' Zurenne took the empty chair as Hosh scrambled to his feet. Since Ilysh seemed perfectly capable of keeping herself informed, she might as well follow her daughter's lead.

'You had better tell me what's happened in Col, most particularly what has convinced Baron Corrain to make such a journey. When did the Archmage last have word from him? Is he travelling with Madam Jilseth or some other mage?'

Hosh looked even more anxious. 'He's with a Mountain woman. She used to be one of these *sheltya* but she was exiled. She still has her Artifice though. But Madam Jilseth says that she cannot find the captain through her scrying and none of the adepts in Col can make the Mountain woman hear them.'

He gazed at the rune bones lying mute and motionless on the table. 'That's why I hoped Kusint might have some way of telling us how he's faring.'

— CHAPTER THIRTY-ONE —

The Upper White River, Northern Ensaimin
4th of For-Spring

'HOW MUCH FURTHER have we got to go? You said that these *sheltya* were bound to meet us if we travelled north of Wrede. That was ten days ago.'

Corrain knew he sounded accusing and he didn't care. He was more exhausted than he wished to admit even to himself. Every successive day tramping through these woodlands had proved that Halferan's baron was nowhere near as fit as a guard captain should be.

They had paused in Wrede where this river swelled the famous lake only to purchase the bare minimum of gear and provisions to sustain them in the wilds. Initially Corrain had been relieved, as they left the smallholdings in the lower valley behind, to see that Aritane's early life in these mountains had taught her the skills for such arduous travel.

Now even this light pack dragged heavily on his shoulders and relentlessly sapped his strength. That wasn't the worst of it. Walking these endless leagues uphill had given Corrain far too much time to brood on the wisdom or folly of this journey. With every passing morning he was more inclined to fear that their quest would prove a waste of time and effort which could have been far more usefully spent elsewhere.

More than that, Corrain knew full well that Jagai's

galleys would be arriving in Col's harbour any tide today or tomorrow.

'Have you used your Artifice to tell the Col adepts where we are? Have they told you what's happening in the city? Do you know what the Archmage is doing in Hadrumal?'

He asked these same questions time and again, always to no avail. Aritane only spoke to him to address practicalities as they established their camp each evening or made ready to resume their journey with each sunrise.

Corrain had had more than enough. He halted on the narrow path worn by deer or whatever other game scuttled through this pine forest at night hoping to escape the wolves which he had heard calling by the cold light of the waxing lesser moon. Corrain had been careful to walk a good distance from any camp before he skinned and gutted the upland pheasants which he had fetched down with the fowling bow he'd bought in Wrede. Finding that particular skill hadn't deserted him was some small consolation.

Aritane continued walking with the same unhurried, unceasing strides. Corrain refused to be drawn after her.

'How much further are you going?' he shouted, feet planted firmly on the frosted mud. 'Until you freeze to death up there?'

The Gidestan mountains loomed ahead, shrugging off their cloak of evergreens to reach twice and three times higher than these foothills which he and Aritane had travelled through thus far. Corrain had seen the high ground between Caladhrian and Lescar on his visits to Duryea in Lord Halferan's guard. He had considered the mighty crags and lofty precipices impressive. Now those hillocks looked as meagre as the Halferan mill pond compared to Wrede's great lake.

The peaks soared upwards, impossibly tall and brutally sheer. They looked so sharp-edged against the pale spring skies that Corrain could believe their ridges were no wider than a knife blade. He didn't imagine he'd ever see for himself. Surely not even the hardiest and most agile of rats could scale those barren heights, still less survive up there.

The dark rocky slopes were shadowed by lethal screes and capped with blinding white snowfields. Rumpled scars marked the course of the avalanches which they had witnessed in the past few days. Such snowfalls filled the empty air with the sound of thunder and blurred the distant peaks with clouds of smothering white.

There was still plenty of snow here at lower levels, whatever Caladhrian almanacs might say of the year turning towards spring. The river remained frozen though Corrain could hear the water rushing beneath. Breaking through it to fill his drinking cup was easy enough to convince him that trusting his own weight to the ice would be folly.

'Why won't you use your Artifice to call out to them?' he yelled after Aritane.

There could be no doubt of her proficiency with aetheric magic. She had carried the two of them to an empty pasture overlooking Wrede as easily as any wizard could have done. More easily? Corrain had no way to judge but he had been struck by how different it had been, compared to being carried over these impossible distances by elemental magic.

As soon as Aritane's hand touched his own, back in that room in Col's Prefecture, Artifice had wrapped him in what seemed like sudden sleep. Opening his eyes, Corrain had found himself on that grassy slope with absolutely no idea how he had got there. For a moment he honestly believed that he had slipped into some dream. Then Aritane had spoken and recollection had rushed back.

And now he was going no further without answers. Most of all he wanted to know if these Mountain Artificers would really help them. This long walk had given him ample opportunity for second thoughts about that.

'Kusint, a man of the Forest Folk, tells me that the *sheltya* oppose the wizards and adepts who serve Mandarkin's tyrants, if they try to outflank the Solurans by cutting through the high mountain passes,' he yelled after Aritane. 'If your people are the Solurans' allies, can we really hope that they will help us?'

Ahead, the Mountain woman finally stopped walking. After a further long moment, she turned around and put back the hood of her heavy grey cape. Buying that had been her only concession to the cold of these heights.

The draper in that Wrede warehouse had certainly regarded Aritane with awe verging on fear. At the time, that encounter had encouraged Corrain to hope that these mysterious *sheltya* might truly have enchantments to equal and to complement Hadrumal's wizardry. But that had been ten days ago.

Aritane looked down the slope at Corrain. 'The *sheltya* are no one's allies. They defend these mountains and their people against any incomers intent on bloodshed.'

Corrain felt a chill which had nothing to do with the lingering frost. 'But these Solurans are threatening Hadrumal and that's six hundred or more leagues away.'

'The *sheltya* are also opposed to any who would use magic to rule over others, be that through wizardry or Artifice. The Solurans are seeking to increase the influence and use of magic among the kingdom's nobility through these ensorcelled items.'

'So the *sheltya* will want to put a stop to that?'

As Corrain sought confirmation Aritane only shrugged. 'I said that I hoped they would hear us if we came here. I made no promises that they would help.'

That wasn't nearly enough to convince Corrain to continue on this path. He needed to know for certain if these *sheltya* were going to prove worthwhile allies.

'If we are to foil this Soluran plot, we have to find these *sheltya* before the day is out. Otherwise you can take me back to Col and we'll devise some other plan with Hadrumal's wizards.'

Aritane shook her head. 'Hadrumal's wizards cannot counter Soluran Artifice without *sheltya* help.'

'Then use your own Artifice to let them know we need their help,' he cried, exasperated.

'I cannot use my true magic here. I have been exiled from these hills on pain of death or worse,' Aritane replied calmly.

'What did you do?' Corrain wondered uneasily what sentence could be worse than death.

'I betrayed my *sheltya* vows.' There was a forbidding edge to her tone.

'What were those vows?' Corrain wasn't going to be deterred now that he had finally got her talking.

Aritane stood silent for long enough to convince him she wasn't going to answer. He even took a step forward, only for her to speak, even if it wasn't to answer his question.

'My brother sought my help in saving our people's hills and valleys from lowlanders who believe that land without walls or fences or some signed and sealed deed of ownership can simply be seized by any who might wish to. He sought to save his wife's family from dispossession and beggary by raising an army to drive the lowlanders back. Events did not unfold as he had hoped.' Aritane surprised Corrain with a chilly smile. 'I believe that you know how that feels.'

'Have you been searching my thoughts?' he demanded

She tucked a wisp of blonde hair back into her thick plait. 'Planir told me.'

Corrain reminded himself that the Archmage trusted this woman. The calculating wizard must believe she could deliver some help from these *sheltya*. Surely he wouldn't have allowed them to make this journey knowing it would be in vain?

On the other hand, if this brother of hers had failed to save his wife's holding from invaders, that didn't say much for Aritane's Artifice. If she had escaped punishment for her misdeeds, whatever those might be, it didn't say much for the *sheltya* magic pursuing her.

She shook her head. 'I didn't say that my brother failed. Merely that events took an unforeseen course, most particularly for him and also for me.'

'Now you are reading my mind.' Corrain scowled.

'If you wish me to answer your questions, I need to fully understand them.' Aritane was unrepentant. 'As far as the *sheltya* are concerned, my brother's crime was not in defending his family's rights to wealth to be won from the forests and mines where they hunt and dig but in convincing me to use my Artifice to help him. My crime was agreeing and worse, persuading others sworn to the grey to do the same. The blood of those who died is on my head and hands.'

Corrain didn't need any arcane enchantments to see the guilt darkening her eyes.

'*Sheltya* can have no family other than those sworn to the grey once they have vowed to serve. They can have no loyalty to any particular valley otherwise they cannot be impartial when judging the disputes which arise and the crimes that are committed among the Mountain Men. *Sheltya* judgement could not be respected if there was any doubt of their neutrality in all respects. When the gravest crimes are judged, *sheltya* must be able to impose the penalties which blood guilt demands. They could not use such Artifice on men and women whom they still considered their kinsfolk.'

Aritane's faint smile told Corrain that she had just used her Artifice to see how unwilling he was to ask her what those crimes and penalties might be.

'How much further should we go on,' he asked instead, 'before we give up hope? The Jagai galleys—'

'The Archipelagans are still two days' hard rowing from Col. We do not expect them to arrive before the dawn tide three mornings hence.'

It wasn't Aritane who answered him.

'Talagrin's hairy arse!' Corrain reached for his sword. A Mountain Man clad in grey had appeared between them; tall for his race though not as stocky as most of the blond men Corrain had encountered over the years.

He appeared to be unarmed but that meant nothing if he was one of these *sheltya*. Equally, if he was a Mountain enchanter, Corrain's blade would be as much use as a loaf of bread in a sword fight. He unclenched his fingers from the wire-wrapped hilt.

The grey clad man smiled with satisfaction. Corrain narrowed his eyes. Did these *sheltya* simply wander in and out of anyone's thoughts as they chose?

'Yes,' the man told him. As he blinked Corrain was

disconcerted to see that the Mountain man's eyelids were stained black with some pigment.

'Bryn.'

Corrain was startled to see how completely Aritane's composure had deserted her. Always pale, now she was ashen with her full lips pressed together, bloodless, and her mouth downturned as though she struggled with tears.

He was entirely unmoved. 'Why have you returned?'

Aritane's voice shook as she answered. 'There are those among Solura's Houses of Sanctuary who are breaking their oaths and using true magic in pursuit of base and greedy ambition. Those of the high peaks should be told.'

'Do you imagine they don't already know?' Bryn asked, scathing.

'I thought—I thought it safest to make certain.' Aritane stumbled over her answer.

'Safe?' Bryn mocked her, harsher still. 'You thought you could return safely to these hills? You didn't imagine you would be called to account for your crimes?'

Something of Aritane's former resolve stiffened her backbone. 'I chose to make this journey because the time has come for me to answer for my offences. I will prove my repentance and show that I have honoured the *sheltya* among the lowlanders.'

'And you?' The grey-robed *sheltya* reached out to touch Corrain.

He tried to step backwards, to pull away. He couldn't move. Even as he fought to resist it, Artifice opened an overwhelming void in his wits that swallowed all awareness whole.

*   *   *

HE WOKE IN darkness, sprawled face down. Tensing his hands, he felt cool stone under his fingertips. Smooth stone, but not thanks to some mason's chisel. This felt more like water-washed rock.

He lifted his head and strained his eyes in a useless attempt to see through the absolute blackness. Abandoning that, he concentrated on listening. The slightest sound might give him some hint as to where he was. All he heard was silence.

He raised himself cautiously to his knees, one hand above his head to avoid knocking himself senseless if the roof proved to be unexpectedly low.

Smooth or not, this stone floor was unforgiving to his bare knees. He turned his body this way and that, trying to feel any breath of air on his naked back or chest. A draft might indicate some way out of here.

He felt nothing so hopeful. Very well. With the same cautious hand held high, he rose to his feet. Arms outstretched before him, he took a careful step, testing the ground before committing his weight and taking a second pace forward. He advanced slowly until his questing fingers found a stone wall.

Moving closer until his bare chest touched the rock, he explored this newfound surface with his fingertips. There were no joints or cracks. This wasn't masonry. He was in a cave. That would certainly explain the unchanging mildness of the air; cool but not uncomfortably cold.

Now he moved sideways, tracing the course of the cavern with his hands. The wall went on and on. For the first time, he felt uneasy. Was he following some passageway or charting a circular course? With no point of reference, he wouldn't know when he came back to the beginning.

He halted and considered this. Without a blade, he couldn't mark the wall. Without clothing, he couldn't leave some token to tell him that he'd made a full circuit. Corrain smiled grimly into the darkness. So he'd piss to mark the spot like some troublesome hound and let whoever had put him in here make whatever they chose of that.

He heard the trickle strike the stone and felt the warmth seep under his toes. These sensations put new heart into him.

Sheltya. Now he remembered. He had been travelling in the mountains with the woman Aritane, trying to find the mysterious Artificers who had exiled her.

His fists clenched at further recollection. He had been seeking these unknown adepts because Soluran wizards had suborned aetheric magic's assistance as they sought to force the Archmage into surrendering the ensorcelled artefacts which the Mandarkin Anskal had discovered in the Archipelago. But Aritane had been afraid that she would be punished for returning.

Corrain gritted his teeth and refused to be dismayed. If he was naked, he wasn't unduly cold. If he was imprisoned, he wasn't loaded down with chains or being thrashed by some whip-wielding slaver. He wasn't guilty of any offence against these *sheltya*. Once one of them read his mind, they would know that and release him.

If he hadn't already found his own way out, to challenge their right to detain him. He continued his slow progress along the wall, trying to determine if it was curving back on itself.

Was this even a real wall? He halted at a further thought. Was he truly here, naked and alone, or was this merely some illusion, like Micaran's deserted vision of Col's Carillon Square or the murderous Soluran's imaginary woodland?

Corrain turned around, leaning his shoulders on the stone as he considered this. If this was an illusion, what did that mean? Little enough, he concluded. He had no magic of his own, so he could hardly overcome such enchantment, not unless he could get his hands around the throat of whoever might be wielding it. So he might as well continue exploring the confines of this prison, real or imagined, and hope to find some means of breaking free.

A voice spoke somewhere in the darkness. 'He is remarkably strong-minded.'

A sardonic voice answered the first. 'Strong-minded or simple-minded?'

'Single-minded?' someone mused.

'Practical at least,' a further speaker commented.

'He is no leader of men,' the sardonic voice said with contempt.

'Look deeper.'

Was that a first speaker replying or someone else? Before Corrain could decide, the overseer's lash bit deep into his shoulder.

He gasped. In the next breath, he bit his lip to stifle the cry which would surely draw the slaver's wrath down on the men sharing this bench. He braced his feet against the wooden plank jutting up from the deck and hauled hard on the oar. The galley pitched and tilted in the wild seas.

Somewhere out beyond the bulwark, the fickle waves dropped away from their blade. The five of them fell backwards as the united strength of their pull met no resistance. Only the chain threaded through the fetters linking his ankles saved Corrain from sprawling into the oar behind them.

Gritting his teeth against the agony of the iron shackles digging into his raw flesh, he struggled upright once again. Shaking the matted hair out of his eyes, he rocked back and forward trying to see past the man who sat between him and Hosh. Was the lad all right out at the end of the bench by the oar port?

'A leader of men, perhaps,' the critical voice allowed grudgingly, 'but he is no ruler.'

His horse's hooves echoed loudly on the new-laid cobbles beneath the archway of Halferan's freshly rebuilt gatehouse. Behind him, Corrain could hear cattle lowing with complaint and sheep making their irritation known as they were herded into the pens erected on the grassy expanse between the manor's wall and the brook.

Emerging into the clouded daylight within the courtyard, he looked first for Kusint. The Forest-born youth hurried out of the guards' barrack hall and raised a hand to acknowledge the troop's arrival. His confident nod told Corrain that all was well within the demesne.

Now Corrain looked for Lady Zurenne. There she was, standing in the great hall's entrance, her children with her at the top of the steps

'Reven?' Reaching back, he snapped his gloved fingers.

'My lord Baron.' After the hesitation over his title which Corrain was so used to, the young sergeant thrust the battered ledger into his waiting hand.

Corrain lifted himself in his stirrups and leaned forward, taking his weight on his hands to swing his booted foot over the horse's rump and dismount. Landing on the cobbles, he took a moment to ease the stiffness in his back, thighs and shoulders. This final leg of their journey back to the manor had been a long and wearisome few days at the end of an arduous half-season.

Walking towards the great hall, he undid the top few buttons of his jerkin. Within a few strides, he became uncomfortably aware of the sweaty reek of his shirt. No matter. He would return to the guard hall and bathe with the rest of the troop while Lady Zurenne addressed herself to the ledger he had brought her.

The farmers who had seen their cattle, sheep and pigs scattered by the corsairs had been writing to her constantly, begging for assistance in determining if their beasts were slaughtered, stolen or strayed. She would know how best to allocate the animals which he and his troop had found wandering unbranded or separately penned with unnotched ears by honest herdsmen as they had made their round of the barony to see how the tenantry fared now that peace had returned. Few farmers had needed persuading to surrender beasts which they had no claim to.

'He is a most loyal man,' a voice approved.

Corrain wrapped his arms around Hosh, doing his best to restrain the boy's thrashing limbs. He could still feel the fever coursing through the lad's veins despite the fact that Hosh was lying here on the beach naked and exposed. Back home an apothecary would advise cold baths to cool him. With sharks in the waters here, even in the shallows, the best that Corrain could do was strip him for the damp winds blowing in from the western sea at this tail end of the Archipelago's unexpectedly chill winter.

Hosh mumbled, incomprehensible, tossing his head from side to side. The lad stared into the distance, his

blurred gaze unseeing. His distorted eye was rimmed
with angry scarlet while the smears of tears and mucus
from his broken nose glistened yellow with pus on his
red and swollen cheek.

Should he soak his own ragged tunic in the sea again,
to swaddle the boy with the sodden cloth and draw
this damaging heat from his bones? As Hosh's struggles
subsided, Corrain looked warily past the twisted and
warty trunk of the ragged-leaved tree hiding them at
this far end of the beach.

He didn't dare leave the lad if there was any chance
that some other slave might wander this way. That they
had nothing to steal was no safeguard. When the corsair
galleys couldn't go voyaging in these storms, the slave
rowers were left to their own devices on this cursed
island. All too many relieved their own anger and fear
by brutalising those weaker than themselves.

Corrain's empty stomach twisted beneath his bruised
ribs. He was always hungry here but now he felt he was
truly starving, after trading his meagre share with the
kitchen slave Imais.

She had promised that her herbs would help break
Hosh's fever. When would that happen? Did Hosh need
another dose? Did he need to sneak close to the corsair
shipmaster's pavilion and find Imais again?

Corrain refused to consider the possibility of Hosh
dying. He would see the boy through this fever and
come the spring, come the sailing season, they would
find some way back to Halferan.

'Loyal indeed,' a different voice agreed.

'Not always,' the sardonic voice sneered.

Her skin was silky beneath his hand, her breast
yielding until his fingertips found her nipple. Her

flesh tightened with desire, just as his own was doing elsewhere. He felt the warm breath of her stifled giggle against his neck as she felt his swelling passion hard against her thigh. Their bodies pressed tight together in the softness of the featherbed, swathed warmly with sheets and blankets.

His mouth found hers. His tongue teased her lips before kissing her long and deeply. He traced the length of her neck with more kisses as she twisted in the bed to offer her breast to his mouth. As he suckled and licked, his hands explored the rest of her body. He could feel her softness, her curves, unlike the firm-fleshed maidens he had dallied with in his youth.

Corrain didn't care about that. Age brought experience to man and woman alike, in the bedchamber like anywhere else. More fool Starrid, if the Halferan manor steward preferred to spend his evenings in the village tavern tossing runes. Corrain was more than happy to keep his neglected wife entertained.

Lord Halferan would disapprove of course, so devoted to Lady Zurenne. Corrain didn't care. No one would tell their lord as long as Starrid's arrogance made him so unpopular among the household while Corrain's newly-gifted rank of guard captain commanded admiration and respect.

Now he had his own bedchamber in the barracks rather than sleeping in the upper dormitory with the rest of the troopers, no one need know whether or not his bed was occupied. Anyway, even if someone discovered his blankets empty and hazarded a guess at whose thighs he was spreading, Corrain was confident that his men would only envy him, tasting this particular ripe peach.

'Arrogant and lustful.' The sardonic voice condemned him.

'Truly?' the first voice mused.

Corrain tensed. His chest no longer pressed against luscious fullness. Instead he felt the merest budding of womanly curves against his ribs. His questing fingers stroked a bony hip before sliding down to find the merest dusting of soft down rather than a richly pelted, plump and moist cleft.

'Now we're properly wed,' Ilysh murmured as she kissed his bare shoulder.

Aghast, he was out of the bed and stumbling backwards across the room quicker than thought. The lingering touch of her lips burned his skin like a brand. He sought to cover his shrivelling manhood with one hand, raising the other to hide any glimpse of the child's nakedness.

How could this happen? Bafflement warred with the horror driving him as far away as the room's confines allowed. Shame overwhelmed him. How would he ever explain such a base betrayal to Lady Zurenne? How could he protect the child now, when every man in the barony would be ready to beat him bloody and Corrain wouldn't raise a hand to stop a single blow—

His shoulders struck the wall behind him. Taken unawares, he lost his footing and fell hard onto his rump. The stone scraped his unclothed shoulder blades raw. Without even the meagre protection of breeches and under linen, the impact of his buttocks on the rock floor jarred his spine agonisingly hard.

Corrain didn't care. The pain cut through his incoherent horror to remind him where he was. He was imprisoned by the *sheltya*. They must have woven that particular nightmare after plundering his memories. To amuse themselves or to test him by laying his character bare?

'Strong-minded,' the first voice repeated.

'Enough.' A new voice spoke, harsh and unforgiving. 'He is of no significance beyond what he can tell us. What have Planir and his covey of conjurors and charlatans done now?'

Corrain stood on the corsair island's beach. The sky shimmered with azure magelight as a gale of brutal wizardry threw him and every man with him against the swiftly disintegrating slavers' pavilion. Amber magelight was tearing the building to pieces from the roof ridge to the deepest foundation. Emerald wizardry foamed amid waves surging upwards from the shore. The waters scattered the wreckage, heedless of frantic men struggling amid the broken rafters, shattered bricks and lacerating shards of tile. Only the scarlet magefire was untouched; burning beams scattering ruby sparks to kindle every scrap of broken furniture or torn fabric tossed amid the turbulent spume.

His face was scorching while the cold sea leeched all strength from his limbs. His heavy boots were dragging at his legs. He swept his arms back and forth, desperately trying to keep his head above the eerie green froth. He didn't know which he feared most; drowning or being burned alive.

A wave washed over his head. Stinging salt water filled his eyes to leave him dazzled by emerald magelight. He blinked to no avail, still blind. Flotsam pummelled him, brutal and bruising. He felt something under his hand. Something floating, not burning.

He grabbed at it, his fingers scraping across the stone floor. One nail broke. The jagged split tore deep into his flesh. Corrain gasped and heard the pathetic sound echo around the empty cavern. He was lying face down in the unchanging darkness.

491

'This is no illusion,' the first voice confirmed. 'This is where you truly are.'

'Enough!' the harsh voice rebuked the speaker. 'What else does he know of Hadrumal's arrogance? That is our only concern here.'

Corrain pressed his unshaven cheek against the floor as a rush of recollection left him lightheaded. The *sheltya* were riffling his memory for every recollection of any meeting with a wizard. Their faces came and went before his mind's eye with dizzying speed.

He tried to cling onto the floor, welcoming the pain of his torn fingernail. He tried to hold onto the sensations of the cool stone against his naked skin, to the raw throbbing of grazes on his knees and shoulder blades.

He didn't succeed for long.

— CHAPTER THIRTY-TWO —

AS HER SPELL faded to show her the first Archmage's ancient tower, Jilseth took a moment to compose her thoughts. So many concerns clamoured for her attention, not least the Jagai fleets which would arrive within the next few tides.

She could only be grateful that the Archmage had finally asked her to return, even if that was only to bring him the latest news from Col. Though there was little enough to tell and nothing which she had not already told him every second day since Aritane had vanished so utterly with Corrain. None of them, neither mentors nor mages, could find either the Caladhrian or the Mountain adept through any spell or enchantment.

Yet Planir had insisted that she stay in the city in case anything should change, so that she could inform him at once. Jilseth tried to curb her irritation as she walked up the stairs to the Archmage's sitting room and went in through the open door. 'Archmage.'

'Good morning.' Planir looked up from knotting a faded black ribbon around a stack of tattered documents on the settle beside him.

Jilseth noted that the broad table had finally been cleared of Kerrit's salvaged archive. Had the Archmage truly read every scroll and volume?

'How are matters in Col?' The Archmage wore a plain doublet and breeches of charcoal grey wool. A dark cloak was thrown over the back of the settle. Had he been out and about this morning, going between Hadrumal's halls and libraries?

'No one has made any enquiries after the dead Soluran. Mentor Garewin suggests we surrender his body to the Elected. Then he will be buried at the edge of the city's burning grounds with his death proclaimed at noon in the principal squares for three successive days.'

Mentor Garewin had explained to Jilseth that this was entirely customary for foreigners who died in the city, whose arcane rites insisted on interment, or for those whose families would have long leagues to travel before they could commit their loved ones to the cleansing release of fire.

'The mentors think that might prompt someone to claim his body.' Too late Jilseth realised how waspish she sounded.

Planir raised an eyebrow. 'Whereas you think they're hoping to catch a floating moon in a net?'

Jilseth shrugged. 'No mentors in any of Col's Schools of Rhetoric, Music or History have been approached by a Soluran adept since the turn of the season, still less by anyone sworn to the three Houses conspiring against us.'

She had had such high hopes initially. Within a few days Col's scholars had identified the symbols which Jilseth had flung on the table before them. The insignia denoted the House of Sacred Serenity in Trudenar, the House of Tranquil Seclusion in Megrilar and the House of Reflective Repose in Safornar. Whatever Mentor Garewin's scruples, Guinalle had been willing to search the thoughts of any of their adepts found within the city. The Prefects were still looking.

'Three Houses of Artifice are conspiring with five Orders of Wizardry across seven Soluran provinces.' Jilseth's frustration got the better of her. 'Have you raised this with Solura's King? With his sworn mages?'

'I hope we can resolve this without compelling King Solquen's intervention, not least because that will inevitably see the Tormalin Emperor involving himself in our affairs.' Planir leaned back against the settle's high cushioned back.

'Why do you suppose I asked you to stay in Col? When we both know that any mage here in Hadrumal could have scried over the docks and told me what you were seeing; the Jagai *zamorin* paying his hirelings to embark on their voyage before measuring their progress at dawn and dusk.'

'I assume you have your reasons, Archmage.' Jilseth had been telling herself that day after day and every time convincing herself had required more effort.

'So I have.' The Archmage nodded. 'Just as I had good reason for telling Merenel to remain in Kellarin with Allin Mere and the settlers' mages, and for sending Tornauld to the Carifate to join Velindre and Mellitha as they negotiate with those Lescari keen to establish their own trading harbours. I've just sent Nolyen to offer his services to Lord Licanin in Caladhria, should some Archipelagan warlord approach him with a view to cleansing his own treasury of unsuspected magic.'

Jilseth looked at him, baffled. 'Archmage?'

'Lady Zurenne hasn't been sitting idle, though I don't imagine she realises how useful her new boldness has been for my own purposes.' Planir grinned before looking more serious.

'Flood Mistress Troanna tells me that the Solurans are

constantly scrying upon us,' he told Jilseth, 'doubtless in hopes of learning something which they can use to force us to yield to their wishes. Naturally we can foil such intrusions but doing so entirely would leave their wizards idle and frustrated, sure to provoke them into devising some other nuisance to plague us.

'Consequently we have allowed them pierce this island's veiling spells from time to time. Troanna is particularly skilled in letting them believe they have done so undetected, thanks to their own subtle magecraft. All they see is fractious mages getting ever more enmeshed in fruitless attempts to divine ensorcelled artefacts' secrets. So they have gone scrying after you and my other confidants, now scattered far and wide, and we can hope that what they are seeing is baffling them completely.'

He raised an apologetic hand. 'I'm sorry I couldn't tell you. With Soluran adepts also ranged against us, I believe there is every chance that they have been using aetheric magic to eavesdrop unbidden on our people's thoughts.'

'Of course, Archmage.' Jilseth felt humiliated. She should have trusted Planir. More than that, she should have worked out his reasoning for herself. She frowned.

'Any Artificer reading my thoughts will know that Aritane has gone with Corrain to ask for the *sheltya*'s assistance. Is that another such diversion?'

'Not at all,' Planir assured her. 'I had very much hoped that dread of *sheltya* displeasure would dissuade these three Houses from working with these wizards.'

'You had hoped so.' Jilseth echoed his words with a sinking feeling. 'Is Lady Guinalle still unable to find Aritane?'

Planir shook his head. 'Guinalle believes that Artifice

is concealing Aritane from aetheric attempts to reach her, and from Usara's scrying besides.'

'Artifice can foil elemental magic?' Jilseth was dismayed.

'So it would seem,' Planir confirmed, 'some spells at least, when the adept is sufficiently proficient. But if the *sheltya* are not interested in helping us, we have other strings to our bow. I brought you here to see the results of some particular endeavours which we've been concealing from Soluran scrying.'

The Archmage gestured towards the open door. Jilseth could already hear footsteps on the staircase and Ely appeared carrying a broad scrying bowl. The Flood Mistress followed her.

'Madam Mage.' Jilseth tried to hide her astonishment. Troanna customarily dressed as comfortably and practically as any other grandmother on Hadrumal's high road. Today she wore a sea green velvet gown beneath a high collared mossy cloak with emeralds glinting amid swirls of gold embroidery.

'Jilseth?' Troanna looked momentarily surprised before turning her attention to the table. 'Ely, fill that if you please.'

'Flood Mistress.' Ely set the bowl down with a thud on the polished wood, prompting an indignant ringing from the silver.

Jilseth took a step forward to offer some help. Ely's face was so ominously pale that she honestly feared the slender magewoman might faint.

Troanna glanced at Planir. 'Three are spying on us at present, from Detich, Noerut and Ancorr.'

'That will suffice.' The Archmage turned to the door. 'Rafrid, I appreciate your promptness, and Canfor, good day to you.'

'Archmage.'

Jilseth was startled to see Canfor's face was deeply lined with exhaustion, his eyes darkly shadowed. Anyone would be forgiven for mistaking the prematurely white-haired mage for one of his own father's generation.

Rafrid couldn't be mistaken for anything but a fearsomely powerful wizard. The Cloud Master had forsaken his usual modest garb for breeches and doublet in azure broadcloth beneath a cobalt blue cloak. Silver thread traced lightning bolts from collar to hem and a heavy silver chain linked the great faceted sapphires of the clasp.

'Kalion and Sannin are on their way up.' Rafrid nodded a general greeting to everyone in the room. 'Good morning.'

The Hearth Master's heavy footfalls drowned out the sounds from the scrying bowl as Ely's magecraft filled it with water. As Kalion appeared, jowls sagging, Jilseth was relieved to see that Sannin looked fresh-faced and more than that, eagerly intent.

'Are you ready?' the Hearth Master asked Planir grimly.

Even for a wizard who customarily dressed with calculated ostentation, Kalion's appearance was dramatic. His robe of scarlet velvet was hemmed with flames worked in gold thread while his crimson cloak was secured on each shoulder of his flowing robe with twin brooches wrought like gold fire baskets filled with ruby coals.

'If you please.' Planir's gesture directed them to the table while he picked up the cloak draped over his settle. The high collar was ornamented with bold devices wrought of fine wire. As he raised his hand to take something from the mantelshelf, the metal shimmered and shifted in the light such that Jilseth couldn't tell if it was silver, gold or bronze.

She couldn't ever recall seeing the Archmage dressed

in such a forbidding garment. The stiff dark cloth framing his face transformed him into an unknowable, unapproachable figure.

Planir's next words doubled her unease. 'Before we begin, Jilseth, you must be ready to join in a nexus with Ely, Canfor and Sannin. You must submit your magic to Sannin's commands without question or reservation. I will be working largely untried magecraft and if something goes awry, she must contain any uncontrolled wizardry—'

'Archmage—' Ely began desperately.

'You can do this. You helped to confine the Mandarkin Anşkal's apprentices.' Planir was as kindly as he was implacable. 'More than that, you are one of the few mages whose affinity was enhanced through union with the quintessential nexus.'

'There's no other water mage who can take your place.' Canfor glowered.

Jilseth wondered if he was regretting his jealousy of mages whom he believed were learning wizardly secrets denied to him. Be careful what you wish for, lest you get it. She should have remembered such age-old wisdom herself, pacing her room in Col, burning with frustration.

'Hadrumal can survive my loss if this wizardry escapes me,' Planir continued calmly. 'Then it will be up to you and the halls to defend this island, if the Solurans can somehow make good on their threats of attacking us by means of this Jagai fleet and its mercenaries.'

'We understand, Archmage,' Sannin said, resolute.

'Flood Mistress,' Planir invited.

Troanna smiled with such malicious anticipation that Jilseth could have believed ice-born magecraft had sent that sudden shiver down her spine.

The Flood Mistress focused her attention on the silver

bowl. The water glowed with bright emerald magelight, though this was no steady green glow but a riot of shifting flares and flashes.

Jilseth felt elemental water magic being drawn into the room from some unimaginable distance. More than that, it wasn't summoned here in service of Troanna's wizardry but compelled by the Flood Mistress's spell. The bowl blazed. Desperate shafts of green magelight erupted to writhe and dissolve into showers of emerald sparks.

Troanna's smile didn't falter as she stared at the bowl. The emerald wizardry hardened. Solid radiance lay across the bowl like a layer of ensorcelled ice.

'I have captured their scrying,' the Flood Mistress said with vindictive satisfaction.

'Rafrid?' Planir nodded at the grizzled wizard.

The Cloud Master cracked his knuckles one by one, looking intently at Troanna's spell imprisoning the Soluran wizards' impertinent spying.

Azure magelight glowed deep within the frozen green. The turquoise shimmer spread and Jilseth felt elemental air force its way into the subjugated magecraft. The unmistakable resonance of a clairaudience spell thrummed against her wizard senses, the invisible threads of sorcery extending far beyond this tower room. Now she truly understood the pre-eminence of Rafrid's mastery. His spell was cleaving through the winds which buffeted waves and land alike to fly, true as an arrow, across five hundred leagues and more.

This spell was compelling the Soluran mages to hear what happened in Hadrumal, just as Troanna's mirrored scrying now forced them to see it. Faint tremors struck Jilseth's affinity as those distant wizards fought in vain to free themselves.

'Hearth Master.' Planir remained by the mantelshelf as Kalion spread his hands.

The fire mage's plump lips thinned, his eyes narrowing, as he applied himself to this unprecedented working. At first, Jilseth could barely sense the subtle breath of fire circling the frozen and interwoven scrying and clairaudience spells. It was easier to feel the rigid boundary which the Hearth Master created to circumscribe the fickle, evanescent element.

As his spell strengthened, Jilseth recognised a bespeaking, a comparatively simple working. So the Archmage had a message for the Soluraans beyond challenging those vainglorious wizards with this display of equally pretentious garb.

Bespeaking might be a straightforward spell but matching this magecraft to the first two spells was demanding all Kalion's expertise. This wizardry must follow the same elemental conduit to those distant towers but if even this modest fire magic was to brush against Rafrid or Troanna's wizardry, then everything would be undone. Jilseth had no doubt that more was at stake than humiliation for Hadrumal.

'Are we ready?' Planir drew on a pair of grey gloves, ornamented and armoured with black leather reinforced with that same eerily ambiguous metal.

'We are.' Troanna confirmed.

As the two Element Masters echoed her, Planir took something from the high shelf above the fire place and looked at the four mages as yet unengaged in wizardry.

Sannin cleared her throat. 'We are ready, Archmage.'

Jilseth tried to echo her but could only utter a hoarse whisper. Canfor's assent was barely any louder and Ely simply nodded, mute, her eyes white-rimmed.

Planir came over to the table and extended his hand above the silver bowl. The swirling circle of elemental fire a finger's width above the frozen scrying glowed brightly as he used the bespeaking spell.

'You will recognise this ring,' he said conversationally. 'It has a climbing spell imbued within it. You or your fellow conspirators were scrying when I demonstrated to my colleagues how impossible it is to destroy such an ensorcelled trinket with even the most intense focus of any single element. I'm sure that you found that reassuring. Watch closely and think again.'

Planir tossed the ring up into the air. He didn't catch it as it fell towards the scrying. Instead he cupped his hands, the width of the bowl apart. Coruscating quintessential magelight crackled from his fingertips, as brilliant as diamond struck by sunlight and glittering with every colour of the rainbow on the very edge of seeing.

A sphere of quintessential magic captured the tumbling ring. Darkness filled the globe, hiding the ring from view. Quintessential magic continued to stream from Planir's fingertips into the sphere. Bright tendrils escaped it, edged with violet radiance which Jilseth had never seen in any magecraft.

As this eerie magelight touched the tower room's floor, the windows or the table, that unknown wizardry dissipated to surrender its magical potential to the natural blend of the elements surrounding them.

In this instant before each tendril vanished, the sensations were intoxicating. Jilseth's affinity told her that she could unmake Hadrumal itself, unaided and as easily as the Archmage's nexus had destroyed the corsair isle, if she dared to command such power.

Except she had no doubt that any attempt to harness

such catastrophic magic would destroy her utterly. Canfor took a hasty sidestep to avoid one of the crackling violet tendrils and Jilseth didn't blame him. She had no wish to risk the dire consequences of such a touch.

All Planir's attention was focused on the sphere of black shadow rimmed with diamond brilliance. Somewhere deep inside, Jilseth could sense an elemental cataclysm unfolding. Her wizardly senses ached with the recollection of the Mandarkin Anskal's death. He had been ripped so utterly asunder, body, blood and bones, that not even dust remained, when his uncontrolled affinity had been unleashed within the adamantine prison which Hadrumal's Masters and Mistress of Element had crafted from their united elemental might.

White-hot light glowed in the heart of the black sphere. Now Jilseth could see the ring caught within the annihilating spell. The radiance was so bright that it was painful to behold but she couldn't look away.

Black smoke escaped the spell; a single wisp but soon thickening, as opaque as ink. Drifting up to the ceiling, it spread across the full width of the room without ever seeming to thin. Jilseth shivered as she felt the excess of elemental magic which had so thrilled her being sucked into the obliterating darkness.

'Sannin?' Canfor was ashen with apprehension but Jilseth saw that he wasn't looking at the ominous darkness spreading above them. He had seen flakes of shattered stone falling from the sphere in a cascade of that violet magelight.

Jilseth answered him. 'No, that's devoid of wizardry.'

Whatever else was happening she could sense these broken fragments were no more than common shale. The frail stone crumbled further as it fell. Before the smallest speck could have struck the frozen scrying, the once-ensorcelled ring was reduced to motes smaller than any eye could see. Smaller than even the most precisely crafted Aldabreshin lens could ever find.

'Your attention, please!' Sannin said sharply.

Jilseth felt the magewoman reaching out with her fire affinity to determine how much wizardry she could command without risking the slightest intermingling with the spells woven around the scrying or, more perilous still, any chance of intersection with the elemental oblivion looming overhead.

She saw sweat matting the Archmage's cropped steel-grey hair. His face glistened in the eerie magelight and a vein in his forehead pulsed. Effort deepened the creases around his eyes and moisture beaded his lashes as his face contorted.

The darkness swirling around the ceiling began to glitter, speckled with all the colours of the elements. The annihilating wizardry which had nullified the magic instilled in the ensorcelled ring now sought to consume any other element which impinged on its shadowy boundaries.

Jilseth established an elemental union with Trydek's tower, ready to draw on the strength of its stones and the foundations reaching down into Hadrumal's bedrock. She could sense Canfor summoning storm clouds from leagues around. Ely had the greatest challenge to surmount; linking her affinity with the waters lapping the wizard isle's shores. Jilseth was both astonished and relieved to feel how swiftly the pale magewoman did so.

The glittering menace subsided. The darkness swirled, plain black with no hint of magelight. As the shadow thinned to grey Jilseth sensed the elemental ebb and flow within and beyond Trydek's tower returning to a natural balance. Nothing now escaped the sphere hovering between Planir's hands; neither the ominous magic nor the remnants of crushed shale.

A pinpoint of white light kindled in the centre of the black globe. It exploded outwards and Jilseth felt a rush of incalculable wizardry unleashed. She laid her affinity open for Sannin to command—

The diamond magelight contained the cataclysm and the sphere vanished as silently and completely as a soap bubble.

Planir's gloved hands thudded onto the polished wood on either side of the scrying bowl. Jilseth could see his arms shaking as he leaned his weight on the table. He stared into the frozen mirror framed by circling fire.

'Now you have seen what Hadrumal can do,' he snarled, venomous spittle flecking his beard. 'Do you truly wish to make us your enemies?'

He pushed himself away from the table. Troanna flung a hand at the scrying bowl to unleash her water magic just as Kalion realised his stranglehold on the elemental fire. Jilseth felt the antagonistic elements clash, only to meet the deafening crack of Rafrid's wizardry. Jilseth sensed the brutal sting whipping across countless leagues to lash the hapless Solurans with one last reminder of Hadrumal's power.

Planir staggered away from the table, tearing off his cloak and letting it fall to the floor. He collapsed onto the settle by the fire, his head thrown back, eyes closed, his face gaunt.

Ely was the first to break the silence. 'What will happen now, Archmage?'

Planir stirred himself to look at her with some semblance of a smile. 'We wait for the Solurans' answer.'

'They cannot persist with this idiocy after seeing such a display of strength.' Troanna frowned nonetheless.

'But I don't suppose they'll use their own wizardry to divert the Jagai fleet. We had better consider which currents we can commit to sending the Archipelagans back to a safe harbour.'

'Not anywhere in Caladhria.' Jilseth hastily found her voice. 'The people are still so fearful of corsairs, there will be uproar.'

'An accidental bloodbath will hardly improve matters,' Rafrid agreed. He looked across the table to Canfor and Ely. 'Let's see what wind and wave can achieve together, to send these poor dupes into Khusro waters. That's the closest Archipelagan domain.'

'Let me send word to Lady Zurenne, to tell Kheda, the Aldabreshin who helped us in Halferan,' Jilseth said at once. 'He may still have a Khusro courier dove, to let them know that this is no Jagai invasion.'

Doubtless he could find some explanation to suit the Khusro wives. Though Jilseth wasn't overly concerned if the Archipelagans chose to enslave those mercenaries from Col. That would serve them right for taking Aldabreshin gold to take up arms against Hadrumal.

'Very well.' Troanna was already walking towards the doorway. Ely followed with Canfor only a few steps behind. Rafrid went after them, thoughtfully cracking his knuckles.

'There are times,' Planir remarked from his seat by the fire, 'when I am sorely tempted to turn our honoured Cloud Master's hands to stone.'

Kalion barked with sudden laughter. 'I thought of giving him blisters.'

Sannin smiled. 'What would you have us do now, Archmage?'

'Keep watch.' Planir heaved a long shuddering breath.

'We've given the Solurans pause for thought but greed and pride can make fools of the wisest men.'

'Until later then.' Sannin inclined her head serenely and headed for the door.

Kalion paused on the threshold to offer Planir a wry smile. 'I don't believe you need to fear Troanna proposing that the Council dismiss you as Archmage.'

'Quite so.' Planir managed a weary grin.

'I will leave you to rest, Archmage.' Jilseth took a step towards the door. She wanted some solitude, to review this astonishing magic, to see what she might glean to improve her own wizardry.

'I would appreciate your assistance.' Planir's request was more a command.

Jilseth wondered what he wanted her to do. 'Shall I make you a black tisane?'

'A very good notion, and while the water's boiling, please renew this tower's wards—' he broke off to take a deep breath '—against any intrusion from some Soluran wizard who has guessed how truly exhausting unmaking that ring's magic must be.'

'Of course, Archmage.' Jilseth hastily wove a cantrip to fill the kettle and stir the fire beneath it.

Sitting at the table, she closed her eyes to concentrate on the warding magic pervading the tower. Though the wizardry was rooted in Planir's own stone mastery, she carefully traced the intricate union of fire, water and air. Quintessential magecraft was poised to overwhelm any spell such as translocation, bespeaking or scrying born of one principal element.

She was unnerved to realise how brittle the warding had become. The Archmage had evidently been using all his strength on other things. This wizardry would still repel one malicious assault but with Planir so exhausted, some second attack might just succeed.

Jilseth drew on the abiding potency of Hadrumal's rich dark earth, on the spring sun warming the moist soil and the gentle breezes stirring the budding twigs, to bolster the defensive spells. She couldn't work this quintessential magic on her own but her skills with quadrate wizardry enabled her to renew it.

She looked at Planir, still sitting limp with fatigue, his eyes closed. Quintessential magic had destroyed the ensorcelled ring but he hadn't been working with a nexus. He had done that alone. How had he achieved such an unprecedented feat?

She frowned. 'Archmage...'

'What is it?' he asked with foreboding.

'Something is wrong...'

At the very edge of her wizardly senses, Jilseth could feel the constantly renewed mists which cloaked the island. Hadrumal bred as well as mageborn, she had sensed this ancient wizardry even before her affinity had manifested itself. Now she felt arcane sorcery scattering that familiar union of water and air to the four winds.

Wizardry in the same vein was assailing the misdirections forged from fire and earth by Trydek's first followers. These spells had long circled the island and its outlying reefs to confuse any compass carried aboard a ship. Further magic blending fire and air had hidden the sun from generations of mariners used to reading their course with cross-staff or quadrant. All this wizardry was being unravelled.

'I believe we have the Solurans' answer,' Jilseth said grimly.

Quick feet ran up the stairs and Sannin appeared in the doorway.

'Archmage—' Clutching at the doorpost, her face twisted with pain. She tore at her high-piled hair, scattering garnet tipped pins.

'Jilseth, bespeak Usara.' Planir tried to rise from the settle and failed, his legs buckling under him.

'No, wait,' Sannin gasped. She held on tight to the door post for a long moment.

Jilseth watched blood trickle down the magewoman's cheek amid tumbling locks of hair. Her varnished fingernails had dug deep into her scalp.

'Artifice?' Planir demanded.

Sannin nodded warily. 'But only when I try to renew the wardings.'

Shouts of outrage echoed across the courtyard below, mingled with incredulity. Jilseth guessed that some other wizards had encountered the same aetheric magic as they sensed this inconceivable undermining of Hadrumal's age-old defences.

'We must have more wizards than they have adepts.' Sannin's lip curled, defiant.

'How long for?' Planir growled. 'Do you doubt that they will start killing us if a mage refuses to yield?'

Recalling the Detich wizard woman's arrogance in this very room, Jilseth was forced to agree. More than that, she knew how many of her fellow wizards would persist until their arrogance was the death of them.

'Though they need not kill us themselves,' the Archmage continued grimly. 'Hadrumal will be just as easily overrun if they merely strike us senseless. When those Archipelagan ships arrive, who will defend the mundane born? When the mercenaries wander unchallenged through this city, who will stop their swords slitting our throats?'

The great tongueless bell over the Council chamber tolled. 'You will have to tell them why this is happening.' Sannin looked apprehensively at Planir. 'Do you think that they will vote to surrender the artefacts to Solura? Once they remember what happened to Otrick.'

For the first time, Jilseth saw uncertainty flicker across the Archmage's face.

'Usara can bring Guinalle and her adepts to counter the Soluran Artifice.' She summoned a taper from the mantelpiece with one air-woven cantrip and propped the empty scrying bowl on its rim with another.

'Perhaps.' Planir didn't sound in the least convinced. 'Sannin can do that. You must find Captain Corrain.'

Jilseth shook her head. 'No one can find him. You said the *sheltya* are hiding him.'

'Not from pendulum magic. Let's hope so, anyway.' Planir struggled to his feet and hauled open a drawer in a side table to find a map and a diamond teardrop on a silken thread. 'You devised the pendulum magic that found him before. I know you can find him again.'

'Even if I can—' Jilseth didn't understand.

'Translocate yourself there.' Planir sent the map and the diamond skidding across the table to her. He sank into a chair. 'You have the skills, even over such a distance. Trust me.'

Jilseth found the Archmage's confidence as terrifying as his intensity. 'What then?'

'Either he's with Aritane or the *sheltya* have them both. Either way, you must tell these Mountain Artificers to remember that we have Trydek's magic.'

'Trydek?' Jilseth stared at Planir.

'Have you never wondered why Hadrumal has no shrines? Every other land where the Imperial Tormalin ever settled or ruled worships their gods. Not here and not because scholarship and rational thought decry such superstition. Because Trydek and his first followers came from far beyond the Great Forest. Trydek was a Mandarkin.'

Planir smiled, gaunt as a death's head.

'Tell the *sheltya* that Solura's adepts are helping the kingdom's wizards to plunder all our lore. Remind them that Mandarkin invariably steals whatever sorcery Solura has within a handful of years. The consequences for the mountains will be bad enough, if the Solurans loot Hadrumal of these ensorcelled artefacts. What disasters will they see if all that Trydek's magic has now become returns to the north?'

The Council bell tolled again. More commotion rose from the courtyard; incomprehensible questions answered with inaudible consternation.

'Archmage,' Sannin warned.

'Scry for Corrain,' Planir ordered Jilseth. 'Truly, you are the only one who can do this.'

'But this is quintessential magic,' she protested.

Sannin looked up from a bespeaking burning scarlet around the silver bowl's rim. 'Canfor and Ely are on their way.'

Once again, Jilseth heard footsteps on the stairs, running this time.

'Archmage?' Canfor was shouting even before they could see him.

'What's happening?' Ely's face was wretched with fear.

'Help Jilseth,' Planir commanded.

Sannin was already spreading out the map. 'We must each hold a corner.'

Ely and Canfor hurried to obey the lissom, scarlet clad magewoman.

Jilseth picked up the silken thread. As the diamond swung over the map, she felt the weight of its aeons-old existence. Using her affinity in that trivial fashion was as natural as breathing.

Now though, she cringed lest some murderous Artifice thrust itself into her mind. How many merciless Soluran adepts could be working hand in glove with the Orders, intent on foiling Hadrumal's wizards' attempts to defend their island and its innocent people? No, she could not succumb to such fears. Unruly emotion was fatal to wizardry.

Her hand shook as she extended it over the blue-inked blob marking Wrede's lake on the chart. That's where Corrain and Aritane had gone so that's where she would start.

Canfor slapped the palm of his hand on to the back of hers. Ely and Sannin did the same, all of them standing awkwardly around the table, their other hands stopping the map curling up to hide its secrets.

Self-doubt assailed Jilseth as the diamond stayed obstinately clear. She couldn't even summon up the quintessential spell that presaged such a search. The Archmage could say what he liked but his words alone couldn't make her equal to this challenge. Unless this was some more subtle Artifice demoralizing her.

Jilseth closed her eyes and used a touch of air magic to muffle the irate voices rising from the courtyard. She had seen vastly more complex magic worked here in this very room today. How had that been done? By turning wizardly custom and practice on its head.

Unbridled emotion was the most deadly of menaces

to the untrained mageborn. But she had long years of training as well as recent experiences that other wizards on this island could only dream of sharing.

Could she harness calculated passion to enhance her magic? Jilseth rejected fear in favour of iron resolve to frustrate these arrogant Solurans. She rejected anger in favour of burning determination.

The diamond glowed with amber magelight. Sapphire swiftly followed, then ruby and emerald as Jilseth bound the other mages into the spell. The diamond burned with white fire.

Trusting some sudden instinct, Jilseth drew on all the power which her earth affinity afforded her. The Archmage was right. Even without the manacle whose resonance Jilseth had bound into her magic before, she found that she could mould this seeking spell to Corrain's very essence.

He was born of Halferan, bred and raised within a stone's throw of the manor whose walls she had reshaped to repel the corsairs. He had eaten beasts reared in the fields where she had thrown up turf-covered ramparts to block the Archipelagan raiders' path. He had drunk ale brewed from the water in the brook flowing past the village and so had she.

The diamond tugged at the thread and she let it lead her to a point on the chart far into the Gidestan mountains.

'I've found him. He's in a cave.'

Somehow Jilseth's affinity told her that Corrain was lying in complete darkness. More than that, the immensity of a mountain surrounded him.

'You cannot translocate there.' Sannin was adamant. 'Following a scrying is dangerous enough but to try finding a cavern underground with no more guide than a pendulum—'

A distraught wail below was swiftly followed by a bellow of anger. A lightning bolt split the clear blue sky with wizardly rage. The Council bell tolled on.

'I can do it if I can draw on your strength.'

Jilseth saw that Planir understood what she was asking.

'No,' Sannin said sharply. 'Let me. Translocation is more closely tied to fire—'

The Archmage struggled to his feet and clamped his hand on top of the four of them making the nexus.

Jilseth focused on the elemental tie between Corrain and Hadrumal now focused through the diamond. She wove the magic which would carry her to his side, doggedly warding her magecraft against any elemental upheaval. As far as Artifice was concerned, she could only summon up her scorn for Solura's deceitful enchantments.

The astonishing breadth and depth of Planir's affinity bolstered her spell. The room in Trydek's tower dissolved into white magelight. She felt herself carried across the emptiness between the island and the mountain more swiftly and surely than she had ever been transported before.

She sensed cool stone beneath her feet as the translocation faded to leave her in utter darkness. Jilseth fought against sudden panic and it wasn't the lack of light which concerned her.

In that last instant, she was left abruptly bereft of the Archmage's strength. Sannin had ripped her own magic away, leaving Jilseth's fingers seared through skin and flesh to the bone beneath. What had panicked the serene magewoman into losing command of her wizardry so violently?

No, that must wait. Now she had to find Corrain, wherever he was in this darkness.

— CHAPTER THIRTY-THREE —

Izmor Descava, Gidesta

14th of For-Spring

'BARON HALFERAN! CORRAIN! Captain!' Her shouts struck him like blows.

Another nightmare? No, he was done with them. Corrain rolled away, hiding his head in his arms.

'Corrain!' A hand seized his shoulder and shook him. 'Wake up!'

He ignored it. Whatever this illusion was, however these unseen *sheltya* bastards wished to torment him; he would have none of it.

The hand grabbed at his hair. Despite his recent efforts to husband his strength, refusing to yield to the desparing rages which left him exhausted and changed nothing, Corrain's anger stirred. He flung out a fist with a warning growl.

'Corr—' The shouting woman broke off with a cough as his knuckles struck cloth over yielding flesh.

His hand encountered another arm. Fingers grabbed at him. He crushed the hand in a brutal grip.

The woman's scream of agony left his ears ringing. A flare of golden magelight stabbed at his eyes before he was plunged into darkness again. It was enough to show him a glimpse of the newcomer.

Corrain scrambled to his feet. 'Madam Jilseth?'

Was this more *sheltya* deceit? Or could this possibly be real?

He heard strangled sobs of pain. A moment later a hiss of indrawn breath cut the gut-wrenching weeping short. A faint yellow flame kindled, no bigger than a thumbnail.

Corrain saw magelight flickering at the tip of Jilseth's upheld forefinger. Below he saw the gashes seared across her fingers and palm, bone deep. No wonder she had screamed when he had grabbed her hand. If those were real wounds.

Why present him with such an illusion? Surely the *sheltya* were done with him? As best he could reckon, they had emptied his head of every last recollection of wizardry three days before.

That was as close as he could reckon the passing time from the rhythm of his hunger and bowels. He'd had six meals of barley porridge flavoured with shreds of meat and stringy dried leaves since he'd woken to find his clothes on the floor beside him along with a ewer of water and a chamber pot. There was no sign of his weapons or gear but that was far too much to hope for.

'Are you truly here?' he demanded.

'Yes,' Jilseth said through gritted teeth. 'Where's Aritane?'

'I haven't seen her since they took us from the valley above Wrede.' Corrain found his own jaw clenching as he recalled the fierce debates over her likely fate which he'd had with himself in the darkness.

She had said that she had been exiled on pain of death. But she was one of their own. Surely the *sheltya* would have read her recollections and seen her remorse. Surely they would have seen the pressing threats which had convinced her to risk returning.

'Can't you scry for her?' he demanded. 'Can't some Suthyfer wizard?'

'We've tried,' Jilseth snapped. The flame at her fingertip swelled to illuminate the entire cave. 'Where's the door?'

'There isn't one, not that I can find,' Corrain amended.

Once he was convinced that this prison was no aetheric illusion, he had searched every hand's breadth of the wall from the undulating curve where it joined the floor to as high as he could reach.

Jilseth looked at him. 'You're not dead of hunger and thirst and you haven't soiled this place—'

'They come and go when I'm asleep,' Corrain said curtly.

He had tried to stay awake, ready to challenge anyone coming to see how he fared. It had been appallingly difficult with the darkness lulling him to sleep. He had searched the cavern for some pebble to sit on, willing to suffer the discomfort for the sake of wakefulness. He hadn't found any such thing and both ewer and chamber pot were made of metal so he hadn't been able to break those for helpful shards.

Jilseth forced a smile. 'My magic will find us a way out.'

'What day is it?' Corrain demanded. 'What's happened in Col? What news do you have of Halferan?'

'It's the fourteenth day of For-Spring,' Jilseth replied swiftly, 'and Hadrumal is beset by Soluran wizards who are unmaking our defences against the Jagai fleet while their adepts attack any mages trying to restore them. These *sheltya* must help us—'

'The fourteenth...' Had he truly lost count of the days so badly?

'Lady Zurenne continues to prosper and there's no sign that our enemies have the least interest in her or her children.' Jilseth was running the fingertips of her unwounded hand lightly over the smooth rock wall. 'You may yet see Halferan take command of renewed trade with the Aldabreshi, in Caladhria at least.'

'What about Hosh?' Surely that simple question should win him an intelligible answer.

'Hosh is restored and returned.' Jilseth frowned at the pale grey stone.

Before Corrain could ask anything further, she stepped into the solid wall as easily as if it was a fog bank.

The mageflame went with her, leaving Corrain in crushing darkness. He hammered on the rock with bare fists, yelling, incoherent with rage and terror.

'I'm sorry!' Jilseth reappeared with the same swiftness and laid her unwounded hand on Corrain's arm.

He saw the remorse in her eyes. Before he could protest that he was no child afraid of snuffing his night candle, she stepped back into the wall and took his arm with her into the solid rock. Corrain struggled to pull himself free. For all he achieved, his hand could have been fixed within the rock like one of those ancient ferns sold in Duryea. Worse, Jilseth was dragging him forward with the strength of a team of horses.

He tried to brace himself with his free hand but his arm sank into the wall up to the elbow. His boots skidded on the cave floor before his feet were inexorably drawn into the stone. His chest pressed painfully hard against the rock before it yielded. Now the wall rasped his unshaven cheek, leaving his skin raw. Pain enveloped him. Every breath was agony, as though he had cracked every one of his ribs.

Corrain closed his eyes, futile though the gesture was. Memory overwhelmed him.

Living on Caladhria's shore, riding the high-banked coast road with pastures on one side and salt marshes on the other, most Halferan men had seen a deer caught in a slough of quicksand. There was no better warning for them to take the utmost care if they ever ventured into the trackless maze of salt-thorn thickets and intertwined streams.

When he had been guard captain, Corrain had once led the pursuit of a man who had killed his brother in a fit of drunken rage. Hunting hounds brought from Taw Ricks had tracked the fugitive into the marshes. Corrain had hand-picked his most experienced men to accompany himself and the kennel master.

They found the murderer struggling in the mire. There had been no way to reach him without risking more and innocent lives. Corrain had stood and watched the man slowly being sucked deeper and deeper so that he could bear witness to Lord Halferan that Talagrin had administered such justice rather than Raeponin's assize and the gallows. He hadn't spoken a word, ignoring the man's piteous cries before the slickness finally closed over his head. There had been no point in offering hope where there was none to be had.

While he had felt no remorse, Corrain had dreamed more than once of such a death in the season that followed. He had woken amid sweat-soaked sheets, struggling against the burden of the mud clinging to every limb. He had tasted the harshness of salt water and sand filling his eyes and nose. He gasped with relief to find that he was free of the choking mud sliding into his mouth and down his throat, stifling every breath—

He was standing in a passage, little different from the cave they had left but for the torchlight beyond the curve of the walls and the promise of freedom in the draft.

Jilseth turned her face towards it. 'I cannot tell how they are keeping the air fresh so deep underground.'

'Have you any idea of the torment you just inflicted on this man?' a woman asked, incredulous.

'Worse than being left alone in the darkness with no way out?' Jilseth retorted, clearly startled.

Corrain opened his eyes. 'Aritane?'

The blonde woman looked at him warily. 'How do you know my name?'

Corrain blinked in the dim light. Now he doubted his own eyes. This woman was tall and while he thought he recognised her twilight blue eyes and her features, her blonde hair had been cropped shorter than the stubble on his own chin. Then he looked a third time. 'It is you.'

'My name is Aritane,' she confirmed guardedly. 'Now come with me. *Sheltya* have granted you an audience.'

However different she looked, her voice convinced Corrain. 'What have you told them? What have they said?'

She looked down at his hand on her grey sleeve, momentarily disbelieving. An instant later, Corrain found his hand hanging by his side with no memory of having released her.

'You are a lowlander so ignorant of our customs. Know that it is forbidden to lay hands upon any *sheltya*.' Though she didn't raise her voice, her rebuke was implacable.

'Don't you know him?' Jilseth raised both hands, beseeching. Corrain noticed that the mageflame no longer burned at her fingertip. 'Don't you remember me? We met in Suthyfer?'

The shaven headed woman frowned, curious. 'Where is Suthyfer?'

'Death or worse.' Now Corrain realised what that meant.

Aritane looked concerned. 'You need not fear execution of body or mind for merely trespassing in the high peaks. Account for yourselves honestly and openly and you will be sent on your way unharmed.'

'On our way?' Corrain stared at her.

Aritane didn't seem to notice anything amiss. 'Follow me.'

As the Mountain woman walked away Corrain glanced at Jilseth. 'Do you want to try some other way to escape? I don't think that would be wise.'

'No,' she agreed tersely. 'In any case, I came to see these *sheltya*.'

Not to rescue him. Corrain told himself he shouldn't have expected it, even as her words cut him to the marrow.

As he gestured for her to take the lead, his hand strayed to his hip but there was no reassuring weight of a blade there.

The passage curved steadily without forking or offering any opening into another cavern. Bracketed torches burned without smoke or flickering.

'Do you know which way we're going?' he asked Jilseth, low voiced.

'Upwards and eastwards,' she murmured, 'however that may help us.'

As Corrain was forced to acknowledge the truth of that, the passageway took an abrupt turn and broadened into a vast cave. High above, the roof was lost in darkness while torches shone against glistening walls of pale stone which seemed to have flowed like water before freezing into rippling draperies and hanging fringes.

A double handful of figures in hooded grey robes stood in a loose circle in the centre of the unfurnished cave. Jilseth halted and Corrain stopped a pace behind her. Aritane, or the woman who had once been Aritane, retreated, to stand at the entrance with her head bowed.

'Good day to you.' Jilseth inclined her head as courteously as any baron addressing the Caladhrian parliament. 'Do I have the honour of addressing your council?'

'Lowlander customs and titles have no place here.' The speaker put back his hood to reveal a shaven head and those eerily darkened eyelids.

Corrain recognised that sardonic contempt. He wondered how to warn Jilseth without drawing the bastard's attention.

A second man tugged at his hood, letting it fall to his shoulders. 'For your current purposes, you may think of us as you would Hadrumal's most eminent mages.'

He didn't look particularly eminent to Corrain; small boned and short even for a Mountain Man, his white hair worn away by age to a few wisps around his ears while one hand hung slack by his side, gently shaking with some palsy.

His voice was calm and confident though and Corrain recognised him for the man who had assured him the cave prison was real.

Did these hoods conceal the other adepts who had riffled through his memories? Who had scoured Aritane's head clean of all that had made her the woman she had once been?

Too late, he remembered how little scruple these people showed when it came to intruding on someone else's thoughts.

A woman lowered her hood to stare critically at him. 'We do not use true magic for our own amusement.'

'Please.' Jilseth raised her hand. 'Time is of the essence. The wizards of Hadrumal are beset by Solura's wizards and adepts from three Houses of Sanctuary. If we don't surrender a store of ensorcelled artefacts, they will strip away our defences and leave us open to attack by countless mercenaries and Archipelagan swordsmen.'

'We have counted the Jagai ships.' Torchlight struck the white-gold sheen of stubble on the woman's head.

'Then you know what we face.' Jilseth looked her in the eye. 'Do you understand what is at stake? Generations of wizardly lore will be lost or stolen away if you do not help us withstand these aetheric assaults so we can defend ourselves.'

'There can be no question of their own adepts defying Soluran Artifice,' the old man declared with absolute certainty,

Corrain saw his gaze shift towards the great cave's entrance. There could be no doubt that these *sheltya* had stripped every last scrap of knowledge about aetheric magic in Suthyfer and Col from Aritane's memory.

Another woman lowered her hood to speak; so thin-faced that her darkened eyes looked like a skull's empty sockets. She was of an age to be Aritane's mother though Corrain recalled that *sheltya* vows forbade them children.

'What is that to us?' Her question was genuine, not rhetorical flourish, though her tone clearly assumed there could be no sufficient answer.

'You fear the loss of your lore.' The first man sneered at Jilseth. 'True knowledge cannot be destroyed and it's of no concern to us if your charlatans' secrets are mislaid.'

She ignored him in favour of addressing the older woman. 'A blade is neither good nor evil. Such judgements only apply when such a tool is used. A knife can slit an innocent's throat or save a man's life in the wilderness. So it is with knowledge, such as Trydek's magic.'

Corrain recognised the first Archmage's name. Now he wanted to know why these *sheltya* now stood as still as the stone icicles on the walls, even those still hidden beneath their concealing hoods.

The tense silence lengthened. The old man spoke first.

'Will you let us read your thoughts and memories? Then we may fully understand the peril which you face and what Hadrumal's fall might mean for these mountains.'

He sounded so matter-of-fact that he might have been asking her to pass him a chapbook to read with his ale in some tavern.

Corrain saw Jilseth's unease but her trepidation didn't convince him that she truly understood the violation she was being asked to endure. Before he could speak, the hostile man shook his head, mocking.

'You ask for our help and yet you will not trust us. Very well, keep your secrets. They are of no interest to us.'

He glanced from side to side and the two women nodded. The elder lifted her hood to shroud her face again.

Corrain saw Jilseth's eyes narrow. She folded her hands behind her back, squaring her shoulders.

'Search my mind if you must.'

Only Corrain could see how tightly she interlaced her fingers, deliberately pressing on those seared wounds. Why inflict such pain on herself?

Before he could find a reason, she collapsed. Corrain sprang forward. Even so, he was barely in time to save her from a bruising fall onto the stone floor. As he hugged her to his chest, she hung in his arms, dead weight.

At least she was still breathing. Corrain lowered her to the floor. Straightening her sprawling legs, he looked up at the *sheltya*. 'What—?'

Jilseth rolled onto her side. She hadn't recovered her wits; her eyes were still tightly closed. Her back arched and her arms tensed, hands clawed. Tremors racked her from head to toe.

Corrain recalled an old guardsman, Brish, from Fitrel's days as sergeant, who'd fallen off his horse and cracked his skull, so the apothecary had said. He'd seemed to recover, until the seizures had started, before an apoplexy had finally killed him.

Jilseth's head drummed on the cave's floor. Corrain saw blood smear her cheek as the unforgiving stone scraped her ear raw. He tore off his jerkin to force the cloth beneath her head.

'What are you doing?' he shouted at the *sheltya*.

'She invited us into her thoughts. The more she fights against us, the more she will suffer.'

The barely veiled satisfaction in the sardonic man's words made Corrain want to punch the swine's teeth out through the back of his head. But he would have to leave Jilseth to do that and still more brutal convulsions were now wracking her. He was struggling to keep his jerkin cushioning her head.

'She cannot help but resist us.' The old man shook his head regretfully.

'These charlatans always panic when they are cut off from their sorcery,' the sardonic man said smugly.

One of the hooded figures said something sharp in the Mountain tongue. Another faceless grey-robed figure answered. If Corrain couldn't understand what they said, he could at least hear their consternation.

Jilseth was whimpering, her lips bloodied. Had she bitten her tongue? Corrain recalled bitter argument in the barrack hall over forcing a spoon into Brish's mouth to stop him choking on his tongue. The poor bastard had broken four teeth on the cursed thing.

Corrain seized Jilseth's shoulders and forced her forwards as a spasm threw her onto her back. He could at least keep her face down to stop her drowning in her own blood.

Her arms and legs thrashed wildly. He would never have believed that such a slightly built woman could prove so strong. She could have no sense of what she was doing, he was sure of that. Her out-flung hand smacked so hard against the floor that Corrain was sure he heard a bone crack.

The *sheltya* stood in their loose circle, conversing in their incomprehensible tongue. Corrain guessed that some argument was developing but Jilseth's whimpers rose to a thin keening, so despairing that hair rose like hackles on his neck.

He gathered her to him in a crushing embrace. If she was lost in some *sheltya* wrought nightmare, perhaps in some way beyond conscious thought, she might feel that reassurance. Hadn't Hosh, when the boy had so nearly died of that fever?

'Enough!'

As the old man spoke, Jilseth went limp. Corrain laid her gently down on his jerkin and rolled her head to one side to save her from choking on bloody drool.

'You are free to go.'

He looked at the golden-haired *sheltya* woman.

'We have debated your fate and conclude that you and your people are of no interest to the mountains.' The man who had been so hostile lifted up his hood to hide his face.

'You may leave this place and she may go on her way when she has returned to her senses. We will not help Hadrumal's wizards.' The *sheltya* woman raised her hood.

Now only the old man with the palsied hand remained with his head uncovered.

'You think I would leave her here?' Corrain didn't care if this old man was the least deserving of his anger.

'No,' the old man said calmly.

Corrain carefully withdrew his jerkin from beneath Jilseth's head and put it on. After a moment's consideration, he squatted and lifted her up. Draping her over one shoulder like a sack of grain wasn't overly dignified but he didn't know how far they might have to go to find shelter.

'Are you casting us out into the wilderness without any gear?' he challenged the old man. 'Can you convince yourselves that's not murder if you don't see our blood on your hands?'

None of the hooded figures reacted. After a long moment, the old man, nodded. 'Wait on the mountainside and I will bring your gear.'

'Which way do we go?' Corrain was in no mood to be put to any tests.

The old man gestured. 'That way.'

Corrain nodded. That could suffice for a farewell because nothing would induce him to thank these callous bastards.

The old man smiled. 'Among the Mountain Men, the insult you should use is "son of his own grandfather."'

Corrain had no answer for that, so he hefted Jilseth more securely onto his shoulder, turned around and left the cavern.

The old man had indicated that he should follow his sword hand. Surely there was no reason for him to lie. Corrain walked steadily onwards, refusing to consider any possibility that he might be heading deeper into this barren labyrinth.

Soon fluttering torch flames and a steadily growing draft of fresh air rewarded him. Rounding two more turns, he saw a jagged cave mouth framing pale blue sky.

Dawn or dusk? Corrain realised he had no idea. Emerging into the thin sunshine, he drew a deep breath of shuddering relief. In the next moment, he shivered uncontrollably. Hastily laying Jilseth down on the dull turf, he buttoned his jerkin and looked around.

They were indeed on a mountainside and nowhere that he recognised. Granted, Corrain knew nothing of the White River's valley above Wrede but the vista ahead looked very different from anything he'd seen on his hike with Aritane. Here the land fell away towards endless trees reaching to the horizon. Where had these *sheltya* taken him?

Could this be the upper region of the Great Forest, on the far side of the broad gap in the mountains where the town of Grynth guarded against any incursions from the Mountain Men living above that region of broken fells and lakes? Corrain had no idea.

First things first and one thing at a time. That's what Fitrel had taught him. Was it morning or evening? That would determine how far he could travel. Once Jilseth recovered her wits, he could hope that her wizardry would carry them to Halferan or more likely to Hadrumal. Meantime, he was certain that the magewoman would want to get as many leagues as possible away from these cursed *sheltya*.

Corrain frowned. It made no sense for the sun to be there.

'You stand on the northward face of the Gidestan peaks,' the old man said placidly.

He turned to see the old *sheltya* in the cave entrance with a blanket-wrapped bundle at his feet. Though neither hilt nor scabbard was visible, the solid length thrust through the middle must surely be his sword. That was a relief, even if he only used it to split firewood.

Corrain contemplated the peak rising up beyond the old *sheltya*. It was easily the height of any of those which he had seen walking with Aritane. Though this mountain stood alone; an outlier separated from the saw-edged range further south by some land he couldn't see.

Whether that rocky shoulder beyond the cave mouth hid a gentle slope down to an accommodating plain or some precipitous drop into murderous ravines made no difference. Corrain couldn't see any hint of a pass through those deadly heights beyond.

'Which is closer? The break in the mountains above Inglis or the Ensaimin lake lands?' He might at least have a direction to walk in while he waited for Jilseth to recover.

'Ushal Tena, the route to Inglis, is two hundred or so leagues eastward. Sekmor Tena, the route to the lakes, is perhaps three hundred leagues westward.'

The old man smiled, though not with the malicious satisfaction Corrain would have expected from his shaven-headed colleagues. The old man seemed pleased, like some kindly grandsire.

'There is a pass closer but you should not risk it at this season, not with such scant gear. It is for summer travel only. Winter chokes it with snow.'

'Good to know.' Corrain wondered how best to carry that bundle as well as Jilseth.

The old man angled his head. 'What do you know of Gidesta?'

'Nothing,' Corrain said curtly. 'As you surely know since you've emptied out my mind as thoroughly as a drunkard's purse.'

'A worthy thrust, swordsman.' The old man was amiably amused. 'Forgive me; it is our custom to teach the young through asking questions. The first step to knowledge is acknowledging ignorance.'

Corrain had no interest in debating scholarly philosophies with the day already half gone. He decided his best approach was to sling Jilseth over his shoulder and then bend his knees little by little until he could pick up the bundle with his free hand.

He scooped up the magewoman and settled her securely before advancing towards the cave mouth and gingerly lowering himself.

'I will walk with you.' The old man picked up the rope-swathed blanket. 'This way.'

He followed a dusty scrape in the frost-bleached turf. 'If you were to head north, you would find any number of streams cutting through those trees.' He nodded towards the boundless wilderness. 'They gather into lakes and rivers cutting through marsh and frozen wastes to join the mightiest of all rivers heading eastwards to the ocean. I do not even know if that river has a name in your tongue.'

Corrain concentrated on his footing as the path grew

steeper. A broken leg or even a sprained ankle could be the death of him and Jilseth.

'We are wise to be content with our land,' the old man continued, reflective. 'Once, long ages ago, there were those who would have used true magic, which you call Artifice, to make that vast plain lush and fertile instead of sodden and sour. Their price was having all others agree to bow their heads and yield to their rule.'

The old man halted, forcing Corrain to stop as well.

'If the people ever tired of that rule, if it turned to tyranny, there could be no undoing that bargain. Not without annulling enchantments which their children's lives relied on. Moreover such disruption coursing through the aether would have unleashed unexpected destruction on every adept beyond the mountains, just as sustaining such selfish magic would have deprived them of all but the most basic enchantments to heal and help their own people.'

The old looked around, his faded eyes reflective.

'Only *sheltya* could stop this madness and so we did. Our many-times grandfathers and foremothers gathered in this solitary place to oppose those who were so arrogant in their magic. In your tongue, this mountain would be called the Peak of Defiance. Our price was committing *sheltya* to vows forbidding the use of true magic to secure personal power or kinsfolk's gain. To guard and guide our own people in perpetuity while guarding ourselves against any urge to interfere in affairs beyond our mountains.'

Corrain held out his empty hand for the bundle, his other arm tight around Jilseth's thighs to stop her sliding off his shoulder. 'I have heard Caladhria's barons' arguments in favour of minding their own mutton. Such high-minded principles left my home undefended and innocent people murdered or enslaved. But you know that full well.'

'I know that your efforts only led to still more upheaval.' The aged *sheltya* made no effort to hand over the vital gear. He pointed instead to a long slope covered with frost shattered rocks. 'You are like a man running for his life across such a scree hoping to escape the calamity which you caused with your own incautious scrambling.'

'What's the alternative?' Corrain challenged him. 'Lie down to be crushed? Besides, the safest-looking ground can shift beneath your feet despite your best efforts to find a solid path. I may not know mountains but I know marshes. I also know to make the most of the daylight so I'll be on my way.'

'True.' The old man smiled amiably. 'May I heal your friend's hand before you leave?'

Corrain considered the offer. Doubtless Jilseth would prefer to answer for herself but if they were out in these woods for a few days, such deep wounds could get infected, even in the depths of winter. Without anyone but him to help her, she might lose her arm entirely and this old man seemed more agreeable than any other Mountain Artificer.

'Please,' he said cautiously. 'Thank you.'

The old man moved to his side and Corrain guessed that he was taking Jilseth's hand. With her head and arms dangling down his back, he couldn't really tell.

The old man murmured softly before returning to the Tormalin tongue. 'There will be scars. This a wizard-wrought wound and that is the antithesis of my own magic.'

Corrain wasn't sure what that meant so settled for asking a question of his own. He shuffled around in order to look the old man in the eye.

'What would you have done with me if the magewoman hadn't come? If no one had come in search of me?'

The old *sheltya* smiled. 'She did come so we will never know. May I heal you before you leave?'

'I have no injuries to speak of.' Corrain's torn fingernails and other grazes were scabbed and dry.

The old man looked quizzically at him. 'I have seen your nightmares. Would you like to be free of such shame and sorrow? *Sheltya* can heal the mind as well as the body.'

Corrain stared at him. All he could think of was Aritane's vacant eyes, her mind emptied of every memory of her years beyond these mountains. What had these merciless adepts done to her?

'That is not for you to know. Her journey is her own.' The old man sighed. 'It was her own choice, to be freed of her burdens of guilt and regret.'

'Is that what happened to her brother?' Corrain wondered.

'That is not for you to know.' The old man's face hardened. 'You are not kin by blood or marriage.'

If Corrain hadn't had Jilseth's weight bearing down on one shoulder, he would have shrugged, dismissive. He settled for holding his hand out. 'If this is as far as you're coming, I'll take our gear.'

The old man handed over the bundle. 'I am Cullam. When you feel that you deserve such healing, tell Lady Guinalle my name. She will not be able to find Aritane's thoughts but I will hear her if she seeks her lost friend. Meantime, you could talk to Hosh. He has wisdom born of humility.'

Before Corrain could ask what he meant by that, the aged *sheltya* vanished.

Corrain drew another deep breath and tried to decide if he was more relieved or more anxious. Resisting a powerful urge to try shaking Jilseth awake, he continued picking his way down the desolate slope towards the uncertain shelter of the closest coppices.

He would head westward, skirting the edge of those sparse woodlands until he must use the last of the daylight to make some sort of camp. If Jilseth hadn't woken by then. If he hadn't walked far enough to escape whatever Artifice was stopping Hadrumal's wizards or Suthyfer's adepts from finding them. If no one was looking for him, Corrain was sure they must be searching for the magewoman.

— CHAPTER THIRTY-FOUR —

Gidesta

14th of For-Spring

JILSETH OPENED HER eyes to darkness. She was still trapped underground. Had the treacherous *sheltya* confined her in the same cavern as Corrain? But they had seen her use wizardry to escape. Had they woven an enchantment to bar her from her affinity? Was this some aetheric prison akin to Micaran's library?

These thoughts coursed through her mind in the blink of an eye. Before paralysing dread could follow, her wizardry sensed cold earth beneath the blanket where she lay. She heard the rustle of the chill wind among the dull brown leaves still clinging to the wintry twigs. A small pond close by was covered with a thick layer of ice and the barest spark of elemental fire sustained the frogs and many-legged creatures buried deep in the mud to wait out the deathly cold.

Now she could see the Greater Moon high above the trees, a day past the full, while the Lesser's quarter gleamed beyond a scatter of stars. Jilseth drew a shuddering breath at this reprieve and thrust out a hand to raise herself up. Too late she remembered her burns.

In the next instant, she realised that her hand was healed. Long healed. Frantic, she sat up and traced the numb, puckered scars with her fingers. How long had she been held captive if the moons had traced their different paths around the heavens to return to the same places where she'd last seen them in Col?

She tried desperately to bring the pages of an almanac to mind. Such concentration was impossible. What disasters had overtaken Hadrumal since she had so miserably failed the Archmage?

'You're awake?'

She heard Corrain's voice and she sensed his body's warmth, feeling the subtle resonance of his approaching footsteps as well as the shift in the breeze circling this dry hollow.

'What day is it?' Jilseth would have got to her feet but she was so vilely light-headed that she stayed huddled on the blanket. She ached in every limb and not just from the penetrating cold. 'Where are we?'

'It's the evening of the same day when you came to find me and we're barely a couple of leagues from the *sheltya* mountain.'

'The same day?' She stared at him, disbelieving.

He dropped an armful of firewood in a hole dug in the turf and neatly ringed with stones. 'You lose all sense of time while they're turning your mind inside out.'

Jilseth shook her head stubbornly, holding up her hand. 'No—'

'That healing was a parting gift from the old man. That's all we're leaving with, beyond blankets, my sword and belt-knife and the remnants of the food and overnighting gear which Aritane and I carried,' Corrain said grimly. 'We're beyond the north slope of the Gidestan mountains, so if you can't use your magic to help us, it'll be midsummer before we get home.'

'There's no fear of that.' Though Jilseth found the thought of returning to Hadrumal, to tell Planir that these *sheltya* would not help them, truly appalling.

Was there any possibility that Lady Guinalle's ancient Artifice and Col's half-trained adepts could stave off the disaster threatening wizardry?

'We have no time to waste.' She tried to stand up but dizziness overwhelmed her.

Corrain caught her elbow to steady her, offering rough comfort. 'It will be a day or so before you're fully yourself.'

'Thank you,' Jilseth said shortly.

She was selfishly thankful to know that he had been subjected to the same aetheric intrusion. It was still more of a relief to see that he was as unwilling to discuss whatever he had endured as she was to revisit her own experiences. Doubtless wizards in Hadrumal would ask her thoughtlessly curious questions but Jilseth had no intention of answering, even if she could.

Whatever had happened since she had come north was a pain-filled blur of confused recollection seemingly drawn from scattered remembrance of her earliest childhood through to the crystal-clear memory of Planir destroying the ensorcelled ring. Trying to focus her thoughts on anything beyond that prompted renewed fear that she would faint, this time with an ominous threat of nausea.

Jilseth thrust the swirling confusion away, concentrating instead on the rich, moist earth beneath her feet. The sense of the vast mountain range so close by swiftly steadied her, in body and affinity alike. She turned to the south.

'We must go.'

She reached for the highest peaks and searched beneath the snows for those knife-edged ridges where the spring sunshine would soon divide the melt-waters. Trickles would join rivulets and they would mingle in foaming cascades tumbling down these mountainsides to join the streams cutting northwards through the wasteland, to blend with a formidable river running to the ocean.

Jilseth followed the waters on the far side of that high divide. Myriad shallow scores undulated across the hard rock. They deepened to carve grooves beneath the ice, guiding the waters ever downward. Some torrents travelled safely through gorges and ravines, others tumbled over abrupt cliffs. By whatever route, brooks and rills found their way to more forgiving slopes dotted with scrub and brush. Soon spindly trees secured a foothold in sheltered gullies. Before long, taller thickets gathered together in broad swathes of woodland. The first hints of axe and fire marked the presence of hunters and trappers.

There was no time to be seduced by the tantalizing traces of ores and rare earths. Jilseth followed the waters to the sea and traced the currents southward. The rock deep beneath the seabed grew ever more familiar, bolstering her confidence even as her misgivings grew over Hadrumal's fate.

Whatever had happened, there was nothing to be gained by delay. She reached for Corrain's hand and white magelight enveloped them.

Before the magic faded, cacophony surrounded them. Doors to wizardly apartments stood ajar, arguing voices within. Magelight made a lantern of the tall windows of Trydek's hall. She looked up to the Archmage's sitting room to see those shutters closed tight, no hint of lamp or candle within.

Corrain angrily shook his arm free. 'You didn't give me a chance to fetch my sword!'

'You hardly need it here,' she protested.

'No?' he retorted. 'With Aldabreshin galleys full of mercenaries hull down on the horizon? Where is Hadrumal's armoury?'

Jilseth had no answer to that so she moved to intercept a hurrying apprentice. 'Where is the Archmage?'

He looked at her as though that was the most foolish question asked on this island since Trydek had built that tower looming darkly over them. 'In the Council Chamber.'

Had the island's most eminent mages been closeted in there all day? What had the prentice and pupil wizards made of that? Had the halls' elders and teachers kept order or had they been too distracted and dismayed by the island's defences' undoing? How many had fought to repair those protections only to suffer aetheric assault?

What fervid speculation was sweeping through the high road's wine shops, drapers and bookbinders to unnerve the island's mundane populace? What of the merchants and artisans in the outlying quarters? Had anyone warned them to gather their families, taking only what they could carry before heading inland to beg sanctuary among the island's villages and farms? How long would that save them once the mercenaries and Archipelagans swarmed ashore? Jilseth didn't bother asking this shivering apprentice any such unanswerable questions.

'Thank you. Corrain—?'

'Lead the way.'

She cut across the courtyard and through the alley leading to the square around the ancient chamber. She only wondered how they might gain entrance as she approached the open archway at the foot of the barrel-vaulted staircase.

'We have to wait until Planir emerges,' she realised aloud. 'The Council will have warded the chamber's door against intrusion.'

Corrain was already taking the flight of steps two at a time. Jilseth hurried after him and found the Caladhrian guardsman contemplating the ensorcelled metal veiling the Council chamber's entrance. Before she could begin to explain its intricacies, Corrain drew his belt-knife and hammered on the barrier with the pommel.

Jilseth felt the stir of flowing wizardry. The featureless metal shaped itself into a face. Black pits in eyes of shimmering quicksilver fixed first on Corrain before looking at her.

'How did you know to do that?' she demanded.

The Caladhrian looked at her, exasperated. 'All I know is that only a fool locks himself behind a door without a knocker or a bell pull.'

Jilseth watched the ensorcelled face melting away as the magical metal returned to serve as the doors' everyday hinges and bindings. She wondered if anyone in Hadrumal, mage or mundane born, would have thought to do something so straight-forward as knocking.

The doors opened. The Council chamber was more crowded with wizards than she had ever seen it. Men and women, from those newly called to teach in Hadrumal's halls through to the most venerable, stood three deep around the circular floor. Those with officially sanctioned seats had no choice but to stand if they wished to be seen or heard.

The last echoes of furious debate faded in the high vault. Every face turned to the door, expectant.

Planir stood on the central dais, gaunt and grey-faced with exhaustion. 'What news from the *sheltya*?'

'They will not help us, Archmage.' Jilseth could only tell the truth.

Countless voices cried out; some despairing, some accusing. As many looked towards her and Corrain as looked towards the Archmage. As many again turned on each other to continue some interrupted argument.

Jilseth was fervently grateful that the chamber's ancient wizardry permitted no magic. With emotions running so high, the perils of unguarded spells must be unprecedented.

'We must sink the Jagai galleys!'

Jilseth didn't see who shouted. Planir had. He spun around to thrust an accusing finger at the belligerent speaker. His voice was hoarse and ragged.

'You wish to make eternal enemies of every Archipelagan? For the present, they can tell themselves we only attacked another wizard while the corsairs had already put themselves beyond all protection of Aldabreshi law with their use of magical artefacts.'

'We can give the Solurans what they want,' another mage shouted angrily. 'What use are these cursed artefacts anyway? We cannot fathom their secrets and they have brought us nothing but grief.'

'Do you think the Solurans will be satisfied with these trinkets?' Cloud Master Rafrid roared. 'If we prove ourselves so craven?'

Other wizards shouted out in support.

'They will menace us until we surrender quintessential magic's secrets.'

'They will threaten us with whatever malice they find in those cursed artefacts!'

'The Tormalin Emperor—' Hearth Master Kalion began.

'The Tormalin will make as many demands as the Solurans before they help us,' a voice prophesied savagely. 'We will be beholden to the Imperial Throne for generations!'

'Then what do you suggest?' another voice demanded, dangerously close to panic.

Planir shrugged. 'You can leave before the mercenaries arrive. You have the magic to do so.'

'Where should we go?'

Jilseth tried to see who had just cried out, shamefully eager to flee to some sanctioned haven.

'Suthyfer?' Planir looked around the crowded chamber and the competing voices fell silent.

'There is Suthyfer,' he repeated, reflective, 'where we might hope those mages who survive this debacle will contemplate the lessons which we seem to have so signally failed to learn in our complacency.'

His face hardened as he surveyed the assembled mages. 'Let us hope that Suthyfer's mages will appreciate the need for wizardry to look towards the mainland unless they want to find themselves as friendless as we have in time of need, when our only hope of help is from those who would exploit us as mercilessly as our enemies.'

He shook his head. The silence in the great chamber was absolute.

'If the mageborn do not prove themselves worthy of respect, how can we demand it? If the mageborn hold themselves aloof, cloaked in secrecy, the mundane remain at the mercy of the fear-filled rumours and confusion which these Soluran Artificers have so cunningly exploited.'

'We cannot leave our hall and libraries to be looted and burned,' a voice pleaded. 'Such knowledge cannot be lost—'

Planir rounded on him, scathing. 'Let us hope that Suthyfer's mages are wise enough to see how the blinkered pursuit of knowledge to the exclusion of all else can leave wizardry fatally ill-prepared to deal with the low cunning of those, mageborn or mundane, who look on their power with greedy eyes or simple ill-will.'

The Archmage laughed harshly and without humour.

'At least we can be confident that Suthyfer's mages won't be so foolish and so arrogant as to discount Artifice merely because they cannot themselves understand it. One lesson we have assuredly learned from the Solurans is how powerful such co-operation can be. It's a shame such realisation comes so late for Hadrumal. Perhaps we would have found some other way out of this maze if we hadn't been so riven by our divisions, so focused on our individual ambitions.'

Planir's condemnation prompted murmurs of protest and abasement in equal measure. Then Troanna's voice rose above the uncomfortable shuffling, wholly unchastened.

'Perhaps we wouldn't find ourselves so hopelessly stymied if you had acted sooner, Archmage.'

The crowd rippled and parted to reveal the Flood Mistress.

'If I had acted sooner?' Planir queried acidly. 'When this Council has proved wholly unable to reach any consensus over what action to take? When a seat in this chamber only seems to confer the right to criticise and to condemn whatever I might do without ever shouldering some share in the weight of responsibility which I bear as Archmage. When a mage actually chooses to take his, or her, seat in our debates,' he added bitterly.

'Enough!'

Corrain's bellow deafened Jilseth. Astonishment silenced the roomful of wizards.

'You have magic to take yourselves away to safety.' The Caladhrian glowered at the assembled mages. 'Who among you will use your spells to save the ordinary folk who keep you living so comfortably; cooking your meals and washing your linen and raising this island's beasts and crops?'

Jilseth saw a good number of indignant faces about to protest. It was some comfort to see that a good sprinkling of her peers had looked beyond their own immediate concerns. Though far too many mages clearly realised that they hadn't given Hadrumal's humble folk any thought until now.

'I reminded those who wish to leave that they have the magic to do so. I said nothing of my own intentions. I will be staying,' Planir assured Corrain.

The Archmage turned swiftly enough to rebuke the whispered incredulity behind him. 'If you think that I only cultivate acquaintances among the halls' servants and along the high road's vendors for the sake of garnering gossip, that shows more of your own character than it does of mine. My friends among the island's non-mageborn know they can rely on me.'

'I am glad to hear it,' Cullam said mildly.

Jilseth spun around so fast that she would have fallen over but for Corrain's swiftly outthrust arm. Standing on the landing at the top of the stairs, the old man smiled affably at her.

'After long and hard-fought argument I have convinced my fellow *sheltya* to allow for some possibility of doubt as to overweening wizardly arrogance.' As he surveyed the crowded room his face wrinkled with disappointment. 'Though I see there is only a little doubt.'

'Have you come to offer some help?' Corrain demanded.

'Single-minded as ever, I see,' The old man smiled again. 'A virtue we prize highly in the mountains, most particularly when a traveller refuses to abandon a stricken companion, however long and hard the journey. Though we have also seen the disasters already provoked by your defiant determination. Wondering what you might try next gives some of us considerable cause for contemplation.'

While Jilseth was trying to work out what that meant, the old *sheltya* looked at Planir, his faded eyes cold.

'We will not save you from the consequences of your own follies. We have seen sufficient proof that you brought this disaster down upon your own heads. However we will not allow true magic, which you call Artifice, to be abused in the base pursuit of Soluran wizardly ambition. Moreover we have no desire to see your perilous sorcery threaten our people's peace and that will assuredly happen with renewed warfare between Solura and Mandarkin. Most especially if such strife is bolstered by these spellcrafted devices shared out amongst those greedy for the elemental powers which nature has denied them.'

As he looked at Hadrumal's assembled mages, his head shook. Jilseth wondered if that was a further expression of disappointment or merely a tremor of his palsy.

'We will discipline those in the Houses of Sanctuary who are so shamefully betraying their learning and their vows to their brothers and sisters.'

'How?' a belligerent voice shouted. Jilseth would have sworn it was Despin even if she couldn't pick him out in the crowd.

'We remove all their knowledge of true lore since

they have proved so unworthy of wielding it,' Cullam replied mildly, though Jilseth was close enough to see his eyes were merciless. 'It will be for their elders in lore to decide if they should be told what they have lost and further, if they should be allowed to study to regain such learning and skills.'

Jilseth remembered Aritane's vacant gaze and had to force herself not to shiver. Fortunately everyone's attention was fixed on Cullam as the old *sheltya* continued.

'We will similarly wipe away all unearned and unsought knowledge of this island from the minds of those sailing towards you. While we respect the Sea Peoples' wish to have no dealings with magic, we believe that our higher duty is to right this particular wrong. As for the hired swords and those ashore who are now so suspicious of your sorcery, we will stifle the enchantment spreading and sustaining such malice. Thereafter it is for you to regain their respect and trust.'

This time he definitely shook his head before addressing Planir with an unmistakable air of farewell. 'Good day to you, Archmage.'

'Wait! What about the Soluran mages?' Once again, Jilseth couldn't see who had called out in the crowded chamber.

Cullam looked straight at whoever it had been. 'You wish us to wipe all knowledge of wizardry from your enemies' minds? Why should we favour one side in this quarrel not of our making which so threatens our people's peace? What have you done to deserve such assistance?'

Jilseth saw the crowd of wizards shuffling as those around the speaker retreated from Cullam's penetrating gaze. She was right; it was Despin.

The old *sheltya* paused, reflective. 'There are those among us who would see the wizardly knowledge which enables your attacks expunged from both sides. I have argued against such drastic action since elemental affinities will remain, inborn as such talents are. Innocents will surely suffer if the mageborn among them no longer have the learning to contain and control their magic.'

He looked at Planir. 'Nevertheless, if you are unable to resolve your quarrels with the Soluran Orders, know that we will not permit elemental warfare to ravage our mountains even if that means unleashing unrestrained magic among the lowlanders.'

As the assembled wizards stared, aghast, Despin broke the silence, sneering. 'So you say.'

Cullam raised his white brows in mild surprise. 'You truly require such proof?'

Despin collapsed to the floor, senseless. Every wizard within arm's length of the obnoxious mage fought to retreat as far as they could.

'What—' Jilseth looked back at Cullam only to see the old man had vanished.

'Archmage?' Someone begged Planir for answers.

The Archmage contemplated Despin lying in a graceless sprawl.

'If anyone else doubts Artifice's power in the hands of such advanced adepts, bespeak Usara in Suthyfer. Guinalle Tor Priminale and Temar D'Alsennin can bear witness to its influence in the Old Empire. Talk to those who knew Cloud Master Otrick and ask them what they remember of his last days and his death after aetheric magic tore his wits to pieces.'

Planir's glare challenged Hearth Master Kalion and

Flood Mistress Troanna, who both nodded slowly. Apprehension around the room visibly increased.

The Archmage clapped his hands, startling everyone. 'Go to your halls and work with your most practised nexus. Troanna and Rafrid, instruct your most trusted and powerful pupils to usher the Jagai galleys to some safe harbour. Everyone else, devote your efforts to repairing our island's defences. Otherwise I fear we'll see Solura's wizards arriving in person to steal what they can't force us to surrender. Let's hope we can succeed before the Mountain adepts decide that their own safety requires our obliteration.'

Jilseth retreated from the doorway as the Council members and other mages hurried from the chamber. Watching Planir on the dais, shoulders sagging and his bearded chin on his chest, she feared that the Archmage's weariness now verged on despair.

He was the last to leave. She stepped forward

'What should I do, Archmage?' Jilseth asked urgently. 'None of the mages I'm used to working a nexus with are here.'

Planir rubbed a shaking hand over his face. 'You had better come with me.'

Corrain had pressed himself against the opposite wall to allow the anxious wizards to pass. He nodded at Despin, still lying unconscious on the stone floor. 'What about him?'

Planir gestured and the doors closed, sealing themselves with ensorcelled metal. 'He can stay there. Trydek's magic will save him from hurting himself or anyone else when he wakes. If he wakes.'

The Archmage headed down the stairs without looking back. Jilseth and Corrain followed.

— CHAPTER THIRTY-FIVE —

Trydek's Tower, Hadrumal
14th of For-Spring

THEIR PATH BACK to Planir's refuge was crowded with clamouring mages, pupils and apprentices of all rank. Thankfully everyone stepped aside for the Archmage. Jilseth found herself running to keep pace as she followed in his wake. It was scant consolation to hear Corrain out of breath at her shoulder.

Most of the throng shouted frantic, gabbled questions at the Archmage. A few yelled Jilseth's name. She had no answers for them. One mage she didn't recognise stepped into her path, enraged at being ignored. He reached for her arm, ready to shake a response out of her. Corrain shoved the unknown wizard backwards to stumble and fall over someone's feet.

'Thank you,' she yelled gratefully.

Planir cut through an alleyway back to the quadrangle below his tower. Once again, he ignored the wizards milling around the entrance until one voice rose above the hubbub.

'Archmage!' It was Sannin, with Canfor at her shoulder. Galen was sheltering Ely from the jostling crowd.

'Upstairs.' Planir jerked his head and the tower door opened. As they hurried inside, no other wizards dared enter without the Archmage's invitation.

The door slammed behind Galen. The only sound in the stairwell was harsh breathing as they walked up to the empty sitting room. Planir entered and the shutters opened themselves, admitting the noise from outside. The Archmage scowled and the racket was muted.

'We need an earth mage for our nexus,' Sannin explained. 'Galen—'

Planir waved that away. 'Jilseth?'

'Of course.' She looked at the burly wizard and was appalled at the misery on his broad face.

Sannin snapped her fingers to reclaim her attention. 'Follow my lead.'

Before Jilseth could reply she felt warmth spread through her, from head to toe, as Sannin's fire affinity bonded to her own earth magic. Now she could feel the lingering glow of those ancient fires which had first moulded Hadrumal's rocks.

At Sannin's nod, she turned to look at Ely and felt the fire magewoman curb her own affinity, so antagonistic to water, to allow the innate sympathy of earth to unite with Ely's magic. Jilseth felt the surge of the waters around the island, smoothing reefs and headlands and shaping the drifting sands.

In the instant their three elements were united, Sannin's affinity surged towards Canfor, claiming fire's ready union with elemental air. Jilseth felt the invisible abrasive power of the wind scouring at the stones of the ancient tower.

In the next moment, she felt the scintillating brilliance of quintessential magic. Jilseth resisted the temptation to take command of the nexus. A sapphire shiver though the magic suggested that Canfor was similarly restraining himself.

'We will not permit the Solurans to come here uninvited.' Sannin was adamant.

She swept their quintessential magic outwards from the tower. As Jilseth stood in the sitting room, looking at the other three mages, her wizard senses soared across the island. They yielded to Sannin's lead as the magecraft cut through the air like an arrow, swift and sure. Hadrumal's magical mists lay ahead; not merely a visible barrier to unnerve sailors but a warding where elemental water blended with fire to confine and confound translocation worked by anyone other than an island mage.

Even with her earth affinity, Jilseth could see that the warding hung frayed and thin. Her mage senses showed her antagonistic spells attacking each individual element within the ancient wizardry. Soluran fire sought to sear away the moisture endlessly drawn up from Hadrumal's seas to replenish the warding, while Soluran water as cold as mountain snows swirled and circled to drain away all warmth.

More than that, she felt a stealthier magic woven from the earth, loading the mist with rocky fragments finer than dust. As droplets formed and coalesced, the malicious burden weighed more and more heavily on the already frail air element of the warding.

Sannin wielded the immutable quintessential magic like a diamond blade. Their united strength bolstered her innate sympathy with fire as she severed the scorching Soluran spells to allow Hadrumal's magic to surge up from the seas once again.

'No!' Ely protested, outraged.

The Soluran water magic fastened onto that renewed strength, sucking at it leechlike. The ice-cold malice swelled and coiled, strangling the fire within the warding.

Jilseth felt Ely take control of the nexus, using her water affinity to focus their quintessential strength and cut through those noxious tendrils sucking the heat out of the warding spell.

'If you please.' Sannin took back the nexus to throw up an impenetrable wall as Soluran fire roared into the elemental void left as the water magic flowed away.

They were making progress but no more swiftly or easily than a man climbing an ice-covered slope, slipping back one step for every two he managed to take.

'Jilseth!' Canfor looked across the room to her.

She nodded. Air and earth alike were poised between fire and water. Like her, he could feel these violent oscillations putting ever more strain on this ancient magic devised to work in harmony with the natural world's eternal rhythms.

She reached through the nexus for his affinity, to combine their strengths and re-unite the warding. First she felt the heat and cold of the Soluran magics revive as soon as the nexus was no longer turned against them. Secondly and more insidious, she felt that subtle earth magic trailing after her, drawn like iron filings to a compass needle. Even so slight an imbalance redoubled the antagonism between air and earth. It took all Jilseth's strength and skill to stop her affinity tearing free of Canfor's and she could feel him fighting just as fiercely.

'Stop.'

Sannin dissolved the nexus so abruptly that they were left gasping.

'What happened?' Planir demanded.

'The Solurans cannot use quintessential magic but they have devised some interesting ways of harrying it,' Sannin said grimly.

'We can sustain the warding,' Ely protested.

Canfor nodded. 'And renew it, little by little.'

'Only as long as our strength holds out.' Jilseth wasn't looking to triumph over either of the others. She was merely stating the bitterly regrettable truth.

'We have more wizards than they do,' Galen growled.

'How long will the *sheltya* allow us to tear at each other, stirring elemental turmoil to corrupt the tides and the wind and the rain?' Planir countered.

Ely screamed and Jilseth barely managed to swallow her own startled shriek. The room was full of wizards.

Not Solurans. Jilseth's first instant of terror subsided as she recognised Merenel and Usara of Suthyfer, though the other three were strangers.

'Shiv.' Sannin ran to embrace the tallest of the newcomers, a sallow man with long black hair drawn back off his face.

Shivvalan. One of the two mages who'd founded the Suthyfer Hall.

'Lady D'Alsennin.' Planir bowed to the unassuming young woman in the same sort of workaday Tormalin garb which Guinalle Tor Priminale wore.

'Just Allin, Archmage, please.' She blushed rosily before turning to her companion, a bright-eyed youth. 'May I make known to you Corristal Austorn, the first of Suthyfer's mageborn to advance from apprentice to pupil?'

'Your affinity is with the air?' Planir stepped forward to shake his hand.

'It is, Archmage.' Even in those few words, his Dalasorian accent was apparent.

Jilseth noted Canfor looking at the youth with measured reservation.

'You are very welcome.' Planir turned to Usara, 'though we are somewhat preoccupied,' he added drily.

Usara wasn't amused. 'So was I, when I had half a hundred mages trying to bespeak me to ask about Mountain Artifice. Then I saw what was happening to Hadrumal.'

'What can Suthyfer offer to help? Sannin demanded.

'Additive magic,' Shiv said promptly. 'You need to utterly disrupt each Soluran spell, not just drive it off. You'll only achieve that through the union of mages with a common affinity.'

'A moment, please.' Jilseth was alarmed. 'Didn't the Mandarkin use additive magic?'

Helplessly enmeshed in Planir's fourfold nexus, she had seen the renegade Anskal ruthlessly battening onto his enslaved apprentices, drawing all their power into his own wizardry, only stopping when they fell dead at his feet.

Shivvalan looked at her. 'He did, but we have perfected its use through co-operation not compulsion.'

'A knife can slit an innocent's throat or save a man's life in the wilderness.' Corrain spoke from the corner where he was standing, disregarded.

Jilseth narrowed her eyes at him. Why were those words so familiar? She couldn't recall, though she couldn't deny their inconvenient truth.

'That's true,' Planir agreed with the Caladhrian. 'But we know the Solurans have additive magic of their own. Can your skills outweigh theirs?'

'We believe so, Archmage,' Allin said earnestly.

'If we can persuade enough of Hadrumal's mages to trust us, and each other.' Usara looked around the room.

Jilseth wouldn't have imagined that his mild eyes could be so penetrating.

'Baron Halferan.' Planir smiled. 'Kindly go downstairs and ask every mage you can see to come up here if they wish to share in Hadrumal's salvation through the use of newly devised wizardry from Suthyfer.'

Corrain considered this. 'They'll ask me what that means.'

Planir shrugged. 'You can't possibly know, so what they have to ask themselves is how urgently they want to save Hadrumal and how much faith they have in their fellow mages.'

Corrain answered with a shrug of his own. 'Let's see.'

As the Caladhrian disappeared down the stairs, Planir challenged the mages in the room. 'Who's willing to be first?'

To Jilseth's surprise, Galen stepped forward to offer Usara his hand. 'For what little use I'll be,' the burly mage said miserably.

'More than you'll know,' Usara assured him as he clasped his wrist.

Galen's eyes widened with surprise.

'Ely?' Shiv offered her his hand. She swallowed hard and took it, exclaiming with astonishment.

As Sannin and Merenel swiftly joined hands with Allin, Jilseth looked at Canfor who was looking askance at the young Dalasorian.

Corristal grinned at him. 'Scared?'

'Cautious,' Canfor snapped as he thrust out his hand.

Now Jilseth realised that Planir was looking at her. She lifted her chin and squared her shoulders and took Galen's other hand.

'Oh!' This was quite unlike blending her elemental strength with those affinities she wasn't born to, balancing their sympathies and antipathies to create quintessential magic.

Jilseth realised that she had never wondered about

other earth mages' affinities. She had assumed their tie to the elemental earth was the same as her own. While she knew full well that some wizards had greater success with some spells than others, she had believed that personal interest and application governed such distinctions within elemental practice. How wrong she had been.

Usara's mage senses were drawn first and foremost to metals; in every state from the rawest ores with barely a pennyweight of crystalline purity in a wagonload of rock through to the finest craftsmanship worked by every sort of smith.

Galen's aptitude lay in understanding the slow processes by which shifting sand and mud became immutable rocks and shales, though at the moment, the stolid wizard's mage senses reeled, as disordered as a man drunk on coarse spirits. Jilseth felt his grip tighten on her fingers as he regained a measure of elemental balance with her on one side and Usara on the other.

Someone took her other hand. She realised it was Planir. Planir the Black as his fellow apprentices had called him when he had arrived, a grimy youth from the coal-hewing valley where he'd been born in Gidesta. Jilseth hadn't thought of that old joke in years. Did that explain why the Archmage's affinity was with living things transmuted into rock through long aeons; trees into coal and diamond, sea-creatures into chalk?

She also sensed that the other three mages were seeing just as clearly into her affinity; into her facility for finding the most infinitesimal traces of minerals. Now Jilseth understood that no amount of study would have led to her mastery of necromancy's secrets without that first quirk of her magebirth.

Before she could pursue that sobering thought, Usara

spoke, his words echoing strangely through her affinity rather than in her ears.

'Let's be rid of these Solurans.'

He led the way just as Sannin had led their frustrated nexus. This time though their united magic travelled through the island's rich dark soil until they reached the shore's rock and gravels. As they reached out for the earthborn spite weighing down the warding, Jilseth felt more and more wizards joining in this unprecedented union. She couldn't tell who they were, links in this chain increasingly far removed from her, but she could feel their strength and the variations in their affinities being added to this new synthesis of wizardry.

It was the work of a moment to strip the furtive dust out of the ancient mists. Whatever its origins; metallic, once-living material or inert mineral, some mage in this elemental communion had the precise affinity to command it. Jilseth and others with similar talents could focus their collective wizardry on the tiniest ensorcelled mote.

Now the assembled mages weighted the dust to make it heavier than lead. It fell out of the air and sank through the water unhindered, plummeting to the sea bed. They didn't let it rest; forcing every last speck into the rocks so far below that Jilseth wondered why she didn't feel the molten heat lurking in the uttermost depths. But she could no more sense elemental fire than water or air.

'Quickly!'

Now Usara was pursuing the dissipating traces of the earthborn wizardry which had carried that dust across land and sea from Solura. With what felt like every earth wizard in Hadrumal behind them, they were easily outstripping the Solurans' frantic attempts to retreat.

What was Usàra going to do now? Apprehension gripped her more tightly than Planir and Galen's strong hands. She could no more pull free of the Suthyfer mage's control that she could have broken either man's hold.

The Soluran wizards fled to their tower, seeking refuge within the elemental strength of the stone walls and the lead-sealed, slate-capped roof. Hadrumal's earth mages shattered such ties with contemptuous ease. More than that, their collective might barred the panicked Solurans from the solace of any further union.

Jilseth winced as she felt those unknown wizards fighting in vain to draw on the elemental earth which had underpinned their affinity ever since their magebirth had manifested. Tears pricked her eyes as their strength failed one by one, their spells flailing, feeble and ineffective.

'Usara!' Planir said sharply.

'I know.' The Suthyfer mage calmly allowed the elemental barriers crushing the Soluran wizards to dissipate.

Jilseth felt her mage senses steadily withdrawing, returning to Hadrumal. That didn't lessen the pain of knowing that those nameless wizards had been left as drained and uncertain as she had been after defending Halferan Manor. Would their magic return as hers had done or were they now condemned to a lifetime of impotent regret, or worse, erratic and uncontrollable demonstrations of the affinity they had once mastered?

Though even as she grieved for their anguish, a dispassionate thought noted that she had poured out her magecraft in saving innocents from undeserved and agonising death. These Solurans had turned their spells on other wizards to find themselves repaid in kind.

The elemental chain broke apart. Jilseth opened her

eyes to see Galen looking thoughtful and unexpectedly hopeful.

'I do believe,' he said cautiously, 'that has helped me.'

Before Jilseth could ask what he meant, the broad-shouldered mage was forcing a path to Ely's side. Planir's sitting room was so crowded that was no easy task even for such a burly man.

Still more mages were lining the stairs and voices in the courtyard below were exclaiming in wonder and triumph. Jilseth wondered how many of Hadrumal's wizards had thrown their different strengths into this last defence.

'It seems that very few of our colleagues were prepared to defy Baron Corrain, even without a sword in his hand.' Planir was amused.

Jilseth didn't feel like smiling as she watched the Suthyfer mages gather by the fireplace, heads close together as they conferred. There didn't seem to be any question that they had succeeded. Merenel and Sannin were congratulating each other while Canfor was looking as thoughtful as Jilseth herself.

She turned to the Archmage. 'So we have proved that we can defeat their attacks on our wardings and further, we can belabour their individual mages with our collective strength until their affinity is exhausted. We still have the artefacts they covet and we still refuse to share the quintessential magic which they lust after. How long before these Orders or some other Soluran wizards devise some new means to attack us, outright or through some new proxy? Will we retaliate with some still more deadly magic? How soon before wizardry destroys itself entirely, saving the *sheltya* the trouble?'

Planir's smile turned rueful. 'Those are good questions.

So few solutions ever turn out to be as final or decisive as those relying on such bold strokes believe. We need only look at Baron Corrain's misadventures to see that.

'Let's hope we have sufficient respite to find the answers. But first,' he said, heartfelt, 'let's find some wine. Perhaps that will inspire us as we plan our next move.

'What?' he challenged Jilseth. 'Surely you're not one of those who believe that I have some overarching masterful plan for every eventuality? I merely do the best I can as events unfold.'

'What do you think will happen next?' she demanded.

Planir looked thoughtful. 'I believe we will have to take the initiative, though that's always a risk when dealing with wizards, especially those so accustomed to conflict.'

As confronting Anskal had proved so calamitously, Jilseth thought with a sinking heart.

— CHAPTER THIRTY-SIX —

Halferan Manor, Caladhria
27th of For-Spring

As a new bride, Zurenne reflected, she had cherished hopes of welcoming Caladhria's greatest lords to the manor as guests and friends. Now she had seen Hadrumal's Archmage, an Aldabreshin warlord's wives, Tormalin nobles and visitors from distant Solura under her roof within a year. If the price hadn't been her beloved husband's death, she might have felt honoured. As it was, she simply longed for tranquillity so she could secure her daughters' future in this wider world which had opened up before her.

She looked up from her embroidery as Corrain entered her private sitting room.

'How are our guests?' Tense, he rubbed the scars around his wrist in unconscious anticipation.

'Recovered.' There was, Zurenne had found, nothing excessively daunting about a noblewoman descended from ancient Emperors or an elderly adept from a House of Sanctuary when they were both laid low by wracking nausea.

Corrain was relieved. 'The Soluran mages will arrive at noon. Do the household know to keep clear of the great hall?'

'They do and I will keep Ilysh, Neeny and Raselle here with me.' Zurenne set her scissors on the low table beside her silk covered settle with a sharp snap as Corrain turned to go. 'A moment, if you please.'

'My lady?' He regarded her with some surprise.

'I would have preferred that you ask my permission, or Lady Ilysh's, before inviting these strangers into our home,' she said with measured calm. 'I would have preferred to hear the Archmage's assurances that this will truly be an end to our trials, for myself.'

'My lady.' Corrain ducked his head.

Zurenne waited for him to offer some justification, to repeat his insistence that Halferan was the only neutral ground on which the Solurans and Hadrumal's advocates would agree to meet.

He didn't speak. She concluded that his silence was the only apology she would get. It would suffice, for the present. She was sure there was more that he wasn't telling her but that rune showed two sides. She had secrets of her own.

'Are you sure that the Archmage isn't coming? No Hadrumal mages at all?' At least Zurenne could hope that reduced the chances of wizardly conniving, if none of them were actually present.

Corrain shoved his hands in his breeches' pockets. 'That's what they've sworn and I don't see Planir breaking his word or allowing anyone else to. Not with these Mountain adepts keeping an eye on them.'

Zurenne couldn't help a shiver. 'Are these *sheltya* truly so perilously powerful?'

Hearing the tale of Hosh's healing in Col, she had thought of Artifice as a gentle, kindly magic. Kusint's stories of the Forest Folk's aetheric magic were similarly benign. Then Corrain had related what he had seen in the far north.

Zurenne remembered standing in the manor's shrine before Saedrin's statue, after the elemental cataclysm had destroyed the corsair island. She begged for reassurance that wizardry's destructive might could somehow be stopped. Be careful what you pray for, so the old warning went.

Corrain surprised her with a grin. 'They are assuredly powerful but I have been wondering how quickly a mage could defeat one by just taking them fifty leagues with a spell.'

Zurenne couldn't help an answering smile. 'I suppose there is that. Still,' she continued, fervently serious, 'let's hope they can come to an accommodation today.'

Corrain looked thoughtful. 'Kusint says that his runes foretell a promising outcome.'

'Good.' Zurenne studied Corrain for a moment. 'Do you know if Lady Ilysh has asked him to seek such omens?'

He nodded. Zurenne waited for him to say something further. As the silence lengthened she took up her embroidery again. 'Hosh tells me that the Jagai ships will have reached harbour safely under unthreatening stars. He says they will be relieved since the heavenly compass will soon turn to a far more menacing configuration.'

'This Kheda, who sent word from Khusro.' Corrain glowered briefly at the thought of the Archipelagan. 'Does he know what those hired swords from Col will do?'

'I have suggested that he spreads word among the Khusro merchants that they could profit by carrying them onwards to Lescar or back to Col when the spring sailings begin.'

'You suggested—' Corrain couldn't hide his surprise.

Zurenne concentrated on placing her stitch neatly.

'Caladhria's barons won't want half an army of disgruntled swordsmen arriving in Relshaz, surely?'

Not now that Lord Licanin and other local barons were looking thoughtfully at the small harbour of Markyate at the mouth of the River Tantel, according to Beresa's most recent letter. Zurenne had mentioned in her own correspondence how Hadrumal's mages were helping the merchants and guildsmen of Attar and Claithe improve their anchorages in hopes of claiming a share of Archipelagan trade.

She already knew from Kheda that the Miris warlord had sent an emissary to Licanin to discuss cleansing his domain's strong rooms of magic. Apparently discovering that such inadvertent contamination was possible, and just as quickly learning that Khusro had discovered how to shed such pollution, had outweighed all arguments in favour of shunning the mainland. Zurenne was confident that her shrewd brother by marriage would secure whatever magecraft Markyate needed in return for helping Hadrumal secure these ensorcelled items.

'True,' Corrain acknowledged before shaking his head in wonder. 'What do you suppose those mercenaries made of arriving in the Archipelago instead of being sent to plunder Hadrumal?'

Zurenne busied herself untangling her silk thread. 'I imagine they will be very relieved when they return to the mainland and learn that these reports of the Archmage and his wizards exhausting their magic were lies.'

According to Kheda, the mercenaries' ire was also being soothed with a judicious measure of gold while the presence of Jagai's own swordsmen was reminding these unwilling guests that they had to get back to the mainland alive to spend their spoils.

Apparently the Jagai warlord was blaming this whole fruitless venture on swindlers from Relshaz who had duped him with well-crafted lies. The Archipelagans were now regarding all Relshazri with profound disfavour.

Any Archipelagan would rather be thought a fool than admit to being influenced by any form of magic but Zurenne wondered if some aetheric adept had put that idea into those Aldabreshi heads. At the Archmage's behest? Not that she had said so to Kheda. He said that the Khusro wives and every other Aldabreshi was entirely prepared to believe in such a deception and there was nothing to be gained by stirring up fear and rumour of Artifice. Zurenne agreed.

She might discuss this with Corrain, once he had become accustomed to her and Ilysh's determination to see Halferan trade with the Archipelago. Meantime, Zurenne had written to her sister Celle, Lady Fandail, on her husband's thickly wooded estates south of Duryea, to ask if the barge-builders who bought Fandail timber knew any merchants who traded into the northern grasslands interested in dealing in quantities of Dalasorian goat hair shawls.

Corrain shifted his weight from foot to foot. Zurenne looked up. Before either of them could speak, they heard shouts down in the courtyard.

'I believe the Esquire Den Dalderin has arrived.' Corrain rubbed his manacle welts again. 'I had better go and greet him.'

Zurenne nodded. 'Offer him my compliments and say I look forward to seeing him at dinner.'

'Very good, my lady.' Corrain grinned and bowed before leaving the room.

Zurenne laid her embroidery down in her lap and

contemplated the shrine-hanging she was working to honour Halcarion. Was it truly possible? Could they be lucky enough to see an end to all this by the evening?

CORRAIN WALKED DOWN the stairs and out onto the steps. The young Tormalin noble was handing his horse into Master Thuse's care. Kusint escorted Den Dalderin towards the great hall.

Corrain contemplated the Forest-born youth. Hosh had been hinting that Kusint was as fond of Ilysh as he was loyal and Corrain had seen for himself how often her eyes followed the guard captain.

At some point, he would have to discuss Lysha's future with Zurenne. An alliance by marriage with some other barony could prove problematic. Some lordling accustomed to unquestioning obedience from a household's women would get a very rude awakening here. Corrain was certain that Lysha wouldn't bend her neck to such autocracy any more readily than Halferan's tenants and yeomanry would yield to a new lord.

Would such a husband try to break her spirit? Corrain wouldn't stand for that. Perhaps a marriage within the barony was still Lysha's best prospect; a true marriage rather than this sham. Doubtless the parliament's lords would mutter and disapprove but Corrain suspected that Halferan's profits from this trading venture Lysha was so set on would muffle most whispers. Meantime he and Zurenne could wait out a handful of years to see if Lysha and Kusint's lingering looks proved more than youthful infatuation.

Regardless, they were already agreed that Tormalin hopes of inveigling a way into Halferan's affairs through this personable and charming young man would be doomed to failure.

'Good day to you, Baron Halferan.' Den Dalderin offered his hand as he came up the steps with Kusint. 'My thanks to you and your good lady for this invitation. You may rest assured of our tangible gratitude as the new trading year begins.'

Corrain answered with a thin smile. 'Let's hope you're still as grateful when this meeting's over.'

Den Dalderin chose not to answer such bluntness, turning to survey the courtyard instead. 'I understood we were expected at noon? May I ask, how will the Solurans make the journey? I understand that a wizard cannot use magic to visit a strange place.'

'One of Hadrumal's mages brought a wizard we trust here first. He's bringing the rest.' Corrain wasn't about to detail the endless arguments before that had been agreed.

As he spoke the kitchen gable timepiece struck its first chime. Before the lingering note was replaced by the second, six figures appeared at the bottom of the steps.

'Elder Raso.' Corrain bowed before turning to the Toremalin youth. 'May I make known to you Yadres Den Dalderin, of Toremal. Esquire, may I make known to you Gaveren Raso, wizard of the Fifth Order of Fornet.'

He didn't bother introducing any of the other five Solurans. 'Shall we go in? The lady adepts are waiting.'

He led the way into the great hall, not looking back to see that they were following. If they didn't this day was as good as over and the Solurans would be the ones to rue it.

Two women sat at the high table; Lady Guinalle in a formal brown silk gown and Sister Alebis, wearing a charcoal robe with a creamy woollen surcoat. An armed and armoured guard stood behind them.

Corrain was still amused to recall the shock on the Halferan troopers' faces when they realised that the Soluran lady adept's escort was a tall and well-muscled girl. Then again, he recalled his own surprise at seeing how many Soluran women wore breeches and sword belts without asking any man's leave.

'Good day to you.' Guinalle Tor Priminale stood and gestured courteously to the high table's empty chairs. 'Please be seated and declare yourselves and the Orders you represent.'

Corrain noted the Solurans' expressions ranged from wary to sulky. That didn't concern him. What he had feared was open hostility. His hopes rose slightly to see them so cowed.

'Ifestal Sansem of the Order of Detich.' The first woman to take a seat looked the most apprehensive.

'Lymas Reson of the Order of Ancorr.' This man's resentment was tempered by fear as he looked at the old woman seated beside Guinalle.

'Stryol Dephad of the Order of Ontesk.' The man huddled in his chair as though that might somehow reduce his guilt.

'Munon Inait of the Order of Noerut.' She looked resigned until she glanced at the Detich magewoman and her eyes narrowed with bitterness.

'Glanoy Trefet of the Order of Temosul.' He dropped into his seat, mumbling his name.

Lady Guinalle nodded serenely. 'As agreed I am here as Archmage Planir's representative while Sister Alebis of the House of Sanctified Repose will bear witness for Solura's adepts. Gaveren Raso of Fornet is here on behalf of the Orders of Wizardry so shamed by your greed and aggression.'

Corrain saw all five mages sit up straighter, shocked to hear such condemnation in her polite tones.

Ifestal Sansem raised a swift hand. 'We—'

'You clearly forgot the obligation laid upon every Soluran Order to rally against any attack on wizardry,' Gaveren Raso said coldly. 'The Elders of the Lake of Kings have made it plain that such obligation is not limited to defending other Solurans. Your attacks upon Hadrumal would entitle us to raze your Orders' towers to the ground and execute you all.'

'No laws forbid the corruption of aetheric adepts,' Sister Alebis observed, 'since such a crime has never occurred. However I have full authority from my House's Revered Mother to administer whatever discipline I see fit, since your selfish actions have seen the most promising adepts in three different Houses lose years of learning in the blink of an eye.'

Corrain wondered how those newly ignorant adepts were faring. He didn't ask.

'We are grateful to Baron Halferan for offering us this meeting place,' Guinalle continued as though there had been no interruption, 'and for bearing witness on behalf of Caladhria's people. We also welcome Yadres Den Dalderin, to bear witness to Emperor Tadriol.'

As she smiled at the Tormalin nobleman, Corrain was pleased to see Den Dalderin looking almost as wary as the Soluran wizards. He ushered the Tormalin youth to a seat at the end of the table and went to stand a few paces away. Kusint took up a similar stance on the other side of the dais.

'Soluran law would see you punished severely. However Planir of Hadrumal has asked that we seek some agreement to avoid any legacy of ill-feeling dividing your two traditions of wizardry. Hadrumal's mages know full well that the most corrupt and vicious magecraft is found in Mandarkin. They acknowledge Solura's invaluable role in confining such malice beyond the mountains.'

Reson of Ancorr couldn't restrain himself. 'Then let us have the means to fight them! These artefacts—'

Guinalle silenced him with an unexpected nod of agreement. 'Hadrumal's Council has agreed to offer those few artefacts which may be of some use in countering the Mandarkin to the Order of Fornet, to be distributed among the other Orders as the Fornet Elders see fit.'

'Do not imagine that your own Orders will see a single piece.' Gaveren Ruso's quick venom wiped an instant of ill-disguised triumph from Ifestal of Detich's face.

Corrain also noted the chagrin on Trefet of Temosul's face.

Once again, Guinalle continued calmly. 'Archmage Planir asks me to remind you that Hadrumal's mages have discovered the secret of destroying these ensorcelled artefacts. They will not hesitate to act if they discover their magecraft is being abused. He encourages you to remember that however arduous discovering such a new spell may be, magecraft becomes easier the more it is repeated, refined and shared.'

'We have asked the Archmage to teach this working to the Elders of Fornet,' Gaveren Raso interjected, 'to help us drive back those Mandarkin tyrants who arm their minions with such purloined magic.'

Now Corrain saw regret choking Inait of Noerut. How foolish she had been to ally herself with those threatening Hadrumal rather than seeking some accommodation with the Archmage.

She would feel more than foolish when she knew the full story, he silently predicted to himself.

'Moreover Suthyfer's mages have recently perfected a range of spells to unite different mages of the same affinity.' A fond smile escaped Guinalle momentarily. 'Since Mandarkin wizards use similar magic in foul and destructive fashion, Usara of Suthyfer offers to teach Solura's Orders this magecraft for their own use.'

Corrain saw Trefet and Inait exchange glances of hopeful astonishment and wondered how often such predatory magic had been used against them in those border forests and mountains.

Then he noticed Ifestal Sansem sit up straight with that same ill-concealed smugness. 'We're pleased to see—'

'In return,' Guinalle spoke over her with implacable courtesy, 'Solura's Orders of Wizardry will forswear the search for and the use of quintessential magic within the kingdom's boundaries and anywhere north of the Great West Road.'

'No.' Sansem slammed her hands down on the table. 'Planir of Hadrumal cannot dictate—'

'You are mistaken.' As Sister Alebis skewered the magewoman with a look, Guinalle sat, deferring to the adept.

Sansem of Detich screamed and clutched her head. Inait of Noerut slumped forward onto the table, her face the colour of sour milk.

Trefet of Temosul sprang to his feet, his toppled chair crashing onto the dais. The wizard's strength failed him and he collapsed to huddle on the floorboards, panting like a dog.

Dephad of Ontesk sat so frozen in his seat, eyes screwed shut, that Corrain was tempted to shove him, just to see if he was alive or unconscious.

Reson of Ancorr whimpered, lips bloodless as he

gripped the sides of his seat with white knuckled hands.

Corrain felt his own palms sweating with apprehension. As he wiped them stealthily on his thighs, he met Kusint's gaze. The Forest-born lad offered him an unobtrusive nod of encouragement and support.

'May I ask,' Yadres Den Dalderin was pale with trepidation, 'what is amiss?' He looked at the empty chair beside him. 'What has happened to Master Raso of Fornet?'

Sister Alebis smiled. 'There is no need to subject him to this demonstration. While our bodies remain in Halferan's great hall under his watchful eye, our minds are now united in an aetheric construct. I see you are familiar with the term, Esquire,' she noted thoughtfully.

'You may not know that such Artifice bars wizards from all contact with their mageborn element. As you see, this can prove distressing. We will allow them to compose themselves.'

The edge in her words made that more a command that mere courtesy. Corrain saw the Soluran wizards struggle to gather their wits. He felt his own heart beat faster as he contemplated what was to come.

Sister Alebis contemplated the stricken wizards until she was satisfied that she had their full attention.

'It is not Planir of Hadrumal who denies Solura quintessential magic,' she told them coldly. 'Your arrogance and folly have drawn the attention of the *sheltya* of the high peaks and their displeasure could have the gravest consequences for us all. This temporary aetheric confinement deprived of your magic is the mildest of the punishments which they could inflict.'

Her voice grew sterner still. 'Since you have proved yourself irredeemably foolish, I will not ask if you believe me. I will show you proof.'

The gimlet eyed old woman looked at Corrain and he braced himself. He fixed his own gaze on Kusint at the other end of the dais.

He would never have agreed to this without seeing the Forest lad endure this Artifice first. Kusint had promised that the trial was nothing Corrain couldn't endure, not after all he had suffered before. Hosh had shared every detail of his own experiences in Col's adepts' company. Both of them had sworn this would seem no more than a dream.

Corrain would have said more of a nightmare. He stood, unable to move, unable to speak, as recollection of all his encounters with the Mountain adepts flowed through his mind.

He had no notion how Sister Alebis was sharing his memories with the Soluran wizards but hearing their distant exclamations proved she was doing just that. His encounter with Aritane after her memories had been obliterated prompted particular consternation.

Finally, his mind's eye lingered on the mage Despin's body, collapsed in Hadrumal's Council chamber. According to Jilseth, the wizard was slowly wasting away, lying senseless in his bed, despite Mentor Garewin's ceaseless efforts to revive him.

A wail from Dephad of Ontesk told Corrain that the merciless old woman had shared that with the five mages as well.

When he feared he couldn't stand it any longer, he felt himself suddenly released from her invisible bonds. He drew a deep, grateful breath and did his best to conceal the weakness in his knees.

Den Dalderin yelped as Gaveren Raso appeared beside him. The Fornet mage contemplated his stricken compatriots, not even trying to conceal his satisfaction at their suffering.

'It would be a grave mistake,' Sister Alebis remarked, 'to think that Solura's adepts don't know the secrets of such Artifice. Rather, you should be grateful that learning aetheric magic is such a lengthy process. By the time we have perfected such Artifice, we are generally old enough to have acquired the wisdom not to use it.'

Guinalle rose to her feet again. 'While I lack the honoured sister's years, you would also be gravely mistaken if you underestimate Suthyfer's adepts. You should also know that we are bound to Suthyfer's mages by the closest ties of respect and affection.'

Corrain was impressed by how threatening such a mild-mannered woman could be, speaking so politely. The Suthyfer adept was more terrifying than Sister Alebis's sword-belted companion still standing silently at the back of the dais.

'Hadrumal has no wish to quarrel with any Soluran mages. Such conflict will cost everyone dear. But know this: if you insist on fighting, you will lose,' Guinalle assured the five men and women, still whey-faced and trembling.

'Very well.' Sister Alebis looked across the table to Gaveren Raso. 'I believe our business here is concluded.'

'Forgive me, sister, not quite.' Guinalle sat down and looked at Yadres Den Dalderin, who was sitting shocked into stillness, his expression haunted.

'When you report what you have seen and heard here to your uncle and the Emperor, please be sure to remind them that the *sheltya*'s enquiry agent was in Ferl, asking after Baron Halferan at the same time as you. You should assume that your interest in this strife between

Hadrumal and Solura's wizards is known to the *sheltya* along with whatever motives you might fondly imagine were only known to you.

'The Mountain adepts will now be well aware of the Tormalin Empire's interest in renewing its knowledge and use of Artifice. If your own adepts are tempted to aspire to the aetheric enchantments which you have seen here today, remember the risks of attracting *sheltya* displeasure. May I recommend the same humility and circumspection in such studies as the mentors of Col and Vanam have always shown?'

She smiled amiably. 'Not least because the continued cooperation of Suthyfer's mages as Tormalin ships cross the ocean will depend on Suthyfer's adepts' agreement. We look forward to seeing Tormalin Artifice abide by the unselfish principles which we advocate.'

Yadres Den Dalderin slowly rose to his feet and bowed low, first to Guinalle, then to Sister Alebis, to Gaveren Raso and finally to Corrain. 'You may rest assured that I will make certain that Tormalin's Emperor understands what I have learned here today.' He sat down heavily.

Corrain was impressed. He didn't think he could have shown such composure at the lad's age, not after witnessing such revelations.

'Good.' Gaveren Raso looked sternly at the five Soluran mages. 'Now, go and tell your Orders how grateful they should be not to pay the penalties which your offences warrant.'

He smiled as the chastened renegades vanished in many-hued magelight and then disappeared himself.

Corrain looked uncertainly at Sister Alebis. 'May I ask how you intend to get home?'

'By way of Col by ship and then north to Selerima and

the Great West Road.' Her smile revealed an unexpected dimple in one soft cheek. 'Your young friend Hosh has been telling me of his friends among the university's mentors. I believe I can offer them some useful lore to improve their healing Artifice.'

'I have business in Lescar,' Guinalle told him. 'Then I'll travel to Bremilayne and take ship back to Suthyfer.' She glanced at Den Dalderin. 'I may call on Emperor Tadriol if there are any matters which he wishes to discuss.'

'He will be honoured to receive you,' the young nobleman assured her.

The Soluran swordswoman stirred at the back of the dais.

'Yes?' Corrain invited her to speak. He wanted to be certain that the day truly saw an end to Halferan's dealings with magic.

'May I ask when lunch is to be served?'

— CHAPTER THIRTY-SEVEN —

'I BELIEVE THAT's all we'll usefully see today. Thank you for your scrying, Flood Mistress, and for your clairaudience, Cloud Master.'

Troanna waved a hand over the silver bowl and the vision of the manor's great hall dissolved. 'Can we trust what we have seen and heard?'

'What would you suggest we do instead?' Planir countered. 'Shall we try trust, until we have reason not to?'

Rafrid looked across the sitting room table to Usara. 'Your wife is a formidable woman. Should I offer congratulations or commiserations?'

Usara grinned. 'I am very lucky.'

Jilseth was wondering what their son Darni might grow into, given such redoubtable parents.

Kalion cleared his throat. 'I suggest that a mage of suitable rank visits the Tormalin Emperor for the Spring Equinox festival. He and Toremal's great princes will have had time to reflect on Den Dalderin's report by then.'

'A good idea, Hearth Master.' Planir nodded. 'The *sheltya* said it was up to us to restore trust in wizardry across the mainland. We may as well start with the most influential people.'

Troanna snorted. 'Meantime, I will continue restoring some order and habits of study in my hall and among those of my affinity.'

'Quite so,' Rafrid agreed with rare accord. 'If you will excuse me, Archmage.'

He followed the Flood Mistress who was already halfway to the door.

Kalion lingered, looking sadly into the empty scrying bowl. 'Let's hope this is truly an end to such strife within wizardry.'

Jilseth wasn't sure if he was talking to the Archmage, to her and Usara, or simply to himself. Before she could decide, Kalion heaved a sigh and departed without a further word.

Planir looked at Usara. 'This whole business has him remembering Otrick.'

'He's not the only one.' The Suthyfer mage paused, reflective, before a half smile lightened his solemn expression. 'If you will permit me, Archmage, I will rejoin my wife.'

'By all means.' Planir urged him on with a gesture. 'Offer her my thanks for enduring the discomforts of translocation to Halferan.'

'Will you be travelling back to Suthyfer together?' Jilseth couldn't restrain her curiosity. 'By road and sea?'

Usara grinned. 'I have found such journeys offer unexpected pleasures. We can be too quick to use wizardry. We don't realise what we might miss.'

Despite that, he vanished with the merest hint of golden magelight.

'Is this really an end to it all?'

Jilseth looked at the Archmage. Planir smiled and the fine creases around his eyes deepened beguilingly.

'You clearly have questions. Let's see if I have answers.'

Jilseth followed him to the settles on either side of the fireplace. 'I remembered, when we were linked through Usara's spell, that you were born in Gidesta.'

'Quite so,' Planir agreed.

'What did you know of the *sheltya*, before you came to Hadrumal?' Jilseth had studied a map in Wellery's Hall, contemplating the distances between the coal mining areas to the north and west of Inglis and that remote defiant peak. If she couldn't recall what had happened to her, she knew precisely where she had recovered her mage senses.

Planir's smile broadened. 'Lowland mothers keep their children biddable with tales of the Eldritch Kin lurking in chimney corners. Upland mothers scare their offspring into obedience with stories of the Grey Watchers. When I met Aritane, I realised what lay behind such myths.'

'Did you always intend involving them to curb these Solurans? Did you know how reluctant they would be? Is that why you allowed me to doubt you? Why you kept so many things from me, so they would think you were failing in your duties when they read my mind?' Jilseth's voice shook despite her efforts to remain calm.

Planir looked at her for a long moment before answering. 'It's said that knowledge is power. That's a double-edged blade. Keeping someone in ignorance can be just as powerful. I have a responsibility as Archmage to use every weapon I can find, especially in such dire straits. I knew only the gravest threat would induce the *sheltya* to act. I'd learned that much from Aritane. I will ask your forgiveness if you want me to but you should know that I would do the same again, with Hadrumal's fate hanging in the balance.'

Jilseth couldn't decide if his frankness made her feel better or worse. 'What would you have done, if they hadn't intervened?'

Planir shrugged. 'There was nothing I could have done. Hadrumal would have been lost.'

Jilseth stared at him. 'Lost? You can say that so calmly?'

'Never think that I take any loss lightly. I have lost more than you will ever know just as I have borne burdens beyond any Element Master or Mistress's endurance.'

His grey eyes were steely and Jilseth was ashamed to recall Larissa's funeral urn upstairs in Planir's private chamber.

'Suthyfer would have survived as a new haven for wizardry. My responsibilities as Archmage go far beyond this island and far beyond mindlessly defending or disciplining every wizard trained by these halls. I want to encourage those wizards to discipline themselves, long after I am dead—or gone.'

He paused, his face reflective in a way which Jilseth found profoundly unnerving. Before she could ask what he meant, the Archmage continued.

'Hadrumal has long needed a stark lesson in humility. Now every mage can reflect on how powerless Mellitha and Velindre found themselves in Relshaz, for all their vaunted magecraft. Now apprentices and pupils won't only hear tales of long-dead menaces like Azazir, driven mad by arrogance until obsession with their element claims them. They'll hear first-hand accounts of Despin's appalling fate.'

Planir leaned forward, intent. 'Wizardry is growing ever more powerful as magecraft is studied and honed, here in Hadrumal, in Solura, now in Suthyfer. I can't do anything to stop that and I don't believe I should. But power so readily encourages arrogance.

'I want every mage to stop and think if he or she should use such powerful spells, not merely if he or she could. I also want every wizard to know that there are those who can stop them abusing the most advanced magecraft, just as I wanted the *sheltya* to realise how powerful elemental magic has become. I only hope they that realise their responsibilities to Artifice go beyond remaining remote and aloof in their mountain fastnesses.'

'As long as they don't decide the swiftest solution to their problems is reducing us all to drooling mindlessness!' Jilseth was alarmed.

Planir grinned, though his expression was no less intent. 'Trust me; the *sheltya* will also learn a few lessons in humility if they choose to come down off their mountains. You should visit Suthyfer again and learn some of the ways Usara and Guinalle have devised for wizards to defend themselves against Artifice.'

'So this isn't over?' Jilseth shrank from the prospect of whatever unknown struggles lay ahead.

'When is anything ever over? When we lie dead upon a pyre or deep in the ground? Not even then, according to the priests and mystics.' Planir leaned back and gazed at her over steepled fingers. 'But I believe that we can hope for calm after these recent years' upheavals. It will be in everyone's interests, from the lowliest peasant to Tormalin's Emperor, to let these ripples die away.

'As to what the future will bring, I don't believe that anyone can ever know that, whether they read the runes or the heavenly compass. What will be will be and we will deal with whatever arises with the means we find at hand.'

GAIL Z. MARTIN'S
THE CHRONICLES OF THE NECROMANCER

"Attractive characters and an imaginative setting combine in an excellent, fast-moving quest novel."
— David Drake, author of the Lord of the Isles series

BOOK ONE
THE SUMMONER

ISBN: 978 1 84416 468 4 • £7.99/$7.99

The world of Prince Martris Drayke is thrown into sudden chaos when his brother murders their father and seizes the throne. Forced to flee, with only a handful of loyal friends to support him, Martris must seek retribution and restore his father's honour. But if the living are arrayed against him, Martris must learn to harness his burgeoning magical powers to call on different sets of allies: the ranks of the dead.

The Summoner is an epic, engrossing tale of loss and revenge, of life and afterlife – and the thin line between them.

"Attractive characters and an imaginative setting."

– David Drake, author of *The Lord of the Isles*

BOOK TWO
THE BLOOD KING

ISBN: 978 1 84416 531 5 • £7.99/$7.99

Having narrowly escaped being murdered by his evil brother, Jared, Prince Martris Drayke must take control of his magical abilities to summon the dead, and gather an army big enough to claim back the throne of his dead father.

But it isn't merely Jared that Tris must combat. The dark mage, Foor Arontala, has schemes to cause an inbalance in the currents of magic and raise the Obsidian King...

"A fantasy adventure with whole-hearted passion."

– Sandy Auden, *SFX*

GAIL Z. MARTIN'S
THE CHRONICLES OF THE NECROMANCER

BOOK THREE
DARK HAVEN

ISBN: (UK) 978 1 84416 708 1 • £7.99
ISBN: (US) 978 1 84416 598 8 • $7.99

The kingdom of Margolan lies in ruin. Martris Drayke, the new king, must rebuild his country in the aftermath of battle, while a new war looms on the horizon. Meanwhile Jonmarc Vahanian is now the Lord of Dark Haven, and there is defiance from the vampires of the *Vayash Moru* at the prospect of a mortal leader.

But can he earn their trust, and at what cost?

"A fast-paced tale laced with plenty of action."

– SF Site

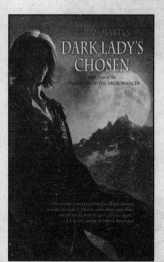

BOOK FOUR
DARK LADY'S CHOSEN

ISBN: (UK) 978 1 84416 830 9 • £7.99
ISBN: (US) 978 1 84416 831 6 • $7.99

Treachery and blood magic threaten King Martris Drayke's hold on the throne he risked everything to win. As the battle against a traitor lord comes to its final days, war, plague and betrayal bring Margolan to the brink of destruction. Civil war looms in Isencroft. And in Dark Haven, Lord Jonmarc Vahanian has bargained his soul for vengeance as he leads the *vayash moru* against a dangerous rogue who would usher in a future drenched in blood.

"Just when you think you know where things are heading, Martin pulls another ace from her sleeve."

– A. J. Hartley, author of *The Mask of Atraeus*

BOOK ONE OF THE CURSED KINGDOMS TRILOGY

THE SENTINEL MAGE

EMILY GEE

"An addictive story."
SFX Magazine on Thief With No Shadow

UK ISBN: 978 1 907519 49 9 • US ISBN: 978 1 907519 50 5 • £7.99/$7.99

In a distant corner of the Seven Kingdoms, an ancient curse festers and grows, consuming everything in its path. Only one man can break it: Harkeld of Osgaard, a prince with mage's blood in his veins. But Prince Harkeld has a bounty on his head - and assassins at his heels.

Innis is a gifted shapeshifter. Now she must do the forbidden: become a man. She must stand at Prince Harkeld's side as his armsman, protecting and deceiving him. But the deserts of Masse are more dangerous than the assassins hunting the prince. The curse has woken deadly creatures, and the magic Prince Harkeld loathes may be the only thing standing between him and death.

"Dark and compelling...
Emily Gee is a storyteller to watch!"
— New York Times Best-Selling Author Nalini Singh

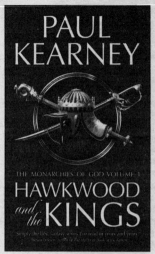
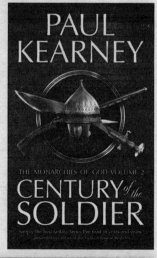

PAUL KEARNEY'S
THE MACHT

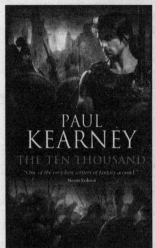

BOOK ONE

THE TEN THOUSAND

ISBN: (UK) 978 1 84416 647 3 • £7.99
ISBN: (US) 978 1 84416 573 5 • $7.99

The Macht are a mystery, a people of extraordinary ferocity and discipline whose prowess on the battlefield is the stuff of legend. For centuries they have remained within the remote fastnesses of the Harukush Mountains.

Beyond lie the teeming races and peoples of the Asurian Empire, which rules the known world, and is invincible. The Great King of Asuria can call up whole nations to the battlefield. His word is law.

But now the Great King's brother means to take the throne by force, and has called on the legend, marching ten thousand warriors of the Macht into the heart of the Empire.

"A bold, strong new voice in fantasy."
– Robert Silverberg

BOOK TWO

CORVUS

ISBN: (UK) 978 1 906735 76 0 • £7.99
ISBN: (US) 978 1 906735 77 7 • $7.99

Twenty-three years after leading a Macht army home from the heart of the Asurian Empire, Rictus is now a hard-bitten mercenary captain, middle-aged and tired. He wants nothing more than to lay down his spear and become the farmer that his father was. But fate has different ideas.

A young war-leader has risen to challenge the order of things in the very heartlands of the Macht, taking city after city and reigning over them as king. His name is Corvus, and they say that he is not even fully human. He means to make himself ruler of all the Macht, and he wants Rictus to help him.

"One of the best writers working in fantasy."
– SciFi.com

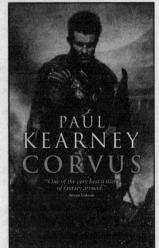

PAUL
KEARNEY

"One of the very best writers of fantasy around."
Steven Erikson

UK ISBN: 978 1 907519 38 3 • US ISBN: 978 1 907519 39 0 • £7.99/$7.99

For the first time in recorded history, the ferocious city-states of the Macht now acknowledge a single man as their overlord. Corvus, the strange, brilliant boy-general, is now High King, having united his people in a fearsome, bloody campaign. He is not yet thirty years old.

A generation ago, ten thousand of the Macht marched into the heart of the ancient Asurian Empire, and fought their way back out again, passing into legend. Corvus's father was one of those who undertook that march, and his most trusted general, Rictus, was leader of those ten thousand. But he intends to do more. The preparations will take years, but when they are complete, Corvus will lead an invasion the like of which the world of Kuf has never seen. Under him, the Macht will undertake nothing less than the overthrow of the Asurian Empire.

**"Very rarely does an author manage to leave you heartbroken while still allowing you to have enjoyed the book you've read... Kearney captures all the best parts of fantasy and combines them together with grit and realism and enough blood to drown a horse."**

– Fantasy Book Review's Book the Month

WWW.SOLARISBOOKS.COM

Follow us on Twitter! www.twitter.com/solarisbooks